THE DECEIVING

THE DECEIVING

The Knowing Saga Book Two

NINIE HAMMON

STERLING & STONE

There are more things in Heaven and Earth than are
dreamt of in your philosophy.
William Shakespeare

Chapter One

Harrelton, Ohio
September 22,
2011

Something was wrong. Sixty-four-year-old Theresa Washington could sense it the way her grandpa could feel the sudden ache of arthritis in his bones when the weather was about to change. She tried to deny it, of course, would likely continue to deny it all the way up until she found out what the bad was.

Lightning shattered the darkness, shards of a broken mirror raining out of the sky. She tensed for the bowling-alley rumble of thunder that would follow as the street ahead appeared and disappeared in rhythm with the wipers' sweep across the windshield.

"Fool!" she muttered aloud. "Out in a storm like this. You deserve to run off the road into a ditch." Course you seldom got what it was you deserved in this life, and most times that was a good thing.

She turned down Elmcrest Circle, where the street-lights glowed through the wall of rain, but all the houses was dark. The storm must have knocked out the 'lectricity. She could see lights in the windows of most houses, though, flickerin' candles or the bright, almost-yellow glow of a lantern.

Miss Minnie got decorative candlesticks in every room in that whole house. Even the bathroom. They's fine!

That was the thing, though, wasn't it? Theresa didn't really believe Minnie and Gerald Cohen was fine at all. Oh, today was Thursday, and she hadn't missed goin' to see the elderly Jewish couple every Thursday evenin' in years. But that's not why she was out in this monsoon. She was here 'cause of the ache of evil in her bones.

The house at 1107 wasn't quite as dignified as the other old homes on the tree-lined street, courtesy of the bronze lions that sat like they was standin' guard on either side of the driveway. The whole yard would have been littered with concrete ducks, garden gnomes and bird baths, too, if Mr. Gerald hadn't drawn a line in the sand at the lions. Oh, how Miss Minnie did love to shop at garage sales and flea markets back when she could still get around by herself! And she hadn't never been able to pass up a bargain. Mr. Gerald said she'd a'brought home a dead horse if she coulda got it for half price.

Theresa's headlights washed the lions in a harsh light when she turned off the street. The house was totally dark. Not a single light in any of the rooms that faced the street. Aw, but that didn't mean nothin'. They had them heavy drapes pulled was all. There was plush drapes in every room. Miss Minnie called the ones in the parlor Scarlet O'Hara drapes 'cause they was made out of green velvet and had tassels on the tiebacks.

Theresa opened the car door and held the mini umbrella she kept stuck up under the front seat out into the cold rain, openin' it to cover her as she got out. Didn't do hardly no good at all, though, soon's she stepped away from the car. Wasn't nothin' mini gonna cover up her maxi. But it did keep her head dry as she went splashin' up the sidewalk through ankle-deep puddles.

The wet rubber soles on her new shoes squeaked on the Moroccan tiles on the porch. The shoes wasn't broke in yet, hurt her feet, but they went with the white Good Samaritan Hospital's Ladies Auxiliary uniform she wore, and the old ones was worn out. She could have stopped by her house for some shoes that didn't pain her—and to get a raincoat!—but that's when the knowing of it come on her, and she drove straight to the Cohens' house.

There was no sound from inside when she knocked on the door. It was a big house, though. If neither one of them had they hearing aids in, they'd miss her knockin' altogether. But they'd be listenin' for it. They was expectin' her. And what about Buscuit? The old couple had took in a mongrel pup a couple of years ago, and now the dog never left Mr. Gerald's side. He always set up a ruckus, barkin' and carrin' on when Theresa come to visit, so excited he'd near wet himself.

Where was the dog?

She started to go around to the side door but didn't want to step back out into the cold downpour. She tried the knob instead. The door wasn't locked. Theresa grunted in annoyance as she pushed it open. It was time for the lecture again, 'bout how they'd oughta lock—

The darkness wasn't from the drapes. Wasn't a single candle lit anywhere. The entry hall was a black cavern, and the house beyond was still and quiet. Theresa's heart kicked into a gallop. She closed her umbrella and stepped inside, and even though she knew it wouldn't do no good, she still reached out to the switch beside the door. There was a crystal chandelier high above her head, all decorated with cobwebs, that had become a word-picture for Theresa of the decay of the huge house the old couple didn't have the means or the energy to care for anymore.

She flipped the switch up and down a time or two, but no light danced in the dusty crystals. Though some part of her didn't want to disturb the silence all around her, Theresa called out, "Miss Minnie. Mr. Gerald. Where you at?"

Wasn't no response, so she stood where she was and listened hard as she could.

Almost drowned out by the pounding of her heart was a small sound, a dog barkin', only muffled, like Biscuit was down in a well. But no demon wails. She sniffed the air. It was musty as always, smelled like old—crumblin' plaster, ancient dust, decayin' wallpaper. But no demon stink.

Theresa had the knowing. She couldn't see demons like Bishop and Andi and Becca could, but she could hear and smell 'em. And sometimes, not always, she could sense they was around even when there wasn't no reason a'tall to b'lieve that was the case. And right now, the alarm bell on that sense was going ding, ding, ding!

Leaving the front door open behind her, she took a couple of steps down the hallway, where rooms with wide French doors or big oak ones opened on the left and right. She couldn't wander 'round in the dark, though, so she set her purse and umbrella on the floor and took out her iPhone, wishin' she'd let Andi put that flashlight app on it the child had wanted to download. Still, when you tapped the digital clock, the screen turned to solid light, and that chased some of the shadows into the corners. She moved toward the sound of Biscuit barkin' in the back of the house.

Apprehension grew in her chest with every step. The dark, the quiet, and now a smell she couldn't identify replaced the old-house stink. It smelled…coppery, like wet pennies. She come to the door of the parlor, strange and foreboding in the shadowy, luminous glow from the cell phone screen. It looked like somethin' out of a black-and-white Frankenstein movie. She put her hand on the door-knob, tellin' herself she'd find Mr. Gerald and Miss Minnie cuddled together on the couch in there, candlelight makin' the room all cozy, as Mr. Gerald read some classic work of literature to Miss Minnie, who couldn't see well enough to read no more.

That's not what she found. Wasn't no flickerin' candles. Wasn't no light of any kind, only a vast expanse of black.

It was a big room with a sixteen-foot ceiling, and the dark ate up the pale glow from her phone. The copper smell was strong here. She could almost tell…it was famil-iar, she'd smelled it before but couldn't place where. She stood in the open doorway for a moment and swept the phone glow in arcs out into the room but it couldn't pene-trate the thick, tar-blackness enough to—was that some-thin' there, somethin' on the sofa on the far side of the room? Someone asleep, maybe?

She moved through the doorway to investigate and started across the room, but had taken only a few steps when her right foot hit somethin' slick, and she slipped. She tried to regain her balance, but her left foot connected with somethin' on the floor and she tripped over it, stum-bled and went down hard on one knee. She reached out to keep herself from face-plantin' on the hardwood floor and ended up on her side, the breath temporarily knocked out of her. Her cell phone flew out of her hand and clattered on the hardwood floor face-side—light-side—down, slidin' across the floor and comin' to rest about fifteen feet away.

Sucking in a gasp of air, then another, Theresa rolled over and got up on her hands and knees, her arthritis screamin' in protest. When she started to crawl toward her phone, her hand brushed somethin'—the thing she'd tripped over—and she reached out in the dark, feelin' around but couldn't lay hands on it. What she did find was that the floor was wet. Sticky wet. That's why she'd slipped. And it smelled like…

Copper. Pennies. Suddenly, she knew what smelled like pennies.

She scrambled the last few feet to her phone and snatched it off the floor. The glass was cracked, but the light still shone, blindin' her for a moment. In its glow, she seen what was on her hands—seen the blood on her hands —for only an instant, then the light on her cell phone blinked and went out and the darkness rushed in all around her.

~

CAVERNA COUNTY, Kentucky

June 5,

1985

Bishop Washington's head snapped up. Unease awoke in his belly, and he looked warily around, glanced over one shoulder and then the other. Something was out there in them trees. Nearby. He could sense it. He'd be able to see it, too, if it come to that. Bishop had the knowing.

A dark cloud of foreboding settled around him, and his mouth suddenly felt like it was full of cotton balls. The evil he was sensing—it was bad—and the kids was in them woods with it, all three of them!

He had dropped Jack Carpenter, Daniel Burke, and Becca Hawkins off on a logging road right after first light, watched the dew that was still on the leaves fall on them like rain when they set out through the trees. Then he'd driven several miles farther north. He'd promised to return to the logging road right after lunch to pick 'em up.

Freezing where he crouched on one knee, Bishop listened with a sense that didn't have nothing to do with hearing. Whatever was out there, it wasn't where them kids was. Couldn't be. It was around here real close by, or he couldn't have sensed it.

The skin on his arms pebbled with gooseflesh.

Bishop stood, a giant of a man, six feet seven inches and working up to three hundred pounds, with shoulders so broad that Theresa'd had to work a seamstress's magic to get his shirts to fit over 'em and around his barrel chest. His skin was as black as the feather of a raven and his face broad, with strong features softened by wide-set, chocolate-drop eyes that even at forty were already sunk in a web of deep smile wrinkles.

Using his thumb to wipe the dirt off the blade of his pocket knife, he flipped it closed, stuffed it in the pocket of his overalls and put the ginseng plant he'd just hollowed gently out of the ground into the cloth knapsack Theresa'd made out of one of his threadbare T-shirts. Ginseng was a wily rascal, hid from you in the shadows. He'd tracked down this patch of it, watching where water trickled out of the rocks, searching out wet ground in the shade of trees or finding it snuggled up beside rock outcrops on the hillside. There was more here to harvest—though you had to be careful, always had to leave some so it could grow back. But he didn't care about the ginseng now as he set out through the trees back to the road, didn't care about nothin' but findin' them kids and gettin' 'em out of these woods!

Jack and Daniel. Just saplings, budding branches of the

men they'd grow up to be—tall and strong and good. Like his Isaac.

The pain of that thought planted daggers in his chest that hurt so bad it was hard to draw in a breath. He couldn't imagine how his sweet Theresa was standing up under it, the not knowing. The boy had been gone more than five months—one hundred fifteen days to be exact—and he didn't need no calendar to tell him that. On every one of them mornings, waking dropped another boulder of time on his chest, and he sometimes felt like he was bein' crushed under the weight of it. Where was he?

Just twenty years old, Isaac had vanished like smoke from a dying campfire on Valentine's Day and nobody—nobody—had seen or heard from him since. Bishop was beginnin' to learn how to wall off the pain of the boy's absence, but Theresa couldn't. She radiated hurt like the side of a stove radiated heat into a room.

When Bishop got to his rusted red pickup, he reached in through the open driver's side window and tossed the cloth bag into the passenger seat beside the baseball cap Becca'd forgot. It was a spare all-stars hat she wore sometimes to keep the hair that hung almost to her waist out of her eyes. She was a beautiful child, fragile, hair the color of corn silk and big sea-green eyes. She'd be a heartthrob one day—shoot, she already had Jack and Daniel following her around like puppy dogs.

It was Becca that Bishop was worried about. Like Bishop, Becca knew. If she was to happen across whatever was out there in them woods, she'd be able to see it. And it would know she'd seen. The sense of evil had been growing on him as he'd rushed through the woods, and now he feared he'd been wrong about it at first. What if it wasn't nearby, wasn't close? What if it was so powerful that he could feel it even when it was a long way off? He shivered. He needed to get to that logging road quick and then lay on the horn, keep honkin' til them kids come runnin'.

He fished the keys out of the pocket opposite the one where he'd stuffed his knife. The truck's old suspension groaned when he got in behind the wheel. He put the key in the ignition and turned it. Nothing happened. He tried again. Not even the grind of the starter—just silence. His old truck had finally given up the ghost or the battery was dead. Either way, he wouldn't be showin' up at that logging road to pick up the kids after lunch.

Right now, they was out there alone with whatever evil creature haunted these woods. And wasn't a thing Bishop could do to help 'em.

Chapter Two
<hr>

Caverna County, Kentucky

June 5,

1985

Twelve-year-old Becca Hawkins had made it all the way to the east branch of the Big Puddle River and found nothing. After Bishop dropped them off at the logging road, she, Jack and Daniel had split up to cover more ground, and she wondered if they'd been luckier than she, had found any of the elusive ginseng plants that grew wild in the Kentucky woods.

She reached down to the brown mutt that stood beside her and scratched him behind one ear. If only dogs could smell ginseng. Not a bad idea, actually. Surely, she could teach McDougal—aka McDoo, McD, Dougie, Dougal Dog and DD—how to do it. He might be a mutt from the animal shelter, but he was smart. First, however, she had to get her hands on some ginseng. Wouldn't take but a little piece. The Three Musketeers—she, Jack and Daniel—had already agreed among themselves that they'd force Bishop to take whatever they made from selling the plants to fix up his rattley-bang old truck that wheezed and chuffed and blew black smoke out the tailpipe.

Becca's stomach grumbled. She'd only had a piece of cold cornbread and a glass of orange juice before she left the house to go to Daniel's to meet Bishop, and now she was regretting that she'd let Jack and Daniel carry the picka-nick basket—which didn't look a thing like the ones Yogi Bear and Boo-Boo spent their lives trying to steal from visitors to Jellystone National Park. Yes, the "basket" was a little heavy, and it was quite gallant of them to refuse to allow her to carry it, but there were peanut-butter-and-jelly sandwiches in it and—

McDougal's ears stood up, and he looked upriver. Then she heard voices. A lone fisherman in a johnboat was floating in the lazy water. He was leaned back, with his hat pulled down over his face, asleep, and the voices were coming from the woods near him. As they drew closer, Becca felt a chill, like ice water had dripped on the back of her neck and was sliding slowly down between her shoulder blades. McDougal whined. The hair on his back and shoulders stood on end. He let out two timid barks before she put her finger to her lips and shushed him.

If there was one command she could count on DD to obey it was "hush"—or he'd have been dead long ago. Her father didn't like dogs, and she couldn't have kept Dougie "out of sight, out of mind" if the dog hadn't learned quick to be quiet. McDougal rubbed against her leg and began to tremble. Becca was suddenly aware of how alone she was. Jack and Daniel couldn't possibly hear if she called out.

But that's not why her heart began to pound so fast she couldn't detect the individual beats and only felt a ragged hum in her chest. There was something wrong with the voices.

Hide.

She moved before she even formed the thought to do it. A shagbark elm tree with crepe myrtle bushes crowded around its base stood on the riverbank about thirty feet from the water. She ran to it, slid in between the limbs of the bushes and crawled as deep into the interior as she could. Then she called out quietly to the dog and spread the limbs so he could join her. She snuggled him up close to her side and put her arm around him. Out through the tangle of leaves, she saw the fisherman stir and sit up at the sound of people crashing through the woods, voices yelling.

Now she was sure. Something was definitely wrong with the voices. Becca knew what it was, too, that sound like chains dragged across a metal floor or the high squeal of the wood-chipper that ripped into her ears at the sawmill. A little squeak of fear slipped out between her lips, even though she had her jaws clenched tight shut, the tiny mewl of a kitten whose eyes weren't open yet, looking for its mother. McDoo wasn't trembling anymore, he was vibrating, making a strange sound deep in his throat that was a cross between a growl and a whine. She put her finger to her lips and the sound stopped, but she could feel the dog's heart hammering in his chest as if he'd come running to her from all the way across a field.

She wanted to squeeze her eyes shut so she wouldn't have to see, had prayed often that God would strike her blind so she couldn't. But it was God, after all, who had made her so she could see. That's what Theresa and Bishop Washington said.

A group of boys about her age exploded out of the woods like a pack of snarling dogs, burst through the trees and ran down toward the riverbank near the fisherman, doffing T-shirts as they approached the river, obviously intent on a swim. But they weren't cheerful, laughing boys having fun. They were yelling—snarling—at each other, all of them. A couple were fighting, shoving and hitting and then falling to the ground in a tangle of arms and legs and growls. Yes, growls. She recognized the boys as members of Jack and Daniel's all-star baseball team, but she didn't know their names. Besides, it wasn't the boys she was looking at.

Becca gawked in horror and revulsion and was afraid she was going to be sick. That many! Six! She had only seen three in her whole life! And each time, the sight had knocked a hole in her belly so she couldn't eat for a week and had given her nightmares that attacked her with hideous monsters until lack of sleep had painted dark, hollow circles under her eyes.

Six!

Six demons.

All the fisherman in the johnboat saw was a gang of rowdy boys that had interrupted his nap.

"Hey," he called out to them. "Hush up that racket now. You think fish is deaf?" Then he must have figured out the boys' intention. "You can't swim here!"

From her vantage point hidden in the crepe myrtle bush, Becca shook her head slowly back and forth.

Oh, don't. Don't draw their attention.

The boys had stopped on the riverbank near the stump where the fisherman's boat was tied up.

"You own this river?" one of them sneered at him.

"It's deep out there in the middle," the fisherman continued. "There's a trench must go down thirty feet or more. Rocks and dead trees on the bottom to get hung up on."

"Butt out, old man," said one of the others as he pulled a blue University of Kentucky T-shirt off over his head.

"We'll swim anywhere we want to swim," said another boy, a kid with his red hair cut in a Mohawk. There was a clear edge of menace in his voice.

But the fisherman wouldn't let it go.

"Go on over to Troll's Hole where all the other kids swim. Get away from here!"

It happened fast. One minute, the fisherman was in his boat right off the riverbank and the boys were on the shore, and the next minute three of them had waded out to the boat, yanked the fisherman out of it and dragged him up onto the sand. The man was big, with a fat belly sticking out in front like he was pregnant, and must have weighed more than any two of the boys combined.

"Hey, what do you think you're doing?" he sputtered when the boys dropped him on his back in front of them. "You can't—"

"Oh yes, we can," cried one of the boys, the redheaded one.

Then another one of the boys kicked the fisherman and the big man howled in pain. That excited them, and they fell on him in a frenzy of blows, with the man crying out and trying to ward them off with his hands.

"Stop!" he wailed, frightened now. "That hurts. Leave me alone!"

But it was like watching a school of piranha. They fed on each other's violence and anger, and the more the man cried out, the harder they punched and kicked him.

Then one of them, the blond one, could be heard above the others. "Ever pull the wings off a fly?" And before anyone could say another word, he placed one foot on the fisherman's chest, grabbed both his wrists and ripped the man's arms off.

HENDERSONVILLE, Indiana
September 22,
2011

Thirty-eight-year-old Becca Hawkins opened her eyes to darkness so absolute she had to reach up and feel her eyelids to be sure they weren't still closed. She was lying on lumps of something, and one of the somethings was poking into her back at such a painful angle it might have been what woke her. Or not. She'd once walked barefoot across shards of glass from a window she'd broken to get into a garage, and if that wouldn't wake you up, what would? She hadn't felt a thing. At the time anyway. She'd felt it later, though. Still felt it when she relived it. That was the horror of flashbacks and night terrors, you didn't just remember pain, you felt it all over again, like you did the first time. That's why she screamed. Who wouldn't scream walking barefoot across broken glass?

Of course, the woman in the bunk next to hers at the shelter had complained that Becca was keeping her awake —disturbing everybody, as a matter of fact—so they'd kicked her out on the street, where she'd had to walk up and down the sidewalk in front of the soup kitchen until it opened at daylight, afraid if she sat still she'd freeze to death. But even that, even walking in the rags of a coat in the bitter cold, her nose running and then freezing on her upper lip, even that was better than reliving the bottoms of both feet cut open with glass stuck so deep it took an emergency room doctor an hour to find all the shards and thirty-two stitches to close the wounds.

She shut her eyes, hoping that the lumpy, leather-stink place was a flashback, and she really was on the army cot in the little room off the kitchen where the cook had said she could sleep until she made enough money to get her own place. Right. Like she'd ever be able to get her own place!

But when she opened her eyes again, she was still there in lumpy darkness. Only now she had figured out where. She was in a closet. Whose closet? Well, a thing like that was hard to say just judging from the generalized stink of a person's sneakers.

A shaft of brilliant light suddenly split the darkness. Somebody had flung open the closet door, and Becca squinted, couldn't see anything in the glare. But she could hear fine.

"Right there," said an indignant woman's voice. "That filthy vagrant…homeless person…whatever it's politically correct to call her kind…it is right there, curled up in a ball in my closet!"

She heard men's voices, the scuffle of feet, and then large hands took hold of her arm and dragged her out into the light.

The closet hadn't been in the woman's bedroom. That was a good thing. Becca'd likely be in more trouble if she'd broken into the woman's house. This was some kind of storage shed, which meant she'd probably only had to push up an unlocked window—or break out the glass!—to slip in from outside. She didn't bother to try to remember what it was she'd done. She'd long since given up doing that. She merely accepted that she'd gone to sleep somewhere and had awakened somewhere else. Badda boom, badda bing. She had no idea where she might have been or what she might have done in between going to sleep and waking up.

"…you doing here?"

A man standing behind the one who'd dragged her out

of the closet was speaking to her. She turned toward him and her heart sank. A cop.

"I don't care what she's doing here," the indignant woman said. "I just want her gone—right now."

"Ma'am, you'll have to come along with me," the police officer told Becca, and led her by the arm out of the building. Once outside, Becca saw that it was a detached garage and that a window on one side stood open.

"Are you arresting me?" she asked.

"You'll know I'm arresting you when I tell you I'm arresting you," he said.

"How can it be called breaking and entering when I didn't break anything?" she said as he propelled her toward a cruiser parked at the curb.

"There's the entering part."

"That window was open," she lied. Or maybe she didn't. Maybe it had been open. "I was only trying to get in out of the rain."

They'd reached the car by then, and the officer stopped and faced her. "I'm taking you in. A jail cell is warm and dry, and they"ll feed you something that bears a resemblance to real food." He looked her up and down. "You're not going to make it if you stay out here."

She wouldn't make it if he put her in there.

"Please don't lock me up," she said. "Can't you just give me a ticket or something, some kind of citation? I'll show up in court, I swear I will." Another lie.

"Don't worry. You'll get out before the DT's get too bad. What else you hooked on besides booze?"

Becca never drank, not a drop, had never even experimented with drugs. Her life was hard enough sober. What it might be like to experience her reality in some kind of dopey state where she had no defenses at all—no, she'd pass on that one, thank you very much.

Might as well run the truth up the flagpole and see if anybody'd salute. "I'm not hooked on anything. I just can't be locked up."

He looked more closely at her, perhaps saw that her pupils weren't dilated and she was steady on her feet and didn't smell like cheap wine or mouthwash.

"You've stopped taking your meds, then. Nobody does what you did without some serious mental issues."

What had she done?

"Either way, you broke the law. I could get you on the breaking and entering charge, vandalism, destruction of public property, terroristic threatening, but I'm only listing the least egregious, vagrancy, on the arrest report so you'll go to district court instead of circuit court. They'll cut you loose on Monday."

"What's today?"

"Thursday."

She couldn't be locked in a jail cell for four days! She had to keep moving, running, or he'd find her.

"You don't understand, I—"

"What's your name?"

Becca hesitated.

"Your real name."

"Becca Hawkins." She hadn't meant to tell him that, but he'd caught her off guard before she had time to make something up.

"Now, I am arresting you. I said I'd tell you." Then he began to recite the mantra. "Rebecca Hawkins, you—"

"It's Becca, just Becca."

It's not short for anything or long for anything or a substitute for anything. It just is.

Who always said that? Jack Carpenter. When they were kids. He said that to teachers and other grown-ups when they got her name wrong. For some reason, it always upset him when people messed up her name.

"…to remain silent. If you give up that right—"

"Don't I have the right to remain sane? You put me in a box, and he'll come for me."

"…an attorney present before questioning. If you cannot afford an—"

"I look to you like I can afford a lawyer?"

"Attorney, one will be appointed for you by the court. Do you understand?"

"You're the one who doesn't understand. If I don't move around, I can't stay away from him!"

"You're going to be in jail, lady. Who's going to break into a jail to get at you?"

What was after her didn't have to break in. He was already there, waiting for her.

Chapter Three

2011

THERESA SAT on the floor in the dark, clutchin' her phone in her wet, shaking hands, frantically punchin' the button on the top to start it again. Nothin'. The button on the bottom of the face, then, the Siri button. She slid her wet fingers down the cracked face and punched that little round dented place on the bottom. No voice asked, "What can I help you with?"

Now, her heart was hammerin' in her chest like some lunatic on a padded door. But she was afraid to try to stand. The knee she'd banged was a hot poker of agony. Old, fat women couldn't fall down without messin' up somethin'. Besides, even if she hadn't hurt her knee, she didn't think her legs could hold her right now. And crawlin' on that bum knee wouldn't likely end well, neither. Couldn't walk or crawl--fine, she'd *scoot* then, across the hardwood floor to the door. She looked around in blackness like bein' blind. Where was the door? Before it went out, the cell phone light had flashed in her eyes, and they wasn't adjusted enough to the darkness to see whatever little bit of light might be shinin' through the doorway from the front door she'd left open.

Her heartbeat ratcheted up another notch and panic swelled in her chest. The door had to be…this way. This was the way she come in, wasn't it? She scooted fast as she could, tried not to let herself know what was on the floor that made it so slick she'd fallen, in the puddles her hand fell into as she scooted. She wiped her hands on her blouse to get the sticky off, feelin' around in the blackness, but couldn't find no doorframe. She'd only come in the room a few steps, then fell, then crawled toward her cell phone. She couldn't have come this far. The door must be the other way. Reversing direction, she started to scoot again, her heart roarin' in her ears so loud she didn't know if Biscuit had stopped barkin' or she just couldn't hear the sound no more.

Her hand hit something else on the wet floor besides a puddle. What her fingers touched felt like…hair? No. Please, no. Her fingers followed the tresses—soft like Miss Minnie's white hair when it wasn't caught up in a bun—but wet and sticky. She reached out farther in the blackness 'til her fingers touched somethin' solid. She felt along its surface until she touched…a forehead—the skin was cold, like a doll's. A scream crawled on hairy black legs up the back of her throat, but she couldn't give it voice 'cause her lungs was full of the air she'd gasped in at the touch of cold human flesh and now she couldn't breathe out.

She reflexively yanked her hand away but her fingers was tangled in the sticky hair. Strugglin' to get her fingers free—panic bursting in bright, colored lights in front of her eyes—air finally exploded out of her lungs, carrying with it a screeching wail like a rip racing down a canvas sail. She staggered upward. Away. Had to get away! She tried to stand and run but slipped and fell again on the slick floor, landin' on her back this time. Her head banged into the floor and shiny spots of white light appeared in front of her eyes.

She tried to blink the spots away, her heart explodin' out of her chest, and when she opened her eyes again, the spots was gone. But they'd been replaced by a red glow high above her. In the corner on the other side of the room, up next to the ceiling, was a strange red light.

She didn't pause to wonder what it might be but rolled over on her side and got to her knees, determined to stand up no matter how bad her knee hurt. The glow got brighter but didn't really light up nothin'. Facing away from it now, she nevertheless saw it spread out across the ceiling, flow across the ceiling like water from a wave glidin' across wet sand. It reached the wall in front of her, then began to…drip down it. It was light, but it oozed down the wallpaper like blood drippin' from the ceiling.

And then she knew she didn't want to look back at that far corner to see where the light was comin' from. Must not. She cringed away from it in the dark, shrank down into the smallest part of herself 'cause she knew what must be there in the corner.

~

1985

Bishop tried one more time to crank the engine of the pickup truck. Nothin'. He could tinker with the engine, of course, and likely get it runnin' again if the battery wasn't dead. He'd been nursin' that old thing along, keeping it runnin' for years after it had ought to have been sold for scrap metal. But he only had his small toolbox in the back, might not have everything he needed. More important, Bishop didn't have time to fix it. Them kids was out there in the woods, and there was a dark ugliness Bishop couldn't identify out there with 'em. This was no time for him to have his head stuck up under the hood of his truck.

He got out. He'd have to walk to the logging road rendezvous point, and it was a long way. It'd probably be the middle of the afternoon 'fore he got there. He glanced up at the mountain to the north and could see Burnt Stump clearly. Whenever he took the kids ginseng huntin' with him, they had to promise two things: to stay together, and if they got lost or somethin' bad happened, they was to go to Burnt Stump. That's where he'd always go to find 'em. Burnt Stump was a huge basswood tree that had been struck by lightning when Bishop's father was a boy. It stood atop the southern end of Bear Claw Mountain like a black lighthouse, visible for miles in every direction.

Bishop stood staring at it for a few moments. It made more sense to go there now and wait than to walk all the way back to the logging road, maybe even miss 'em there. They'd show up at Burnt Stump eventually when he didn't meet them on the logging road. He didn't like that plan a'tall—just leavin' 'em in the woods with whatever was out there, but what else was he gone do?

Bishop set out west through the woods, not runnin'— couldn't run in these tangled trees and vines or you'd trip and break your neck—but loping in long strides that ate up the distance. He hadn't never encountered a demon in the woods before. He'd seen 'em in town, though, ridin' some poor soul like a beetle attached to their back, suckin' the life juice out. More often, what he seen wasn't demons possessing people but demons influencing people. Wasn't the same as a demon taking over a person's will and heart. That was a process, didn't happen overnight—unless they was a child. A demon could overpower the will of a child. But demons whisperin' in folks' ears, telling 'em lies—what you seen then was lights kinda flickerin' around a person or sometimes a shadow or eye-shine like the glassy sheen of an animal's eyes in the dark.

His grandpa had told him about them lights, the shine and the darkness when he was just a boy and had first figured out that what he was seein' in the world around him wasn't necessarily the same thing other folks was seein'. Grampa Rufus had warned him years ago there wasn't but a few places in the world like Caverna County, Kentucky. This here place was special, but not in a good way.

The whole family has gathered at his grandparents' house after church. They've finished lunch, and the women are congregated in the kitchen, cleaning up and chattering woman-talk while the men gather on the back porch to smoke stogies, spit tobacco and tell lies.

Bishop is seated on the porch swing, pushing it back and forth with his toe when Grampa Rufus comes out the screen door that protests with a loud squawk, and sits down beside him.

"You's having trouble with what you seen this mornin', ain't you boy?" Grampa Rufus had no patience with folks who'd "shimmy-shammy" around the point. He always got right to it.

Bishop nods but says nothing, keeps his head lowered, looking at the planks of the porch floor because he's afraid if he opens his mouth, he'll cry. He's eight years old and would rather die than burst into tears like some sissy girl.

"You seen the spirit lights on them field hands that came in late and sat in the back row in church."

It wasn't a question, but Bishop nods again nonetheless. He saw them all right, had turned in the pew when he heard the rustle of feet coming in from the vestibule. Four men stood all respectful-like with they hats in they hands while they located seats on the pew in the back. Lights flickered around all of them, blinked on and off, and he could hear ugly sounds that didn't have words, whispers. The fourth man had a darkness that…it was like a snake, and it slithered all over him, around his neck and down the front of his shirt. Bishop had looked away then, horrified. It wasn't that Bishop didn't know what the lights and dark thing was. He and Grampa Rufus had talked about it many times.

But in church!

Sometimes Bishop fears his grandfather can actually read minds. This is one of those times.

"And you can't get it in your head how come they'd show up in the house of God."

Bishop looks at him then for the first time, the anguish inside him bursting out in a torrent of words.

"Ain't there nowhere you's safe from them creatures? I know you said they's everywhere, but how can demons come in God's house and sit down nicey-nice like they was all holy, and why—?"

"Satan's the prince of this world, son, you got to get that in your head. God give it over to him—for a time —and—"

"Why would God do a thing like that?" Bishop demands.

"The next time you see God, you need to ask him that question," his grandfather snaps. "But 'tween now and then all you got is that much." He studies Bishop. "I s'pose you old enough to hear this. I's 'bout your age when Mama told me. Son, you got to shake hands with the fact that demons is everywhere, but Caverna County is a special kinda bad place."

Bishop feels an odd airy feeling in the pit of his stomach and an unreasonable desire to leap up off the swing and run as fast as he can so he can't hear the words that are about to come out of Grampa Rufus's mouth. At that same time, he feels a steadiness in his soul, like some part of him has known this all along.

His grandfather starts out tellin' him what he already knows—that there's a barrier between the spiritual world and the world of men.

"It's what you cross over when you die so it ain't solid, not like no brick wall. For a demon to get into this world, he got to go through that barrier, too." His grandfather pauses and collects himself before he continues. "Well, in some places in the world, 'pears that barrier's thinner than it is in other places, and for reasons I don't understand, they's ways for demons to pass back and forth there. That's how they possessed the folks Jesus talks about in the Bible. That make sense to you?"

Bishop nods.

"What else you need to understand is that sometimes you happens to be right up next to some place in the spiritual world where the fabric 'tween us and them ain't strong." He shudders in revulsion. "They's right there on the other side, maggots, crawling all over each other."

"Like a city full of them?"

"The Bible don't say nothin' 'bout demons livin' in cities!" The old man is annoyed. He don't stand for nobody playin' fast and loose with the Scripture. "And other than what the Bible does say, all the rest of what anybody knows about demons is what they figured out they own self based on the evidence they could see—so they might have got it right and they might not. But I 'spect

Caesarea Philippi in the Bible was likely one of them places. And folks say they's parts of Haiti where the membrane separating our world from the darkness is so thin it ain't hardly there a'tall."

Bishop has no idea where Haiti might be.

"Son, from what I've seen—and my mama, and her daddy before her who was brought here as a slave—Caverna County is one of them places, too. Maybe bad as Haiti, dangerous in a way that only those of us who know can see."

As he hurried through the woods, Bishop sensed now the danger his grandfather had described all those years ago, felt the presence of evil around him, a shadowy darkness that other folks couldn't see. He could see it, though. So could Isaac. And so could Becca.

Chapter Four

1985

Becca heard a horrible sucking sound when the blond boy pulled the fisherman's arms off—or imagined she did—and her stomach lurched. She spewed the remains of this morning's cornbread and orange juice onto the ground in front of Dougie, wrenching and gagging. The boys surely would have heard her if the fisherman hadn't been making so much noise, screaming a high-pitched wail that went on and on.

"You idiot! You want to get us arrested?" cried the redheaded boy with the Mohawk as the other boys yipped and yelled in glee! He reached out and grabbed the boy holding the now-unattached fisherman's arms and tossed him down the riverbank, where he landed on his butt in the sand. The boy dropped the gory arms and leapt up, angling for a fight, started to lunge at the redheaded boy but must have thought better of it and merely stood glaring at him.

"Do you realize what you've done?" the redhead said. The fisherman was still screaming. He lay on his back where they'd left him, his head thrown back, shrieking at the top of his lungs. "Do you want to explain—?" The redheaded boy stopped and cast an annoyed glance at the fisherman. To the boy standing nearest the man, he said, "Shut him up." The boy dutifully took a step toward the man and placed his foot on the man's throat. With a jumping motion, like you'd crank a motorcycle, he shifted his weight to that foot, and the screaming ended abruptly in a strangled sound. The fisherman went limp.

The redhead continued where he'd left off. "To explain why we didn't find him—that we had to stop looking because we were all in jail?" His voice had risen in pitch and volume until he was yelling. The other boy said nothing, and the others fell silent with him. Then the redheaded boy shifted gears. Looking around, he said, "We have to make this all go away, clean up this mess. Get rid of the body."

"Just throw it in the river," said a boy in a gray T-shirt that had a Hard Rock Cafe Memphis logo on the front.

"Riiight." The redheaded boy sneered. "So it can float downstream and bob up on shore somewhere missing both arms?"

"How will anybody know we were the ones who did it?" said a dark-haired boy. The others were instantly arguing, yelling at each other, shoving. A brawl threatened to break out any second.

"Stop it!" roared the redheaded boy as he separated two boys who'd balled their hands into fists and were about to start slugging it out. "We have to figure this out or…do you want to tell him?"

The boys fell silent until one of them offered, "The guy said the water was deep here, with stumps and stuff on the bottom. We could use this rope"—he indicated the line that attached the johnboat to a scraggly bush on shore—

"to tie the body to a stump down there, pile some rocks on it, maybe."

"And bury the arms in the sand," said another.

The redheaded boy considered, then nodded. Turning to the boy who liked to pull the wings off flies, he said. "You get to do the honors, Dumas. And you better tie him tight."

Becca watched in fascinated horror as the boys busied themselves cleaning up the carnage. One filled the fisherman's minnow bucket in the river and used the water to wash the blood off the sand while the others wound the rope securely around the body and hauled it out into the water. It took several dives before the boy declared that the body wasn't going anywhere.

Then two of the boys lifted a rock the size of a Volkswagen—picked it up like it was made out of Styrofoam—and tossed it into the water over the spot where the body was submerged. They threw other big rocks in, too, rocks as big as washing machines, like little kids tossing pebbles into the water. One boy used his fist to smash a hole in the bottom of the boat near the motor in the back and then shoved it out into the river to float downstream until the weight of the motor pulled it under and sank it. Someone must have buried the arms, but Becca didn't see who or where. When they were finished, the leader surveyed the riverbank, his red hair as stiff as the straw in a broom in a narrow strip from his forehead to his neck. Nothing remained to show that anybody'd ever been there.

Satisfied, the boy nodded. "Come on," he said.

The other boys fell in beside him as he started down the riverbank—headed right to the spot where Becca was hiding in the crepe myrtle bush.

2011

In the beginning, jail wasn't as bad as Becca feared it'd be. There were only a couple of other prisoners, and one of them was so drunk she did nothing but babble nonsense, sing golden oldies in an off-key soprano and cry about losing "Billy," who was either her boyfriend or her bulldog.

The other woman was a fat Hispanic woman who'd apparently been picked up for shoplifting, and it struck Becca that the woman could have stuffed a microwave down the front of her dress and nobody'd have noticed. You played the cards you were dealt, though, and did the best you could with whatever you had. That was what life was, doing the best you could.

In Becca's case, that had never, ever, been enough. She always came up short at the end of the day, but she never quit trying, either. And that was something. You got points for that, didn't you?

Then they'd brought in the prostitute. Long before Becca saw her, she felt the wave of cold that flowed out from her, frozen lava from a volcano of ice. The frigid air instantly slathered the floor and walls and cell bars with frost—not white frost but ugly dark-red crystals, a color frost could never be but was. The air was so cold it hurt to breathe, felt like those bloody crystals were forming in her nose and throat and lungs, cutting her open so she bled, her warm blood instantly frozen into more jagged red crystals. The cold bit into her flesh and chilled her to the bone, and it would have done the same thing if she'd been wearing an Eskimo parka of sealskin and polar bear hide instead of just a T-shirt and jeans. This was cold from the other, and it knew no boundaries, was as inexorable and unstoppable as a rising tide.

What the prostitute really looked like to other people, Becca didn't know. She never saw people the way others did. She'd caught a glimpse of dirty dark hair and squinty, too-small eyes. But as soon as Becca spotted what was attached to the woman's chest, all the woman's features changed.

Her eyes opened up and became deep, dark pools with no color at all—just the black irises and no eyelids—like a lizard. Her nose melted and ran down off her face so nothing was left behind but two wet holes that oozed green goo to drip down her lip. Her teeth sharpened, razor edge, and her fingers grew claws.

And some part of Becca had always known that wasn't real. People's features changing—that wasn't really happening. She understood that what she perceived was not objective reality. Maybe the demons had some power to distort the reality that Becca saw. Or maybe—and this had always been a scary thought—maybe what she saw was reality, a manifestation of what the person had become in response to the evil inside them. Maybe the rest, the veneer, was illusion.

Becca wanted to run—that's why she couldn't be locked up, what the officer didn't understand—she had to be able to run because the others could always sense her, could feel Becca's knowing.

"What have we here?" said the thing sucking the life from the helpless woman. Its voice was gravel grinding under a truck tire.

Becca sat on the floor in the corner of her cell, squashed up tight against the concrete block wall, her eyes squeezed shut.

"Oh, juicy," it said, its voice changing to a high shriek

like the cry of gulls at the beach. "Come talk to us, Miss Pretty."

Becca felt her eyes opening. She hated that, hated that she had to look and couldn't close her eyes and stick her fingers into her ears and chant "I can't hear you!" She had to see. If you could see, you had to see. That's the way it was.

It was a creature of slime, the filth at the bottom of a sewer pipe, with many hairy black legs, like a mutant spider.

"You do see me," it said from a great maw of a mouth that opened up across its whole chest. "Can I come and play with you? Be with you? Be inside you?"

Becca cried, "No!" in spite of herself, even though she knew it was wrong, oh so very wrong to engage a demon. She wailed the word as loud as she could, and it came out a strangled whisper.

"You know who I am and where I come from, and you know I can have you if I want."

It couldn't, of course, but that was small comfort to Becca now, locked in here with it, unable to get away.

It began to jeer and laugh at her, its slime running all over the woman it was attached to, and Becca watched because she had to. She cringed back into herself, into the smallest crevice in her mind. Tried to prepare for the onslaught of dirty, black evil that would so paralyze and suffocate her that she would die, die, die a thousand times only to come back again and again to suffer more.

Now, he would come, the Monster Other would come. He would know where she was, and he would slither dark and stinking into her mind and steal every lovely thing from it until it was a wasteland, utterly bereft of goodness and beauty. She would look at it and speak to it. The touch of pure evil would feel slick and smooth, like the belly of a spider.

~

2011

Theresa cowered in the profound dark that was somehow not lit at all by the red glow above, the glow that was dripping down the walls.

"You're early this evening, Mrs. Washington," said a voice from behind her. "I was just finishing up."

The voice.

She was utterly paralyzed by the sound. It was more than mesmerizing, stronger than hypnotic. It was pure evil, wrapped in a pleasant baritone, honey poured over shards of broken glass, so totally other that the foreign sound took Theresa's breath away.

"Look at me," the voice said. And Theresa felt her body and head turning toward the sound. Only she wasn't doin' the turning. She fought against it, tried to resist, but her pitiful little effort meant nothin' at all. She suspected—no, she was sure—that if she could somehow have kept her head still, her neck would have snapped from the pressure.

What slid into view when she turned was impossible. The red glow came from the corner of the room up near the ceiling. It radiated in undulating waves from a man, distorting him the way heat waves in the desert warp the horizon. He hung there, suspended, dressed in a business suit, tie straight, pants creased. His hair, the color of a ten-penny nail, come down to a widow's peak on his forehead and it was combed neat and tidy. Well, what hair there was. Much of it on the right side had been burned off and a jagged piece of scar snaked down across his face like red barbed wire. His eyes was an odd shade of light green under a prominent brow and thick black eyebrows.

She was no more surprised that a man hung suspended in the air than she was by who the man was. Chapman Whitworth. He was the man who'd summoned a monster demon when Jack, Daniel and Becca were twelve years old, more than a quarter of a century ago. The man who just last week the president had nominated for a vacant seat on the United States Supreme Court.

"Do you think you can stand against me?" Whitworth asked. "Seriously? You and your ragtag lackeys—is that what you think? Because if you do"—his voice changed then, became the voice of an elderly black woman with a soft Southern drawl—"you got a whole heap more thinks a'comin', missy-girl."

It felt like he'd slapped her.

"You will pay—each of you—for opposing me." Then the voice ceased to be mesmerizing and hypnotic. It turned raw and guttural, so harsh and jagged her ears might bleed from hearing it. "I will not take your lives...I will destroy them."

Theresa's thoughts scattered, random, leaves hit by a breeze.

Don't let me cry.

Reckon anybody ever died from being afraid?

I wish Bishop was here.

His strong presence would have changed everything. She was certainly a poor second choice to stand up to a demon. Bishop spoke his last words to a demon before it killed him. And he could see the monstrous thing, not just the man form it was living in. Jack said Bishop's voice had sounded strong and firm.

Help me!

"We will beat you," Theresa said. "Just like we did the last time."

Where did that come from? Theresa had absolutely not formed them words in her mind or pushed them out of her mouth. Not in a steady voice—she was shaking like a half-froze hummingbird. The thought, the intent, the words, the will to say them—none of it had come from Theresa. And that was both the most comfortin' and most frightenin' thing that had ever happened to her.

The red glow grew so suddenly intense that she could have seen it clearly with her eyes closed. Something formed around the man, a red shape, a monster face twisted with anger and hatred. Like Andi'd seen that day they all found out the war wasn't over yet, that their battle against the monster demon that possessed Chapman Whitworth was only beginning. The hideous face grew, became more solid loomed above—

Light suddenly flooded the room, along with the sound of music—literally The Sound of Music—blaring from stereo speakers brought to life by returning electricity. The glare struck Theresa blind, staggered her like a blow. She squinted through a forest of eyelashes, but her mind refused to put them flashing images into anything that made any sense.

Red everywhere. Blood! On the furniture, the floor. All over her own hands and arms and clothing. Miss Minnie lay on the floor a few feet away, covered in blood. Mr. Gerald lay sprawled spread-eagled by the door—she'd tripped over his foot. An ax was stuck in his chest like a lumberjack had left it in a tree stump.

She screamed again, tried to scoot toward the door she could see now. But her way out was blocked. A man dressed in black sweatpants and a black hoodie was standing in the doorway.

"What are you doing here?" Whitworth roared at the man, who was staring into the room with a look of… surprise, maybe? Or fear. Whitworth spoke in his own voice, a human voice. She turned to see him standing in the corner of the room, where an instant before he'd been suspended near the ceiling. The red light was gone; Whitworth looked normal, though he still seemed almost to be outlined in red Magic Marker.

The man made a move to come into the room, had one foot lifted.

"Stay out of here, fool," Whitworth said. "I told you to turn the electricity back on and then wait in the car. Go!"

The man vanished out of the doorway.

Whitworth turned his attention back to Theresa, but her mind had gone to a place where even a demon from Hell couldn't call her back. Reality had finally elbowed its way into her consciousness. The old couple she loved, that she'd looked after all these years—sweet Miss Minnie and gentle Mr. Gerald—had been hacked to death.

And suddenly, Whitworth was standing in front of her, though she didn't never see him take a step. His feet wasn't touching the floor.

Then the ax in Mr. Gerald's chest moved, wiggled slightly and pulled out of the bloody chest with a distinct smuck sound. It moved through the air like a kid's helium balloon on a string 'til it was there beside Whitworth.

He was gonna kill her after all, bury the blade in her like he'd done in Mr. Gerald. Theresa lifted her arm up above her head and cringed away from the blow.

Whitworth kicked her leg, not to hurt her but a nudge to get her attention. She opened the eyes she'd squeezed shut and looked up at him, his scarred face clear in the light from the pole lamp beside the chair. Mr. Gerald's chair, where he sat and read the sports page of the Cincinnati Inquirer every morning after breakfast.

"Take it," he said and nodded to the ax. When she didn't move, he spoke again, an edge of threat in his voice. "I said take it."

She reached up a trembling hand and took the ax by the bloody handle, then sat unmoving, holding the ax in front of her.

"...every mountain, ford every stream, follow every rainbow..." Julie Andrews's voice filled the room, almost drowning out the sound of faraway barking.

"Have a nice rest of your day," Whitworth said.

She felt herself being flung forward and her head connected with the oak floor and the world was gone.

Chapter Five

2011

On the other side of Webster County from the old house where Theresa Washington lay unconscious on a blood-splattered floor, Daniel Burke stepped out of the lounge onto the polished floor of the lobby of the Cincinnati Centurion Hotel.

He was not in the best possible frame of mind. He was speaking tonight at the Tri-State Ministerial Association Pastors' Conference in the hotel's Emerald Ballroom, and late in the afternoon, he'd gotten a voice mail asking him to show up an hour early for a preconference gathering. But when he got to the hotel—no gathering. The conference registration desk wasn't even set up, so he'd cooled his heels in the lounge, using his phone to make notes on his message for Sunday.

Now, there was a silver-haired woman working behind a table bearing the sign "TSMA Register Here." He slipped his phone into the breast pocket of his jacket as she handed him a blank nametag and a pen. He filled out the tag and stuck it to the pocket over his phone. He'd give it half an hour before it fell off.

When the woman read it, she recognized him. "You look just like you do on TV," she said.

Daniel was a handsome man with a friendly, square-jawed face, kind brown eyes and hair the same chestnut-brown as his daughter, Andi. His six-foot frame was trim and three-times-a-week-in-the-gym fit. He waited patiently while the woman oohed about his church building—"It looks like a coliseum!"—and aahed about his congregation—"How do you know anybody with twenty-five-thousand people?" And as soon as she paused to take a breath, Daniel excused himself and crossed the lobby to the bank of elevators.

The one on the far right in the set of three was sitting with the door open, a young woman dressed all in red—blouse, skirt and shoes—inside. She smiled broadly at Daniel, like they were old friends, and as soon as he stepped in, she pushed the Close Door button even though there was a man making purposefully for the elevator, obviously intent on getting on. Wherever the woman was going, she was in a hurry to get there.

Daniel pressed fourteen for the Emerald Ballroom and settled back to stare at the lighted numbers as elevator courtesy required. The number four had just lit up when the woman pushed the emergency stop button, and the elevator halted with a jerk. What followed was the oddest few minutes of Daniel Burke's life.

The woman was tiny, barely five feet tall, with long blonde hair and a single diamond stud in her left nostril. Daniel turned to look at her, preparing to ask why she'd stopped the elevator, but the words died on his lips. She was gawking at him like she was the one who was surprised. And not only surprised, but frightened.

After that, absolutely nothing the woman did made any sense at all. She suddenly pitched backward toward the back elevator wall, would have fallen if he hadn't reached out to steady her. She grabbed his tie, pulled him toward her, then wrenched her head from side to side furiously and pushed him away. After that, she disengaged the emergency stop button and turned and huddled in the back corner of the elevator, facing away from him.

When the elevator doors opened on the fifth floor, the woman tripped—on what?—going out and sprawled on the floor. When he reached to help her up, she snatched his cell phone out of the breast pocket of his suit jacket and held it behind her while she scooted away from him toward the wall. Trying to get it back from her was like dealing with a five-year-old playing keep-away. He'd ask politely; she'd shake her head no and act scared. She suddenly jumped up and dodged past him into the hallway, where she held the phone out, then snatched it back again and again. When he cornered her at the end of the hall and threatened to summon security, she finally gave it to him, then snatched at it to get it back before bolting toward the elevator and vanishing.

Daniel stood alone in the hallway for a few moments after she was gone, totally confused.

What just happened here?

Then he shrugged—the woman was definitely off her meds—and returned to the elevator. He pushed the Up arrow, smoothed his hair, straightened the tie the crazy woman had pulled askew. Moments later he got in the elevator and rode to the top floor with an elderly couple in polite elevator silence.

When he stood before the crowd of about five hundred people, pastors and their wives and elder board members ten minutes later, he had collected his wits and was on his game. He began with a story.

"A man sits down on an airplane beside a stunningly beautiful young woman and knows instantly they were made for each other," Daniel said. "So the man asks her, 'What kind of men do you like?'"

The audience listened in rapt attention.

"The bombshell told the man, 'Well, I'm very attracted to Native American men with those big eyes and high cheekbones.' Then she stops and considers. 'But I think Jewish men are sexy, too. They're so intense and determined.' She pauses again. 'And Southern men—I love the sweet drawl when they talk.'"

"Then the woman flashes the man a breathtaking smile and asks coyly, 'And what did you say your name was?'"

Daniel paused for a beat and delivered the last line with perfect timing.

"Geronimo Bernstein…but my friends call me Bubba."

When the laughter died away, Daniel opened his mouth to begin the talk he'd prepared about how pastors and other church leaders were required to wear many hats, to be "Geronimo Bernstein" to the members of their congregations and their communities.

But he didn't say any of that. He couldn't. The problem was that Daniel wasn't the same man who'd accepted this speaking engagement six months ago. After what he'd seen, after Emily's murder, he couldn't seem to put it on autopilot anymore, couldn't manage to open his mouth and let the same old crap fall out.

The silence lengthened, became uncomfortable. The crowd moved restlessly in their chairs, looking around in consternation. Finally, Daniel made a decision and began speaking before he could change his mind.

"You don't really believe what you say you believe," he said, his voice calm and deliberate.

That got their attention. You could have heard a mouse tiptoe across a cotton ball. He leaned over the podium and spoke very softly, the microphone amplifying his quiet words.

"If you did, you'd know that the forces of evil are at work among us all the time, that as you coach your daughter's soccer team or watch movies on your iPad, mow the grass or hit a hole in one—beings made of pure evil are watching, eager to cause you misery and heartache. And their greatest weapon is the one you have given to them."

When he whispered the last line, every person in the audience was unconsciously leaning forward to hear it.

"You don't even believe they exist."

Daniel went on in that vein, giving himself over to his words in an intimate abandon, his voice louder and then softer in a kind of musical cadence that'd made him the "golden boy," a rising star in the ministry.

But few people hung around to chat with the golden boy after he finished speaking. He wasn't surprised. If he kept telling people what they did not want to hear, his days as a megachurch pastor were numbered. And he tried to make himself care about that, to make it matter, but he couldn't seem to manage. Was it just grief? All the experts claimed you shouldn't make any major decisions or changes in your life during the first six months after the death of a loved one because you weren't in your right mind. But it seemed to Daniel that he'd never been more in his "right mind" than he'd been in the three months since Emily died. All the pretense, the phoniness was gone, been burned away in an instant by the sound of the gunshot that killed her.

Jack Carpenter had lost his wife, too, years ago. He

understood. He'd been there for Daniel in the early days when the razor edge of pain sliced him open so viscerally he could hardly stand. Jack had told him then, "Every morning, you'll open your eyes, and it'll be the first thing you think about. And then one morning, it'll be the second."

For Daniel, it was still the first.

"Excuse me, are you Daniel Burke?"

The question came from behind him. When Daniel turned around, he found two uniformed police officers.

Daniel gestured down at his nametag.

"That's what it says right—" His nametag was gone.

"We need you to come with us, sir," said the one on the right and took him by the arm. The jerking movement sent a little bolt of pain down into his wrist, the one Victor Alexander had snapped like a twig that day in the belfry after he'd shot Emily. It was still casted from the final surgery and scars would forever encircle it in white bracelets.

Then the officers hauled Daniel out of the building.

2011

Harrelton, Ohio Police Department Sergeant Jack Carpenter had seen worse gore in ten years as a police officer and six in Special Forces—but not on someone he loved.

Theresa Washington sat on a table in an exam cubicle in Good Samaritan Hospital emergency room covered in dried blood. It was smeared all over her—hands, arms, legs, face, hair, and had turned her white hospital auxiliary uniform pink. When she saw him, she burst into tears, and he put his arms around her and pulled her tight to his chest while she cried. He was a big man, six feet four inches, with skin a couple of shades lighter than Theresa's. Though not handsome, his face was distinctive—rugged—with penetrating eyes and a determined set to his square chin.

"Oh, Jack, they's gone. Miss Minnie and Mr. Gerald is dead," she said.

Jack knew that already. An anonymous 911 call had reported screams coming from a house on Elmcrest Circle, and the responding officer had found two dead bodies and an unconscious Theresa at the scene.

He rocked her gently back and forth as sobs racked her body. Up close, he could see that there was one clean spot on her. A white bandage covered some sort of wound on her forehead.

"Are you all right?"

"No, I ain't all right." She pulled back out of his arms and looked up at him. Her tears had cleaned the blood off her cheeks in twin streaks. "It was him. He done it."

"Who?"

"Chapman Whitworth! He was there."

"At the Cohens' house?" Jack was flabbergasted.

"Won't nobody but me ever know it, though. Won't be no trace he ever set foot in the place, like he was a ghost."

Jack listened in growing wonder as Theresa told him what had happened. Light dripping down the walls? And Whitworth?

"They can do that?" he asked. "Demon-possessed people can float in the air?"

"S'pose they can," she snapped. "He did!" Then she sagged and put her face in her hands, didn't cry, just shook her head slowly back and forth. "If Bishop was here…he tole me once that powerful demons, what Scripture calls authorities, can tele—tell—what's it called?"

"Telekinesis. Moving things by thinking about it, by mental power."

"Bishop said that was a power come from the demon hisself—not like when a demon dumps a person's own adrenaline in they veins to make 'em impossible strong."

Jack, Daniel and Theresa had fought for their lives three months ago against demon-possessed men like that.

"What other kind of things them creatures might be able to do, I got no idea. Bishop did say that regular old demons is bound by natural laws but an efreet ain't. It can be in two places at the same time—possessing somebody and yet still at the place where it was summoned into the world." She paused. "They can control animals, too. You seen that part when you's a kid."

What comes behind. The hiss of snakes and the whisper of spiders crawling all over them. Yeah, Jack had seen that part. He remembered almost nothing from the summer when he was twelve years old and wished that memory was not one of the few he'd reclaimed.

"Bigger ones than bugs, I think. Dogs and cats. They can lift up things, too, not just theirselves. Like he done that ax. Pulled it right up out of Mr. Gerald's chest. It was…stuck"—tears threatened to claim her again—"and he had to wiggle it."

They were both silent for a beat. Then Jack spoke carefully.

"You do know why he gave you that ax, don't you?"

"Duh! Course I know. He wanted my fingerprints on it. His sure wasn't! I bet he never touched it at all. Just used it to…probably floating up in the air when he done it so's he wouldn't get no blood on his good suit."

She reached out and grabbed Jack's hand with both of

hers. They were trembling. "They ain't gonna find no trace of him anywhere in that house. You know they ain't. Just me. All over the place. And that man in the black hoodie— I bet they ain't gonna find no trace of him, neither."

"Man in a black hoodie?"

"I told that other officer about him, but I don't think he b'lieved a word I's sayin'." She described the man to Jack. "They gone say I killed them old people. That I took that ax…and then the electricity went out, and I slipped in the dark and hit my head."

"What possible motive could you—?"

"He's got that part figured out, too. You'll see."

"Why go to all this trouble? Why not just kill you?"

"'Parently things has changed somehow since he sent Cole Stuart and them others after us. He's changed his mind, don't want us dead no more. He wants us alive…so's he can make us suffer."

She was silent again, and then the suggestion of a smile tugged at her lips. "I said the day we put my Bishop in the ground that Miss Minnie and Mr. Gerald would go out of this world together. That when one of they hearts stopped beatin', the other's would, too." Tears filled her eyes and slid slowly down her cheeks. "They'd a'liked that part."

Chapter Six

2011

Daniel felt a sense of foreboding as he sat in the back of the police cruiser, what Bishop Washington would have called "the presence of evil" when he was a kid.

As the policemen had ushered him toward the doors of the Emerald Ballroom, he'd finally found his voice and bleated, "What's all this about?"

One of the officers had said they needed to talk to him in connection with—and then rattled off a string of charges. Daniel had heard only one word: rape. After that, he'd been so stunned that nothing else registered.

But now, sitting in the back of the cruiser, he focused, tried to get it straight in his head.

Rape. And aggravated assault. Why on earth would they suspect him of—then it came to him, fell into place like the last tumbler of a lock that springs it open. The little blonde woman in the elevator! She'd been so crazy, there was no telling what she might have said.

Surely, the police wouldn't believe the story of a

whack-job like that, take her word over his. But he couldn't shake the sinking feeling in the pit of his stomach.

At the police station, Daniel was relieved of the contents of his pockets. He handed over his car keys, a handful of change and his wallet out of his pants pockets.

"Everything," said the officer, nodding toward his suit jacket.

Daniel took his cell phone out of the top pocket, then stuck his hands down into the bottom pockets as he said, "I don't carry anything in--"

There was something in the left pocket, something cloth. He pulled it out and gaped at it in stunned disbelief. It was a pair of lacy bikini panties! Pink ones, torn. The officer snatched it out of his palm and held it up like a mouse by the tail.

Daniel was almost too flabbergasted to form words. "I don't...I have *no idea* how that got there. I didn't--"

"Save it," the officer said, then ushered Daniel unceremoniously into a police lineup. He was number four of five men standing in front of a height chart facing a mirror.

He didn't have to wait long for the verdict. As soon as he stepped out into the hallway, a plainclothes officer he'd not seen before told him, "Daniel Burke, we need to ask you some questions. The victim has picked you out of the lineup as the man who raped and assaulted her earlier this evening."

"Someone says I…raped…?" Daniel's breath caught in his throat, and he couldn't continue.

"Do you wish to have an attorney present before questioning?"

"I didn't do anything!"

"Are you saying that you give up your right to an attorney during questioning?"

"What do I need an attorney for? This is a mistake. I didn't hurt anybody."

Without so much as a "come with me," the officer took him by the arm and ushered him down the hallway to a door at the end. The room behind the door looked like every interrogation room in every cop show or movie Daniel had ever seen.

A wooden table, bare. Three chairs around it. There was no two-way mirror on the wall, though, and Daniel was disappointed about that. Wasn't there supposed to be a mirror? He should demand a mirror. No mirror, no questioning. Game over.

Daniel grabbed his thoughts, sensing a freight-train rush toward hysteria and tried to think rationally. What evidence could they possibly have against him? He hadn't done anything. What kind of idiot cop would take the word of a crazy woman over the minister of one of the biggest churches in America?

Daniel was told to have a seat, that somebody would be with him shortly.

"Shortly" turned out to be more than two hours, during which Daniel cycled through every conceivable emotion, broke into a cold sweat, almost hyperventilated—all for the edification and amusement of the video camera that was obviously this room's equivalent of a two-way mirror. It had been strategically placed too high for him to rip it off the wall had he been the kind of man disposed to ripping things off walls. During the last fifteen minutes of his stay in the room, however, he was considering whether or not he could reach it if he climbed up on one of the chairs.

Two men in sport coats came into the room. One was about fifty, balding, with sharp, angular features, and the other was short, with a face like a ferret. Daniel decided on the spot that he suffered from a raging case of little-man syndrome.

"I'm Detective Donald Bizanski," said Angular Face. "And this is Detective Herb Fowler."

Fowler didn't even nod, just placed a folder and a laptop on the table, pulled out a chair directly across from Daniel and sat down.

"Would you like something to drink—coffee, water, a soft drink?" Bizanski asked.

Good cop. Which meant the little ferret was Bad Cop.

"No, I'm not thirsty. I want to get this all straightened out so I can go home. My little girl's with a housekeeper, and she'll be waiting up. I always tuck her in bed at night and say her prayers with her."

Daniel couldn't help that last bit. If ever in his life he'd felt the need to sound "religious" and "holy" it was right now.

"We'll give you time to make arrangements for your little girl," said Fowler. "You're going to be staying with us for a while."

Daniel felt that pounding again, the hammer blows of heartbeats he was sure moved his shirt with every stroke. He didn't mean to sound frightened when he spoke, but he knew he did, and he hated it.

"Why? I haven't done anything."

"You'll have a chance to tell your side of the story," said Bizanski.

"What story? I don't have any idea what you guys are talking about."

Bad cop opened the folder on the table in front of him and removed a nametag and pitched it across the table toward Daniel.

"Recognize this?"

"Of course I recognize it. It's my nametag. I lost it when—" When had he lost it? He couldn't recall.

"When what?" Fowler pressed.

"I don't know for sure. But I think it was…Why does it matter where I lost my nametag?"

The detective reached into the folder again and pulled out the pair of torn pink panties Daniel had found in his coat pocket.

"I don't know how those panties got in my pocket," Daniel said, hearing how phony that sounded even in his own ears, like a line of bad dialogue from a black-and-white movie. "I know how that sounds, but it's the truth. I never saw those--"

"The victim has identified them. She said the guy who raped her ripped them off her and kept them--as a souvenir."

"Victim?" Daniel's mind was spinning so fast the friction might set his head on fire.

The officer reached into the folder a third time and brought out four eight-by-ten photographs and placed them on the table in front of Daniel, one at a time, like a Las Vegas blackjack dealer.

Daniel stared at the photos, and for a moment the images didn't even register. They showed front and side views of a woman who'd been beaten up—badly. Her left eye was black—swollen completely shut—her lip was split and her nose appeared to be broken. The sleeve of her dress was ripped at the shoulder.

"Do you know this woman? Her name is Lily Saunders."

Then it hit him. It was the woman from the elevator.

"Yes. I mean, no. I don't know the woman, but I recognize her. I rode up in the elevator with her at the Centurion Hotel tonight. What happened to her?"

"We're hoping you can tell us that," said Bizanski. "So you admit being in the elevator with Miss Saunders at the Centurion?"

"I didn't know her name was Lily Saunders. It's not like she introduced herself, but yes."

"She didn't tell you her name when you spent half an hour in the bar with her before you got into the elevator?" Fowler asked.

Daniel was incredulous. "I wasn't in the bar with her!"

"The parking lot stamp for your car says you arrived at the hotel an hour before you were scheduled to speak. Where were you?"

"I got a voice mail asking me to come early—"

"From whom?"

"I don't know, there was no name and—"

"Can we hear it?"

"I didn't save it."

"Why were you to come early?"

"For a gathering…but I couldn't find anybody…there must have been some kind of misunderstanding, so I sat in the lounge. I was not in the bar. I never saw that woman before I got into the elevator with her. But I certainly remember her. She was nuts!"

"How so?" Bizanski asked in a gentle tone. Yeah, Good Cop. Definitely Good Cop. "What did she do that was strange?"

"Everything she did was strange," Daniel said. Then he told the officers what had happened in the elevator and in the hallway outside the elevator. It didn't take long. There wasn't a whole lot to tell. When he finished, the two officers were silent. They exchanged a look, Good Cop passing the ball back to Bad Cop.

"So you're saying this was all her fault?" Bad Cop said. ""That she stopped the elevator, she grabbed you, she came on to you?"

The purposeful disbelief dripped off his words.

"She didn't come on to me. She…like I said, what she did didn't make sense. None of it."

"Pull up your sleeves," Bizanski said. "I want to see the top of your hands."

The officer picked up his phone and took three shots of the scratch on Daniel's right hand while Daniel tried to explain it.

"I had to threaten her to get her to give me the phone." He saw their reaction and added, "Threaten to call security. So she handed it to me, then grabbed to get it back and scratched my hand."

"How'd her underwear get in your pocket?"

"She must have put it there."

"Why would she do a thing like that?"

"I don't know--ask *her!*"

"And that's your story?"

"It's not a story. It's the truth."

"You do know, don't you, that there are surveillance cameras in the elevator and the hallway?"

Daniel hadn't noticed the cameras. Now, he let out a huge sigh and relaxed back into his chair. He saw that Good Cop noted his reaction. Bad Cop didn't. "Then what am I doing here?" he demanded. "If you've seen the tape, you know I didn't do anything."

"That's not what the surveillance videos show."

Daniel was shocked into silence.

"That's crazy…impossible."

"Take a look for yourself," Fowler said.

The detective punched a button on his laptop, typed

something in, then turned the screen to face Daniel. He reached around the screen and clicked play on a video.

The picture was gray and grainy. The video was jumpy, so the movement you could see was jerky and halting—like every other surveillance camera image he'd ever seen on television. But it was clear that it was Daniel and the woman Fowler called Miss Saunders, alone in the elevator.

Daniel watched in mounting horror at what was obviously a perfectly choreographed dance, played out for an audience of one—the stationary security camera mounted in the front left corner of the elevator. It was perfectly staged so the movement that was within the range of the camera told a story that was nothing like the reality he'd lived for the few minutes he'd spent with Lily Saunders.

The woman greets Daniel with a welcoming smile as he gets on the elevator. The doors close, the elevator moves. Then it suddenly jerks to a stop. The row of control buttons on the front wall of the elevator is outside the range of the camera. The video shows the back of Daniel's head because he's turned to face the woman. She looks at him, facing the camera and appears both surprised and afraid. Then the woman is flung violently into the back wall of the elevator, with Daniel, filmed from the back, bent over her, holding on to her shoulders. He leans closer in an obvious effort to kiss her. She shakes her head vehemently no, shoves him away and lurches toward the front of the elevator, her hand out to disconnect the emergency stop button. Then she hurries back to the corner, turns away from him and hunches her shoulders as if she were trying to melt into the wall.

When the elevator stops, she hurries toward the door to get away. Though it's out of the range of the elevator camera, it's obvious Daniel tries to grab her because she sprawls out face-first on the floor in full view of the hallway camera. He gets out of the elevator, leans over her, and she backs up away from him until she hits the wall, totally terrified, shaking her head no.

Daniel advances toward her. She shakes her head no. He reaches down to grab her, but she scoots out of his grasp and makes a break for it down the hallway. Daniel follows her.

Then what is obviously another piece of the tape rolls, the time stamp later than the first one. In it, the woman runs back through the range of the hall camera and out the stairway door. Her face is turned away from the camera, but it is clear that the sleeve of her red blouse has been ripped. The last shot is of Daniel waiting for the elevator, straightening his tie and smoothing his hair.

Daniel stared unbelieving at the gray screen after the officer switched off the video, his mind reeling, so many thoughts racing through it he didn't have time to stop and think any of them.

"Still say you didn't do anything?" Bad Cop asked. "We've got forensics lifting prints off the snack room where you shoved her down beside the ice machine and raped her. You telling me they won't find your prints there?"

"Of course, they'll find my prints. She ran in there with my phone and slammed the door in my face. I went in after her."

Bad Cop sneered. "It's a shame you came prepared, used protection. A video and prints—the only thing we don't have is a DNA sample."

Reality dawned on Daniel laboriously, like lifting something heavy, and he couldn't seem to find his voice for a few moments after that. But when he did it, was surprisingly level and clear—what Jack had called his "ministerial voice" when they were kids. Over the years, it had become the default.

"I'd like to talk to an attorney," he said.

"Don't bother," Bad Cop said. "We don't need to ask any more questions right now. You've told us everything we need to know."

Chapter Seven

1985

Becca held her breath as the demon-possessed boys approached her hiding place. Cold spread out in front of them, an arctic blast that made instant white plumes out of McDougal's panting breath. She put a trembling finger to her lips to keep the dog quiet and felt each individual beat of her heart as it banged in her chest. The bush hid the two of them well, blocking them completely from sight. She told herself she was safe, the boys wouldn't see her.

And they didn't.

But they did smell her.

"Yuck," said the boy nearest the bush when they passed. He pulled up short. "That smells like puke!"

Becca looked at the wet spot where she'd spewed out her breakfast. Why didn't she think to cover it up with dirt? It was too late to do that now, though. She had to stay as still as a baby rabbit. Any movement would shake the limbs of the bush.

"Fresh puke," said the boy next to him.

They all stopped running. She could see their feet as

they stood together talking—arguing—no more than ten feet away.

"I don't smell anything."

"You got a nose? It's gross."

Shoes shuffled on the rocks as the boy who didn't smell it apparently shoved the boy who did.

"Somebody's been here." Becca recognized the redheaded kid's voice. "Look around."

Then it was over in a matter of seconds. One of the boys crouched down, peered in and spotted her.

"What do we have here?" He stepped to the bush, parted the limbs and reached for her. She cringed away, but he snagged a hank of her hair and started to drag her out of the bush. McDougal didn't bark or growl, just sunk his teeth into the boy's arm above the wrist. The boy howled in pain, let go of Becca's hair and fell backward, dragging the dog with him. He landed on his back, bellowing, and shook McDougal off with a violent motion that sent the sixty-pound dog flying through the air. He landed with a plop fifteen feet away. The boy leapt to his feet and lurched toward him.

"I'm gonna kill—"

McDougal bolted into the woods in the direction he and Becca had come.

The boy took two steps after the dog, but the redheaded kid grabbed his arm and gestured to Becca, still crouched among the bush's branches.

"We got bigger fish to fry."

The redhead reached in, grabbed her arm, dragged her out of the bush and flung her to the ground in front of them.

She squeezed her eyes shut tight. Her frantic thoughts scattered like the tiny white seeds of a dandelion puffball hit by a breeze.

We should have stayed together like we promised Bishop.

Run, DD, run!

I don't want to die.

When she opened her eyes, she changed her mind. She did want to die. Right here and right now. She didn't want to live for even a moment in the same world with the creatures that crawled all over the six boys, more horrifying than monsters that stalked nightmares in the deepest ditch of midnight.

Riding the back of one of the boys was a winged creature with the face of a deformed ape and the hairy legs of a spider. One eye was lower than the other, both were red and looked out from under a brow ridge with no forehead at all, only a slanted lumpy skull with horns.

The boy who'd pulled the fisherman's arms off looked like he was pouting, his lower lip puffed downward, his upper lip pointed like a bird's beak. He was carrying a rat-shaped demon made out of wasps, its skin as alive as maggots, its eyes the pale yellow of pus, with red centers.

The boy McDoo had bitten carried a lizard-faced monster with tentacles wrapped around him and red eyes without irises. It was oozing a brown goo that smelled like a backed-up sewer, and a sticky strand of it slid down the boy's face.

The one on the owl-beak boy surveyed her, tilting its head to the side in a motion that disturbed the wasp shape, and it momentarily came apart.

"You can see me," it said. The voice ripped into her ears, a sound full of hatred and loathing.

She didn't speak, couldn't speak. But it could tell she heard from her shuddering reaction to the voice.

"You can, can't you!" it said triumphantly. Then it threw its head back and laughed, making a sound the antithesis of real laughter, jagged and ugly, that for some reason made Becca think of rotted meat.

All the demons were focused on her now. The boys they inhabited stood, their arms at their sides, their faces blank, their eyes sightless.

"Let's eat it," offered a demon that looked like a worm with slimy wet skin and a mouth that held six rows of needles instead of teeth that stretched all the way back down its throat. "Eat it alive. I get the eyeballs!" A wave of that ugly laughter rolled through the assemblage, and the smell of rotting meat made Becca nauseated, and she was afraid she was about to start heaving again.

"She saw," said the boy McDoo had bitten. He ignored the wound as if it weren't there. The boy might have howled, but the demon hadn't felt a thing. "We'll have to kill her, tie her body down with the other one."

That solution didn't appear to appeal to the other boys —no, the demons, it was the demons who were fighting— they were just using the boys to do it. It particularly didn't appeal to the boy who'd had to tie the body down in the river.

"We don't have any more rope," he said.

The argument about the nature of her death and the disposal of her body went on. The redheaded boy's demon didn't participate, just cut its eyes from them to her. The demon resembled a dragon, its face elongated, providing a mouth with fangs and double rows of shark teeth beneath a nose with wide black openings and bulging eyes that moved independently, looking everywhere at once. Its body was vaguely lizard-shaped with scales, but its tail was like a scorpion's. It lifted up over the demon's body, twitching back and forth, ending in a spike stinger more than a foot long.

"Shut up," the redheaded boy said and casually backhanded the boy standing next to him. "Killing everybody we come in contact with isn't exactly low profile." He leaned closer to Becca, and the stench of him gagged her. "This baby pig is an asset, and we're going to keep it. At least for a little while."

That surprised them all into silence.

"She knows," the dragon demon said. "Don't you get it? She can help us find the summoner. We'll take her back to…him"—all the demons cringed—"she'll tell him whatever he wants to know." As an afterthought, he added, "Then we can eat it."

2011

Jack Carpenter walked into his kitchen and tossed the manila envelope on the counter. Ignoring it, pretending it wasn't there. He had swung by the station after taking Theresa home from the emergency room and found it on his desk with a Post-it note saying it'd been delivered by a courier while he was out.

He opened the refrigerator door and stood staring into its almost empty interior. There was a half-full jar of bean dip, some mystery meat in a plastic bag that might once have been pickle-and-pimento loaf, a box of leftover pizza that he was sure had been there for the better part of a month—as had the box of carryout Chinese deli rice beside it—a quart of milk that looked suspiciously solid, and three cans of beer in the racks on the door.

Bad milk or beer? Duh.

He lifted a can of beer out of the rack and closed the door, swearing as he did so that he really was going to go to the grocery store tomorrow—not the Jiffy Stop down the street but a real, no-kidding, actual supermarket with aisles of fresh fruit and vegetables. Ok, so he never ate vegetables, but there would at least be frozen dinners there. Yeah, tomorrow for sure.

But tonight…

He'd put off opening the envelope for as long as he could. Good news was seldom delivered by courier in an anonymous brown envelope. Jack sank down into a comfortable overstuffed chair besieged by a circling herd of fast-food remains. With a sweep of his arm, he cleared the old newspapers and unopened mail off the footstool in front of it, opened the envelope and spread out the contents on the Naugahyde —"the skins from a dozen dead Naugas," he heard Daniel's little-kid voice say. Then he sat looking at a handful of black-and-white photographs.

In the same way you can sometimes sense something hurtling at you in the dark, Jack could feel a blow coming. The intensity of the feeling suggested it might be staggering.

The third picture appeared to be exactly the same as the first. Same scene—wide steps with a black wrought iron railing leading up to a sprawling porch. The time stamp was different, though, a few minutes later than the first two pictures.

Jack started looking at every other picture, only the enhanced ones. In the bottom of the frame of the next picture, a person was visible on the bottom step. From that point on, the pictures were not only enhanced, they were enlarged and cropped so all that was visible was the person on the steps. Enlarged like that, Jack could see that the person was a black boy and that he was carrying something, though it was not immediately clear what it was. What was clear, however, bright and shiny clear, was the name printed in big, block letters on the back of the boy's shirt: Carpenter.

The final picture showed a close-up of what the boy was carrying. Jack's stomach rolled, he might even have been sick if his cell phone hadn't rung. He fished the phone out of his pocket. Crock.

"Sergeant Carpenter," Jack said, trying to sound official.

"You want to tell me what in the Sam Hill's going on with Theresa Washington?" Crock offered no preamble.

"She went to visit two old friends and found them dead. What's to tell?"

"You're going to stand on that?"

"It's what happened."

Harrelton Police Department Major Charles Crocker was silent. Jack could picture him brooding. A round, bald, bowlegged man, the major was as formidable as he looked harmless and as clever as he looked goofy. He had a keen wit, a discerning spirit and absolute loyalty to the officers in his command.

He had something else, too. Crock got it. He had let Jack know after the bizarre circumstances that had put Jack in the hospital in July, that he understood there were sometimes forces at work that defied explanation.

"Is this…part of that other?" Crock asked. "What happened before?"

"Uh-huh."

"Goody," Crock said.

"I was thinking of more colorful descriptions, but goody will do for now."

"And the rest of it? The part that's a zit on your backside—is that part of the other, too?"

"What 'rest of it'?"

"You don't get out much, do you, Carpenter? Do you even own a television set?"

"What for? When one of those read-a-teleprompter talking heads describes a 'situation,' it's like they didn't even go to the same crime scene I did."

"Well, you might want to give this story a look-see before the press gets hold of your address and turn up at your house."

"Why would the press come to my house?"

"They showed the video on the six o'clock news," Crock said.

The pictures—they were screen shots from a security camera video.

"It was the top story, and the media sharks and anti-hug-a-policeman puppets have already started crawling out from under rocks."

"I haven't seen the video," Jack said and his own voice sounded strangely tinny in his ear. "Just…screen grabs. Still photographs." He really didn't want to ask the rest of it, but he had to, of course. "What does the video show?"

"Oh, they hedged their bets. Threw around 'allegedly' like tossing feed to chickens, pointed out that security camera footage does not constitute proof of wrongdoing. But I figure the story in tomorrow's Inquirer will read something like 'The local hero cop who singlehandedly stopped a psycho from massacring a room full of helpless children three months ago allegedly set a fire that massacred a nursing home full of helpless old people when he was a kid.'"

The Twin Oaks fire.

Flames all around him. Harsh heat and red light. Screams of agony.

There's a figure in the flames. Jack can only see him

from behind. The flames back up from the figure, move out of his way as if shoved by an invisible hand. Then the figure turns slowly to face Jack.

"Jack?" Crock spoke his name in the tone of voice you use when you've already said something several times and gotten no response. "Are you all right?"

All Jack's spit had dried up so suddenly that pulling his tongue off the roof of his mouth to speak felt like disengaging two strips of Velcro. "Not really."

"So you were there at the fire? What were you doing with a—"

"I don't know. I…don't remember. Any of it. That whole summer. It was wiped out of my mind."

Crock paused to let that soak in. "You do realize, don't you, that it won't be long before it's not just the press asking questions about that fire."

"Goody," was all Jack could manage.

"I was thinking of more colorful descriptions, but goody will do for now." Crock paused again, and when he continued, there was urgency in his voice. "That fire, you and Theresa—all of it—eventually, you're going to have to tell me what's really going on here."

"You don't want to know."

"Try me."

"The longer you can live your life without knowing what I know, the better off you'll be."

The major let it go for the time being but he was a kid looking for the prize in the bottom of a Happy Meal. He'd keep digging until he found it.

Then Crocker shifted gears. "There's one more thing."

"Anybody ever tell you the story about straws and camels' backs?"

"Relax. This is random info. You just got a hit on an

alert you sent out a couple of months ago. The sheriff's department in Hendersonville, Indiana—that's between Columbus and Bloomington, I think—has locked up somebody you were looking for. Her name's Becca Hawkins."

Crock hung, up but Jack stood for half a minute with his cell phone still pressed to his ear, listening to the nothing. There used to be a dial tone that told you the line had gone dead. On cell phones there was…nothing. He hadn't realized until now how much he missed the dial tone.

Jack's mind filled up the void of no-dial-tone nothingness in his head with a single word—it lit up across the expanse of his whole consciousness like it'd been written on the night sky by the flaming tail of a comet.

Becca.

When snippets of memory from that lost summer had begun to return, Jack had recalled that he had been desperately in love with Becca Hawkins when he was twelve years old. So was Daniel Burke.

Chapter Eight

1985

As the two twelve-year-olds walked together through the woods, Jack was listening in what he hoped looked like rapt attention to what Daniel was telling him: details of Daniel's grand plan to do what nobody had ever done— draw a map of the hundreds, no, probably thousands of miles of interconnected caves beneath Caverna County. Daniel was always coming up with one harebrained idea or another.

Daniel was tall for his age, taller than Jack but not as strong. Jack thought he looked like Sonny Crockett in *Miami Vice*--just needed a sports coat over a T-shirt and enough facial hair for beard stubble to complete the image. Daniel's was a square-jawed all-American face, and you could read there whatever he was feeling as clearly as if it'd been written in green ink on his forehead.

Jack's face was unreadable—some would say stern—a good-looking boy, though his features were too strong and blunt to be handsome. He was compact and well-muscled, but he radiated a kind of rugged toughness that made him seem bigger than he was.

Jack was black; Daniel was white.

"Of course, it'd take a lot of rope," Daniel said, "but you could go out to the end of a piece of rope, draw a map of how you got there, then move the rope—"

"It's like a honeycomb," Jack said. "Layers and layers going down nobody knows how far."

"We'd start with the top level and then—"

"And then fall through to the next level or the next, break a leg and get stuck down there. That rock's unstable. The water's still dissolving the limestone."

"Yeah, but—"

"How can you draw a map of something that's constantly changing? One minute, there's a cavern and a wall. And the next time you go in, the wall's gone and it's two caves. You don't see a long line of spelunkers itching to crawl around in the caverns, Danno, and there's a reason for that."

"So you think it's a dumb idea?"

"Well…" It was really hard to lie to Daniel. Even if you were a good liar, he could spot it. Jack suspected that was because Daniel probably hadn't told half a dozen lies in his whole life, and that included the ones you had to tell about the knitted scarf your aunt sent you for Christmas or when some lady in a store wanted to know if a dress made her look fat. "Not dumb, exactly, just—"

"Shhhh," Daniel said. "Listen."

Jack heard the sound of a dog barking on the other side of the hill. Dougal Dog after a squirrel. He was surprised that Becca was so close by. The three had split up after Bishop let them out, but later he'd happened upon Daniel in the woods. Dougal Dog appeared at the crest of the hill and came down it so fast that you'd think his tail was on fire, barking machine-gun fire all the way. The dog slid to a stop in front of them, panting, and never stopped barking. This was the most sound Jack had ever heard come out of the animal's mouth. He looked up at the crest of the hill, expecting to see Becca. She wasn't there.

The dog turned and ran a few yards back the way it had come, stopped and barked. Then did the same thing again.

"I think he wants us to follow him," Daniel said.

Jack burst out laughing so abruptly that he almost spit in Daniel's face. It was a baritone rumble now that Jack's voice had started changing. He roared. Couldn't stop, dropped the picka-nick basket he was holding, leaned over and grabbed his belly. He wanted to share the humor with Daniel but couldn't get his own mirth under control enough to talk.

Between bleats of laughter, he finally managed to say, "You sound like…on Saturday mornings…" He spoke in a high-pitched falsetto. "I think Lassie wants us to follow her. Maybe Timmy's in trouble." Which sent Jack into another peal of hysterics.

Daniel smiled, but didn't see as much humor in the remark as Jack did. The dog kept barking, running a few steps and barking some more.

"Maybe Becca is in trouble," Daniel said.

Jack would have laughed at that, too, if not for Daniel's sober attitude. And if there was something wrong with Becca… Suddenly, none of it was funny at all anymore.

"Has she taught him that?" Jack asked. "To go get people?"

"Dogs do all kinds of things nobody trained them to do." Daniel was already turning to run after the dog as he said it. Jack stopped only long enough to grab the picka-nick basket. He and Daniel had built it in shop class before school let out, making the top part into a lid with hinges and a catch, lining the inside with pale yellow felt—Becca's favorite color—and polishing the outside until it sparkled. They'd given it to her for her birthday, a replacement for the two yellow wicker picnic baskets that had fallen off the back of Jack's bike and exploded, firing sandwiches and fruit like shrapnel all over the street. You could drop the picka-nick basket off a building, and it would still hold on to your sandwiches. But it was heavy, and loaded as it was now with lunch for the three of them, it banged painfully against Jack's leg so he had trouble keeping up with Daniel and the dog. But DD always paused to wait for them when they fell behind.

Even though both boys were in good shape, Jack was beginning to feel a painful stitch in his side when the dog quit barking like you'd turned off a water faucet, then stood panting at the top of a gentle rise that fell away to a gash-cut valley beyond. When the boys joined him, they saw why he had stopped barking. About sixty yards down the trail, walking away from them, was a group of boys— with Becca in the middle of them.

Jack's gut turned to concrete.

"Aren't those the guys from Brewster Academy?" Daniel asked.

It was them alright. Couldn't miss the red-headed kid with the Mohawk--Carl or Cody something, maybe--and the one trying to look like Eddie Van Halen with long, poofy brown hair. They'd only met the other members of the Bradford's Ridge All-Star baseball team once at the cookout the day after the team roster was announced. And it hadn't gone well.

"How would she know those guys?" Daniel continued.

"She wouldn't."

Jack felt sick. Everything about what he was seeing was

wrong. Not only strange but somehow…sinister. One small blonde girl walking in the middle of a group of six boys. He didn't have to say any of that to Daniel.

"What do we do?" Daniel asked.

"We act like this is the most normal thing in the world, that's what we do…and go get Becca."

Jack draped a smile between the corners of his mouth like hanging a sheet on a clothesline and started down the slope.

"Hey, hold up a minute," he called out cheerily.

The boys all snapped around in surprise. Jack had never before seen anybody move that fast. He'd never seen the kind of naked malice and aggression he saw in their faces and body language, either. If they'd been animals, they'd have been snarling. Maybe they were snarling. But that wasn't what made it suddenly impossible for him to catch his breath. He'd never seen anybody look as scared as Becca looked. He felt Daniel tense beside him and knew he'd read it all, too.

With Dougal Dog at their side, he and Daniel trotted down to where the others stood. The Eddie Van Halen wannabe spotted DD and started toward him, his hands balled into fists, his face a picture of rage. Jack noticed then that the boy had a wound on his right arm above his wrist. Not bandaged, it was dripping blood. It looked like a dog bite.

The tallest boy, the redhead with the Mohawk, grabbed the other boy and yanked him back a step. They exchanged a look, and then the first boy stayed where he was. Jack noticed that several of the boys had black stains on their jeans that could have been—what? Blood?

"Hi, Becs," Jack said casually as he set the picka-nick basket down on the ground. Jack had never called her that. He'd never heard anybody call her that, so he hoped the foreignness of it would alert Becca that he and Daniel understood something was terribly wrong. "What are you guys doing out here in the woods? If you're after ginseng, looks like you came up as empty-handed as we did."

The other boys were silent, glaring at Jack and Daniel. Up close, they didn't look right. Jack couldn't quite put his finger on why not. They were strangely unkempt, stank like they hadn't had a bath in a month. It was a…wild smell. Something about their eyes, too, like the reflective shine in an animal's eyes at night. Or the defiant set of their faces—faces that seemed harder and older than they had only a couple of days ago at Bishop and Theresa's cookout when they'd mocked Daniel and Jack for refusing go out drinking with them. They'd been cocky and rebellious then, too, angling for a fight. If Bishop hadn't stepped in and separated them, they might even have come to blows—bloody noses all around. Those weren't the stakes now, though. The boys they'd faced in Bishop's backyard weren't dangerous. These boys were. Jack hadn't been afraid of those guys. He was unreasonably and inexplicably terrified of these.

"Mind if we tag along with you?" Jack tried to look chagrined. "Truth is, we got lost. I hope you know how to get out of here."

"Yeah, we mind," the redheaded boy said.

Cole. His name was Cole Stuart.

"Find your own way out."

Daniel spoke for the first time. "Aw, Jack, we can see Burnt Stump from here." He pointed to the black sentinel on the mountain to the south. "We'll be all right; let's stay." He turned his eyes on Becca. "You want to stay with us, Becs? Help us look for ginseng?"

"She's going with us," Cole said.

"That's not your decision to make, now is it?" Daniel

replied, pleasantly enough. "If she wants to stay with us, she stays."

There it was, then—the gauntlet on the ground. Daniel held his hand out to Becca.

The redheaded kid was all over Jack and Daniel in a heartbeat. Jack only had time to think two words before a fist slammed into his belly. Mad dog.

It was finished almost before it started. You could reasonably expect to lose a fight six against two, but this fight was just one against two. Cole Stuart's speed and ferocity hammered punches into Jack in such rapid succession that Jack never even had time to make a fist. The next thing he knew, he was up against a tree fifteen feet from the nearest boy with no idea how he'd gotten there. Jack knew how to take a beating. His father had taught him well. But this…

The other boys started to surround Jack where he lay. Even with his heart strumming in his ears muffling sound, he could hear Cole Stuart yelling and Becca screaming.

He only caught snippets, pieces of what Cole said. "… enough …can't hurt…" Becca's cries sliced into his heart with a pain far greater than what he felt in his belly.

Then it was quiet, except for the roaring in his ears. There wasn't even the usual huffing and puffing after a fight. Cole Stuart wasn't breathing hard, hadn't broken a sweat.

Becca's voice had been silenced abruptly, cut off. He looked around, found her. One of the boys had his hand over her mouth. His eyes locked with hers for a heartbeat, and the raw terror he saw there gave him the strength to start struggling to his feet.

"Stay where you are," Cole said. "Mind your own business and stay out of our way, or I'll let the rest of them have at you."

Jack kept struggling, scooting upward with his back against the tree until he was upright. He took a wobbly step toward the group of boys. They seemed to inhale at the same time for a group lunge that some part of him was certain he would not survive.

Becca pulled the boy's hand off her mouth and cried, "Stop it. I…don't want to stay here and hunt for ginseng. There's no reason to fight anymore." Her eyes caught Jack's again, then cut to Daniel, who lay on the ground an impossible twenty feet away, curled around the blow Cole had landed in his belly. "My mom's supposed to pick me up at that logging road out on Route 31. You know the place. If you happen to see her there when you leave, would you tell her…that I'm at Jubal's house. She knows where Jubal lives." Becca looked around at the boys surrounding her. "They're going to give me a ride there."

Becca's mother had died when she was four years old.

The boy who'd had his hand over her mouth, the one with the pouty bottom lip and a skinny rat-tail of blond hair hanging halfway down his back—Jacob something—grabbed her arm and yanked, and she turned to follow him. She must have seen Dougal Dog start to come along, and she made a slight hand motion to the dog, her palm out: stay. That was a command she had taught him, and he obediently sat down, whining softly. After that, she didn't look back, just continued down the valley with the boys surrounding her on all sides. Jack watched them until they were out of sight, then pushed off from the tree, staggered to Daniel and knelt/fell in the dirt beside him. Daniel had uncurled and was trying to push himself up onto his hands and knees.

"We can't let them just take her—I'm going to follow them," Jack said, hearing his own intention for the first time as spoke the words.

He started to rise, but Daniel grabbed his arm. "I know where they're taking…" he said, with not quite enough air to push out all the words. "Help me up."

Jack staggered up, grabbed Daniel's arm and hauled him to his feet. "How do you know?"

"She told us," Daniel was still gasping. "She said she was going to Jubal's house."

That hadn't made any sense to Jack. Becca didn't have any girlfriends named Jubal. She didn't have any friends at all except for him and Daniel.

"Remember in Bible study last week—in Genesis—Jubal was the father of music." Jack didn't remember but wasn't surprised that Becca and Daniel apparently did. "Music…the Melody Creek Rest Area—get it?"

How'd Becca manage to come up with all that on the spur of the moment—scared as she was? Jack's admiration for her swelled in his chest.

Daniel took in a painful breath and continued. "They must have parked their bikes there."

"If they did, they walked all the way around the south side of Bear Claw, and it's going to take them awhile to walk back. We have to get Bishop."

"The logging road's that way." Jack pointed back over his shoulder in the direction opposite where the boys were taking Becca. "And he's not even supposed to pick us there until after lunch." Jack didn't have a watch, but Daniel did.

"It's not even eleven o'clock," Daniel muttered.

"Yeah, and then we'd have to drive all the way around Bear Claw Mountain."

The mountains of Caverna County were crisscrossed by hundreds of miles of roads that meandered through the valleys and hidden hollows in no particular hurry to take anybody anywhere. This cluster of mountains was stretched out north/south around the base of Bear Claw

Mountain—so named because it was roughly shaped like one. They'd left Hester Road for a logging road on the east side of the blunt end of the claw—where Burnt Stump stood sentinel. Then the highway turned north and circled around the pointed end. Melody Creek, where the six boys had entered the mountains, was on the west side of Bear Claw.

"They'll be long gone before we could get there in a car to stop them."

Jack stood, gasping and thinking.

"But if we climbed up to Burnt Stump, we could go back down the other side to Melody Creek—with Bishop! — and cut them off." he said. "When we don't show up at the logging road, Burnt Stump is where he'll go looking for us."

Daniel turned his eyes toward the scorched tree pointing at the sky on Bear Claw Mountain's southern summit. On three of the mountain's sides, the land was a fairly gentle upward slope. But the east side facing Jack and Daniel was a craggy, boulder-strewn ridge that looked— from here at least—all but impassable. "Climb up the east face of Bear Claw and then sit there, waiting for Bishop?"

"It's a gamble. We just have to hope Bishop gets impatient quick when we're not on time at the logging road." Daniel looked dubious. "It's a chance. Meeting Bishop as planned has no chance at all. You got a better idea?"

Daniel didn't.

"Then come on!" Jack reached down for the picka-nick basket and stumbled off toward the mountain. Though Daniel was still slightly bent over, his belly muscles apparently spasming from the blow he'd taken, he kept up with Jack.

"What"—Daniel was panting—"just happened here?"

"I have no idea."

Chapter Nine

2011

Ten-year-old Miranda Burke was sobbing. She lay with her face buried in her pillow on the Princess Bride bedspread Mommy had ordered from that store that had old stuff you couldn't get anywhere else. She didn't know Andi was listening and then Andi'd had to pretend to be surprised on Christmas morning.

The first night she'd slept under it, Mommy had pulled it snug up around her neck, kissed her on the nose and said, "Night, night, Buttercup."

The memory made Andi cry harder, and she let it all out, didn't try to hold her feelings in like she did when Daddy was around so she wouldn't make him sad, too. But she bet he was doing the same thing.

She lifted her head and cried out at the ceiling in a tear-clotted voice, "I'm mad at you, God." And she was, too. So mad it almost was stronger than the hurt deep in her belly that felt like she was about to throw up.

"You let that bad man kill Mommy, and you didn't do a thing to stop it. And you could have. You could have sent a big white angel with a sword or something. You could have kept Mommy alive, but you let her die. I hate you!"

Ossy hopped up onto the bed beside her. The big calico circled around twice before curling snug up against Andi's side. He wasn't supposed to get cat hair on Andi's bed, but he slept with her every night.

She put one arm around Ossy, buried her face in his fur and fingered the small gold cross she wore—Mommy's necklace that Daddy said her mother would want her to have. Daddy's wrist had been in a cast so Uncle Jack had put it around Andi's neck the day of Mommy's funeral. She swore she would never take it off, never for her whole life. The thought of her mother's funeral made her cry harder. She didn't just miss Mommy, she needed Mommy —to braid her curly brown hair because Daddy's big fingers couldn't get it right, to finish teaching her how to iron a shirt and how to make pancakes shaped like rabbits and snowmen.

And now she couldn't even smell Mommy anymore! At first, her perfume was still in her clothes, and Andi would go into her closet when Daddy wasn't home and let the skirts and blouses hang down around her and pretend that Mommy was only at the grocery store and would be home any minute.

Now, even the perfume smell was gone.

"Why, God?" she cried out, pleading. "Why did you take my Mommy away?"

Andi finally cried herself out, cried so long and hard that her chest hurt. The sorrow was still there, of course, but crying had made it a little better. Not much, but a little. It was something she could hide when Daddy got home and came upstairs to tuck her in and say her prayers with her. She sat up and took a tissue from the box the house-keeper, Mrs. Beavers, always made sure to leave there for her. She blew her nose noisily, but before she could reach for another tissue to wipe her eyes—the same light blue her mother's had been—she felt something soft on her cheek. Not a tissue, some kind of cloth that was softer than velvet. She heard it then, the sound she had no name for—singing with no words and music made with no instrument she had ever heard.

Sitting beside her on the bed was Princess Buttercup in a dress made of light, her long blonde hair flowing down her back, shining—with sparkles. It wasn't Princess Buttercup at all, of course, but an angel who was wiping Andi's tears away. And Andi thought she could see tear streaks on the angel's cheeks, too.

"I want to show you something, Andi," she said. It was the voice that had spoken in her head the day her mommy died, told her to ring the bell to save Daddy's life.

"Shapes and lights like before?"

"No, something different. But you must look at it very carefully and remember as much about it as you can."

Then the walls of the room vanished, and Andi was somewhere that didn't have a bed or piles of soft stuffed animals or boxes of tissue right there beside her. She was in a room with no bed at all, just a pile of blankets on the floor and bare wood walls and a single light bulb hanging down on a wire in the middle of the ceiling. There were boards over both the windows, nailed on the outside, so you couldn't see out. Well, maybe you could see a little bit if you got up real close and looked through a crack. Andi went to the nearest window and put her eye to the biggest space between the boards, about as wide as her thumb.

There was nothing to see, though, only woods and off to the edge where she could barely see it, a gravel driveway. Then a car pulled up into the shadow of the house on the driveway, a blue car that had a bright-yellow license plate all splattered with red mud. There was an Indian design in the middle below the words "Land of Ench…" but the rest was covered with mud.

She couldn't see who got out on the driver's side, but she heard two doors open and close so there must have been somebody in the back seat on that side behind the driver. She could see the other side of the car, though, and the person in the front on the passenger side was a young man wearing a Pittsburgh Steelers T-shirt. He was a black man, but his skin wasn't as dark as Miss Theresa's, which was the color of the piece of coal Andi had picked up off the ground that time she went with Mommy and Daddy on vacation in the Smoky Mountains and stopped on the way to see the coal mining museum in eastern Kentucky. He was more the color of Uncle Jack, except his hair wasn't cut off like Uncle Jack's, so short there was barely any curl left to see. Just the opposite! This man's hair hung down around his shoulders in long things called dreadlocks that Andi thought looked as disgusting as the bottom of a bird's nest.

The men were talking, but she couldn't hear what they said at first. Their voices were drowned out by another sound. Clickety-clack, clickety-clack, clickety-clack. A train. No whistle, just the cars going by somewhere close on the other side of the house. It was a nice sound, friendly somehow, but Andi couldn't have said why that was. Then the clickety-clack faded, got softer and softer as the train pulled away.

In the quiet, the scene faded, too. It didn't blink off like somebody'd turned off the television. It got more and more dim, until you could see the images, but you could also see through them. She could see the window with the wood nailed over the front, and she could see her My Little Pony dressing table through it.

"Will you remember what you saw?" Princess Buttercup asked.

Andi nodded, then burst out, "I'm mad at God, and you can tell him I said so!"

She reached out her hand and cupped Andi's cheek. "He knows."

Then she was gone, and Andi was sitting alone on her bed in her room.

And she couldn't feel the anger or sadness anymore. They'd been replaced by a cold emptiness that wasn't something you cried or yelled about. It was something that settled in around you so you couldn't smile or laugh or see anything bright and good and happy in the world.

Andi wondered if she'd ever stop feeling that way or if when somebody you loved died, you didn't ever feel like smiling again for the rest of your life.

~

DANIEL WAS DISORIENTED, as if he'd stepped out of the flow of time and was a step behind reality. He awoke to a world that had shifted in such a profound way its movement surely would have been captured on a seismometer if one had been handy.

No, he didn't wake up to that world. To wake up, one must first go to sleep, and Daniel hadn't closed his eyes all night. He had become aware of the shifting of his world, the realignment of the planets in his solar system the night before when he'd had to call the head of church security to bail him out of jail.

Bail him out of jail.

Every time those words popped into Daniel's head, he

wanted to giggle. Wasn't a thing funny about it, but the words put him in mind of a black-and-white gangster movie from the forties starring James Cagney.

Ok, he hadn't been in jail. You had to be arrested to go to jail, and he hadn't been charged with anything—yet.

Daniel looked at his watch again. Still too early to call Jack. But perhaps not too early for Theresa. She always said she was a "bird sleeper"—went to bed with the chickens and was out of bed, dressed and had a load of laundry in the washing machine before the rooster'd had its first cup of coffee.

She answered on the second ring.

"What's wrong?" she asked.

"How do you know something's wrong?"

"Phone don't never ring when the sun ain't shone on the day 'less'n somethin' bad's happened. What is it?"

He told her.

"He put the hammer down on both of us in less time than it takes to cook a pot roast. He's been planning this for a right smart while."

"Both of us?"

"Mr. Gerald and Miss Minnie…they dead." She told him what happened.

"Why doesn't he just try to kill us, Theresa, like he did before?"

"Jack was wondering the same thing. I don't know for certain, but I 'spect he wants us alive so he can make us miserable. Payback. But I think he also wants us so busy with our own problems that we won't have no time to make trouble for him. We got to talk, you, me and Jack. Figure out how we gone get ourselves out of the fixes he's landed us in so we can get on with what we set out to do."

That seemed so ludicrous at that moment Daniel had to bite back a laugh. Right. What they'd set out to do—

stop Chapman Whitworth from becoming a Supreme Court justice. The man who, in an evening's work, had managed to totally devastate Theresa's life and his own. Oh, and once that was done, they'd turn their sights on finding the efreet responsible for all this and destroy it or defeat it or banish or it take its batteries out or whatever it was they'd done to it when he, Jack and Becca were twelve years old. Except permanently this time. Piece of cake.

"You boys need to come over for lunch. You call Jack. I'll make chili."

Theresa's chili. Oh, how he and Jack had loved Theresa's chili when they were kids. Daniel felt a sudden aching longing in his chest for a time and a life and a world that could be set aright by a bowl of chili.

He tiptoed into Andi's room and sat for a long time, just watching her sleep before he woke her to get her ready for school. Looking at her face in repose, he was always struck by her uncanny resemblance to her mother—except for the dimples and the sprinkling of freckles on her nose that Emily said looked like she'd been dusted with cinnamon. When Andi was awake, the animation of her face hid the resemblance. There were always emotions playing across it. The child felt the world and everything in it in such an intense way that her face mirrored joy, sadness, pain and fear like the waters of a still pool.

Andi could see demons, and when she did, the horror on her face mirrored the evil she could see. Looking into her eyes then was almost like looking at the devil himself.

Emily's face had not been nearly as mobile as her daughter's. He'd always thought Emily looked like a china doll. Her face, so chiseled and beautiful, was seldom marred by any emotion—except for the night he'd confronted her about her affair with Jeff Kendrick.

The thought knifed into him with such ferocious pain

he almost moaned out loud. Daniel had never had a chance to make things right between them before she was murdered. He'd been on the phone to her when she died, heard the gunshot that killed her. It was a sound that still tore open his soul if he let himself think about it. A sound—

"Daddy?"

Andi looked at him from the bed, still in that nether-world between sleep and wakefulness. Her hair was a jumble of chestnut curls; a sleep crease on her left cheek sliced right through her dimple. He loved her so much at that instant his heart might explode right there in his chest.

"Is it time to get up?" she asked.

Andi hated to get up in the morning about as much as she hated to go to bed at night. Sleeping had been an issue with the child since she was a baby. They'd tried to divide and conquer, he and Emily. Daniel had the unenviable task of getting the child to stay in the bed and go to sleep at night, and Emily faced the grumpy, whiny, sleepy little girl in the morning.

Now, Daniel woke Andi, usually with a kiss on the forehead. And Andi never complained, merely got up and got dressed. She wasn't hard to put to bed anymore, either. Since her mother's death, she had become Little Miss Perfect, maybe because she feared she had to be perfect to keep Daddy from going away, too. Or maybe because she knew her mother had died to save her life. He knew he shouldn't let that behavior continue, but he neither knew how nor had the energy or will to do anything about it yet.

He crossed the room and sat down on the edge of her bed.

"No, actually you can go back to sleep for fifteen minutes if you want to," he said. "I'm a little early this morning—since I didn't get to see you last night. I intended to be home before supper, but—"

"Where were you, Daddy?"

I was in jail, sweetheart, arrested, handcuffed and led away in chains.

"I got busy and the time got away from me, I'm sorry."

"That's ok, Daddy. Mrs. Beavers and I had fried chicken, and I even went to bed early."

Yes, he definitely needed to do something about Little Miss Perfect.

"If you want to snooze a little longer—"

"She came again last night. Princess Buttercup. And I had another one of those dreams that you have when you're awake. What Miss Theresa calls visions."

Andi had started having visions when she woke up in the hospital after she…died—from a stray bullet that had lodged in her chest when Jack killed a demon-possessed shooter in her school. Her visions of shapes had saved his life and Jack's, so Daniel knew they were important messages, warnings. But he still couldn't get his arms around the weirdness of it, coming from his own little girl, with scabs riding both knees and hair that looked tousled five minutes after you brushed it.

"What did you see?"

Andi told him about the boarded-up window and the car and the man with bird-nest hair. The visions were as real to Andi as the walking-around world, and she reported what she'd seen in minute detail. It made absolutely no sense, of course. This vision had people in it, though, not just images, and it left Daniel with a disquiet he couldn't put his finger on.

"And you never saw the man before? At school maybe or at the grocery store or in the mall?"

Andi made a face.

"No! If I'd ever seen him before, I'd remember his hair. It was gross, Daddy."

He smiled at that and held out his arms to her.

"We'll talk about the guy having a bad hair day later. Right now I am in serious need of a great big good-morning hug."

She sat up and flung her arms around his neck and squeezed hard. Like she didn't ever want to let him go. He didn't want to let her go, either.

Chapter Ten

2011

Jack's media hurricane made landfall at the police station before Jack got to work. Grazing on the front steps was a small herd of reporters, and the parking lot held two behemoth broadcast trucks. Jack drove slowly past them and went around the block to the back entrance.

Unfortunately, one enterprising news agency had seen a chance to snag a good parking space, and their gargantuan truck, complete with a satellite dish Frisbee attached to the roof, was pulled up—illegally—behind the building. It was the low-watt local station, the ambulance-chasing, three-headed-baby-stolen-by-aliens station. As soon as they saw his cruiser and recognized Jack, they were on him like powdered sugar on doughnuts.

He opened his car door, and a microphone was thrust in his face by a twenty-something reporter who looked like a fashion model. Didn't ugly fat women have brains and charm and wit?

"Sergeant Carpenter, what do you have to say to allegations that you set fire to the Twin Oaks Nursing Home in 1985 because the residents there were almost exclusively white?"

Jack looked at her in utter astonishment.

Seriously?

Jack had watched the eleven o'clock news the night before, managed to catch the story on two different stations that had produced his manila envelope of screen shots.

It began with the introduction of Anderson Rowland, a freelance journalist who had been putting together a series on the worst fires in American history when he "happened upon" something extraordinary.

"There have been so many advancements in film and photo enhancement in the past quarter century that footage shot at the time of some of these fires—blurred, grainy or out of focus then—now reveals usable images," Rowland said.

A shot filled the screen of an inferno, a blazing three-story building so engulfed in flames it was unrecognizable. Jack recognized it, though.

"The Twin Oaks Nursing Home in Bradford's Ridge, Kentucky, burned on June 22, 1985, killing one hundred forty people—one hundred fifteen residents and twenty-five staff. There were no survivors."

And there it was, the iconic photo seared into the minds of America like the photo of the fireman carrying the dead baby out of the Alfred P. Murrah Federal Building in Oklahoma City ten years later.

In the photo, a young man whose hair is on fire carries the burning body of an elderly patient out of the flames.

It was so gripping, the look of anguish on the young man's face so heartrending that the picture won Louisville Courier-Journal photographer Brent Atkinson a Pulitzer Prize for news photography. It also won the flaming-hair hero an appointment to West Point. His name was Chapman Whitworth.

News film footage and still pictures of the burning building from different angles filled the screen as Rowland continued speaking.

"Arson investigators call Twin Oaks the Mystery of the Century Fire. The main phone line to the building was cut. Firefighters found doors chained shut on the inside. Bureau of Alcohol, Tobacco and Firearms agents went over the remains of the building with toothbrushes. They said gasoline was used to start fires in multiple locations simultaneously, but years of investigation have provided nothing to indicate who was responsible."

Then Rowland began to explain about the parking lot surveillance camera, and grainy images of parked cars filled the screen.

"The parking lot camera survived the blaze because it was located on a light post near the street. Though it was trained on the lot, a small portion of the building—the front steps and door—is visible in the far edge of the camera's range. But blowing up that portion of the film in 1985 revealed nothing but images too blurry to make out anything."

Next was computer-enhanced footage. Though still grainy, the steps and the front door were clearly visible.

"The time stamp shows this was shot less than an hour before the fire started," Rowland said. He paused, then continued dramatically, "Now…watch."

At first the steps were empty, but then a figure appeared and started up them, his movements a herky-jerky surveillance camera dance. The person was a black boy wearing a T-shirt with the name "Carpenter" printed in block letters on the back. He was carrying something and the final image was a freeze-frame close-up of what the boy had in his right hand. It was a five-gallon can of gasoline.

"That's a Bradford's Ridge All-Star team T-shirt, and Jackson Randal Carpenter was the pitcher on that team in 1985," Rowland said. "Fast-forward twenty-six years. The same Jack Carpenter, now a sergeant in the Harrelton, Ohio, police department, killed a school shooter at Carlisle Elementary School three months ago."

Other images on the report had not been included in the manila envelope, previews-of-coming-attractions photos. Rowland said that after he saw the security camera footage, he went digging in the archives of the three television news stations that sent helicopters to the fire—and "got lucky" again. Inspection of a WLOU News First wide-angle shot of the burning building revealed someone standing in the edge of the woods on the south side.

The footage flashed on the screen. The quality of the news film was far superior to the surveillance camera. Blown up, it provided an image clear enough to see that the figure in the woods was the boy who'd entered the building earlier. He was wearing the same T-shirt and jeans, but the clothing was filthy. The T-shirt was no longer white. Dirt and maybe soot stained it. The right knee was torn out of his jeans and the bottom portion of both legs was blackened, had been scorched.

"Jack Carpenter was in that building when it was burning and is the only survivor of the fire, but repeated efforts to reach Carpenter and ask what he was doing there and how he managed to escape were unsuccessful."

Nobody had called Jack about anything.

"A quarter of a century after the Mystery of the Century Fire killed a hundred and forty people, we discover that a twelve-year-old boy carried gasoline into the Twin Oaks Nursing Home minutes before the fire started—and then escaped the flames. That boy has never told a soul and has maintained his silence for twenty-six years. Why?"

Maybe because he was as surprised as you were to find out he was there.

Jack had spent most of the rest of the night staring at the ceiling above his bed, trying to remember. Which was futile and he knew it. He'd been struggling to remember that summer ever since the day he'd stood staring at a Little League team picture that belonged to a man he'd just killed—a man who intended to shoot a room full of school children. Jack had been on that same Little League team and so had Daniel Burke, but neither of them had any memories of that summer. In the weeks after that, memories had been thrust out of Jack's mind, ejected—Theresa said by an angel—and the images in them were clear, but nothing much else was. Since then, Jack had begun to see holes in the blackout cloth that hid that time from him, like a pair of worn jeans where the last frayed threads finally break, and the fabric separates. But they weren't normal memories that play like a movie and you can see details— what someone was wearing or what the ocean looked like behind them. Jack couldn't remember what his bicycle looked like, couldn't see it—even in a memory where he was riding it! Daniel said his memories were shrouded in fog. And neither one of them had been able to retrieve a single memory just by concentrating, trying to remember.

So all he could do was refuse to answer questions about the fire—certainly not questions as willfully stupid and inflammatory as the one this Barbie doll in a human being suit had just asked him.

"No comment," he said and tried to go around her toward the back door of the building. She not only didn't back up, she stepped closer, blocked him in, literally pinned him into the space between the open car door and the vehicle. The only way to get around her was to knock her down, a deliciously tempting option.

"Are you afraid to answer my question, Sergeant Carpenter? Or are you refusing to give me information because I'm white?"

"Please, step back out of my way, ma'am," he said, in the tone of voice reserved for uncooperative drunks. "I do have a statement to make."

She leapt back to free him from where she'd imprisoned him, almost shoved the microphone up his nose and waited with a look of carnivorous anticipation.

"What is it you have to say to WRDE Action News?"

"Your van is illegally parked," he said and gestured toward the huge "Official Vehicles Only" sign the van was parked beside. "And it's obstructing a public walkway." The back bumper of the huge vehicle hung out over the sidewalk. He reached into his hip pocket, pulled out his citation pad and began to write as he stepped to a spot behind the van where he could see the license plate, trailing the chattering reporter like the tail on a kite.

"If you have nothing to hide, why are you unwilling to answer questions? Did you have accomplices? Why didn't you come forward twenty-six years ago?" And finally, the question she'd obviously been saving for last, "Is it true that your wife died in the 9-11 attacks on the World Trade Center, along with most of your fellow officers—but you refused to respond to the call out?"

Jack ripped off the ticket.

"You're to appear in Webster County District Court at nine am September 28 if you wish to contest this charge. If you don't, you can mail in a check for the amount of the fine. The address and the fine schedule are on the back of the ticket."

He stepped around to the front of the news van and slipped the ticket under the windshield wiper.

"If you fail to appear in court or pay the fine, a warrant can be issued for your arrest." He paused, leaned into her and said the rest slowly, with emphasis. "And then it would be my sworn duty as a police officer to serve that warrant and take you into custody."

The challenge in his eyes was so unmistakable that it unsettled her, and she actually took a step back. Jack brushed by her and walked into the building, even managed not to slam the door in her face, a feat of self-control worthy of a Meritorious Service Commendation.

Major Crocker was standing in the doorway of his office, and when he spotted Jack, motioned for him to come in.

"My sources in forensics tell me they're not finding a trace of anybody in the Cohens' house except Theresa Washington. So how did somebody else kill those old people without leaving so much as an eyelash behind, and she walks out of there looking like an extra in a slasher movie?"

Jack shrugged noncommittally.

"You know more than you're telling me."

"I don't know anything you'd believe."

"Try me."

Jack said nothing. Crock reached up and popped Cher out of his right ear. He'd dubbed his hearing aids Sonny and Cher, and Cher'd been giving him trouble for a week.

"What happened in that house, Major…was super-natural."

"Really." It was a statement, not a question.

"I'm not talking about some wave-a-fairy-wand, now-you-see-it-now-you-don't, hocus-pocus magic trick. I'm talking about…supernatural."

Crock stuffed Cher back into his ear.

"As in…like a demon or something? Somebody's possessed?"

"Something like that."

Crocker face was impassive, his voice level. "I suppose that would go a long way toward explaining the psycho who knocked out doors and walls chasing you through warehouses three months ago."

"That's the whole explanation. It's why a psycho shot up a school and killed Bishop Washington. And why another psycho killed Daniel Burke's wife."

Crocker let out a low whistle.

"Don't bite off more than you can chew, Crock. I have no idea how to do a spiritual Heimlich."

"So Daniel Burke's part of all this, too?" Crock asked.

Jack nodded.

"Maybe that explains why he got busted last night for rape."

"Rape?"

"This morning's paper, you haven't read …? Let me guess—print media never shows up at the same crime scene as you do, either."

Ten minutes later, Jack was sitting in the break room drinking coffee that tasted like the runoff from a nuclear waste dump, reading for the third time the story about Daniel in the morning's newspaper. He'd tried to call Daniel but settled for a voice mail message saying he was available whenever Daniel wanted to talk.

Patrolmen Paco Rodriguez and Sam Peterson came in together from a domestic violence call.

"I just don't see how you can call hitting somebody with a Wiffle-ball stick assault with a deadly—"

Peterson stopped when he saw Jack. "There he is, our resident celebrity," he said. "But it doesn't sound like those loudmouths out front are angling to become Jack Carpenter groupies."

He pulled out a chair facing Jack, spun it around and straddled it with his arms resting on the chair back. Ramirez stepped up to the soft drink machine.

"So…what gives, sergeant?" Peterson asked.

He tried to make the question sound offhanded, but Jack could see how focused he was on Jack's response. Ramirez paused, didn't drop his change into the slot.

"Wish I knew," Jack said, trying for offhandedness and failing, too.

"That was you in the video, wasn't it?" Peterson prompted. "You were carrying—"

"It was me, but I don't know why I was…taking gasoline into the building. I don't remember. My childhood is a void, a blank space. All the memories of that summer are gone."

"You have amnesia?"

"Seriously?" Paco put in. Unintended skepticism was slathered over his words thicker than cheese on a burrito.

"I know it sounds …strange, but it's true." Jack didn't like the defensive quality he heard in his voice. "I really don't remember."

A denial was what they were looking for, fishing for. If Jack had said he flat-out didn't do it—that the video was a fake or he wasn't the person in it—they'd have believed him in the face of a mountain of evidence to the contrary, would have stood by him and defended him. But he couldn't say he didn't burn down that building because maybe he did.

That's what they were thinking, too—maybe he did.

Chapter Eleven

2011

Daniel's media hurricane made landfall five minutes after he got to the church. In fairness, most of his synapses were diverted to the phone call he'd had with Jack on his way in and he was distracted.

Miss Minnie and Mr. Gerald dead and now…

Jack had carried gasoline into Twin Oaks?

Had he? Jack had asked him, but Daniel had no more idea than Jack did. He'd given up straining to remember that summer. It was hopeless. Snippets, pieces of memories downloaded into his mind like files off the Internet every now and then—blurred, foggy, and he couldn't make out details. He had no control over what he recalled or when he remembered it.

What was it Theresa'd said when he'd talked to her this morning? "Chapman Whitworth put the hammer down on both of us in less time than it takes to cook a pot roast." Make that all three of us.

The first reporter just showed up. A staff writer for the Cincinnati Post-Gazette, he strode in unannounced and told Daniel's secretary he had an urgent matter to discuss with the church's senior minister.

"I understand you were arrested last night—is that true Reverend Burke?" he said as soon as he stepped into Daniel's office.

"You didn't tell my secretary you were a reporter." Daniel stood. "The church has a public relations person who handles all our dealings with the press. He'll issue a statement this afternoon."

The reporter didn't drop a beat.

"The charges were assault and rape—how long had you known the victim before the alleged incident took place?"

Less than thirty seconds, but Daniel didn't say that. What he did say was that he would call security and have the man forcibly removed from the building if he didn't leave.

Daniel called his secretary into his office after the man left, told her not to allow anyone from the press in to see him, not to answer any questions, to call a staff meeting for right after lunch and to try to reach Clayton Abernathy, the chairman of the board of elders.

Two hours later, Daniel was sitting at his laptop watching the cursor blink, blink, blink on a white screen when Clayton Abernathy knocked on his office door. At seventy-seven, the man didn't look sixty, had only a touch of gray in his black hair at the temples and the trim physique of a marathoner. Emily'd always said the old man had no wrinkles because you had to smile every now and then to crease the skin, and that the reason he stood up so straight was that he had a pool cue stuffed down the back of his shirt and one leg of his pants.

Emily.

"I didn't return your call, but I thought we needed to

sit down and talk face to face," Abernathy was saying when Daniel tuned back in.

"Of course, Clayton. Please sit down."

Clayton seated himself in one of the big, comfortable chairs in front of Daniel's desk, and Daniel sat in the other one.

He knew what was coming. Still, expecting to get hammered and actually feeling your skull crack were very different things, and Daniel couldn't help tensing for the blow.

"I called a special board meeting this morning, and it is our unanimous view that it would not be in the best interest of Voice of Hope Community Church for you to be in the pulpit this weekend. Greg can take over for you. We've already contacted him."

Daniel nodded. Clayton just sat there. The man could sit so amazingly still.

"Come on, Clayton, let's deal with the elephant in the room. I should have told you myself, but it's clear you know what I've been accused of, right?"

"Assault and rape."

Hearing the words still sent a punch into Daniel's belly.

"You only need to know one thing. I didn't do anything wrong."

He sounded artificial and phony even to his own ears. There was flat-out no way to say, "I didn't do it" and not sound like every other man who pleaded his innocence after he got caught with his hand in the cookie jar.

"Of course, you didn't, Daniel. We have the utmost confidence that you can resolve this matter quickly." The old man's face was impassive, like talking to a mannequin. "Just a case of mistaken identity, I'm sure. As soon as this woman has time to make a positive identification, you'll be cleared, and you can put this whole ugly mess behind you."

"I wish it were that simple." Daniel was about to tell the elder board chairman that the woman had already picked him out of a police lineup, but before he had a chance to share that particular piece of damning information, Daniel's cell phone rang. He pulled it out of his pocket to turn it off and saw that it was Jack.

"I apologize, but I have to take this call," Daniel said, knowing that Abernathy would consider it exceedingly rude for him to allow this kind of intrusion.

"Jack, I'm in a meeting right now. Can this wait un—"

"No, it can't," Jack said. "That woman, Lily Saunders, the one from the elevator. I was doing some digging on her this morning, trying to find her connection to Whitworth. The Cincinnati PD called me a few minutes ago because I'd been asking questions about her earlier—and now they're the ones with questions."

"I don't understand."

"They found her this morning in the river, Daniel. They're calling it a homicide."

Daniel couldn't speak, could feel the color drain out of his face. His stunned silence filled the room like pressure that threatened to blow out the windows.

"They're going to think I…aren't they, Jack?"

"You wouldn't happen to have an alibi for last night, say between two and six am?"

"I was home in bed."

"That's not an alibi. We'll talk later." Then Jack hung up.

Daniel slowly returned his phone to his pocket.

"Something's wrong, Daniel. You look…are you all right?"

"Yes and no. Yes, something's wrong, and no, I'm not all right." Daniel knew what he had to do.

"Clayton, you need to fire me. I could resign effective

immediately and draft a formal letter of resignation, but it would look a lot better for the reputation of the church for you to fire me."

"I don't understand, Daniel. I—"

"This situation is not going to get better. In fact, it's about to get a whole lot worse."

"Tell me what's going on." Clayton seemed genuinely concerned and that touched Daniel.

"That phone call was from a friend who's a police officer. He told me that the woman—her name is Lily Sanders, I think—who accused me of...who said I..." Daniel couldn't say the word rape. He just couldn't. "The woman who has made allegations against me—she's dead."

Clayton's only visible response was a slight intake of breath, not quite a gasp.

"They think it was murder, and I'm guessing they're going to think...I did it."

"And you told your friend you were home in bed at the time. Not much of an alibi."

Daniel was surprised at the way Clayton was taking the news.

"That's what Jack said."

"You didn't do it." It wasn't a question, but Daniel answered it anyway.

"No, I didn't. But I'm not sure I can prove that I didn't."

"Far as I know, in this country you're innocent until proven guilty. Not the other way around."

Again, Clayton surprised him.

"What's happening, Daniel? The thing with this woman, it wasn't some kind of indiscretion on your part or a misunderstanding was it?"

The only explanation was the truth, ridiculous as it was going to sound when he said it.

"No, it wasn't. Someone is trying to—there's no other way to put it, Clayton—he's trying to destroy me. He's utterly ruthless. I don't know how...I don't have any defense against..."

Daniel fell silent and looked down in his hands in his lap. He felt totally defeated. The silence drew out, would have felt uncomfortable if Daniel had been in a place where he noticed such things. When the old man finally spoke, his voice was firm and resolute.

"My grandfather had a saying, Daniel. 'Don't just do something, stand there.'"

Daniel looked up, confused.

"When you don't know what to do, you stand, Daniel. You hold your head up, and you stand."

Daniel gaped at him.

"If you want to resign, I can't stop you. But this church won't fire you, not as long as I'm the chairman of the board. And we will support you whether you're still our minister or not."

"Clayton, why would you—?"

"That business this summer with the man in the belfry...and Emily. It never made sense to me. What happened wasn't random violence, was it?"

Daniel shook his head.

"There's only one reason to try to bring down a man of God. And there's only one who'd have any reason to want to, one who destroys for destruction's sake. The Father of Lies. You stand against him, son, and this church will stand right there beside you."

Daniel felt suddenly close to tears. In all his years at Voice of Hope Community Church, he never knew there was this kind of spiritual depth anywhere in it. But how would he have known? Deep calls out to deep. The reverse is also true. Daniel had only seen the side of the church that reflected back to him his own image.

"Clayton, I…thank you."

Clayton reached over and put his hand on Daniel's shoulder. He leaned close, and Daniel could have sworn he saw a light flicker in the old man's eyes, the glint of sunlight off polished steel.

"We know who wins in the end," he said. "You need to remember that. Now, tell me what's going on."

Daniel did. All of it.

~

2011

"Hawkins," said the guard outside his cell. "You ready?"

Billy Ray sat up and pinned on the face he'd worn every day since he was transferred to the Kentucky State Penitentiary in Danforth from the federal prison in Lexington ten years ago, the docile-prisoner face, the repentant-prisoner face, the rehabilitated-prisoner face, the face that had gotten him released on parole at his very first parole board hearing after he'd served the mandatory twenty-year federal sentence he got for being—what was it they'd called him?—a drug czar.

"You gonna miss me when I'm gone, Baxter?" he asked the guard.

"You know, I might," the guard said. "You're the first con in a long time who's been respectful."

"Pays to respect the law," Billy Ray said.

I ever see you on the outside, I'll slit your throat soon's your back's turned.

"What you gonna do now that you're free?" Baxter asked. "Use all that money you got buried in a boxcar somewhere to buy yourself a dry cleaner's, maybe, or a likker store?"

Billy Ray laughed a resigned laugh. It sounded totally sincere. It should; he'd been practicing it for years.

"You believe in fairy tales, do ya, Baxter? The Tooth Fairy and the Easter Bunny? Shoot, if I had a nickel for every person who's asked if I got a pile of money out there waiting for me, I wouldn't need the pile of money!"

That elicited a chuckle from the guard, who unlocked the cell door then, and held it open. Billy Ray followed the guard down the catwalk in front of the row of cells, hollering out to all the other prisoners he'd sucked up to for years to stay out of trouble—prisoners too stupid to stop shooting themselves in the foot with their own reckless behavior and untamed tempers. There was a time and a place for violence, for payback, for retribution. Prison wasn't it, unless you wanted your cell number to be your permanent address.

Billy Ray was smarter than that. That's why he was leaving, and all the other morons were staying. That's why he was going home to the buried boxcar full of money that he'd managed to convince the whole world was a fantasy. Money he intended to use—every dime of it if he had to—to find his sweet daughter, Becca.

There was, after all, a place for violence, for payback and for retribution.

Elmer Pruitt, known as Possum, picked Billy Ray up outside the prison gate in an old Ford pickup truck with a front bumper held on by duct tape. He'd called in a favor to get Possum to come get him and let him use the truck for three days. Billy Ray had a lot of markers out there. He'd taken the hit for all of them—got ten years tacked on his sentence for refusing to name his accomplices and turn over his "assets." But he'd given his word he'd remain silent, and Billy Ray Hawkins always kept his word. No exceptions. Oh, he wasn't abiding by some lofty moral code. He'd just figured out early on that men who kept their word were respected. Do exactly what you say you're gonna do—every time——and after a while even stupid people understand that when you threaten 'em, you ain't bluffin'. That's when respect turned into fear, and being a man other men feared was a good thing.

Inside an hour after he dropped Possum at the pool hall on Main Street, Billy Ray had a shiny new driver's license, new clothes from Walmart, and a prepaid cell phone that he used to make two calls.

Then he had to report to his parole officer, a fat, stupid civil service idiot named Clarence Bohanan. Bohanan or somebody like him would have control over Billy Ray's life for the next decade, could yank him back into a prison cell if he so much as went squirrel-hunting—parolees couldn't own a gun. Or had a beer with old friends—wasn't supposed to associate with known felons. Shoot, Billy Ray didn't even know anybody who wasn't a felon! Well, Billy Ray Hawkins was not willing to live like that—and he'd figured out a way he wouldn't have to.

Billy Ray had a job as a farm hand working his own farm! The state didn't know that, of course. He'd signed the deed of the land he'd inherited from his daddy over to Horace Turpin before his trial so the feds couldn't seize it as the ill-gotten gains of a drug enterprise. They took everything else, of course. Or tried to. But danged if there wasn't a mysterious fire at the mansion he'd built on ten acres off Hawthorne Mountain Road—house, barn, outbuildings—everything burned to the ground the day after he was convicted. Billy Ray couldn't have been paroled if Turp hadn't provided him "gainful employment and a place to live." And he could count on the man to swear on a ten-foot stack of Bibles that Billy Ray'd shown up every day on time, worked hard, hadn't caused no trouble and was home in bed in the little house on the back of the farm where he'd grown up by nine o'clock every night.

And while the law thought he was out digging post-holes and milking Turp's cows, Billy Ray'd conduct his business just like he always done.

He hadn't let himself worry about his "treasure" all these years. It was safe or it wasn't, and he couldn't do nothing about it one way or the other. But until a couple of weeks ago, his riches had mostly been his way of keepin' score. Then an opportunity had come up so sudden and unexpected, it still didn't quite seem real. Now, he had something to spend his money on that mattered. He could use it to buy freedom. He could purchase the next ten years of his life back. That's what he'd been promised, and the man who'd done the swearin' had fairly well better be a man of his word, or he'd wind up buried in a hollow alongside the bodies of that guard, Baxter…and Becca.

The sun had just dropped below the level of the mountain to the west of the farm when Billy Ray finally stood in front of the butt-cheek rocks at the base of the mountain that backed up to U.S. 31. At the sight of them, he felt a little thrill in his belly that was almost like being aroused. There was anticipation mixed with fear as he climbed up the rocks and dropped down into the small space between them that you couldn't even see until you was right on top of it. He liked places like this, secret, dark places, was always digging around to find them when he was a kid.

The memory hit him like a bolt of lightning.

Shiny black walls and a star shape drawn on the floor. He steps over the chalk line that blurs as his eyes try to focus, and he struggles to remember where he is. He's drunk. The room is spinning, and he falls on his face, hears the sound of breaking glass. It sounds far away, but it's not. It's the amulet, the vial he wears around his neck. It has shattered beneath him on the stone floor.

Then it comes, the nightmare creature appears in a red glow. He looks up at it, leaps to his feet and staggers backward over the chalk line on the floor, his eyes riveted to an unimaginable horror. A scream tears out of his throat, and once he starts screaming, he can't stop even after he has shredded his vocal cords.

Billy Ray stood stock still for a moment, frozen by the memory. He hadn't done that, remembered that awful day, in years. It was a nightmare he'd had about a monster once when he was drunk. Just his imagination.

Then how had he damaged his voice?

He'd been to a handful of doctors over the years but couldn't none of them do anything about it. He'd "shredded his vocal cords," they'd said. He'd speak in a gravel-throated bark for the rest o' his life.

He resolutely banished the question and the implications of it from his mind. He had way better things to think about right now than a fantasy monster. He had money to find.

He rolled the wheel-shaped stone away from in front of the metal grate he'd affixed to the rock at the entrance to the cave. He dug in the Walmart sack until he located the hacksaw. After all this time, the padlock would be rusted shut, and he'd come prepared with a new one. It didn't take long to saw through the old lock and push the door in squeaky protest inward. He stepped inside the cave, inhaled the suddenly cooler air and was certain without needing any further confirmation that in all these years, no one had been here. He suddenly threw back his head and laughed out loud. How crazy was that, some doper burying a boxcar full of riches?

He stood in the cave entrance, laughing, for a long time.

Chapter Twelve

1985

Bishop Washington paced beneath the blackened stump. Theresa was the one in the family done the pacing, and when he'd tell her to sit down and relax, she'd give him a look sharp enough to cause internal bleeding and tell him her worries was chasing her and if she sat down, they'd catch her.

Bishop's worries about the three children he'd brought to the woods were chasing him, roaring through his mind like monsters on Harleys, and if he was to sit down, they'd run him down and kill him.

He shouldn't have brought 'em! Shoot, he probably shouldn't have taken them fishing a week ago, neither, or to the pond to skate and to Long Drive Hill to go sleddin' last winter. But them children soaked up the attention and affection he and Theresa lavished on them like butter on warm toast. Jack, the tough guy, who went home every night to a beatin' by his good-for-nothing father. Daniel—from a perfect Christian home where his father cared way more about the pain in his congregation than he did the loneliness of his own son, and his mother cared only about his little sister—period. And Becca, fragile as a china doll, who lived in the house with the biggest and meanest dope grower in the county. They'd been drawn to the warmth of the Washingtons at the annual Christian Youth Rally two years ago. When Isaac had started a Bible study every Thursday evening in their home afterward, the dozen kids who came originally dwindled in a couple of months down to the Three Musketeers—Jack, Daniel and Becca. Becca came because she knew, and Bishop was the only person in her life who understood. Jack and Daniel came because Becca did.

Those three had hero-worshipped Isaac, thought he was—

Can't go there.

He heard a scrambling in the rocks behind him on the cliff side of Bear Claw. Then up popped Daniel Burke, climbing over a boulder and jumping down the last few feet to the ground. Jack was right behind him. Their hands and knees was scraped, they shirts soaked in sweat. Dougal Dog leapt up on the back side of the rock and down off it, but Becca was nowhere in sight.

"What are you doing?" He stuttered in disbelief in unison with the boys' jubilant cry: "Bishop!"

It was hard to tell which one of them was the most surprised—or the most thrilled—to see the other.

Daniel come runnin' across the distance separating them and flung his arms around Bishop's waist. Jack looked like he wanted to do the same thing but didn't, and after a moment, Daniel musta decided his was a little-kid response, and he stepped back.

And then they was talking, babbling and interrupting each other, close to tears, telling a horror story so scary it shoved aside the speech that'd been forming in Bishop's head about their promise to stay together in the woods and the dangers of climbing up the east face of Bear Claw Mountain.

Fear stood in the center of his mind now, hot and stinking. This was the evil in the woods. Unless these boys was just exaggerating gettin' beat in a fight—and they wasn't— Cole Stuart was possessed by a demon so powerful that Bishop could sense the evil of it miles away.

But how could it have happened so fast? He'd seen the boys from Brewster Academy three days ago, and they was fine—chests out, blustering boys but not bad kids. So how did one of them get possessed?

"Bishop, those boys weren't…right," Daniel sputtered. And Bishop understood the difficulty of trying to describe the "otherness" of someone whose body and will had been taken over by a creature from Hell. "I never saw anybody who looked that mean, that—"

"Filled up with hate," Bishop said. "With his face all closed up shut and ugly."

Jack was better at reading people than Daniel was.

"You know something about this, don't you, Bishop? What? How could Cole do…and why would they kidnap Becca?"

"I don't have no idea why they'd take Becca, son." Then his growing fear and anger boomed in his James Earl Jones voice. "But they ain't gone take that child nowhere!"

The boys jumped at the rumble, but he could tell they was glad. They was just kids themselves, after all, too young to have to deal with a thing like this, and whether they'd admit it even to themselves, they was eager to hand the problem off to a grownup who could fix it. "I'm gone go get her!" His voice quieted. "And you two gone stay right here with McDoo."

He raised his hand to quiet the instant protest. "No

discussing to be done. You boys would just get in the way. You sit and have some lunch, and I'll come back"—he stopped and amended—"Becca and I'll come back and get you."

Then he was runnin' through the woods. Yeah, runnin'. Fear propelling him as he set his face for what he was going to have to do—stand up to a demon and defy it. In all life's fears, wasn't nothing worse.

~

2011

Theresa looked hollow-eyed when she greeted Jack with a big hug at the door. The wound on her forehead wore only a Band-Aid now, but the swollen lump was plainly visible. Daniel looked like he hadn't slept in a week, said he'd already had a run-in with the press but didn't want to talk about it. Jack was sure he looked just as bad. The lame, the halt and the weak. Up against one of the most powerful demons in the universe.

Goody.

After she said grace—eating unblessed food'll give you the runs, she'd always said—Theresa produced a pot of chili that tasted even better than it smelled. Once they were all seated, Jack dragged it out, couldn't help it. He'd been able to think of nothing else since he watched a boy with "Carpenter" written on the back of his shirt mount the steps of Twin Oaks Nursing Home carrying a can of gasoline.

"I know I've already talked to both of you about this… but videos don't lie," he said in a low voice full of pebbles. "I was there. I— "

"Them pictures don't tell the truth of it," Theresa said.

"Daniel, are you sure you don't remember anything, any reason why…"

The helpless look on Daniel's face was answer enough. "Sometimes things swirl out of the mist, but even then I can't see them clearly," Daniel said.

"Real truth's in here," Theresa said, patting her bosom quietly. "The things of the world'll lie to you and confuse you, but your heart don't lie. You know in your heart you couldn't never have done such a thing,"

That was the trouble. Jack didn't know that. Didn't know that at all. But Daniel and Theresa would never understand. Jack wasn't like them. There was a darkness in him he'd seen even as a boy. He'd always been on the outside with his nose pressed up against the glass, looking in at the others enjoying a…peace he could not fathom. And where he stood on the outside, there was darkness all around. Had he…joined forces with it?

But for now, Jack let it go and changed gears. He hadn't told either one of them yet about Becca—who might remember everything.

"I have news," he said.

"So do I," Theresa said. "Is yours good news or bad news?"

"Good news."

"Then we'd ought to hear mine first. Always like to end on a positive note." She cleared her throat.

"You said last night in the emergency room that I didn't have no motive to kill Miss Minnie and Mr. Gerald, and I said Chapman Whitworth would arrange one. Well, he did. That sweet old couple didn't have a whole lot in this world—just that big old house they couldn't look after, a car, personal things."

She squared her shoulders.

"I got a call about an hour ago from Mr. Gerald's

lawyer. He was right upset. Said he got in this morning's mail a 'revised' copy of Mr. Gerald's will—mailed yesterday!—and everything'd been changed on it so their whole estate would come to me. It'd been signed by Mr. Gerald, but that lawyer let me know right quick he knew that wasn't Mr. Gerald's signature."

"If the estate's not worth beans, why would Whitworth think he could convince the police you'd commit two murders to get your hands on it?" Daniel asked.

"That's the thing of it, see. Come to find out, they estate was worth lots of beans."

"How many?" Jack asked.

"A couple of million."

Daniel whistled.

"They had gub'mint bonds. Stacks of them, that lawyer said. I never knew about none of it, and I'm not completely sure they knew how much them bonds was worth. All's I do know is they had a boatload of money, and it 'pears somebody changed their will so's it'd all come to me when they died."

"Yep, that's a powerful motive for murder," Jack said.

"Demons is smart and crafty. And this 'un has had a long time to come up with his game plan," Theresa said.

"And we've been on the receiving end of it for less than twenty-four hours." Daniel sighed. "A disgraced preacher, a rogue cop and…"

"And a fat, old black woman," Theresa finished for him.

"What could the three of us possibly do to stop an efreet?" Daniel said.

"That's been poured into Chapman Whitworth's soul like cream into coffee," Theresa said. "Ain't no way to tell where one starts and the other one stops."

"And what that means, boys and girls," Jack said, his

voice soft but firm, "is the only way we're going to stop Chapman Whitworth from taking a seat on the Supreme Court"—he took a breath and plunged ahead—"is to kill him."

Theresa gasped, but Daniel didn't.

"We got to try everything we know to do 'fore we start talking 'bout killin' people!" Theresa said.

"Everything we know to do is…what?" Daniel asked. "He's already five steps ahead of us."

Jack got up and went to the pot of chili on the stove and ladled a second massive portion into his bowl. "Anybody else want some?"

"I don't know how you can eat," Daniel said.

"Ranger training. Eat whenever there's food because you never know when there won't be. Homemade chili is waaay more gastronomically pleasing than carryout pizza or Chinese egg rolls. Besides, I'm the one with the good news, remember?" He paused for a beat. "I found Becca."

That was a conversation stopper.

"How? Is she all right? Where?" Theresa and Daniel chattered at him so frantically that he couldn't get out an answer.

"Really close by, as a matter of fact. Hendersonville, Indiana," Jack said. "The rest of it…I don't know. She was arrested last night for vagrancy. Now you know everything I know."

"Vagrancy?" Daniel said.

It was clear he didn't like what that charge said about the current state of Becca's affairs.

"Do you think she remembers what happened that summer?" Jack asked Theresa.

"Oh, I 'spect she remembers a whole lot more'n she wants to remember about it. Some'm happened 'tween her and that efreet. Some'm went wrong. She…failed somehow—didn't get it right—or else it couldn't have come back. You boys' minds wiped out the awful of that demon—or God did—but Becca…Becca was talkin' to it." Theresa sighed. "She never was right after that. Never got over it that I could see. You moved away; Becca stayed. But she was different."

"Different how?" Jack asked.

"Just…different." It was obvious that Theresa didn't want to talk about it, at least not right now.

"So now there are four of us," Daniel said. "Add to the disgraced preacher, the rogue cop and the…sweet-spirited old black woman…a vagrant who hasn't been 'right in the head' in twenty-six years. That's it? That's our army?"

"Uh-huh." Theresa smiled a little. "Remember how God reduced Gideon's army so when they won the battle, it'd be clear it was God done it."

Jack's frustration slipped out then. He tried to keep it from Theresa and Daniel the best he could because he knew it upset them to know that spiritually—how was it Theresa had put it?—"you and God's not on good terms."

"Yeah, this is all part of the game God plays," Jack said. "He won't tell you what he wants you to do. He tells you some of it, a leading here, hints, clues—but you're never really sure."

"Does wonders for your prayer life," Daniel said, and Jack couldn't tell whether he was serious or being sarcastic.

"And he won't even help you do what he's told you to do. He waits until the very end, then shows up and gives you barely what you have to have to survive," Jack struggled to keep the anger he felt from showing in his voice. "If whatever you're facing is something you can do, he'll diminish your resources—or increase the challenge—so you can only do it with his help."

"You may see it as a game, but God don't," Theresa said.

"I spent four years in seminary," Daniel said, "and I still can't come up with a good answer when Andi wants to know why God didn't save her mother."

"Who's to say he didn't save her mother hundreds of times 'fore that demon come for her?" Theresa said. "That he hasn't saved all of us? We oversleep maybe, and miss the bus that crashes. Or we can't find our car keys so that drunk driver blows through a red light right before we hit the intersection. Thing is, we don't see those times. We only see the times when he don't save us."

"There's no sense rehashing all this," Daniel said. "The bottom line is we don't get a say in any of it. Period. That's how God rolls. We have to keep a demon from sitting on the Supreme Court. And other than killing Chapman Whitworth, I don't know—"

"There is something else we could do," Jack said.

"And that is?" Daniel asked.

"We could go to Senator LaHayne, the chairman of the committee investigating Whitworth."

The senator had come out in staunch opposition to Whitworth's nomination the day after the president's announcement, though he'd never given any reason for his disapproval. Whitworth was as squeaky clean as a new rubber duckie.

"What can we say to him?" Daniel said. "Something like, 'Senator LaHayne, the man you're about to confirm as a justice on the United States Supreme Court is possessed by a demon.' Right. That'll work."

"We don't say Whitworth's a demon. We say he's a criminal—and that we can prove it."

The other two said nothing.

"What if we told the senator that we know something

damning about Whitworth's background—we don't have to tell the senator what it is—and Whitworth found out we knew and is out to get us. What If we had—and I know this is a tall order—proof that Chapman Whitworth framed Theresa for murder and Daniel for rape to keep you too busy to go after him, and dragged out that old video of me to destroy my credibility so nobody'd believe me if I opposed him? What if we outfox the fox, use what he's done to us to bring him down?"

"How could we possibly prove to Senator LaHayne that Whitworth did all this?" Daniel said. "How will we even get the senator to talk to us?"

Theresa smiled beatifically. "Now don't you be worrying about the small stuff," she said. "God's got this."

That thought brought Jack no comfort whatsoever.

"But before we start planning our strategy, we got to have ourselves a sit-down with Becca," she continued.

"I've already made arrangements to go tomorrow," Jack said. "Who's coming with me?"

"I'm in," Theresa said.

Daniel shook his head.

"Sorry, Jack. I'm performing a wedding tomorrow morning." He stopped for a moment. "But I think you need to take Andi with you."

Andi. Jack hadn't thought about that.

"You're right," he said, "Andi needs to meet Becca."

"And I s'pect maybe Becca needs to meet Andi, too," Theresa said.

Chapter Thirteen

1985

Bishop figured he probably sounded like a herd of elephants crashing through the woods when he burst out of the trees onto the asphalt of the parking lot at the rest area called Melody Creek that the state'd put here to give folks access to the woods. This was a national forest, so they didn't build nothing among the trees themselves, but there was three concrete picnic tables and benches and a fire pit in the grass beyond the parking lot and worn down hiking trails leading away from it on both ends. Bishop hadn't been on no hiking trail. He'd grown up next to these woods and a lifetime spent here drew a map in his head that was more sure and true than any trail. He leaned over with his hands on his knees, panting, fear leaking into the sweat that soaked his shirt and ran in rivers down his face, giving it the peculiar stink like was all around you in a war.

Then he began searching the undergrowth just off the road, looking for—

Six bicycles, different sizes, was hidden in the brush

under a tree just off the highway. You wouldn't have seen them 'less you knew to look. He'd beat them here! At least partly relieved, he sank down on a guard rail post near the bikes to catch his breath.

How they figure to get Becca out of here when they only got six bikes?

But the bigger question, the more horrible question, the one that had been chewing at his guts like a hungry rat all the way down the mountainside was why they'd taken her in the first place. She could see that demon, sure, which it'd been Bishop's experience shocked and unnerved a demon. But that wasn't no reason to run off with her. And how'd that Stuart kid get the rest of them boys to go along with it? They was reasonable kids and had sense enough to understand this was kidnapping. How could they possibly think they could get away with such a thing? And why would they try?

A car pulled into the rest area parking lot on the opposite side from Bishop, and a family tumbled out, Mom and Dad, two little girls, a baby and a dog. Dad started unpacking the trunk of the car as Mom put a paper tablecloth on one of the concrete picnic tables, gesturing for the little girls to put rocks on the four corners to hold it down while she set up basic baby gear.

Bishop took in a big gulp of air and let it out slow to calm himself.

I know ain't nothing that's happenin' here today escaped your notice, Lord. You ain't surprised. But I sure am! Surprised and so scared I'm spittin' cotton balls. And I know fear don't come from you. It comes from the Father of Lies, and every time we give in to fear, we's moving in his direction and not yours. I got all that. But I'm fresh out of courage, Lord. I need you to give me some—or at least strike that demon blind so he don't see how scared I am.

Bishop heard voices coming from the trail that ran south from the pull-off. Here it was, then. He steeled himself for what he'd face when that demon realized he knew. Tried to prepare himself for what was about to happen. But wasn't nothing in Bishop's life, nothing he'd ever seen or done—not even Vietnam—that could have prepared him for what he seen when six boys come out of the woods with one terrified little girl.

It was the single most shocking, horrifying sight his eyes had ever beheld, a frozen frame image destined to populate his nightmares with monsters for the rest of his life. Wasn't just one demon. They was a demon sucking the life out of every one of them boys! They was swarming on them, thicker than maggots on road kill. Bishop had never seen so many at once and couldn't remember his mother or grandfather ever saying they'd faced more than one at a time—well, two. That time the white men come for his daddy in the night, wearing sheets to cover up they faces. They was two demons, then—one on the man who dragged Daddy out of the house, yelling that wasn't no nigger gonna register to vote in this county long as there was a breath left in his body and one on the man who tied Daddy to a tree. And the flickerin' lights of other demons whisperin' in the ears of the other men who took turns punchin' him til he hung limp from the ropes, his face looking like ground meat. Bishop and his mama clung to each other on the porch, feeling in their souls every punch that landed, watchin' the demons who was so busy they didn't notice that he and Mama knew.

These demons wasn't in such a good mood. They wasn't laughin'. They was arguing, yelling at each other. The raw ugliness and evil in their voices had a darkness of its own separate from the words. Each jagged black clot of sound hit his ear and tore through it into this brain with a savagery that left him breathless. Every time Bishop had ever heard a demon speak, he expected his ears to gush blood from the brutality of the attack.

The sheer force of their combined ugliness was overwhelming. One was made out of wasps, another looked like a horribly deformed gorilla. The demon on Cole Stuart, the ringleader, was a dragon with a scorpion's tail, a lizard's tongue in a mouth full of shark teeth, and bulging black eyeballs big as baseballs that moved separately, looking in different directions at the same time. The cold that flowed out ahead of them hit Bishop in an arctic blast, chilled his bones and frosted his breath. He sucked in a gasp from the cold. This was Hell, right here, right now, in a roadside picnic area in central Kentucky. How the real thing could possibly be worse than this—and he knew it was, indeed, infinitely worse—was beyond his wildest imaginings.

As soon as the boys emerged from the woods, the dog at the other end of the parking lot began to bark.

Then Becca saw Bishop. She was deathly pale and seemed somehow to have shrunk, was much smaller than she'd been when he'd let her and the boys out on the logging road a lifetime ago. But her face lit now with a wonder and joy that stabbed right through Bishop's heart and straight into his soul.

"Bishop!" she cried and started to rush toward him. One of the boys grabbed her by the arm and stopped her. The boys was looking at each other, confused, but the demons were all looking at Bishop, their ugliness multiplied by ten by the rage and loathing on their faces.

"It knows," snarled the deformed gorilla demon. "You see us, don't you, nigger pig?"

"I could say I don't, but that'd be kinda stupid, wouldn't it, since I heard the question."

Cole Stuart said evenly, coldly. "Why hello, Coach Washington. What brings you out here"—he glanced at the lone vehicle at the other end of the lot, where a little girl was trying with no success to quiet the basset hound —"on foot, apparently?"

Bishop didn't answer the question, didn't want to say any more than he had to for fear the demons would hear the tremor that surely must be in his voice. Instead, he spoke to the boy holding Becca's arm.

"You'll want to let her go now, son." In Bishop's mind, his voice trembled like the warble of an old-lady soprano. But what come out his mouth carried a level of steely authority that was right impressive. The boy, Jacob Dumas, was taken aback by it; the demon on his shoulders only sneered. None of the other demons was cowed in any way by Bishop.

"Let's eat it," cried Jacob's demon, a creature made of wasps. "I like dark meat. Let's stick it and make it squeal." All the demons cavorted around in glee except the dragon demon on Cole Stuart. It spoke through Cole.

"The little girl is going with us, Coach," he said. His voice would have sounded pleasant to a passerby. "So you need to get out of our way."

"And if I don't? When I don't?"

"You have no idea what the six of us could do to you."

Bishop knew, all right. Demons didn't have no super powers of they own, but the humans they was possessing did. You seen it on the news from time to time—a story 'bout somebody who'd picked up a car off'n a child and the like. Release enough adrenaline into a person and they could do just about anything. And the demons didn't feel no pain. Superhuman strength and no pain was a powerful combination.

"Oh, I know full well what you can do to me, but you'd

best be givin' some thought right now to what I can do to you."

Cole just stared at him.

"You think I'm gone stand aside and just let you boys kidnap a twelve-year-old child?"

"It's not kidnapping if she wants to go!" Cole snapped, triumph in his voice. Apparently, he'd been working it out in his head.

"Riiiight," Bishop said. "Try that on Judge Carter and see how well it works out for you. You need to remember, you's just a bunch of kids. I'm a grownup. People gone listen to me and b'lieve what I tell 'em. You beat me half to death and then run off with this little girl, won't be no rock anywhere in this county you can hide under."

"Kill him like we did—" began the slug demon, but Stuart's dragon quieted him with a casual whip of his tail that knocked the creature off the boy he was riding and left him dangling from the tentacle he'd sunk deep into the boy's chest.

"That ain't a bad idea, come to think of it," Bishop said. "Go on ahead. Kill me. You ain't gone get her past me less'n you do, anyway. I ain't gone go down 'thout a fight, though, and it's gone be messy. So you're gone have to kill them, too." He pointed to the family enjoying a picnic at the other end of the parking lot. It was the absolute providence of God that they'd shown up when they had. "The mama, the papa, three little children and a dog. And if somebody else was to pull up while you's massacring that family, you gone have to kill them, too." He paused. "You so stupid you think you can leave a trail of dead bodies all over the county like that and ain't nobody gone notice?"

Then Bishop took a shot in the dark. An idea that had begun to form, lost in the shock and horror of seeing six demons at once surfaced now, elbowed its way to the front of Bishop's brain and demanded attention. Why was these demons all together? Demons hated everybody and everything in all creation, including—especially—each other. They'd never stay together, work cooperatively like this—not willingly.

"I 'spect your boss ain't gone be too happy when they haul you all off to jail."

His words silenced the demons, who'd been jumpin' around and chatterin'. They all looked to the dragon. Bishop struck while the iron was hot. Stepping toward them, he avoided the eyes of the demons and spoke directly to the boy holding on to Becca. "I ain't gone say it again. Let her go."

Jacob didn't look to the dragon for leadership, just opened the hand on her arm, where giant pink indentations remained that'd be purple bruises by tomorrow. Becca exploded out of the group of boys and crashed into Bishop, flinging her arms around him and holding on fiercely.

"You haven't seen the last of us," Cole said, not menacing but matter-of-fact.

"I'm sure I ain't," Bishop said, striving for the same pass-the-salt tone and hoping he'd at least got close. "You do remember baseball practice gone start next Wednesday, noon at the ball field." He paused, stood up to his full six feet seven inches that dwarfed even the biggest of the twelve-year-old boys. "Better not be late, or you gone have to run laps 'round the field."

There was no response. Cole and the other boys wordlessly pulled their bicycles out of the brush. Bishop's legs finally collapsed out from under him, but he managed to make it look like he'd just gotten down on one knee so he could hug Becca, who threw her arms around his neck, choking him. He glanced only once at the demons. He'd have sworn there was no way in the world they could be uglier or that he could be more frightened than he already was. But he was wrong. The looks of rage and loathing changed their ugly faces into hideous masks of evil so horrifying he instantly looked away and busied himself patting Becca on the back as if she was crying, which she wasn't.

Cole only spoke once.

"Whatever she tells you…remember, it's her word against six of us." Then the boys mounted their bikes and rode silently away.

Only then did the little basset hound stop barking. But that's when another dog began. Dougal Dog burst out of the undergrowth near where Bishop had exited the woods, barking wildly as he ran toward Becca. She didn't bend to pet him, though, refused to release her grip on Bishop. Jack and Daniel came out of the woods right behind him.

"Don't you boys never do what you's told?" Bishop said. Now the quaver he'd feared would be in his voice put in an appearance and he shut up. They wasn't listenin' to him anyway. They didn't see nothin' but Becca, they eyes gobbling her up like she was peppermint ice cream.

"Are you ok?" Daniel asked her.

But she wouldn't look at him, just buried her face deeper in her arms around Bishop's neck.

"Becca?" Jack said.

Bishop caught the two boys' attention, then looked down meaningfully at the little girl attached to his neck. "I need you boys to do somethin' for me," he said. "I need you to go to the house of a friend of mine, lives a couple of miles from here."

"Isn't there some place closer we could go to call the sheriff?" Jack asked.

"The sheriff? And report what?" Bishop said.

"That those guys kidnapped Becca!"

Bishop shook his head. "No, son, that's not the way it went down," he said. "What happened here was some kids got into a fight in the woods, and the winners took one of the losers 'captive' for a little while—you know, like playin' army—and when the game was over, they let her go." Bishop looked from Jack to Daniel. "You all is twelve years old. The sheriff ain't gone see no crime was committed."

"But—" Jack began.

"I need you to go to my friend's house and ask him can he run us back to the truck and help me fix it. It won't start."

"But—" Daniel began, but Jack elbowed him and cut his eyes toward Becca, and Daniel said no more.

Bishop described a farmhouse a couple of miles down the road where they'd find a middle-aged man named Bernard Tackett.

"Ask Bernie real polite if'n he'll come, and tell him I need for him to bring his jumper cables and his tool box— you got that?" The boys nodded. "Go on now. I got to get that truck fixed so's I can get you children home."

When the boys were out of sight, he sat back in the dirt and pulled Becca into his lap. "They won't be back for a while. Bernie don't do nothing fast. Whenever you ready, sugar, we can talk."

But she just clung to him, mute, and continued to shake.

Chapter Fourteen

2011

"Who's Becca?" Andi asked her father as he finished putting the ribbons on the ends of her braids. She'd get Miss Theresa to redo them in the car.

"She's an old friend of mine and Jack's. We all went to elementary school together. Becca and Jack and I were the Three Musketeers."

"You had swords? I didn't know they still had swords when you were a little kid."

Her father grinned. "People called us that because we were three friends like the Three Musketeers."

"Oh." Andi was disappointed. She still didn't understand why she was going to have to miss the wedding—Andi loved weddings, even if she didn't know the bride or groom—to go with Uncle Jack and Miss Theresa to meet this "Becca" person, but she'd have liked the whole idea a lot better if Becca'd had a sword.

Becca.

Andi suddenly felt cold all over.

"Daddy, is this Becca…is she who the demons were looking for?"

She tried never to think about that time, about what she saw through the crack in the storage room door that day in school—the monster of wasps that stuck a claw in the bad man's head and made him shoot Miss Lund. He had asked, "Where's Becca?" before he killed Mr. Bishop. So had the demon who killed Mommy.

Andi is clinging to her mother, holding on as tight as she can. Mommy turned her head away so she wasn't looking at the fat man with the gun, but Andi can see what Mommy can't—a monster stuck to the man with tentacles in his cheek and neck—and even with her eyes squeezed tight shut, the image won't go away. She sees the lizard face with slanted red eyes that don't have a black spot in the middle and no eyelids at all—no nose, either—and a mouth full of teeth that look like knives. She can smell the monster, too, the greenish-brown goo running down the bad man's back that stinks worse than a baby's diaper. And she can feel the cold, like standing in front of the open freezer door.

"And you know where Becca is, could lead me right to her?" the fat man says to Daddy on the phone, but he doesn't believe what Daddy tells him. "You're the worst liar I ever heard. I ain't gonna get it out of you that easy. But just 'cause you're being so cooperative, I'm gonna give you a choice. You get to decide who I kill."

Mommy tells the man that if he touches Andi, she will rip his throat out with her fingernails. "You will kill me and let my little girl go," she says.

Then Mommy takes her hand and leads her to the choir robe closet. When Mommy kneels down, Andi grabs her around the neck and bursts into the tears she's been wanting to cry since she saw the fat man with the monster on his back in the fellowship hall. Mommy pulls her arms away and takes her face into her hands. She kisses her on the forehead and whispers in her ear, "When I close this door, you run. And you hide. Find some place he'll never find you." She looks into Andi's eyes for just a moment. "I love you," she says. Then she opens the door and shoves Andi inside.

Andi stands in the dark in the closet, wishing she'd told Mommy that she loved her, too.

"Yes, honey," Daddy said. "She's the Becca they...... were looking for." He had let go of the ribbon he was tying into a bow on her right braid and it hung loose, dangling.

"What did they want her for?"

Daddy took a deep breath, and Andi knew he didn't want to tell her, but he did.

"For the same reason they wanted your Uncle Jack and me. They wanted to kill her."

But they hadn't killed Daddy or Uncle Jack—or Miss Theresa, either. They got away. They beat those demons and got away! Andi was suddenly glad that Becca— whoever she was—got away, too.

Daddy finished tying the ribbon on the end of her braid. She could tell he didn't want to talk about that bad stuff anymore, and neither did she.

"Well, how'd I do?" he asked. He stepped back and looked at both braids, proud they were the same length. "What do you think?"

"They look great, Daddy." Maybe she could get Miss Theresa to teach her how to braid her own hair so she wouldn't have to keep lying to Daddy.

"Get your raincoat, pumpkin. It's supposed to rain today. They'll be here in a few minutes."

Andi started for the coat closet.

"I hung it in your closet upstairs."

She started to say something, then didn't. Just went up the stairs to her room. Her raincoat was supposed to be in the coat closet! Mommy said not to put it in her closet when she came in out of the rain because it would get all her clean clothes wet and drip on her good shoes. But Daddy didn't know that. Mommy would have told her to get her rain boots, too. There were so many things Daddy didn't know.

She gathered up her coat and boots and heard a car door slam in the driveway below her window. She went to the window to see if Uncle Jack was in his police car. Daddy said he wouldn't be, but maybe. A ride in a police car would be better even than a sword.

She pulled back the curtain to look out, but she didn't see a police car. She didn't see a rainy day, either. In the blink of an eye she wasn't in her room at all. She was in the room with bare walls and blankets in a pile on the floor, looking out through a tiny slit between the boards nailed over a window.

She could hear the clickety-clack sound of a train getting softer and softer, and in the quiet she could hear the voices of the men outside the window who were unloading stuff, groceries in BetterBuy bags.

"Not my fault I get carsick," said the man with dreadlocks. "If I'd stayed in the backseat on these winding roads, I'd have chucked up my whole supper. You want to smell recycled Tony Baronni pizza?"

Another voice spoke then, one of the men on the driver's side of the car. He walked behind the car's open trunk and began unloading groceries. She could only see part of the man, his arm and shoulder, as he handed Dreadlock Man a six-pack of beer. She couldn't read the name on the label, but there were two black Xs on it, and she could see little beads of sparkling condensation on the sides of the cans. He was white and had a big tattoo on his arm of a dragon or maybe some kind of sea serpent, red and black and green. The spiky tail came down to his hand and the head covered his lumpy round shoulder muscles.

"If you ever threw up in my car, it'd be the last food you ever ate," Tattoo Man said. "Had a girlfriend once got drunk and threw up in the heater vent. Had to wait til summer and then sold the car to some poor smuck who didn't find out until it got cold that every time you turned on the heat—"

"I tole you we should have had Mi Madre's Tacos," said a voice that sounded like Speedy Gonzales from the other side of the car. Andi knew "mi madre" meant "my mother." She had started taking Spanish in second grade.

The trunk of the car slammed shut, and Dreadlock Man came around the passenger side carrying groceries—she could see chocolate ice cream in one bag—and the six-pack.

"I want to watch the game," he said as he passed the window. "You sure the reception's good on the south side of the river?"

"It is if the dish is working," said Tattoo Man.

After a moment, she heard a door slam. Then it was quiet again.

"Andi," a voice spoke her name, and she turned around to see who else was in the room. But she wasn't in the room with bare wood walls anymore. She was in her own bedroom, where a sprinkle of rain was now tapping on the window.

She wasn't alone in her bedroom, though. Ossy hopped down off the windowsill and rubbed up against her leg and began to purr softly. He always purred when he saw the lady made out of light.

WHEN JACK PICKED up Theresa at her house for the trip to Indiana Saturday morning, she'd just returned from the visitation for Gerald and Minnie Cohen at Warfield's Funeral Home.

"Them folks musta knowed about the will," she said. "I tried to tell that snotty daughter of theirs who lives down in Florida what her parents would have wanted—we'd talked about songs and such—and she let me know wasn't none of my business what she done, thank you very much. She's in a hurry to get back down to Florida to work on her tan."

"Ever wonder why white people always want to be darker, and black people always want to be lighter?"

She gave Jack a look, and he shut up and let her vent.

"And they wanted they graves to be under a tree somewhere so the leaves could fall on them in the fall, and they could lay side by side forever. But she's gonna have them cremated, maybe set they ashes on her mantle or—" Theresa stopped short. "Biscuit!"

She responded to Jack's unasked question. "A shaggy mutt they took in, called him Biscuit—Miss Minnie said 'cause that was the color of his fur, and Mr. Gerald said it was 'cause he was so flaky. What's that awful woman gonna do with the dog?"

They didn't talk about it anymore after they picked up Andi. Nobody had to worry about holding up their end of the conversation after that.

"Here's how you play the Alphabet Game," Andi said, her grin stapling twin dimples in her cheeks. "You pick a side of the road—let Miss Theresa have the right side because she doesn't see too good. And then you look for letters of the alphabet—in signs and stuff."

After the Alphabet Game came Twenty Questions, the Theme Song game and the Restaurant Game. Jack earned the first five points by spotting Burger King when they pulled off to get gas. He was grateful for the distraction of the games. He suffered from raging claustrophobia. He'd learned to control it during Ranger training, but he was never comfortable in a confined space and long car rides were punishing.

A gray drizzle still fell from a sullen mass of clouds that bruised the sky, harried by a cold wind, briefly veined every now and then with lightning. Jack and Theresa waited in the car for Andi, who had gone into the convenience store to use the bathroom.

Andi suddenly rushed out to the car, yanked open the door, leapt into the back seat and slammed the door shut behind her.

"What's wrong, child?" Theresa asked. But before Andi had a chance to answer, Theresa wrinkled up her nose and frowned, shook her head like there was something she was trying to shake out of it.

"Who?" she asked Andi.

"Him." Andi pointed to a young man who'd just stepped out of the store. He was muscular and athletic, looked like he was probably a high school football player.

The young man looked toward their car, just looked. Jack started the engine and pulled away, shaken.

Of course, he knew Andi could...but it hadn't occurred to him that meant everywhere. He wanted to stop the car and take the kid in his arms and tell her he wouldn't let any of those horrible monsters get anywhere near her. Instead, he said, "I have a game; it's called Rooty Fruity."

"How do you play?" Theresa asked with just a bit too much enthusiasm.

Jack had no idea. He was making up the rules as he went along.

"Well...you name a fruit and...the first person who spots a car that color gets five points."

Andi's voice from the back seat was soft and a little tremulous, but determined.

"Banana," she said.

Jack loved her at that moment more than he'd ever loved anybody. Except Lyla.

~

1985

Becca Hawkins cowered in the back corner of her huge walk-in closet. It was her special place. It was back behind the long hanging clothes like bathrobes—she had three of them, one with a Macy's tag still dangling from the sleeve—the full-length fur coat Daddy made her wear sometimes even though the thought of the poor animals who'd been skinned to provide the fur almost brought her to tears, long dresses and a silk kimono thing Daddy'd brought back from somewhere. She'd strategically placed a mound of stuffed animals in front of the clothes so that when she slipped through the dangling fur and silk, there was an open space about six feet square that you couldn't see from the door, not even with the closet light on.

She'd made it after she got McDougal. It would have been scary back there in the dark if she hadn't had his warm presence to reassure her, the smell of his doggie breath and the soft whump, whump, whump of his tail on the carpet. She kept a big, powerful flashlight in a corner, the kind that would probably light up a satellite, but she didn't often turn it on because the brilliance cast ugly, harsh shadows, and she preferred the warm velvet black.

Darkness was her friend, provided a refuge even when she wasn't here because she used its inky nothingness in her mind to wipe out the lamp's glow when the bad stuff happened. Daddy always left the lamp on, said he liked to see.

Sitting beside her, McDoo whimpered softly, and she realized she was squeezing him so tight it must hurt so she loosened her grip but kept her arms around him and her face buried in his fur. She wanted to pray. She came here often to talk to God—had been thrilled when Bishop said Jesus told people to pray in their closets. But she couldn't pray now. She couldn't cry, either, though she'd been wanting to cry for hours. Sometimes crying eased the pain of the horrible lump in her belly that she didn't have a name for—the fear/dread/sorrow/guilt/shame lump. Like throwing up makes you feel better for a little while after.

She'd tried hard to cry when she told Bishop what had happened, well not all that had happened.

Ever pull the wings off a fly?

She couldn't tell him that part because she couldn't stand to have the image painted in her head with the telling. She was afraid she'd start screaming, like she'd wanted to do crouched in the bush with McDoo. And if she ever did start screaming, she knew she would never stop. So she couldn't cry or scream—only shake—and speak with a very small voice that didn't seem like hers at all. The voice had been calm and precise, coming from somewhere down in a deep well where it had gone to hide from all the feelings that boiled and bubbled inside her.

The horror of one demon was almost more than Becca could stand. But six, their images, branded forever in her brain! Becca Hawkins didn't know much about the way things worked in this world, but she did know that what she

had seen and heard today had damaged her in a funda-
mental way that could never be repaired, had ripped her
apart somewhere deep in her soul, had torn loose something essential. Now she was bleeding—was it called
hemorrhaging?—from a gaping wound there, and no
bandage existed for such an injury. She'd just keep
bleeding and bleeding until there was no blood left. She
would die then, from no other cause that anybody would
be able to find, and it would be over—dark and quiet, like
it was here.

Then the darkness in her special place, as deep and
black as tar, suddenly began to lighten with a rich golden
glow—that was also music. Light couldn't be music, but it
was—voices with no words. The air smelled like a spring
rain and the light on her cheek was the touch of velvet as
soft as the down in her comforter. The golden brilliance
that cast no shadows grew brighter until she could see DD
clearly. He had slipped out of her grasp and risen to his
feet and was looking at the glow, wagging his tail
frantically.

There was a person in the glow. Or the glow was a
person. Becca couldn't tell which.

Becca's special place was too small for her and McDoo
and this woman to fit in together. But she couldn't see the
sides of the space enclosing her anymore, couldn't feel the
wall she was leaning against. The clothes were gone, the
stuffed animal wall was gone. It was dark outside the glow,
but it felt like the darkness was wide and deep and went on
forever. She probably should have been afraid, but she
wasn't. In fact, she actually blurted out a little peep of a
giggle because resting on the long, glossy black hair of the
woman dressed in light—it flowed around her like fabric,
shimmering and sparkling with sequins—was the floppy
red-and-white striped hat of The Cat in the Hat. The book

had been Becca's all-time favorite, and she cherished the handful of memories she had of sitting in her mother's lap, listening to her read it aloud.

"You're not the Cat in the Hat," she blurted out.

"I'm whatever doesn't frighten you," the glowing woman replied. She cocked the hat forward at a jaunty angle and did a joyful little dance, holding the hat so it bobbed up and down but didn't fall off.

Becca smiled.

"You're not afraid, are you, Becca?"

Becca shook her head.

"Good. You've seen enough scary things for one day."

"How do you know that?"

"I was there."

"In the woods today? I didn't see you."

"There's much that you don't see, Becca, battles you can't begin to imagine, all around you, all the time."

"I see them," Becca said. "The…bad ones. Demons."

"Yes, you do." The woman reached out a hand and cupped Becca's cheek tenderly. Her touch was warm and soft. "And that's too scary for a little girl to handle. That's why I'm here."

"To get rid of the bad ones?" A candle flame of hope flickered in Becca's heart.

"No, I can't get rid of them. But I can stand with you and hold your hand when you know so you won't be afraid. And I can heal your heart and protect it."

"But I don't want to see them."

"God designed you to see them. He put the sight in you for a reason."

"Wha—?"

"I don't know the reason. I only know there is one."

There was a sudden fierceness in her beauty that was both wonderful and terrible to behold, and Becca knew that never again in her life would she see anything as lovely and as dangerous as this being…this woman of light…this angel.

"Their ugliness will not destroy you, sweet Becca. I won't let it!"

The glow grew so bright that Becca had to close her eyes, but she could see it through her eyelids. Then it began to fade, and the darkness washed back in behind it. McDougal gave a small bark, a single yap, and the angel was gone.

Chapter Fifteen

2011

When they got to Hendersonville, Indiana, Jack pulled up in front of the jail, got out and went inside. It was a small jail, served only one county, and probably didn't have half a dozen cells. He had called to ask about visiting Becca as soon as he found out where she was.

The deputy who was on duty was gruff and grumpy, and no amount of cajoling on Jack's part could get him to allow Andi in to see the prisoner.

"Rule's thirteen years old," he said.

Jack went back out to the car.

"I'll go first," he told Theresa and handed her the car keys. "You two go get some burgers and bring them back. I think the shift changes at three, and maybe whoever takes over from this bozo will let us take Andi."

Theresa, left and Jack allowed himself to be patted down, emptied out his pockets and left the contents in a metal bowl, and was led up a set of old, metal stairs to the floor above where the cells were located. The jailer seated Jack in a room one step up the contagion ladder from a bus stop restroom and came back almost imme-diately.

"I should have asked her before I went to all this trou-ble," he said. "She don't want no visitors."

"Did you tell her who—?"

"She didn't give me time to tell her nothing. I said she had a visitor, and she said she didn't want to see anybody. End of story. Come on."

As they started back down the metal steps, Jack couldn't help himself. He tilted his head back and shouted, "Becca! It's me, Jack!" as loud as he could. The deputy gave him a dirty look.

They were all the way to the bottom of the steps before a voice from the floor above called out. Tentative. Small.

"Jack?"

The deputy grumbled something unintelligible, turned around and started back up the stairs.

The thin, frail woman with dirty short blond hair, dressed in Goodwill clothes, bore so little resemblance to the vibrant little girl he'd known all those years ago that Jack would have passed her for a stranger if he'd bumped into her on the street.

She stepped tentatively into the room, head down, and she didn't lift it to look at Jack even when the deputy had left after a brief speech about how he'd be right downstairs and that they'd better not try to "get it on" because that was a violation of jail rules and he'd throw Jack in a cell, too, if he caught him.

The deputy didn't have the authority to arrest him, but Jack was polite and docile—fearful the little runt would toss him out on his ear—which he did have the authority to do.

The room was silent after he left. Jack didn't have any idea what to say. Oh, it wasn't that he hadn't come up with a dozen different scenarios about how the conversation would go. But he was so taken aback by her appearance and demeanor that he couldn't make any of his prepared intros work. He'd thought up speeches to make to the little girl he knew all grown up. This woman was very different, much less or perhaps much more than that.

Finally, he blurted out, "Let's sit down, Becca." He indicated one of the two wooden chairs on either side of a plain wooden table that were the only pieces of furniture in the room. "And just talk."

He went to the table, pulled out a chair for her and then sat down in the chair on the other side of the table to urge her to follow.

Finally, she moved toward the chair, every step reluctant, and sat down on the edge of it.

"It tormented me all night, wouldn't let me sleep. I only came here to get away for a little while."

She still didn't look up.

"Who tormented you, Becca?"

"The demon on the prostitute."

He thought about Andi at the convenience store.

"That must be horrible to be able to see them."

She lifted her head and looked at him in wonder.

"It is you, isn't it, Jack."

"It's good to see you, Becca."

She was still gaping at him.

"I can't believe it's really you." Then it appeared that she just that moment realized how she must look. She dropped her gaze. "I'm sorry," she said, her voice soft. "I shouldn't have agreed to…you shouldn't have come." She looked up. "How'd you find me? And why'd you come looking?"

He'd known she would ask, of course. He'd had a convenient excuse all cooked up about a Three Musketeers reunion. But he could see now something that inane would sound as phony as it was.

"I…we wanted to see you. A couple of months ago, Daniel and I connected for the first time in more than twenty years, and of course we thought about you."

"Daniel?" The same wonder.

"And Theresa, too. In fact, she's here today. Right now. They said you were only allowed one visitor at a time, but she's down there, waiting."

Becca put her face in her hands and shook her head.

"Can't." Her words were muffled by her hands, and her voice had become thick with unshed tears. "No." She took in a trembling breath but neither looked up nor took her hands away from her face. "You need to go now, both of you. Just go."

"Theresa won't leave here without seeing you. She'll sit down at the foot of the stairs and stay there all night and all day tomorrow and…however long it takes. You know Theresa. You can't get rid of her just by saying you don't want to see her."

She looked up at him then, and twin streams of tears cleaned off some of the dirt on her face as they slid toward her chin.

"Please don't do this, Jack. Just leave me alone. Go away and don't come back."

"No."

"I don't want to see you, either of you!"

"Yes, you do, child," Theresa said from the doorway. "You want to see us so bad the wanting of it aches in your heart like a rotten tooth."

Becca froze as solid as a hood ornament, then closed her eyes, lowered her head and covered her face with her hands like she wanted to hide her whole self behind them.

Jack looked a question at Theresa.

"I brought that deputy a Big Mac and talked him into letting me come on up," she said simply.

Jack could not begin to imagine that conversation.

The old woman moved ponderously across the room until she was standing beside Becca, then put her hand tenderly on the young woman's shoulder.

"Why don't you cry, sugar. 'Pears to me you need it, been needin' it for a right smart while."

Becca sat, unmoving, so still Jack couldn't even see her breathe.

"Go on ahead."

Theresa's was the voice he knew she'd have used to soothe a fretful baby.

"You safe with us."

Jack only realized Becca had been holding her breath when she let it out in a trembling sigh. Then her shoulders began to shake, though he could hear no sound of crying. Without opening her eyes or looking up, she suddenly reached out and threw her arms around Theresa, turned in the chair and buried her face in Theresa's dress. Then she sobbed. Not loud or hysterical, but gut-wrenching, so full of every imaginable emotion the raw pain of it was utterly heartbreaking. On and on she cried. Theresa swayed gently back and forth and smoothed back her dirty hair. Jack felt like he was watching a holy moment.

Becca finally exhausted herself. Jack had the sense that if she'd been physically able to, she would have continued to cry for hours. When the shaking stopped and she had been reduced to hitching breathing, she continued to cling fiercely to Theresa.

Theresa sniffed and wrinkled her nose. "Demon stink," she said. "They's one here about, close. We gone get you out of here, child. You gone come home with me. You ain't gone spend another night locked up in this bad place with that monster." She looked up at Jack. "Jack, you go see to it."

He looked at Theresa in mute astonishment. Just like that? He carried a Get Out of Jail Free card for such occasions? She flashed him a beatific smile.

Well...maybe he could bail Becca out, get her bonded into his custody or something. He'd have to find a judge willing to do it. On Saturday afternoon. He got to his feet and headed toward the door.

"Andi's downstairs talking to the jailer," Theresa said.

When Jack got to the bottom of the stairs, he saw Andi perched on the end of the visitor's bench in earnest conversation with a uniformed man he didn't know—must have been the jailer.

She giggled. The man smiled broadly. Jack just shook his head.

It took Jack almost three hours to find a judge—he was sitting drenched in the stands of his granddaughter's rain-delayed softball game—and get a release order signed. Andi elected to stay behind with her new best friend, Bud the Jailer.

Theresa spent the whole time upstairs with Becca.

It was late afternoon by the time Jack got back to the jail. The judge had postponed Becca's court date for two weeks. The jailer went upstairs, and a few minutes later Theresa followed him back down. Behind Theresa was Becca.

Jack wasn't at all prepared for what happened when Andi saw Becca.

~

IT WAS A GRAY, drizzly Saturday, with rain spitting down from low-hanging clouds and a gusty wind combing the leaves off trees. Billy Ray listened to it and to the silence in the woods and was certain he was completely alone before he climbed up onto the butt-cheek rocks again and dropped down into the crevice behind them. He pulled the can of WD-40 out of the Walmart sack and gave each hinge on the grate a good squirt, worked the gate back and forth a time or two, and the hinges stopped squalling.

He'd brought a car battery with him and used it to replace the old, dead one. Then he had electricity.

The boxcar was standard—fifty feet long, nine and half feet wide and eleven feet tall. In one end of it Billy Ray'd made an office of sorts, had an oak desk with a wide top and drawers on both sides and a comfortable chair with wheels—he'd never quite got it why office chairs needed wheels. He pulled open the shallow drawer in the center of the desk, and it was right where he'd left it—a stack of money, used tens and twenties—two thousand dollars. That would tide him over until he could connect with his new business associate to begin converting his other assets here into spendable currency.

The treasure Billy Ray'd hid away in a buried boxcar all these years wasn't money or dope. It was gold. Solid gold. Evenly distributed along shelves he'd built with concrete blocks and two-by-twelves were two hundred and fifty kilo bars of it—a thousand grams or 32.15 troy ounces. When he'd loaded the gold away in the boxcar, each of the bars had been worth about eleven thousand five hundred dollars. He had found a smarmy little banker in Louisville willing to procure the gold for him—at a hefty percentage off the top, of course, to keep quiet about where the gold was going.

That man had gouged Billy Ray on gold transactions

for seven years. When the law came down on Billy Ray, he had gone around to all his business associates and settled up accounts, so to speak. He'd paid the little man in Louisville a visit then, too. They found him a week later floating in the Ohio River. Throat cut.

Five hundred pounds of solid gold. Now worth twelve million dollars. Four times what it had been worth when he climbed down into the crack between the rocks every month or so and deposited another bar on a shelf.

About three years ago, he had contacted the brother-in-law of an inmate who'd been Billy Ray's bunkmate until he died of cancer. The brother-in-law fenced jewels and precious metals, and over time he and Billy Ray had set up a business relationship without either one of them ever mentioning the exact nature of the transactions they'd be conducting.

That's how he'd come by the big deal, the important deal, the one that would buy back his future. One of the phone calls Billy Ray had made was to the man who'd be running the big deal. Left him a message saying his end of the bargain was set in place. The second was to his "business partner." By the end of the week, Billy Ray would cash in one of the bars, and he'd have all the money he would need to fund his own personal venture, the only venture that mattered to him. Finding Becca!

But it occurred to him that he might not have to spend a dime in that endeavor, that what he wanted to know might be just one conversation away.

Chapter Sixteen

2011

Andi was seated on the counter where the jailer had set her so he could show her the antique jail keys he kept on display on the wall.

"That one looks like the key to the castle that Yellin gave them after Fessik burst into flames and pretended he was the Dread Pirate Roberts and scared the Brute Squad, and they ran away," she told Jack, swinging her feet back and forth beneath her.

Princess Bride. Had to be. Though he had neither seen the movie nor read the book, Jack could quote most of the dialogue, courtesy of Andi's obsession with it.

She was studying the key and didn't look up when the jailer came back down the stairs. Theresa came next. Becca was behind Theresa, so small Jack didn't see her until Theresa moved out of the way.

That's when Andi saw her, too.

She instantly let out a squeal, hopped down off the counter and bolted toward Becca. The force of her impact when she threw her arms around Becca almost bowled her over. Becca seemed to melt. She disengaged Andi's arms from around her waist long enough to sink to one knee in front of the child. Then she grabbed Andi in a mighty hug, and they clung to each other.

"Haven't seen each other in a while, huh," the jailer observed.

"Actually, they've never met," Jack said and dragged his eyes away from Becca and Andi long enough to look at Theresa. She was staring at them too, of course, as shocked as he was, only she was smiling. Jack found himself smiling, too.

"Never met?" the jailer said.

"Princess Buttercup said I'd meet you today," Andi said, holding Becca every bit as tight as Becca held her. "Well, she's not really Princess Buttercup. The lady made out of light just looks like Princess Buttercup so I won't be afraid of her. But she didn't say it would be you. I mean, I didn't know the person we were coming here to see would be who she was talking about. Sometimes, she tells me things that don't make any sense, and then when I figure them out, it's not what I was thinking at all."

Becca didn't say anything, just held Andi tight with her eyes squeezed shut and such a look of joy on her haggard features that Jack again had the sense that he was witnessing a holy moment.

"You telling me those two don't know each other," the jailer asked, and the question seemed to break the spell and the light in the room dimmed. It was only then that Jack realized there had been a luminescence coming from Becca and Andi, a glow. It was a brightness that didn't cast shadows, lit up everything it touched, front and back sides. The glow had replaced the ugly yellow light cast by the overhead fluorescents and had been reflected in the dark windowpanes, like a warm fire on a hearth, only not flickering.

It wasn't the first time Jack had seen a glow like that. That day at the burning warehouse when he'd rushed into the impenetrable smoke to find Theresa, he'd been guided to her by the same kind of glow. And years before, he'd seen it, that summer when he was twelve years old.

After they left, they stopped to grab carryout pizza and hadn't driven five miles before Andi and Becca were sound asleep in the back seat. Andi's head was in Becca's lap.

"Do you know what all that"—he waved his hand back toward Hendersonville in a kind of all-inclusive gesture —"was about?" Jack asked Theresa quietly.

"Not for sure, but I can guess. Can't you?"

Jack said nothing.

"I swear, son, you 'spect the good Lord to drop a piano on your head?"

"No, actually, I had in mind skywriting," Jack said. "'Dear Jack, I showed you that demons exist. Well, guess what—so do angels. Sincerely, God' In purple. In Hebrew."

"You read Hebrew, do you?"

"Only in purple. So…you're saying there was an angel in that room?"

"You didn't see it?"

"You did?"

"Not the form of it, but the light. The joy. You didn't feel the good?"

"There could have been a whole herd of angels, and I don't think I'd have felt…the good. I think only good people are aware of that, and I have too much…dark in me."

Theresa made a humph sound in her throat.

"Everybody always thinks they own bad's worse'n everybody else's. They let they bad block out the light so's they can't see it even when it's shining in their very own faces. I 'spect that's what happened to Becca."

"What did she tell you?" Jack couldn't hold on to the question any longer, had to know if Becca still had the memories of that summer that had been wiped from his and Daniel's minds—if she remembered how three children had defeated a monster demon. And if she knew anything about a nursing home and a can of gasoline.

"Not as much as you'd think and a whole lot of it didn't make no sense, or ain't real. I think I know what's wrong with her, though, at least, part of what's wrong. PSTD…or PDTS or whatever—"

"PTSD. Posttraumatic stress disorder."

"Yeah, like soldiers get who've just come home from a war—seein' things that ain't there, reliving things. If anybody ever earned PTSD, it's Becca Hawkins. The battle she was in took her a whole lot further out there into the dark than I ever plan to venture my own self."

She saw the confused look on his face.

"Becca touched pure evil. She went up against it and it got to her somehow and now she can't get away from it. Or thinks she can't and that 'mounts to the same thing."

"Does she remember?"

Theresa looked at him sadly. "No, she don't," she said. "She's as clueless about what you children did that summer as you and Daniel—a piece of memory here, a snip there. I'm sorry, Jack."

They drove on in silence for a time, Jack trying to come to terms with the reality that nobody could tell them how to destroy the efreet. And nobody could tell him what part he might have played in the fire that killed one hundred and sixty people in the Twin Oaks Nursing Home.

"Where's she been, Theresa? What's she been doing?"

"Ever'where and ever'thing. I didn't get but a little peek into it. She spent a goodly amount of time locked up."

"In prison?"

"In a mental hospital."

"Why?"

"Why do you think! Her goin' round talking about flaming monsters and demons made out of flies. They come after her in legions, armies of them, trying to beat her down. And she didn't have nothing to hold to so they trampled her."

"Nothing to hold on to…?"

"I don't know, but best I can make out is that somehow…Becca let go of the light. The light didn't let go of her, of course. It don't never let go. But long's she wouldn't look at it, couldn't see it through her own dark…they come at her then."

"And after the mental hospital?"

"She wandered. Homeless. She'd get her some job washin' dishes or cleanin,' stay until a demon come along, and then she'd run, don't even remember where all she went."

Jack thought of the clean-cut football player at the convenience store.

"I think she does remember a lot about when the three of you took on that efreet, but them memories is distorted now, real all tangled up with not real. Forgetting was a blessing, son, make no mistake about it, and Becca didn't get that blessing."

"Forgetting isn't a blessing for me. Those pictures of me going into Twin Oaks…" He paused and tried not to sound as troubled as he really was. "What did I do there? Did I…participate? Did I…join the Bad Kids?" He laughed with no humor at all. "Had to learn the secret handshake and wear the magic decoder ring."

"Course you didn't."

"You don't know that and neither do I."

"You will. When you need to, the Lord's gone show you."

"I need to now. The ATF called Major Crocker and said they'd be sending an agent down to talk to me. I need to be able to answer questions with more than 'I don't remember.'"

There was one thing he did remember, though, had been remembering for months. He remembered Isaac, a tall, broad-shouldered young man with Bishop's strength and Theresa's kind eyes. He could hear the sound of his laughter—rich and full, and recall how he could throw a pitch so fast it'd burn right through the leather of a catcher's mitt. Theresa had been so shattered by her son's disappearance she was in a daze that whole summer, too tuned out to know what was going on around her. What Jack remembered about Isaac he couldn't share with Theresa, had never told anyone. Whatever it was that had happened to Isaac......it had been Jack's fault. He didn't know about the fire, but he was absolutely certain about Isaac. And one day, he would remember what he'd done.

WHEN THE POLICE came for Daniel on Saturday afternoon, they didn't truss him up in handcuffs, but he was still glad he'd sent Andi off with Jack and Theresa that morning, grateful she wasn't there to see him ushered out of the house and hauled away in a dark sedan with men in suits on either side of him in the back seat.

They'd made it clear he wasn't being arrested—yet.

They just wanted to ask him some questions. If Clayton hadn't insisted on it the day before, Daniel wouldn't have had the good judgment to tell the officers that he wanted to have his attorney present for the questioning.

"You use every weapon at your disposal—which in your case means getting the best legal advice money can buy." Clayton said he'd handle that part, that the church would pay for all Daniel's legal fees, would find the best criminal lawyer in Cincinnati to represent him and Theresa Washington, too, since she was in the crosshairs of the same evil Daniel was.

Daniel hadn't even had time to think of legal representation, had no idea it would all happen so fast. In the back of the police car on the way to the station, the officers allowed him to use his cell phone to call Clayton, who hadn't been in. Daniel left a message saying the church's "top legal advice" needed to meet him at the police station this afternoon because he had been taken in for questioning.

Daniel was left alone in a different interrogation room this time, one that looked like it'd come right off the set of CSI—table, chairs and one-way mirror included. He sat there for a time before he heard muted voices in the hallway outside.

"Unless you intend to lodge formal charges against my client, I want him released right now." Though Daniel couldn't hear the voice well, the air of authority in the words would make any client glad to have the man on his side. "…haven't even had a chance to speak to my client…" The voices moved on down the hallway and Daniel caught "…insist on questioning him today, I will advise him not to utter a single syllable."

A few minutes later, one of the officers who'd come to

pick Daniel up opened the door and told him he was free to go.

When Daniel turned the corner at the end of the hallway outside the room, he got his first look at the attorney Clayton had hired for him. He was dressed in a polo shirt and khakis, like he'd been ready to go play golf. And perhaps he had been, but the rain had canceled his plans for the afternoon. Daniel stopped still, but the man was too engaged in conversation to notice.

"My client will be glad to cooperate with the police in any possible way in this investigation and will work with you to come in for an interview sometime next week. Do you gentlemen have a problem with that?"

The attorney turned then and saw Daniel standing in the hallway, still as a statue. A look crossed his face that was utterly unreadable. Then he told Daniel simply, "I'll give you a ride home."

Daniel found himself nodding, mostly out of surprise and shock, then walked toward the elevator beside the attorney Clayton and the church had hired to represent him, who was, indeed, the best legal advice money could buy. And who was also the man Emily had been having an affair with right before she died.

As soon as the elevator doors closed, Jeff Kendrick said, "Because Clayton is an old family friend and when he asked me, I couldn't come up with a good reason why not on the spot." He didn't look at Daniel. It flashed through Daniel's mind that he really ought to make it a personal policy from now on to take the stairs. Some of the worst moments in his life in the past three days had been in elevators. "I knew you'd refuse my counsel and that would be the end of it, but Clayton called me a little while ago and said you'd been taken in. On Saturday…there was no time to find somebody else."

The elevator reached the basement, the doors opened and both men stepped out into the parking garage. Kendrick turned to Daniel and looked him in the eye. Daniel felt a surge of emotions as tangled up as last year's Christmas lights.

"Short and sweet," Kendrick said. "From what Clayton told me, the assault and rape charges are your biggest problem. A murder charge would be a stretch. They may have motive, but they'd still have to come up with evidence linking you to the crime and not having an alibi doesn't constitute evidence. But the other—the surveillance camera footage is evidence and so is the lineup. And—"

Daniel hit him.

He smashed his fist into Kendrick's face. The attorney staggered backward, collided with a concrete pillar and slid down it to the floor. Blood poured out of his nose and split lip, ran down his chin and began to drip on his clean polo shirt.

The sudden violence probably surprised Daniel as much as it did Kendrick. He'd never hit anybody—not as an adult—had never even considered it. And he hadn't "considered" hitting Kendrick. He'd just done it. The images that haunted his waking and dreaming moments ever since he found out, images of Emily and…he'd just let go.

Kendrick sat dazed for a moment, then reached into his pocket for a handkerchief and began wiping the blood off his face. Daniel gradually became aware of the thundering of his heart in his ears and the smell of exhaust fumes mixed with the clean scent of rain. His knuckles throbbed.

The man on the dirty concrete looked up at him.

"I take it this means you don't want me to represent

you." He started to rise, then sank back. "Can I get up, or do you plan to deck me again?"

Daniel said nothing. Kendrick got slowly to his feet, holding the bloody handkerchief to his mouth with one hand and using the other to brush the dust off his khaki pants.

"Don't expect me to be noble and say I deserved that," he said and continued to brush at his pants. "But maybe I did. Yeah, I probably did."

Still Daniel remained silent.

"You need to know—I am going to take your friend's case, Theresa Washington's, if they charge her," Kendrick said.

"Why?" Daniel realized that was the first word he'd spoken to Kendrick since he'd seen him standing in the hallway upstairs.

"Because Clayton Abernathy came to every one of my baseball games—when every other little boy had a father in the stands, he was there for me." He swiped at the blood still running out of his nose and then pressed the handkerchief hard to his split lip. "He paid my way through law school." He sniffed, but still the blood flowed. "And because I believe she's innocent." He looked Daniel in the eye. "I think you're both innocent."

"Why?" Daniel asked again.

"Because Clayton believes you, that somebody is trying—"

"No. Why…Emily?"

Her name still tore a hole in his gut every time he said it. He was surprised by the look of pain—grief?—that crossed Kendrick's face.

"You're not entitled to that one," he snapped. "It'd take more than one sucker punch to make me go there." Then he shook his head, gave Daniel a wry smile. "I'd have taken her away from you, Daniel. I absolutely would have, in a New York minute! I tried to take her away from you."

Kendrick leaned over abruptly and began fussing with the papers that had scattered on the floor, like he wanted a moment to gather his composure. Daniel remembered then that Kendrick was a champion kickboxer. Sure, Daniel caught him totally off guard, but the man could have wiped up the parking garage floor with Daniel if he'd wanted to.

Kendrick collected the last page and stood.

"Because of who you are, I'm betting the prosecutor won't want to get anywhere near this one. He'll make the grand jury take the heat, present his evidence and let them issue an indictment. So you've got a week, maybe ten days. But whether he charges you or they do, you are in deep poop, my friend." He handed Daniel the papers. "The 'victim' picked you out of a lineup, and with her dead, her initial statement to the police stands as is. No chance to go after her in a deposition, get her to explain why she never screamed, why she refused a rape kit. No chance to pick her story apart piece by piece on the stand. There's just her statement and it sounds pretty damning."

"I didn't touch her."

"Of course you didn't. But it's a bear to win a case when there's a videotape of your client committing the crime and the victim's underwear is in his pocket."

He swiped at his lip and looked at the handkerchief. It had finally stopped bleeding. He reached into his suit coat pocket and took out a business card. "I'd appreciate it if you'd give this to Mrs. Washington," he said, and handed it to Daniel. "Tell her I'll call her early next week so we can talk."

Daniel accepted the card wordlessly. Then Kendrick gestured toward the far end of the parking garage.

"There's a cabstand on that end. If you don't have cash, they take plastic." He paused. "Good luck, Daniel." But he didn't offer to shake Daniel's hand, just turned with the effortless grace of a big cat, and headed off toward the nearest row of cars.

Chapter Seventeen

2011

Theresa let Becca sleep on Sunday morning long as she wanted to. The scrawny woman who'd come out of the bathroom after her shower last night had looked like a kitten got dropped in a puddle—hair all spiky like, sticking out all over. And on a clean face you could see the huge circles under her eyes and how pale her skin was. Theresa'd actually tucked her in bed in her spare bedroom in the basement like she was a little girl. She left the bedside lamp on when she turned to go, but Becca stopped her.

"Would you turn it off, please," she said. "I...I've never liked a light on beside the bed."

Theresa was tired, too, had dragged herself out of bed Sunday morning, her old back aching so bad from sitting in the car the day before that she had to put on her "cookie sheet corset." She'd hurt her back years ago, had almost got trampled to death by a mob—at a funeral home! Bishop'd had to rush her to a hospital in Louisville the next day where they'd done some kind of back surgery. She'd had trouble with her back ever since. A couple of years ago, a doctor had given her a brace to stabilize it, but it wasn't near stiff enough once she'd got it wound around her big belly. Bishop had fixed it, though, added three little steel struts attached to a small piece of metal to it, and she'd told him his contraption looked like a cookie sheet. He'd got right tickled, but his laugh'd been gentle, like it always was, only poking fun, never being hurtful.

She put on her black dress over it—the one she'd worn to Bishop's service—humming the song they'd sung that day. A Mighty Fortress is Our God. Bishop had liked that part about "a bulwark never failing." Theresa'd always been gonna look up "bulwark" and see exactly what it did mean but had never got around to it.

The memorial service for Miss Minnie and Mr. Gerald was as dark and gray as the wet day. Theresa sat in the back so she could slip out, didn't figure the family'd appreciate her showing up at the brunch they's having in the church basement after. But the couple's other daughter— the nicer one who didn't live in Florida—stopped her at the door before she had a chance to leave.

"Stella's going to have their dog put to sleep," she said without preamble. "I don't think my parents would have wanted it…to die. Would you take it?"'

Theresa was too surprised to say anything.

"It's in their backyard. Stella tied it to a tree."

In the rain?

"If you want it, you'll have to go get it right now while the family's having brunch."

Translate that: Stella don't know I'm doin' this.

Then the woman hurried away.

A dog? Me?

But Miss Minnie and Mr. Gerald did love that mutt, and Theresa couldn't very well let their harpy daughter kill it! Well, she'd just have to go get it, take it home with her and then take it to the animal shelter tomorrow where they could find it a good home.

Rescuing Biscuit was actually easier than Theresa was afraid it was gonna be. Gratefully, the rain had let up so only her feet got soaked, and soon's she opened the back gate, that poor old wet dog started wagging its tail and yappin'.

Somebody'd ought to tie Stella out in the rain!

She reached down and unhooked the leash from his collar, and Biscuit started running around and around her in circles, and when she opened her car door, he hopped right in, sat down on her backseat and filled the car with wet dog stink. Well, she'd smelled worse things—lots of worse things.

On her way home, Theresa stopped for dog food and to get something for Becca to wear—she'd thrown Becca's clothes in the trash. Dang near crippled her to walk around Walmart in them wet high-heeled shoes that pinched her bunion. The second Biscuit hopped out of the car in Theresa's garage, the dog did one of those doggie full-body shakes to get the water out of his fur. And it occurred to her that he'd been sitting there in the car soaked to the skin ever since she'd picked him up…so had he waited to do that shaking thing so's he wouldn't mess up her car? Did dogs do things like that? She'd intended to leave the dog in the garage, but when she went to get a bowl for his dog food, Becca was standing in the kitchen and spotted him. Her face lit up like a kid on Christmas morning.

"What's his name?" she asked.

"Biscuit. He's right flaky."

Becca dropped to her knees on the kitchen floor, and the dog padded right up to her. She flung her arms around him, didn't care that he was wet. With her face buried in his fur, she whispered, "I had a dog once. His name was DD."

~

1985

Daniel had not spoken to Becca about what had happened in the woods three days before. And he wanted to, was desperate to. But he hadn't seen her since then. Bishop and Theresa's Bible study on Thursday had been canceled because Theresa had been "feeling poorly," which they'd all learned was code for "upset about Isaac." This morning, when she and Jack had shown up at the flagpole in front of the courthouse, she'd looked so fragile, like blown glass, and he was afraid to do anything to upset her or she might shatter right there before his eyes. So they rode to the park, and nobody mentioned what had happened to them. They all were aware that nobody was mentioning it, too, which made it awkward. They'd never been awkward with each other, but when they got off their bikes, they walked along in strained silence.

Daniel and Jack had talked about it to each other, of course, for hours. During their walk to Bernard Tackett's house—which, oh by the way, was closer to three miles away from the Melody Creek Rest Area than two—they had worn the subject out—and none of it made sense.

There were any number of reasons why the six Brewster Academy boys had been in the woods. Maybe they'd been hunting ginseng like he and Jack and Becca, or they'd gone to swing on the huge grapevines near Castle Rock or to catch frogs in Miller's Pond or crawdads in the creek. But what possible reason was there for them to snatch up Becca and run off with her? What were they planning to do with her? He and Jack had quickly dismissed the most obvious explanation—partly because they couldn't bear to think of such a thing!—but mostly because it didn't fit the circumstances. If that's what they intended to do, they'd certainly had time and opportunity enough right there in the woods. Why drag her off with them? No, it was something else. And whatever it was, Bishop understood it, but didn't share that understanding with him or Jack.

Daniel shot a glance at Becca as she walked beside him across the soccer fields to the tennis courts where they liked to knock the ball back and forth across the net—not real tennis. Mikey Rutherford was probably waiting for them there since he invariably showed up wherever they went. Mikey was an ok kid, and Daniel felt sorry for him because he was fat and people teased him about it, but his constant chatter could be as annoying as a buzzing fly

Suddenly, Becca's eyes got wide. He followed her gaze to an oak tree where six boys were lounging lazily around the trunk. The Bad Kids—that's what the boys from Brewster had become in his head. Daniel faltered, slowing his step at the sight of them. But Jack and Becca forged ahead as though they'd seen nothing, and he quickly caught up.

"Well, hello, hello, hello," said Walter Stephenson. Daniel knew all their names now. He and Jack had looked them up on the team roster that had a school picture of each player. Walter and Ronnie Martin had the cuffs of their pants rolled up tight around their ankles and Walter had a bandanna tied around one leg above the knee. Brewster Academy was for rich kids. They always had the latest *whatever*, and dressed in fashions the public school kids only saw on Friday Night Videos. Roger Willingham reached over to a boombox the size of a steamer trunk and punched a button, and "Iron Man" by Black Sabbath blasted out the speakers.

"Who do we have here?" Cole Stuart said.

In movements too swift to be normal, the boys suddenly surrounded them. They seemed…different…in a way Daniel couldn't define. They were definitely cleaner than they'd been in the woods. They didn't stink, but there was also a …civilized…quality that'd been totally missing in the wild animals they'd encountered in the woods. They seemed almost…restrained, somehow.

Cole Stuart poked a finger in Daniel's chest, and it felt like he'd been stabbed.

"The good…" He turned to Jack and poked his chest. "The bad…" He turned to Becca. "And the ugly!"

Daniel felt Jack tense beside him. When they all burst into raucous laughter, Jack launched himself at Cole, caught him in the chest and knocked him down. Jack knew exactly what he was getting into, and he flat-out didn't care. Never had Daniel admired Jack's brazen courage more than he did at that moment. Cole hit the ground with Jack on top of him, and Jack landed a good solid punch in Cole's face. His nose squirted blood.

Then Cole flung him off. From flat on his back on the ground, Cole launched Jack into the air, and he landed fifteen feet away. The other boys picked Jack up and tossed him like a rag doll back into the dirt in front of Cole, who grabbed him by the hair with one hand and lifted him up so their eyes were level. Then Cole slammed a hammer blow into Jack's belly. Jack groaned and Cole hit him again.

"Leave him alone!" Daniel heard his voice speak words before he had a chance to form them, but they were the right words and he stood by them. Cole let go of Jack, and he collapsed in a heap.

"You want some of this?" Cole snarled.

The image of Jack's courage was fresh in his mind. "If you think you can take me, yeah."

Cole swung at him, but Daniel managed to dodge most of the force of it, just catching a glancing blow to the cheek. But even that was staggering, and he fell backwards —into the waiting arms of Roger Willingham and Ronnie Martin, who had circled around behind him. They suspended Daniel by his arms between them, and Cole homed in on him.

Jack lurched off the ground at Cole, and Cole backhanded him, knocking him flat. Victor Alexander and Jacob Dumas, the two boys not holding Daniel, attacked Jack, kicking and stomping him, and he curled into a ball in the dirt to protect his head.

"Stop it!" Becca cried. "That's enough."

What happened next must have been a product of the ringing in Daniel's head because it seemed to him that Becca's voice changed somehow. She spoke with a power and authority it was hard to envision coming out the mouth of the frail little girl.

Everyone froze. Time itself seemed to falter. The two boys holding Daniel's arms let go so suddenly that Daniel collapsed, a beanbag in the dirt. He and Jack both squinted up at Becca from the ground, the sun in their eyes. Daniel knew with the kind of certainty that belongs only to absolute truth, that there existed nowhere else in the world a girl as beautiful as Becca Hawkins.

"Leave, all of you," she said. "Go!"

"And if we don't?" Cole slathered the words in contempt, but there was no power in them. Just a blowhard hurling an empty threat. It was meaningless, and even he seemed to know it.

Jack rolled over and staggered up, then reached out a hand and helped Daniel to his feet, too.

"Let's go," Cole said. "Gotta be careful. Can't hurt anybody. Can't leave a mark."

All the others turned to leave, too, except the blond kid, whose bottom lip stuck out as if he were pouting. Jacob Dumas spit in the dirt and took a step toward Jack, his eyes open way too wide.

"Uh-uh. I'm gonna get me some dark meat."

Cole was on him in a second, grabbed his arm and spun him around.

"You're not—!"

That's all Cole got out before Dumas attacked him with stunning brutality. And instantly they were at each other—all restraint gone—biting and hitting and kicking like animals. The others joined in the fray, either trying to drag them apart or getting in their own licks. The savageness was stunning, as was the ferocity and strength of the combatants. Blood and hunks of hair flew. A boy was launched six feet into the air—amid grunts and sounds like growls.

Daniel found himself backing away with Becca and Jack at his side. They'd been totally forgotten in the spontaneous combustion that set the group of boys against each other.

When Jack turned to Becca, Daniel saw on Jack's face the same adoration that must have been painted on his own. Adoration mixed with awe and wonder now.

At church on Sunday, Daniel was sporting a glowing shiner from his second encounter with the Bad Kids, and Bishop wanted to know how he'd gotten it.

"Same fist, different day," he said.

Bishop's eyes widened, but he was most interested in hearing about how Becca had…well, done whatever it was she'd done. Daniel picked up on the delight his description of that part painted on Bishop's face.

"You understand more than you're telling Jack and me, don't you? How could Becca…?"

There was a sudden commotion in the vestibule in the front of the church. First a scream, and then a clamor of upset voices. Then Marty Pritchard pushed his way through the crowd, searching the remaining people in the sanctuary for—

"Dr. Clements," Marty called out when he spotted a tall, balding man in the far aisle. "Can you come—Mrs. Milligan—I think she's had a heart attack. Ken's calling an ambulance."

The doctor hurried away and information slowly washed back down the crowd exiting the church.

"A hog snake, musta been three feet long…"

"It's hog nose snake, and the poor woman almost stepped on it."

"What's a snake doing on the church steps?"

"Somebody musta put it there."

"What kinda person'd do a thing like that?"

Daniel looked at Bishop. The big man was thinking the same thing he was.

Chapter Eighteen

2011

It was going on ten o'clock on Monday morning and Becca hadn't stirred, though Theresa'd heard the kitchen door open and close right after sunup, so she must have taken the dog out to do its business. Theresa smiled at the way them two had took to each other. Guess she wouldn't be taking the dog to the animal shelter after all. Biscuit had spent the night on the floor beside Becca's bed. And besides, Theresa was getting right fond of the fur ball her own self.

When the doorbell rang, she figured it was that package of flower seeds she'd ordered. She'd been expecting it for a week.

What she found on the other side of the screen was something else she'd been expecting instead.

"Are you Theresa Washington?" asked one of the two police officers who stood at her door.

That fool knew full well who she was. And she'd have told him that, but all the spit suddenly dried up in her mouth and she couldn't say nothing, only nodded.

"Theresa Washington, you are under arrest for the murders of Gerald and Minerva Cohen. You have the right to…"

Theresa's heart started to pound like a cook whacking on a pot with a spoon to call the hands to supper. She heard "arrest" and "murder" and "attorney."

Attorney!

"I want to call my lawyer," she bleated, sounding every bit as scared and desperate as she felt.

The officer let her get the business card Daniel'd given her that she'd stuck to the refrigerator door with a magnet. She called the number, and Jeff Kendrick's secretary told Theresa she'd give him a message. She scribbled a note for Becca that she left on the table by the front door. Then the first officer took her arm, turned her around and fastened cold, steel handcuffs on her wrists.

"What? You think I'm gone make a run for it?"

He said nothing, merely propelled her down the side-walk toward the police cruiser parked in her driveway. "If I's to run, they'd have earthquakes in California."

When the car pulled away from her house, Theresa started to cry, but softly so the officers in the front seat couldn't hear.

They fingerprinted her.

They took her picture—front and side views.

They removed her jewelry—earrings, a necklace and a watch. Her wedding band was sunk so deep in her flesh if they wanted it they was gonna have to cut her finger off to get it. And they took her belt—you know, so's she wouldn't decide to hang herself with it.

And then they put her in a jail cell. Ok, technically it wasn't no jail. Only had two cells. It was a "holding facil-ity" attached to the police station, but if the real thing looked, felt or stunk any worse than this, she could understand why they took prisoners' belts away.

Wasn't no lonelier sound in the whole world that the bang of a jail cell clanging shut.

And then it was quiet, and she was alone. No, not alone.

She spoke aloud. She always prayed out loud.

He's got his armies coming after us now, Lord. And I'm so scared I ain't gonna have a solid bowel movement for the rest of this week! I need help.

She forced herself to look around at the unrelenting gray of the cell's walls/ceiling/floor/furniture, needed to come to terms with the reality of it. 'Less God intervened, she was gonna spend the rest of her life locked up in a place like this. Wasn't no jury in the world would find her not guilty! Shoot, she'd convict her own self based on the evidence they was gonna hear.

Her lip began to tremble, and she bit down hard, determined not to cry for fear she might not be able to stop.

I know the Apostle Paul was locked away in a place a whole lot worse than this so I ain't got no room to complain. But…please—

A sob escaped that she couldn't hold on to, and it brought all its friends with it. Her shoulders began to shake, and she put her head in her hands and let go.

She'd been in the cell for long enough to have a good cry and get it out of her system when the door at the end of the hallway opened and one of the police officers who'd brought her in returned. Behind him strode a man so smooth he made Teflon look lumpy. His shoes must have cost more than Theresa got in Social Security for a year. Shoot, his suit probably cost more than her house was worth. Though his nose was red and swollen, like maybe somebody'd popped him one in the face, he had a kind of presence, which meant they was either locking him up in the other cell 'cause he was a crook or he was a lawyer.

"I'm Jeff Kendrick, Mrs. Washington," he said. "Call me Jeff. I'll be representing you."

"You come to get me out of here?"

"I'll have it all arranged to get you out on bail after your arraignment in the morning."

"What's an arraign—"

"Arraignment. On a charge as serious as murder, you—"

Then it hit her. In the morning!

"You mean I got to stay here all night?"

"No, not here…"

They hauled her off to the Webster County Jail in Cincinnati trussed up in handcuffs like she was Al Capone. Soon as they took her into the building, she started shaking. She scolded herself for it—wasn't nothing bad gone happen to her here. But she was wrong about that part.

She and two other women prisoners was taken into a room with half a dozen guards where orange jumpsuits hung on pegs all around the walls.

"Ok, ladies," said a big guard by the door. Theresa supposed she was a woman 'cause all the other guards was —but it coulda gone either way. "You know the drill —strip."

"I got to take my clothes off?" Theresa blurted out, stunned.

"How many things can 'strip' mean?" said the guard. She had a black nightstick in her hand and was rhythmi- cally slapping the end of it into her palm as she began to chant a singsong mantra she'd probably said hundreds, maybe thousands of times, her voice too loud, like maybe they was all deaf.

"Remove your outer garments and place them in the numbered metal baskets provided for that purpose against the far wall, socks and shoes on the bottom. Take off your bra and panties and hold them in your hand as you will be putting those back on when you are issued a jumpsuit. Any contraband recovered during this search will be seized and you will be charged..."

She kept talking while Theresa looked around the room. Wasn't no dressing rooms she could see.

"Where we s'posed to change?" she asked. She knew, of course, just couldn't make herself face the fact of it.

"Where do you think?"

"Right here in front of ever'body?"

Two of the guards laughed, but the guard with the nightstick didn't, just poked Theresa in the side with it.

"Get a move on, fatso," she said. "Big as you are, this could take a while."

"Just do it," urged one of the prisoners who'd come in with her. The woman was already down to her bra and panties.

"Yeah," said the other prisoner. "They gotta make sure you ain't got a bazooka in your armpit."

Theresa stood, frozen.

"Don't make them force you," warned the first prisoner.

Theresa was wearing a bright print blouse over black slacks. She reached up and began mechanically to unbutton the blouse. She wasn't aware of crying but could feel big tears streaming down her cheeks. Her movements slowed as she got near the bottom and when the blouse was unbuttoned, she made no move to take it off.

The other prisoners were already naked, standing as

directed with their arms out to their sides while guards wearing plastic gloves poked and examined them. On command, they both spread they feet out and bent over at the waist for a "cavity" search.

Theresa couldn't seem to get a breath. Wasn't no air in the room.

The big guard ran out of patience and gestured toward Theresa with her nightstick and a little redheaded guard stepped in front of her and began to yank her blouse off. Theresa reflexively pushed the guard's hands away. That's all it took.

It happened fast. The big guard stepped to Theresa and whacked her hard on the side of the leg with the nightstick, on her thigh a couple of inches above the knee. That leg collapsed, folded up like a broken twig, and Theresa fell to the concrete floor. Then they was all over her. Three or four guards, she couldn't tell how many, snatching and grabbing and her trying to make them stop. She didn't intend to fight them, but it was like a reflex, like you push somebody away when they's trying to tickle you.

It didn't take them guards long to overpower her. Before she knew it, Theresa was lying naked on the floor, spread-eagled, with a guard holding each leg and arm. The guard with the nightstick stepped in between her legs.

"You should have listened to your friends," she said and gestured with the nightstick toward the two other prisoners standing by the wall dressed in orange jumpsuits.

Then the guard snapped on plastic gloves and done the exam personally, done it rough as she possibly could for payback. Touching Theresa, jabbing and poking her, deliberately hurting her in her private places, but Theresa bit her lip and didn't cry out. Just lay there and felt the hot tears run down the side of her head and into her hair.

Then they took her in her orange jumpsuit and shoved

her into a cage with five other women. It was a cage, too, lined up with other cages like the monkey house at the zoo.

Theresa had smelled it out in the hall before they even got to the cells. But here, the demon stink was overwhelming—rot and decay, the reek of moldering corpses. And the demon wailing numbed her heart—eerie, high-pitched screams, otherworldly and utterly desolate, sounds like the shrieks of ravaged souls writhing in agony or the keening cry of lost children wandering alone in the dark.

Could have been prisoners, could have been guards. She didn't know which, couldn't single out any one demon 'cause she couldn't see them like Becca could. No wonder that child couldn't be locked up! And this was just jail. What must prison be like?

The world grayed out after that under the combined effect of what them guards had done to her and so much evil close by. But she was aware of some things.

Heat. Lazy fans moved hot air around sweating bodies.

Filth. Ground-in grime slathered everything she touched.

Noise. The squeak of the fans, the clang of cell doors, the babble of conversations, voices raised in anger, crying, even singing formed a mindless cacophony that assaulted her senses.

All painted on the backdrop of the evil Theresa didn't need ears to hear or a nose to smell.

That night, Theresa tried not to see or hear what two of them women was doing while the others watched and laughed. Then she lay on a bottom bunk—a little white girl traded it to her for the top bunk, said she didn't want a "fat nigger woman" to come crashing down on her in the middle of the night. Theresa cried then, hard but quiet. Wouldn't do to let them others know how scared she was.

As she lay in the dark cage, wondering if the sun had

yet come up out there in the real world, she recognized how cunning was the evil that had put her here. She'd much rather Chapman Whitworth had hacked her to death than live the rest of her life locked away in a place like this. And he knew that.

The next morning, they took her to a courtroom somewhere and Jeff Kendrick was waiting for her. She was so exhausted and traumatized she was only vaguely aware that she was standing with him in front of a judge on a raised dais.

"Theresa Maxine Washington, you have been accused of two counts of aggravated murder. The state of Ohio charges that on or about September 22, 2011, with prior calculation and design, you caused the deaths of Minerva Lucille Cohen and Gerald Alexander Cohen. How do you plead?"

Images blew through her mind, a whirlwind of thoughts. Trying to grab one and hold on long enough to think it was like trying to pick out a single bird when a whole flock took flight.

Miss Minnie with the hand-painted ornament she'd given Theresa for Christmas.

The smell of the pineapple upside down cake fresh out of the oven they'd brought to the house when Bishop died.

Mr. Gerald lying on the floor with an ax stuck in his chest.

"Not guilty." Jeff was whispering in her ear. "You need to say—"

"Not guilty," she said. "I wouldn't never hurt them sweet old people."

Half an hour later, she was standing with Jeff on the steps in front of the building—hot asphalt and exhaust fumes smelling like roses in her nostrils.

"Do you understand what has happened, Mrs. Washington?" he asked, as the cab he'd called to take her home pulled up to the curb.

"It's Theresa," she said. "And I understand all I need to." She took in a deep, trembling breath and let it out slowly and deliberately. She'd made her peace with it sometime in the middle of the night. "I understand that what happens to me ain't gone be decided by no judge and jury."

He didn't comment, only said they needed to talk and told her to call his office and make an appointment with his secretary.

"Maybe me and Daniel could come see you together. We got different problems, but they both come from the same source."

The man's face tightened. "You need to know that Daniel isn't…thrilled to have me as his lawyer. He made that clear Saturday." The attorney reached up and touched his swollen nose. "But the man who hired me is used to getting what he wants and apparently, he…made Daniel an offer he couldn't refuse this morning."

"Why don't Daniel want you on the case?"

"That's a question you'll have to ask Daniel."

Chapter Nineteen

2011

Jack was on a split shift and didn't come to work until noon, and by then, Theresa was already gone. When he heard she'd been arrested and taken to the county jail in Cincinnati, he went straight to Crock's office, stormed in without knocking and then paced back and forth in front of Crock's desk, so angry he didn't dare speak.

Crocker leaned his chair back on two legs and reached into his pocket for a cinnamon toothpick. He'd just quit smoking and said chewing on toothpicks helped with his "oral fixation." On a bad day, Jack had seen him gnaw down a whole box of them.

"Guess I should have called you when they brought Theresa in," Crock said. "But what could you have done if you'd known?"

Nothing. That was the sticking point. There was nothing Jack could do, nothing anybody could do. Whitworth was holding all the cards—five aces.

"She's being railroaded."

"Who's driving the train?"

Jack knew none of it would make any sense unless he tied it all together with the story of Chapman Whitworth—and if he did that, he'd have to take the major on a journey he couldn't come back from.

"You waiting for a drum roll?" Crock asked.

"Chapman Whitworth."

"You should have waited for the drum roll."

"He's been nursing a grudge against us for twenty-six years. We...know something about him, and he wants to keep us too busy to rain on his Supreme Court parade."

"And what you know is ...?"

"The part I can't tell you."

Crocker dropped the front legs of his chair back onto the floor with a thud.

"Aw, come on, Jack. How do you expect me to help?"

"You don't have to know that part to help me."

Crocker looked at him hard, studied him. "And if I say I want to know that part?"

The man had no idea how that would rock his world, and Jack felt a sudden need to protect him from it. To keep him in—well, if not blissful ignorance, at least comfortable ignorance.

The problem was, it was true. That was the whole problem—it was true. Jack sighed.

"In that case, I'd say pizza's in order."

"Make mine pepperoni with extra cheese."

"Tomorrow night at Theresa's. Say...seven o'clock."

"How do you know she's having pizza tomorrow night?"

"Because that sweet old woman is going to need her friends around her after"—Jack ground his teeth—"spending the night in jail! So I'm going to tell her she's having a party. You got a preference, Domino's or Papa John's?"

"They'll both keep me up all night."

The group gathered around the big table in Theresa's kitchen Tuesday night was anything but festive. Daniel and Andi had arrived the same time Jack did.

"Uncle Jack," Andi cried, "Daddy said Miss Theresa has a dog!" Her grin planted dimples in her cheeks deep enough to eat pudding out of. Then she ran ahead of them into the house.

Daniel watched her go with a sour look on his face.

"Somebody pee in your Cheerios?" Jack asked.

"I woke up this morning with a dead horse's head in my bed—metaphorically speaking," Daniel said, then strode silent and fuming into the house.

Jack would find out what that meant later.

Theresa did, indeed, have a dog, a brown mutt so happy to greet every new guest it hopped up and down and ran around in circles, tail wagging. Jack figured it was going to wet itself any minute.

Theresa looked completely spent. Her vibrant brown eyes, always as bright as twin pilot lights, were cloudy, with a haunted look he'd never seen there before. Her whole countenance had changed. She seemed to be hunkered down, tensed for a blow.

Becca looked…now that was hard to say. If you meant comparatively, just "clean" was a huge improvement over the last time he'd seen her. But objectively, she was hollow-eyed and frail, with a fearful, hunted look that never left her face, even when she was listening attentively to Andi's babble.

The only time she'd brightened was when she saw Daniel. He'd given her a big hug, held her out at arm's length and gave her another, long and affectionate. If he was taken aback in any way by her appearance or demeanor, he showed no sign of it, appeared genuinely delighted to see her. Clearly, she was equally delighted to see him.

For a moment that bothered Jack. Why? Well, duh, he'd spent his whole childhood, at least the part of it he could remember, being jealous of Becca and Daniel. And he learned later that Daniel had been equally jealous of him and Becca. Now, here they were twenty-six years later, still playing the parts they'd played as children. Some things never changed.

Theresa told him she'd filled Becca in on the little kids in Bradford's Ridge who had set spiders loose in a Sunday school class and pulled up rose bushes with their bare hands. And about the attacks of the now-adult Bad Kids three months ago—who'd been searching for her. Then he understood why Becca looked so frightened.

The grown-ups kept up a facade of lighthearted banter until Andi was ensconced in a beanbag chair in the den, her arm around her new best friend Biscuit the dog, with idiot sea creatures cavorting around the screen in front of her. Theresa set a bowl of popcorn beside her, came back into the kitchen and sat ponderously down in her chair.

"I spent last night in jail," she said. There was wonder mixed with horror in her voice. "I got photographed and fingerprinted—good thing I'm black 'cause that ink don't come off, don't know how white folks..." She trailed off. When she spoke again, her voice was clotted with unshed tears, barely above a whisper. "I can't be locked up in a cage like that with the stink and the wailing." He could hear the terror in the words. "We got to do something 'cause I can't—" She stopped herself, looked around, cleared her throat, then turned to Crock. "I understand you interested in knowing what's really goin' on here," she said.

"Jack says I'm not going to like it."

"He tell you you ain't gonna b'lieve it once you do hear it? Most folks don't, anyway."

"I'm not most people."

"How so?"

He looked at Jack as she had looked at him. "I've seen…things I haven't told Jack about."

"What things?" Jack asked.

"You show me yours and then I'll show you mine," Crock said.

Jack took a deep breath. "Once upon a time," he said, "there were three musketeers—Becca, Daniel and Jack…"

~

1985

Ella Fletcher was secretly flattered when people said she looked like Tweetie Bird's grandmother. Small and round, her gray hair pulled back in a bagel-sized bun at her neck, with plump rosy cheeks and rimless glasses perched on her nose, the resemblance was striking. She liked Tweetie Bird and goodness knows she qualified for the grandmother designation. Fourteen so far, and Mary Jane had looked like she was ready to pop any minute when Ella saw her at church on Sunday. And those didn't even count the ones born to all her other children, those she'd had in classes during thirty-two years as a third grade teacher. Count them, and you'd be up in the hundreds, maybe thousands.

The sun was already coming up, which meant Ella'd slept late. She slipped quietly out of bed so as not to wake Harold. He needed his rest. The doctor'd said he'd get to feeling better real soon after his heart surgery, but he was still listless and grumpy, and Ella was worried about him.

Soon as she fed Jelly, she'd make herself a cup of coffee. Jelly's complete name was Jelly Belly, a cocker spaniel whose big brown eyes had melted even Harold's heart—and he didn't much fancy dogs. Ella would find him snoozing in front of the door in the kitchen where a doggie flap allowed him access to the backyard, so he could do his business without her having to let him in and out all the time.

She flipped on the kitchen light. Jelly wasn't on the rug where he slept. Must be out watering the rose bushes. She filled his dish with doggie chow and gave him fresh water in his bowl—though it was almost full. He usually had it licked dry in the morning from lapping at it all night.

When the coffee was done, she added a dash of cream to a cup, wondering why Jelly was taking so long in the yard. She unfastened the deadbolt and pulled the door open.

"Jelly!" she called out. "Come on in and have some break—"

That's when she chanced to look down. Sitting on the porch at her feet was a cardboard box probably twice the size of a shoe box. It had brown stains down one side, and the lid was ajar. Ella bent over and lifted the lid off the box.

Her hand went numb, and she didn't even feel herself drop the cup. Didn't hear it clatter to the floor. Didn't feel the hot splash of coffee on her foot.

Then Ella Fletcher began to scream, to shriek, her face so contorted with horror that she didn't look a thing like Tweetie Bird's grandmother anymore.

An hour later, Caverna County Sheriff William Cunningham stood in Ella's kitchen doorway, staring at the contents of the box that still sat on the porch where she'd found it. The sheriff wasn't a tall man, but he was broad and thick, built like an oil drum. The premature gray in his hair had washed down into his lumberjack beard that extended two inches below his chin, and hound dog jowls made him look ten years older than forty-five. Today he felt even older than he looked.

Ella was upstairs. Dr. Clements had come by and given her a shot of something to calm her down, and two of her daughters were with her now, trying to soothe her. Harold Fletcher stood by the sheriff's side, dressed in a robe and slippers. The sheriff didn't think he looked good —his face was gray—but he'd been the one who called 911.

"What kind of person does something like this?" Harold asked.

"I got no idea," the sheriff said. He hadn't touched the box, of course. It was evidence, and the boys from the Kentucky State Police forensics lab would be here soon to go over it with tweezers—a grizzly job, he thought. He wouldn't want to have to remove the pieces of that dog one by one from the box. And from what the sheriff could tell, there were lots of pieces—two set apart from the rest. The dog's eyeballs rested in two paper cupcake holders between its severed head and tail.

One of the sheriff's deputies came into the kitchen and touched the sheriff on the shoulder. "Dispatch says you need to go to Franklin's Department Store," he said.

"I'm busy here. If they got a shoplifter, tell them to—"

"It's not a shoplifter. It's…something else."

"Something else" turned out to be three hysterical customers, two frantic store employees and one three-foot-long black snake. Well, one snake they'd found before they called the sheriff. Since then, employees and deputies had turned up four more snakes—two in shoe boxes, one in the pocket of a man's suit jacket and another draped like a necklace around a mannequin in the storage room. They were still looking for others.

As soon as the sheriff walked in, all three women started babbling at the same time in an unintelligible cacophony that resolved itself into simple story. Mildred Hart, Rose Tungate and Sophie Walsh had been at the door when the store opened this morning, eager to take advantage of the store's Buy One, Get One Free sale. Mildred had headed toward the dresses while Rose and Sophie busied themselves digging through a large bin piled with clearance priced "accessories." Scarves, purses, patterned pantyhose, gloves—that kind of thing.

"I was digging around in the bin," Rose said, "and I found—I thought it was a belt!" Her face screwed up in a look of revulsion. "I touched it—pulled it out and—" Her voice broke, and she fell into Mildred's arms and started to sob.

While the sheriff was taking statements from the employees, that same deputy—the one who'd been at the Fletchers' house—stepped up beside him and spoke softly in his ear. "There's more," he said.

"What more?" the sheriff blustered, then turned away when he saw that everyone in the building had heard his outburst. "What more?" he asked again, softer.

"We just got a call from the manager of Bracken Park," he said. "He's closed the city swimming pool."

"There aren't snakes—"

"No, sir. No snakes. He closed it because somebody dumped a barrel of sewage in the water."

The sheriff looked at his watch. It wasn't even ten o'clock.

By six o'clock that evening, when he added up what he hoped was the final tally, there had been half a dozen acts of vandalism besides the pool sewage—spray-painted swastikas, desecrated churches, blood poured all over the altar at St. Dominic's, slashed tires on fire trucks and ambulances, a trash can full of garter snakes in the girls' bathroom at Harper's Drive-In. Stevie Holiday's pet rabbit had been set on fire. And eleven dogs had been executed.

All the dogs had been mutilated in some way for the maximum horror effect, and their bodies left for their masters to find. Four were big dogs—two German shepherds, a Rottweiler and the Websters' guard dog—a pit bull that patrolled the backyard, guarding the small marijuana patch George was under the illusion nobody knew he grew for his wife who had cancer. All had had their throats slit. There'd been no forensic evidence to speak of. They'd made casts of footprints at three of the crime scenes—that could have been anybody's—found no fingerprints at all. Everything has been wiped clean. The state police lab would go over everything and issue a report, of course, but the sheriff knew in his gut they'd find nothing.

The whole town was teetering on the brink of mass hysteria, and he did not have a single suspect. Not one. Nobody had seen or heard anything!

When the knock came at his closed office door, the sheriff considered not answering it. He only wanted to sit in the late afternoon sun streaming through his window and not talk to anybody about anything.

"Come in," he said.

Bishop Washington opened the door and stepped in, quickly filling the small space. At least he seemed to. The huge man was as gentle as he was big, though, and the sheriff had come to like and respect him during the past months' futile search for Bishop's missing son.

"You got a minute, Bill?" he asked.

"No. But sit down and I'll find one."

Bishop eased down into the small chair, looked as uncomfortable as an elephant sitting on a football.

"I heard what's going on."

"As far as I can tell, the only person in the whole county who hasn't heard about it is Ambrose Pendleton, who went out fishing last week in the east branch of the Big Puddle and nobody's seen him since."

"You got any idea who's responsible?"

"Not a clue. Do you?"

Bishop looked uncomfortable. He'd taken off his baseball cap that read Bradford's Ridge All-Stars and was unconsciously crumpling it in his big hands. "Not no evidence, nothing like that. But you might want to…look into the whereabouts of some boys that's on my team. They's six of them from Brewster Academy."

"Because …?"

"They's mean as snakes, that's why. I am one hundred percent certain there ain't no limit to the awful they's capable of."

"Wait a minute…aren't you coaching twelve-year-olds?"

"Uh-huh."

The beginning of hope that had surged in the sheriff's chest, quickly drained away. "That lets them off the hook, then. Just kids. You must not have heard—four of the dogs that were killed were big dogs, German Shepherds and a pit bull. I don't imagine those animals went gently into that good night. They only found the last one a little while ago. I figure the owners were using it for dog fighting. I can't prove that, but what other reason would they have to own a ninety pound Rottweiler so vicious they have to keep it locked in a kennel behind a twenty foot protection fence? They finally found it with its throat slit. It took them all day to find it because the body was left draped across a tree limb twenty-five feet off the ground. No kids in the world could have pulled that off."

"These could have."

The sheriff's smile was tired, but not nearly as tired as he felt. He stood and looked at Bishop—a good man, only trying to help. "Don't I wish it was as easy as a gang of rowdy boys. Right now, I can't figure how a platoon of Army Rangers could have pulled all this off in one night. No sign of a struggle anywhere. No blood spatter, no mess. Everything clean and neat. Got into locked buildings, backyards and over fences. Unless one of your kids is Superman…"

Bishop looked uncomfortable. "Just check 'em out, Bill. That's all I'm sayin'. Find out where they was when all this happened."

The sheriff sighed, made a mental note to add this to the list of crackpot solutions he'd been hearing since sunup.

Of course, Bradford's Ridge made the news the next day, would have been the lead story on every channel if the governor's helicopter hadn't crashed right after lunch. The stations sent the big guns to cover that, but two second-stringer crews of TV reporters showed up in Bradford's Ridge toting cameras on their shoulders, filming interviews with the sheriff and the people whose dogs had been killed. The story didn't make the six o'clock, but it did make the eleven o'clock news as well as the front pages of the Louisville Courier-Journal—a big story because it was Ohio's governor who was nearly killed—and below the fold in the Cincinnati Inquirer. The reporters came up with all manner of wacky theories—might as well have blamed a tribe of gypsies or space aliens. Or a gang of twelve-year-old boys.

Chapter Twenty

2011

Harrelton Ohio Police Department Major Charles Everett Crocker wasn't sure exactly what he'd been expecting when he told Jack he wanted to know "what was really going on," but whatever it was, it fell way short of this.

There were a lot of ways you could go with a story like Crock'd just heard. A shared delusion. Happened, sometimes. He'd seen it.

But that explanation didn't feel right in that place in his belly somewhere slightly south of his navel, the residence of what police officers the world over called "a cop's gut." Crock's was particularly sensitive. He almost always knew when a situation was about to go sideways so you'd best jump out of the way before you got hit by the shift, or when some squirrelly little dude with a small brain and a big gun was actually going to use it. His cop's gut had kicked in three months ago when the goings-on with Jack hadn't stacked up any neater than a pile of cats.

The major's gut was telling him right now that these

people weren't crazy. He was sure he'd sleep better nights if he could convince himself they were, but the trouble with your gut was it never shut up. Like a nagging wife, it kept after you until you finally listened to the truth. Crocker suspected…no, he knew he'd just heard the truth in long-johns with the butt flap down. And the only thing his nagging internal organs would allow him to do with that was adjust his own thinking to the reality of it. What was true was true, and that was that.

Besides, there was the other side that had brought him here tonight. He had his own stories to tell about the…go ahead, quit chewing on it and spit it out.

"I've had some experiences myself with the…super-natural."

He held the word out there for a moment like a dead fish on a stick. Nobody flinched. Well, one of them flinched. He flinched, but the others didn't bat an eye.

"What I thought happened to me…what did happen to me…wasn't like what you're describing, though. There are armies on both sides of this war and I believe I've had a run-in or two over the years with the white-hat dudes, the good guys."

"Angels," Theresa said.

Again, nobody but Crocker batted an eye. He batted both of them, flapped the lids up and down like he was trying to send smoke signals. He opened his mouth to say that "angels" was a stretch, but said instead, "I've never told anybody about it."

"Course you ain't." Theresa was impatient. "Don't nobody ever tell anybody else 'bout such things. They's happening all over the place but everybody's so afraid of lookin' foolish, they don't say nothin', which is just the way ole Clubfoot likes it."

"Have you seen creatures of light?" The words came

from the emaciated young woman sitting beside Daniel Burke on the couch, her fingers unconsciously entwined with his, a bid for comfort in a world where all comfort was gone. She leaned forward as she asked the question. It was clear a lot was riding on his response.

And Crocker knew he was about to disappoint.

"It's not like that. I haven't seen 'creatures' of any kind—light or dark. What I've seen have been ordinary people…but somehow more than that."

Nobody offered any comment on that so he plunged ahead.

"The first time was when I was a kid. Just eight years old and I knew I was going to die."

He'd sneaked off to go swimming alone and had gotten a cramp.

"I could barely keep my head above water when this guy came out of nowhere. He wasn't there and then he was. A big guy, dressed in a T-shirt and jeans and boots—big, tall cowboy boots made out of shiny black leather with red trim on the top. I remember that part distinctly because I knew he couldn't swim with boots on."

The man raced across the strip of mud in front of the swimming hole just as Crock went under and couldn't get back to the surface.

"He grabbed me, dragged me to the shore and carried me to the top of the riverbank. Then I closed my eyes—just a blink—but when I opened them again, the man was gone.

"I tried to convince myself that he was some passing stranger, but that didn't work." Crock paused for a beat. "See…there weren't any boot prints in the mud. You could see one set of prints, bare feet—mine. Those big ol' cowboy boots would have left prints."

Crocker was looking down at his hands in his lap as he

told the last part, suddenly embarrassed by the simplicity of his story.

"You's thinking that what you seen ain't dramatic or nothing so it can't be real," Theresa said, her voice soft. Chill bumps pebbled Crock's arms. That's *exactly* what he'd been thinking. "Most times when the Lord sends his angels, it ain't dramatic. They don't float in the sky, a whole flock of them like they done over the baby Jesus. They just keep a little boy from drowning when God's got bidness he wants that boy to do later on in life."

Crock didn't like that 'business later on in life' part, but he kept talking.

"There were other times. I was in a car wreck, came to with a broken leg and flames all around me. Then somebody yanked the car door open and dragged me out—right before that car went off like a bottle rocket. I was lying on the grass at the side of the road with so much blood in my eyes I couldn't see anything...except black cowboy boots."

He had other stories but they all begged an answer to the question, a polished stone of wonder he'd wallowed around in his mind for so long all the rough edges had been sanded smooth. He'd never before had anybody he could ask the question because he'd never before told anybody about the...say it, go on say it...the angel.

"Why?"

He didn't mean for it to come out sounding as anguished as it did, but the torment he'd felt in his soul all these years gushed out with the question. "Why would... God...send an angel to save me when—"

"When they's so many other people he don't save? Important people, maybe, like Dr. King." Theresa glanced at the framed picture of Dr. Martin Luther King on the wall. "Innocent children like —" she looked at Daniel--

"Mary Anne." Crocker saw Daniel wince. "Or necessary people like my Bishop, people other folks need to help them do what God's assigned 'em to do?"

She'd been talking to all of them, but now she spoke only to Crocker. "Why'd God save you and not them?"

He leaned forward, not breathing. Finally an answer!

"I ain't got no idea, sugar."

"You don't know? You mean there's no reason—"

"I never said there wasn't no reason. God don't do nothing 'thout a reason. But you got to understand somethin' or you gone spend your whole life miserable, lookin' for answers when ain't none to find." She looked deep into his eyes. "Major Crocker, the God of the universe don't owe you an explanation for what he does. He's God. You ain't."

The room fell completely silent. Then Jack's voice, sharp and pointed, stabbed into the quiet.

"You're not required to like that explanation, by the way," he said. "You can still do what has to be done and not like it one bit. As a matter of fact, you can do what you're supposed to do and be so furious..."

It was almost like Jack suddenly realized he had actually spoken out loud, and he dropped his gaze to the floor.

"Some things haven't changed in twenty-six years," Daniel put in, sliding into the conversation effortlessly, shielding Jack. "He didn't like it when we were twelve years old—did he, Becca?"

Daniel continued to talk, and Crocker saw a look of gratitude wash over Jack's face. He suspected this might not be the first time Daniel Burke had swooped in and taken the heat off his friend.

Theresa spoke to Crock again. "Major, a man totally taken over by a prince of darkness is 'bout to be made a justice on the United States Supreme Court—unless we stop him." She looked pointedly at every person in the room. "Just the four"—she fixed her gaze squarely on him —"the five of us. That make any sense to you?"

~

FIRST THING WEDNESDAY MORNING, Jack was summoned into Crock's office. The major'd had all night to chew on what he'd heard, and Jack wondered—

"Appears it's up to you and me to figure out how Chapman Whitworth orchestrated getting all three of you up to your tighty whities in alligators—in one day." Crock popped a cinnamon toothpick into his mouth. "Which is probably a record of some kind if there's a Guinness Book of Dastardly Deeds."

Just like that, Crock was in.

"Soo…" Crock cleared his throat and spoke in his police-major voice. "Sergeant Carpenter, because the Bureau of Alcohol, Tobacco and Firearms is investigating you in connection with a mass murder case, I am putting you on temporary suspension. You're off patrol. You'll be assigned duties…at my discretion."

"Can you do that?"

"I just did. Of course, if the captain finds out I've got you digging around in the Cohen case when he thinks we've already found that bone, the guano will definitely hit the air-conditioning."

"The only place we have to dig is the man Theresa saw at the Cohens' house," Jack said. He thought for a moment. "Anybody owe you a favor at the FBI?"

"If you're asking did I take a bullet for somebody or throw myself on a grenade, no. But I'm a personable fellow for all that, and I made a few friends."

"Think maybe you could arm-twist one of them into loaning you a sketch artist? Theresa got a good look at the guy."

"You want me to get a sketch artist—for a closed case." A statement, not a question.

"Uh-huh. And the use of their facial recognition software."

"Sure you don't want me to ask for somebody's first-born son?" Crock blew out his breath in a whoosh. "Ok, I'll see what I can do."

Jack got up to leave.

"Jack," Crock said, "we're twisting in the wind here. You know that, don't you. No backup, nothing official."

Jack looked Crock in the eye and nodded. Crock nodded back.

The moment passed.

"Well, while you're out investigating a closed case, I'm going to stick my nose into one that's out of our jurisdiction. I just called the Centurion Hotel and asked—you know, the suspect being a hometown boy and all——if they'd mind if I took a look-see at the surveillance footage from the elevator and hallway cameras for the week before Daniel hopped in it with Miss Goody Two-Shoes."

Jack didn't get it.

"I've watched that clip you gave me four times. That woman did a pre-tty impressive little dance, don't you think? Had it perfectly choreographed. No way she pulled that off without practicing it. At the very least, she and whoever she's working with scoped out the camera angles. Maybe they got caught on camera, too."

"How do you know Lily Saunders has a partner?"

Crock cocked an eyebrow at Jack. "You ever try to black your own eye, bust your own lip and break your own nose?"

Before the end of that day, the sketch artist met with Theresa, and by mid-afternoon Thursday the facial recognition software had done its magic.

Jack marched triumphantly into Crocker's office.

"You either just won the lottery or had a really good bowel movement this morning," Crocker said. "Which is it?"

"We have a name," Jack said, and handed Crocker a mug shot. "Edgar Wallace Boskowitz, Bosko to his friends and fellow inmates at Lebanon Correctional Institution. Served a dime there in 1995 for a string of burglaries. Has a rap sheet the size of Cleveland, property and drug crimes, and was just paroled from Marion on a controlled substances charge. But the thing is, he should have been otherwise occupied when Theresa's friends died, locked away permanently as a persistent felony offender."

"But he wasn't because…"

"He was the driver in a Three Stooges bank robbery. Police capped his partner, but the guy'd killed a security guard. Bank robbery, dead guard——case gets kicked up to federal court and…"

"The judge in the case was Chapman Whitworth," Crock finished for him.

"Give the man a kewpie doll. The gun his partner used was entered into evidence the first day of Bosko's trial and then somehow got 'misplaced.' Defense demanded a mistrial and without the fingerprints and the murder weapon…"

Crock reached over his desk and gave Jack a fist bump as he got up from his big leather chair. "The Centurion Hotel called a few minutes ago," he said. "Seems the cameras in that elevator and hallway that worked flawlessly to record Daniel's assault on Thursday night didn't work so flawlessly the previous Monday. That whole day's tape from those cameras is blank. And that's exceedingly odd, the manager told me, because the security company sent a technician to do an unscheduled inspection of the system the day of Daniel's rendezvous. Clean bill of health. No mention of erased tape." Crock picked up his little vial of toothpicks from the desk and slipped it into his pocket. "So I'm on my way to McComber Security Systems."

Jack nodded.

"We caught a break on Bosko," Jack said. "Our civic-minded federal judge shops locally--Mr. Boskowitz lives right here in Harrelton. I got the names of a couple of his 'known associates' from his parole officer, and I'm going out to shake some trees and see if anything falls out, maybe find a tie to Lily Saunders before I pay him a visit." Jack paused. "After I discuss with an ATF agent an event he probably knows more about than I do."

Chapter Twenty-One

2011

"I don't like this any more than you do," said the voice on the other end of the line, and Daniel Burke sincerely doubted that was possible. "If you can see a way out, I'm all over it. But as it stands, you can't tell Clayton Abernathy no and neither can I."

Daniel had met a stone wall when he'd tried to talk to Abernathy about Jeff Kendrick.

"That young man is the best criminal lawyer in Cincinnati, and you're getting the best." That was the old man's final word, and short of telling him the real reason why he didn't want Kendrick to represent him, there was no getting around it.

Daniel had to admit—grudgingly—that they both were stuck. "Fine, then," he said. "You're my lawyer."

"Agreed."

Silence again.

"There's no lemonade to be made of this that I can see, so let's just suck up the sour and get on with it," Jeff said. "We have to talk. Soon. Carve out a big hunk of time because there's a lot to go over. Clayton says you and Mrs. Washington are being framed, and I have to know why. And who."

"You're not going to believe it."

Daniel heard anger replace annoyance in Kendrick's voice.

"Let's get one thing straight right now, Daniel," he snapped. "I will believe it because you're my client, and if you say it's true, it's true. That's how attorneys roll."

"Fair enough. My secretary can work it out with yours."

"Done," Kendrick said and hung up without saying goodbye.

When his secretary buzzed in a few minutes later, Daniel assumed she was confirming with him the appointment with Jeff Kendrick. She wasn't.

"There's a man here who wants to see you," she said. "He's not a reporter. He says he's an old friend of yours, Billy Ray Hawkins."

Billy Ray looked just like he had the day Daniel and Jack had visited him in prison—absent the prison garb, that is. In fact, he looked like he'd always looked, like he looked when Daniel was a kid tiptoeing with Becca through her living room, trying not to wake her father as he slept off a bender. He was one of those men who'd never looked particularly young, so as he aged, he never looked particularly old, either. He could have been anywhere between thirty-five and sixty. The only mark the years had left on him was a sprinkling of gray in his hair and wrinkles around his eyes that crinkled the tear-drop tattoo beneath the left one. Crow's feet, not smile wrinkles. Billy Ray hadn't earned smile wrinkles.

Dressed in jeans, work boots and a short-sleeved plaid shirt that displayed the full-sleeve tattoos, he was as comfortable in Daniel's plush office as he'd have been in a chicken coop.

"You got nice digs, Reverend," he said in a gravelly voice that was always startling no matter how many times you'd heard it. Daniel gestured toward the leather chair, and Billy Ray sat. He glanced around at the lush carpet and cherry desk, and his eyes came to rest on the floor-to-ceiling shelves filled with leather-bound tomes. "You read all them books?"

Actually, Daniel had read precious few of them. They had been selected painstakingly by somebody—some decorator, he supposed—to indicate a level of education and erudition he didn't have. They were for show.

"Every last one."

Billy Ray looked at him, made no comment, and Daniel had the uncomfortable feeling the man knew he was blowing smoke. It was dangerous to underestimate men like Billy Ray Hawkins. Daniel suspected that for most of the man's life, other people had done just that and had lived to regret it.

"Can I get you anything?" Daniel asked in stony politeness. "Coffee, a soft drink?"

"The only thing you can get for me is my little girl," he said, as easily as "pass the salt." "I want her home with her daddy where she belongs, and I figure you know where I can find her."

"Becca is a thirty-eight-year-old woman so I fail to see how 'home with her daddy' is where she belongs," Daniel said.

"Now there you go, making all kind of assumptions and judgments. She's my little girl, and I just want to take care of her and see she has everything she needs."

"Why on earth would you come here looking for her?" Daniel asked. "If I'd known where to find her, why would

Jack and I have gone all the way to Danforth to ask if you knew where she was?"

"You's looking for Becca then, and you figured to start with me. Well, I'm looking for Becca now, and I figure to start with you—because it seems to me if you's so determined to find her back in July, you've surely had success by now."

Wrongo, Moosebreath—that's what Andi always said when she was playing Go Fish and was bluffing.

"Sorry to disappoint you, Billy Ray, but we've come up snake eyes. Don't have any more idea where she is now than we did when we talked to you."

"See, there you go again. Making assumptions."

"What kind of assumptions?"

"Assuming I'm too dumb to know when a man's lying to me and when he's telling the truth. Sitting in a cell twenty-four/seven for twenty years, studyin' people, how their eyes twitch when they're lying—like yours just done."

Oh yes, it was a dangerous thing, indeed, to underestimate Billy Ray Hawkins.

"I don't care if you use eye-twitches, nose wiggles or projectile vomiting as an indicator, I'm not lying. But I also don't care one way or the other whether you believe me." He paused. "Ask Jack if you want to, but I can save you the trouble—he doesn't know, either."

At the mention of Jack, Billy Ray face closed up tight. "Don't need to talk to that black buck. I done found out what I need to know."

"Suit yourself. If you want to leave me your number, I'll give it to her if I ever do find her. Right off the top of my head, though, I'd say it's a safe bet she won't use it, that she doesn't want to have anything to do with you."

"The wanting of it ain't the point here. There's what's right and what's true that matters. It's right and true that

I'm her daddy, and she's my kin." He leaned a little forward in the chair. "And she will come right on home with me soon's I have a chance to convince her she'd ought to."

"Well, I wish you luck, Billy Ray, but I can't help you." Daniel stood to indicate the conversation was over. Billy Ray remained seated, looking up at him through dark eyes as cunning and ruthless as a ferret's.

"Take a word of advice from an old friend who's known you since you's a pup—probably be a good idea if you's to stick to the truth from now on 'cause you ain't no good at all at lyin'. I wasn't sure of it before I came here, but I am now—you do know where she is." His voice got softer, meaner. "Listen up to what I'm telling you for true. I'm only gonna say it just this one time, Daniel. You need to tell me what you know. Right now. You will regret it if you don't."

The cold edge of threat in his voice sliced through the air like a dagger.

"I can't help you, Billy Ray," Daniel said, and was glad his own tone was not only firm, but unafraid. Of course, his lack of fear was like the leather books that lined his office—all for show. "Now, if you'll excuse me, I have another appointment."

Billy Ray stood silently, went to the door, then stopped, looked back and shook his head sadly. "You're gonna be real sorry you didn't give me my girl when I asked, Reverend." His voice was soft. "Real, real sorry."

Chapter Twenty-Two

2011

Jeff Kendrick always believed his clients. Even when every word coming out of their mouths was a bald-faced lie, he still "believed" them. It all came down to the definition of believe. He'd had to redefine the term a long time ago to mean simply to behave in a manner that does not contradict what your client says and present to the world the words of your client as gospel.

Neither of those definitions required that he, personally, had to blindly accept that his client was telling the truth—whatever that happened to be. In most cases, Jeff was lucky if his personal belief system lined up with his client's on any part of their story. At least in Daniel's and Theresa's cases, he didn't believe his clients were guilty of the crimes they'd been accused of committing. Clayton Abernathy believed in Daniel, and that alone would have been good enough for Jeff to bet his life and fortune on. Even without that, though, it was impossible to believe that the Boy Scout minister had committed rape.

Boy Scout. That's what Emily had called him. Not that

they talked about Daniel when they were together. Their time was too precious, so delicious and limited that they seldom squandered so much as a drop of it on any other human being but each other.

He jerked his mind away from thoughts of Emily like his hand had touched a hot stove. He could not go there, not with her…husband…sitting across the desk from him, putting his life and future into Jeff's hands. Theresa was talking and Daniel was looking at her, and in that unguarded moment Jeff saw a ragged pain in Daniel's eyes that he was sure mirrored his own unguarded self. It occurred to him to wonder how Daniel kept from thinking about Emily when he was sitting across the desk from the man who'd tried to take her away from him.

Jeff's belief in Theresa's innocence was a gut reaction he'd have bet his life on, too. She didn't have Clayton Abernathy's endorsement to speak for her, but the old woman didn't need the endorsement of anybody to stand tall in her own righteousness. Theresa Washington was good—whatever that meant. Maybe that's what made her so amazingly intuitive.

As soon as they were seated, Theresa looked at him with such discernment he was sure she could read the tag on his boxer shorts. She looked at Daniel and then asked, "What's goin' on 'tween the two of you?"

He figured he'd let Daniel field that one. Daniel didn't say a word.

"You two been posturing around each other, peeing on bushes ever since we got here," she said. "Any fool can see they's way too much testosterone in this room. What's wrong?"

The silence drew out until Jeff finally broke it. "You've both told me that there are things about this case you're not willing to share with me. I agreed to represent you anyway. So you're going to have to accept that there are things about it I'm not willing to share, either."

Her black eyes continued to bore into him like a slow-speed dental drill. "That's fair enough, I suppose," she said.

But he'd bet his country club membership she'd keep probing until she had an answer.

And then they'd started telling him their story, and as the tale spread out before him, the question of "believing your client" flitted around in his head like an irritated wasp.

"So…let me get this straight. You're telling me that Chapman Whitworth is somehow involved in all this?"

"No, that's not what I'm saying a'tall," Theresa said. "He's not 'involved.' He's the puppet master pulling the strings, and neither one of us would be here if it wasn't for him."

"This is payback for something you did to him twenty-six years ago—that you're not willing to tell me about. And because the two of you know something about him—that you're also not willing to share with me—and he wants to divert your energies so you won't use it against him, and maybe to discredit you so no one would believe you if you did?"

He must have allowed the skepticism he felt to creep into his voice because Daniel lost it at that point. He'd been sitting quietly after he'd described the incident with the woman in the elevator, not contributing much to the conversation, letting Theresa tell the tale. Suddenly, he slammed his fist down on the desktop hard enough to set the balls in the Newton's Cradle on Jeff's desk whacking frantically at each other.

"There's a monster controlling Chapman Whitworth, and that's why Emily's dead," he said, his quiet voice a violent howl of emotion. "He had her killed. Are you listening to me, Kendrick? He murdered my wife while she was on the phone to me, telling me she loved me. I heard the gunshot…and then there was…silence."

Jeff could do nothing but stare at Daniel. Clearly, the man's grief had unhinged his mind.

"No, it wasn't some 'random act of violence' like the police and the press said. It was premeditated murder. She died to save Andi's life, killed by a creature sent after me."

Jeff glanced at Theresa, looking for the sympathy in her eyes he knew he'd see there for a dear friend who'd obviously had some kind of breakdown. She met his gaze square.

"We wasn't gone tell you all of it 'cause we knew you wouldn't b'lieve us if we did. We only wanted to give you enough so's maybe you could represent us against these lies." She looked at Daniel and sighed. "But he's done opened this can, so looks like we gone have to eat all of it."

And then they told him the most amazing tale he had ever heard. It took more than an hour to weave all of its parts together. The police sergeant, Jack Carpenter, the school shooter, the man who'd kidnapped Theresa and tried to kill Carpenter in a warehouse. And other killings— a man in a hospital bed in some little town in Kentucky, a bomb and a fire in…it all began to blur at that point. But he heard the important part loud and clear: the mental hospital escapee who'd shot Emily was a man who was possessed by a demon.

He only realized they'd stopped talking when the silence began to roar in his ears. He focused again, his eyes caught by the coal-black ones of the old woman.

"Don't 'spect you to b'lieve it, but you said to tell the truth, and there it is."

Diminished capacity.

Wouldn't have been his first choice for a plea—particularly when he was convinced his clients were innocent. But it might be the only one that would get them off. Because it was clear now that these two people who seemed otherwise normal were the victims of some grand shared delusion. He'd never seen anything like it in his life.

Daniel's cell phone rang. He looked at it and then glanced at Theresa. "It's Jack," he said, and took the call.

Theresa sat patiently, looking at him as Daniel spoke. The expression on her face disturbed Jeff, rattled him all the way to the core. It wouldn't have had it been lunacy. It wasn't. It was compassion.

Daniel hung up and addressed them both.

"Jack and Crock, Major Crocker, found the man from your drawing." He must have seen Jeff's confusion. "Crock arranged for an FBI sketch artist and then used facial recognition software."

"The police found the man you said was in the house that day?" Jeff asked.

"Not the police. Jack. He and the major were working on their own."

"Why?"

"For the same reason we couldn't tell you what was going on," Theresa snapped. "'Cause wouldn't nobody believe them."

"They identified the guy—an ex-con named Boskowitz. He should be in prison right now for murder, but 'key evidence' in his case got 'misplaced.' The judge was Chapman Whitworth."

Jeff felt all the wind sigh out of him like somebody'd stuck a nail in his air mattress.

"Look Mr. Kendrick…Jeff…you don't got to believe the why of it, but surely with all this, you can see that Chapman Whitworth ain't who he claims to be." She shook her head. "What happens to Daniel and me, that don't matter. What matters is us stoppin' him from sittin' on the Supreme Court!" A tremor seemed to pass through her body. "You ain't got no idea what pure evil can do when it's took over a powerful man."

"And you're going to stop him?" It was a simple, direct question. By now, Jeff's incredulity meter had so over-heated it had blown a fuse and shut down completely.

"Not us. Senator LaHayne," Daniel said. Then he looked like all the air had whooshed out of his air mattress, too. "If we could figure out a way to talk to him."

Theresa reached over and patted him on the knee. "Don't you fuss. God'll provide a way. He always does."

"Would you like his cell phone number?" Jeff saw the others staring at him and realized he'd said the words out loud. He was so rattled, he clarified. "Not God's…Senator LaHayne's."

"You have Senator Thomas LaHayne's cell number?" Daniel asked. From the look on his face it was clear his incredulity meter was still functioning just fine.

"Well, he's not on my favorites list, if that's what you mean. But I can get it for you. His son and I were fraternity brothers at Harvard."

THE MANAGER of McComber Security Systems was more than happy to help the friendly police officer who bore an uncanny resemblance to Elmer Fudd with his bald head and big ears. She gave him the address of the technician who'd inspected the Centurion Hotel's system Thursday morning, a trainee who hadn't been back to work since, and handed Crocker a photocopy of the man's driver's license.

Well, attention K-Mart shoppers.

It was the second time today Crocker had seen that name beneath a picture: Edgar Wallace Boskowitz.

He tried to reach Jack with the news, but he must have had his phone turned off during his meeting with the ATF agent. Crock settled for leaving him a voice mail. The address on the photocopied license was a rundown apartment building in a part of town not shown on Harrelton, Ohio, Chamber of Commerce brochures.

Approaching the third-floor apartment, Crocker began to feel that tingly sensation in the pit of his stomach that was either a cop's gut warning or incipient diarrhea, and even though he didn't have enough probable cause right now to give the guy a parking ticket, Crocker drew his weapon and flattened himself against the hallway wall beside the door.

He reached over and rapped on the door. Nothing. But Crocker thought he heard movement inside. He knocked again and was sure of it this time. So he banged his fist on the door and called out, "This is the police. Open the door." If you're going to bluff, bluff big.

Three shots splintered the wood on the cheap door, the sound a cannon roar in the narrow hallway. Hand gun, not semiautomatic, six shots if it was a revolver, and he'd just used three of them.

Crocker stepped sideways, keeping his body well out of the line of fire, leaned back—he was way too old to be doing this—and kicked the door a couple of inches above the door knob. The jam shattered, the door flew open in a hail of splinters and he flattened against the wall again.

"Put the gun on the floor and slide it out," Crocker

called, knowing that was about as likely as water flowing up hill. "Then put your hands on your head and—"

He heard the squeal of metal on metal and instantly recognized the sound. The guy was on the fire escape, had just hit the release on the ladder that would extend the last fifteen feet to the ground. Crocker spun into the room, crossed it to the window. Below, he could see a man leap off the bottom of the ladder and take off down the alley. Crock couldn't chase him. He was definitely too old for that.

His heart still felt like a lunatic woodpecker'd got loose in his chest, the adrenaline rush still pulsing as he holstered his weapon and concentrated on slow, regular breaths. Just then, Sonny and Cher informed him he was about to have company. Sirens, too far away for anybody else to hear, meant somebody in this neighborhood had actually called the police. Must have been a 911 butt call.

He turned from the window and looked around. The place was amazingly neat and clean. What sleazeball polished his metal refrigerator, for crying out loud? The dishes were set meticulously in the dish drainer. Not a couch pillow out of place. Safe bet this dude was over-the-top OCD.

And a classic movie nut. On a shelf in the bedroom was a model of the Millennium Falcon along with action figures—Princess Leia, the white orc from The Hobbit and a huge raptor. Beside the bed was a life-size replica of R2D2. The walls were adorned with movie posters. Not in frames, but held on the wall with white stick pins, and every poster had a torn movie ticket stub stapled neatly to the bottom. Star Wars—the original—Luke watching Yoda lift his ship out of the swamp. Lord of the Rings—Sam fighting Shelob. Jurassic Park—lizards with big teeth and small hands. The Hobbit, Titanic, Avatar. The biggest was for Harry Potter and the Deathly Hallows—Part 2 which hung directly across from the bed—Harry, Hermione and Ron looking all grown up. That poster had no torn ticket attached.

When you toss a house, you're looking for evidence in two categories. One—something the perp doesn't realize could be incriminating, like a parking garage stub that puts him at the scene of the crime. Two—something the perp knows is incriminating, like the murder weapon or stolen property. You'll find Category One things in trash cans, glove boxes and coat pockets. You'll find Category Two items hidden some place the perp thinks you'd never think to look—such as taped to the back of a picture frame or on top of fan blades, beneath a floorboard and even…yes… under the mattress.

Crock had learned during his years as an FBI agent not to try to outsmart the bad guys he chased. The point wasn't to out-think a criminal. The trick was to in-think one. Get inside his head. Try to figure out what he would do by seeing the world through his eyes.

Crock concentrated. An OCD neat freak wouldn't likely hang on to Category One items. What about Category Two? Where would a guy like Bosko hide something he didn't want anybody to see?

Crocks eyes surveyed the room slowly and came to rest on the life-size replica of R2D2. You don't suppose…?

He crossed the room and knelt on protesting knees before the robot. Stifling an urge to cry in a falsetto voice, "Help me, Obi-Wan Kenobi, you're my only hope," he inspected the front of the life-size reproduction, looking for an opening. He found what looked like a CD slot right in front and stuck his fingers inside it. No CD, but something was definitely jammed into the slot. He could just catch the edge of it with his fingernails.

When he dragged it out, he held it by the corner. An envelope.

The sirens were probably a block away now.

Using his car key, he opened the flap of the envelope by the edge, looked inside and noted the contents. Then he lifted the mattress on the bed and placed the envelope on the box springs. He went into the living room and was standing by the shattered door when the siren blipped off as a squad car slid to a stop out front.

The uniform who'd responded was Peterson—good. There were sharper knives in the drawer than Peterson.

"I tried to call for backup," Crock told him. Trying to look as chagrined as possible, he held up his phone. "Dead. But all the action's over now. I only stopped by to have a little chat with Mr. Boskowitz because a friend on the Cincy PD likes him for a series of burglaries, and I owe the guy a favor." Plausible enough unless Peterson wanted to know who his friend was. He didn't.

"I figure the guy wouldn't have opened up like half-price day at the firing range unless he's got something to hide—stolen merchandise, maybe drugs. Let's poke around and see what we can turn up."

Crock let Peterson find the envelope under the mattress.

Chapter Twenty-Three

1985

Michael Rutherford grunted as he pulled a big box of baseball caps down off the top of the stack. He'd been here maybe three minutes and already his shirt was plastered to his back and his hair hung down wet over his forehead. His mother said fat people sweat more than thin people. If that was the way it was, he was as stuck with sweat as he was with fat, and he'd made his peace with fat a long time ago. It was what it was, no sense moping about it. You could make a place for yourself in the world as a fat, sweaty kid. You just had to try harder.

Trying harder was how he came to be unloading boxes of Little League uniforms. Michael couldn't hit a baseball off a golf tee with a tennis racket. But he'd made the elite All-Star team by using his brain. He'd figured out Bishop Washington was going to need help maybe even before Bishop did. Everybody knew Isaac was supposed to be his father's assistant coach. So Mikey showed up at just the right time and got himself appointed team manager. He was the bat boy.

And he had to be on the team. Daniel and Jack were on the team. And wherever they went, Becca Hawkins went. Being on the team meant Michael got to be near Becca, and that was the sum total of everything that mattered to him in life. Becca was unlike any girl he'd ever known. She didn't dress like all the other girls--in T-shirts with the neck cut out, hanging open over the shoulder, and a lone lace glove with the fingers chopped off. She didn't tease her hair, spray it solid and stick a big bow in it, either. Becca's hair hung straight down her back to her waist, looked like corn silk. He knew if he touched it--he longed to but had never dared--it would be as soft as a baby duck's bottom. Becca wasn't interested in being a Madonna look-alike. She was just...*Becca.* The most beautiful girl Michael Rutherford had ever seen.

The uniforms he was unpacking consisted of a cap and pants and a T-shirt with each player's last name in big block letters on the back above the Bradford's Ridge All-Star team logo. On the front, Bradford's Ridge Rangers was printed above the logo of Prather's Insurance Company, the local business that had purchased the team's equipment in exchange for advertising space on the players. Team members were encouraged to wear their team T-shirts everywhere they went, not just during games. Michael intended to wear his every day all summer.

"You doin' a fine job, son," Bishop said when he arrived and saw how much Mikey'd accomplished.

Bishop was like that. He always had something kind to say, always made you feel good about yourself. Michael was sure most of the rest of the team joined him in hero worship of the man-mountain. Jack and Daniel certainly did. They met at his house once a week for a Bible study—which Michael would have sold his left leg to be able to attend, too. But Michael's family was Catholic. End of discussion.

Team members started arriving before noon when practice was officially set to start.

Michael was leaned over digging in a box of T-shirts when somebody kicked him soundly in the backside and sent him flying into the dirt.

"Hel-lo Mi-key," said Ronnie Martin. "How's Fatty Cakes, the team fat boy—I mean bat boy—today?" Ronnie had taken a dislike to Mikey the day of the cookout at Bishop's house.

Michael Rutherford didn't miss much. When you were fat and slow, you better be alert or you'd get trampled. He'd been close enough, kept his mouth shut, listened to Daniel and Jack talking and figured out they'd gotten into a fight with the boys from Brewster Academy in the woods last week. And he'd been at the park—got out of sight at the first sign of trouble—the day the Brewster Academy boys had attacked Jack and Daniel. The day Becca had… Mikey didn't know what she'd done. He didn't understand any of what he'd seen that day. But he knew enough to keep his head down and look like he was minding his own business after that. He was scared of those guys in a way that was totally unreasonable.

Mikey got up off the ground and dusted his pants, planted a grin on his face.

"Doin' just fine, Ronnie. I got your uniform all ready—right over there."

Mikey felt like some small, black thing had sneaked in the back door of his head and was crawling around in there—slithering around in there. His heart was pounding. Why was he so afraid—terrified—for no reason at all?

Everything seemed…off…after that. Bishop handed out the equipment and assembled the boys in front of him.

"We gone get warmed up today, catch a few pop flies and have a little batting practice," Bishop said. Mikey watched closely. The big man didn't look at the six boys from Brewster Academy when he spoke and seemed to be straining to stay focused, concentrating hard. It reminded Mikey of watching his mother try to have a telephone conversation while his little brother and sisters were fighting. "They's aerating the field Thursday and Friday so next full practice is Monday. Noon to five every day after that. Just got a few weeks to whip this team into shape. You boys need to come ready to play ball."

The coach clapped his hands and sent the boys into the outfield to catch flies.

What happened shortly after that had more clarity than what came before, even though it happened so fast it was over in seconds.

Bishop called the boys in for batting practice. "Everybody wants to swing all-out and knock one over the center-field fence," Bishop said. "Don"t nobody want to practice bunting. But in the strategy of baseball, you got to know how to look like you's about to swing for the moon, but end it in a bunt instead. That's what we gone work on now."

Jack fired pitches into Daniel's glove. Bishop stood beside the first few batters, showing them how to bring the bat down out of a full swing and hold it properly to bunt. Then he stepped back and watched—mostly lame attempts that landed somewhere between Jack and Daniel for what would have been an easy out at first base during a real game.

Roger Willingham was the first of the Brewster Academy boys to step into the batter's box, and Mikey could see Bishop, Jack and Daniel tense. Jack threw the first two balls wide but the third was right in the strike zone, and Roger didn't even try to bunt, just swung at it, a full roundhouse that caught a little piece of the ball and sent it foul along the baseline.

Before Bishop could dress him down, Roger mumbled, "I'm sorry. I didn't mean to do that. Toss me another one, and let me try again."

Jack started his windup. Only Mikey, Bishop and Daniel heard Roger mumble, "I'll get it right this time."

Bishop moved, like he was going to grab Roger or maybe knock him out of the box. But the ball was already in the air, and he was already swinging. The bat connected with the ball with a mighty crack. The ball whizzed past Jack's ear, a bullet five feet off the ground, a line drive into center field.

The outfield had been goofing off since bunting practice wasn't likely to send any balls their way. Joshua Harper saw the line drive coming, though, and went for it, running and diving, reaching out his gloved hand toward the ball.

The ball slammed square into the center of Josh's glove, forced his hand backward and snapped his wrist. Mikey had particularly keen vision and saw it, like in slow motion: the ball striking the glove, the glove bending backward from the blow, the hand inside the glove snapping off the wrist like a dry twig, leaving the hand dangling from Josh's arm, connected only by tissue and tendons. Josh crashed to the ground with his gloved hand under him. Didn't even cry out until he rolled over and saw his hand bent crooked. Then he began to scream.

Mikey wasn't the only one who saw what really happened. Others did, too, but they couldn't translate what they'd seen into any frame of reference they had. Nobody could aim a ball like firing a bullet the way Roger had done; nobody could hit a ball so hard it would break the arm of whoever tried to catch it. So when somebody yelled that Josh had fallen on his wrist and broken it, even the ones who'd actually witnessed what happened up close altered their memories to match that explanation. Yeah, that's what they'd seen. Joshua Harper fell on his wrist and broke it.

Mikey, Jack, Daniel and Bishop knew their eyes hadn't lied. They also knew Roger's aim had been a little off. If it had flown true, the baseball would have smashed into Jack's face. His head would have snapped off his neck like Joshua's hand off his wrist.

~

2011

Ever since the meeting with the agent from the Bureau of Alcohol, Tobacco and Firearms, Jack had been stifling an almost uncontrollable desire to do something violent—hit something or throw something or go beat the crap out of somebody with a pool cue. But Crock's voice mail was almost as satisfying as beating the crap out of somebody.

So the guy who helped a demon kill the Cohens was also involved in the plot to frame Daniel.

"Booyah!" he said aloud.

When he got back to the station that evening after chasing down Bosko's buddies—none of whom were even remotely helpful—Ramirez, Samuels and Peterson greeted him at the door as they were going out. Cool. Reserved. The sergeant who'd lead them on dozens of SWAT calls—not the least of which was to cap a school shooter—was not the man they'd believed him to be. Apparently, they'd drunk the Kool-Aid, believed the story that he'd helped burn down a nursing home with all the old people locked inside. And he couldn't tell them it wasn't true because maybe it was.

Crock was seated behind his desk, chewing on a cinnamon toothpick, rubbing his bloodshot eyes.

"I've been bird hunting," Jack said, "chasing wild geese."

"How'd it go with the agent from—"

"I don't want to talk about it," Jack said, cutting him off. "What'd you find out?"

Crocker looked at him for a long moment, then let it drop.

"Did you hear there was a shooting at the residence of one Edgar Wallace Boskowitz this afternoon?" Crock asked. "Attempted murder of a police officer definitely violates his parole. Which makes him a fugitive. Which means we not only have the legal right but the responsibility to look under every rock in Webster County to find him—a task that will be assigned to Sergeant Jack Carpenter…at my discretion, of course."

"Shooting? Were you—?"

"A search of his apartment turned up an envelope full of money, twenty crisp one-thousand-dollar bills, stuffed under his mattress."

"Clever hiding place."

"There's more. How about I hit the high points? After four hours of staring at security camera footage, a couple of critical synapses are about to misfire and leave me in a coma."

Crock said he'd gone from Bosko's apartment to the Centurion Hotel.

"We're assuming Bosko erased Monday's footage in that elevator and hallway because he and Lily practiced her little dance in it that day—right? But would he bother to erase Monday's film on all the other cameras in the building, too?"

He hadn't. Crock found several cameras with shots of

Lily or Bosko—separately. But only the parking garage camera showed the two of them together, and the lighting was bad, the picture particularly grainy. They stepped out of the building, looked around the area by the door as if they were searching for something and then exited in different directions.

"So I figured—if Bosko's in this with Lily, doesn't it make sense he was the one who provided the necessary black eye, split lip and broken nose? And where better to provide it than in a dark parking garage?"

Sure enough, only minutes after the seven forty-eight time stamp on the elevator camera, Lily emerged from the building into the parking garage. She looked around, then stepped into the shadows behind a concrete piling by the door. A couple of minutes later, she reappeared, staggering, her hands on her face. After she went back into the building, Bosko came out from behind the piling and hurried away. A few minutes after that, a black car with Bosko at the wheel pulled in range of the camera and then drove out of the garage.

"I know what a fan you are of still frames from a surveillance camera," Crock said, and Jack scowled at him. "So I had these made especially for you." He picked up a folder off his desk. "First, let me tell you what I didn't get." He pulled a picture from the folder showing a woman coming out of the building. But her head was down and turned so her long hair covered her face. "You can't tell that Lily's face is unmarked when she came out of the building, though it's pretty clear she was a hurtin' turkey when she went back in. So none of this clears Daniel."

Jack again felt the desire to hit somebody with a pool cue.

"There's more, though. I started doing the math. Theresa got to the Cohen's between six-thirty and seven.

Bosko had to be in that parking garage to rearrange Lily's face after she ambushed Daniel—who was scheduled to speak at eight. So Bosko was cutting it close."

Jack began to connect the dots, and his heart kicked into a gallop.

"And you figure he might not have had time—"

"To drop off his passenger." Crock dealt the final picture. It was a blow-up of the black car exiting the garage. A shadowy shot of the person in the backseat of the vehicle. Might not have been conclusive on anybody less distinctive, but the scar was clearly visible. It was Chapman Whitworth.

"Before you start throwing confetti and making a mess everywhere, you need to know I saved the best for last. That envelope full of money they found under Bosko's mattress—I got the FBI to do a quick run on it for prints. And, by the way, I've leveraged every relationship I have in the whole federal building. If you want me to work any more magic with them, we're going to have to sacrifice a chicken.

"They found two clear set of prints. Ran them both through NCIC, and it only coughed out Bosko, nobody else. Then I told them to run the not-Bosko prints through the military database." Crock sat back and sucked on his cinnamon toothpick. "Two people touched the envelope I dug out of R2D2's gullet this afternoon. One was Bosko. The other was former U.S. Army Lieutenant Colonel— and you'll-have-to-go-through-me hero—Chapman Wainwright Whitworth."

"Booyah," Jack said softly. He was silent for a moment, adding it all up in his head. "So we can prove Bosko and Lily Saunders were in on something together. We can prove Whitworth paid Bosko for something and that they were together the night both crimes were committed. But right now we can't prove Bosko has done anything except try to ventilate a police officer. Not a speck of evidence to put him at the Cohens' house or link him to Lily's murder."

"Unless we can dangle immunity, get him to talk."

"We have to find him first."

Chapter Twenty-Four

2011

Jack sat in the dark in his living room, staring out a curtain-less window at the cratered face of the moon, at stars as big as ice chips and twice as cold. He wanted a drink and that was scary. He could see himself becoming a hard drinker—defined as a man who drank to help himself cope—who slid down the slippery slope into alcoholism. A drunk was, after all, a man who drank because he couldn't cope.

He'd dreamed of fire every night since he saw the surveillance video of a kid in a baseball shirt with "Carpenter" written on the back carry a can of gasoline up the front steps and into Twin Oaks Nursing Home. They weren't narrative dreams, at least not that he could remember. Just images, flashes, and then he'd wake up panting, drenched in sweat.

He'd watched the video—what? A dozen times? Two dozen?—and the sight of his younger self walking up those steps had torn something loose inside him, some mooring of self-image that had held who he was snugly together. He could feel it there with every breath, flapping in the breeze, getting more and more tattered until eventually there'd be nothing left but rags.

Bottom line: he must have helped the Bad Kids burn down that nursing home. What other explanation was there?

Bottom-er line, if there was such a thing: he couldn't prove to himself or to anybody else that he didn't because he flat-out didn't know.

ATF Agent McCarthy had not been satisfied with the I-can't-remember answer to every question. A narrow-shouldered, bespectacled little man carrying a file as big as a Merriam-Webster Dictionary, he'd sneered when Jack said he'd forgotten that whole summer.

"That's convenient," he'd said, and it was clear he hadn't come to find out what had happened. He'd already made up his mind what had happened. He had come to see that "justice was done."

He'd done most of the talking, much of it about the "thorny legal issues to resolve" because Jack had been a juvenile "at the time he committed the crime." But his final words had been strangely devoid of the sarcasm that had slathered everything else he'd said.

"You do know, don't you, that Kentucky is a death penalty state? Oh, nobody's going to put a needle in your arm. You were twelve years old."

He leaned closer.

"But you won't skate on this one, either—not when more than a hundred helpless old people burned to death while their families watched. The wheels of justice grind slowly, Sergeant Carpenter, but they grind exceedingly fine. It will take a while, but eventually you will pay for what you did that day. With your career, your reputation—maybe even a wrongful death lawsuit that'll take everything you own."

A little smile had flirted with the corners of his mouth.

"And if we get reeeeal lucky, a jury in Caverna County, Kentucky, might just lock you up for the rest of your life."

~

2011

United States Senator Richard Thomas LaHayne looked like he'd come late when body parts were distributed and had been constructed from whatever happened to be left over in the garage. Nothing seemed to match. Tall, with thin arms and legs that would have given him a terrific jump shot if lifting his body off the ground hadn't required lifting his torso, which was roughly the size and shape of a propane tank. His head was disproportionately large, pumpkin-esque, balanced on a pencil neck in which an Adams apple bobbed up and down like a cork on a fishing line.

The man certainly didn't have the most powerful office in the world within his grasp based on his looks. And you knew that wasn't the case as soon as he fixed his eyes on you—charcoal gray, the color of ashes in ice, and there was a spark in them sometimes like the glint of sunlight on a gun barrel.

The eyes were nestled in a delicate spider web of smile wrinkles, in a face so oddly kind and wise that the good in his heart instantly called out to whatever was good in yours.

Five minutes in his presence and you understood how he'd won landslide victories three times to become the senior senator from the state of Ohio, how he had risen through the ranks of power in the power broker capital of the world, how he had bargained and compromised, stood firm and given in with a kind of life rhythm to it.

Ten minutes in his presence and you understood that behind that kindly exterior existed a brilliant mind, a man who was as tough as boot leather and utterly fearless. A man who could beat you up with his furrowed brow and bushy eyebrows. A man who did not suffer fools well and did not tolerate unscrupulous behavior in any form—an unheard-of trait for a politician.

Half an hour in his presence and you knew you would be wise indeed to shoot absolutely straight with this man because he would know instantly if you didn't. And you would be foolish indeed to cross him because retribution would be swift and sure if you did.

Jack and Daniel spent more than half an hour with Senator LaHayne, and both would later say that they had come to the man to give something to him but had left with the sense that they'd gotten more than they gave, though they couldn't have articulated what that was.

They had been outrageously lucky—"Luck don't have nothin' to do with it!" Theresa had said—to get time with the senator. His calendar was booked somewhere into the next decade, but he was from Cleveland and his daughter's early labor had called him home and cleared his schedule. Somehow Jeff had tracked all that down and worked magic to wedge them in.

They met the senator in a small parlor off the maternity waiting room of St. Barnabas Hospital in Cleveland, where he was awaiting the birth of his first grandchild, a boy, he told them, who would be named after his grandfather.

"I'm old school. I prefer the days when you didn't know if a baby was a boy or a girl until you examined their body parts naked after they were born." His voice had a pleasant, gravelly quality to it, and he peered at them over the top of rimless Ben Franklin glasses. "Anymore, that's about the only surefire way to tell if somebody's a boy or a girl. And sometimes even that doesn't work. You didn't hear that, by the way, because I didn't say it."

The senator looked at his watch. "You've got however long it takes that little boy to make it into the world—give or take a potty break or two. My son says I can trust Jeff that it really is important that I hear what you have to say. Still, I'm telling you that two words got you here today. Chapman Whitworth. And whatever it is you have to say, I would bet Aunt Josie's bloomers he is not happy that you're here saying it."

"Chapman Whitworth doesn't know we're here," Daniel said.

The senator chuckled mirthlessly.

"This is an election year, son. Everybody knows who talks to everybody—when, where and for how long. Maybe not what's discussed, but that something was. Your something is about Chapman Whitworth. What is it?"

Then he settled back in a chair as if he were totally relaxed, chatting with old friends. Only the absolute fixed attention in his gray eyes gave away his concentration.

Jack and Daniel had talked on the drive to Cleveland about what they were going to say and had come up with a plausible, step-by-step explanation. But when Jack opened his mouth to begin that explanation, those words weren't what came out of it.

"He's evil," Jack said simply. "Pure evil. But you already know that part, don't you, senator."

The man seemed to skip a breath. That and a blink were his only reactions. "I do."

"And you're fighting so hard to keep him from being

confirmed because you know that."

"I am."

"But that's all you know, which is why you've never been able to give any definitive reasons—to the committee or the press or anybody else—for opposing him."

There was a beat of silence before the senator spoke slowly. "It is."

The senator sat forward in the chair, the better to fix Jack and Daniel with the penetrating look for which he was so famous, the look opponents feared and friends respected. "You boys want to tell me why you believe he's evil?"

"Does that matter?" Jack couldn't believe he'd said that. Daniel was looking at him like he'd grown a third eye in the middle of his forehead. "In total honesty, senator—"

"Nobody's totally honest, son. Don't make a promise you can't keep."

"I may not be a totally honest man, but what I am about to tell you is the honest truth: you don't want to how we know what kind of man Chapman Whitworth is. A very wise woman named Theresa Washington told me once, 'You can't unknow the truth. Once you know it, you're responsible from then on for doing something about it.'"

"Are you a spiritual man, son?"

The question caught Jack totally off guard and he dodged it. "Daniel here is a minister. He's the pastor of—"

"I didn't ask about Daniel. I asked about you. Are you a spiritual man?"

That was tough. He could bluff or blow smoke or… "Yes, I suppose I am, but not because I want to be. Not because I want to have anything to do with any of this." He hadn't meant to sound so angry, but it had come out that way, and it was honest. "I don't have any choice.

Given what I know, what I've seen…you can't unknow the truth."

"I respect that. I'm not sure I'd call myself a spiritual man, either."

"Sir," Daniel spoke then, winging it, just like Jack was. They hadn't come within rock-throwing distance of what they'd intended to say since the first words out of Jack's mouth. "You don't have to know all that we do to understand what's happening, to believe us. And it's better for you if you don't know."

They were in a kind of dance, each of them saying much more than his actual words conveyed and each understanding far more than what he heard.

"Ever heard of the Reverend Eli Pendleton?" the senator asked. Daniel nodded; Jack shook his head. "He was my grandfather. I bet you didn't know that." The senator could see the reference was lost on Jack.

"Eli Pendleton was a missionary to the Aweti tribe in the Brazilian rainforest in the 1930s. Lived in their huts, loved them, served them, sacrificed for them, and one day they turned on him. They beat him until he was unrecognizable. They broke both arms and both legs. They cut off his fingers. And then his toes. And then his…After that, they dumped him naked into a canoe and shoved it out into the river. It was a miracle he survived."

Jack couldn't help gasping. From the look on Daniel's face, he had known something about the man, but not that part.

"My grandfather was…I've always had trouble tacking words on to it. That man was…holy. Good in a way people just aren't good. At least, not anymore. I was only around him a few times, maybe spent a total of a week of my life in his presence. But when he touched me, put his hand on my head to ruffle my hair"—the senator reached up and rubbed his bald head—"and I did have hair once! Or when he held me in his lap, I could see his goodness, a bright light that shone in his eyes. Like looking at the sun—the spots are still there even after you look away. It… changed me."

Jack and Daniel said nothing. Didn't move. Didn't breathe. The intensity of the man's words was mesmerizing. He had drawn the three of them into some special place, had wrapped a cloak of common understanding around them that bound them together and separated them from the rest of the world.

"Over the years, I have seen something like that light in other people. Not often. But sometimes. Only twice as bright as my grandfather's—the day Billy Graham shook my hand and the day an old woman working in a soup kitchen reached up and touched my cheek. I can see its absence, too. Not often. I shake a man's hand, and I can see when there is no light at all. Just empty, gray nothing. Fog and shifting shadows. A void."

He paused then, and his gaze seemed to drill all the way down to the bottom of Jack's soul. "But I have only once in my life seen actual darkness. Not the lack of light, but an entity in itself. A black thing. That was on the senate floor the day Chapman Whitworth came up to meet me after the president's nomination was announced. He put out his hand to shake, and he held mine a beat too long. He knew that I saw. And he was glad."

The three of them sat in silence then, time suspended. Senator LaHayne sat slowly back in his chair and returned to the relaxed state that wasn't relaxed at all.

"All right. I don't need you to tell me how you know Chapman Whitworth is evil. I suspect I am better off not knowing. But you came here to tell me something I can use against him. What is it?"

They told him all the things they'd rehearsed telling him, the part that was finally what they'd agreed they'd say as they drove up Interstate 75 from Cincinnati. That Chapman Whitworth was trying to ruin them. That he had framed them. That he had hacked to death two harmless old people.

"This Bosko is the key," Jack said. "First we have to find him, and then we have to get him to talk. I don't want to mislead you, senator—both of those things are long shots. And even if we manage to pull it off, I know he's not exactly a credible witness. But back his story up with the case against him in Whitworth's court where the evidence disappeared, the surveillance footage that puts Whitworth in Bosko's car the night of the crimes and Whitworth's fingerprints on an envelope full of money found in Bosko's apartment, and I believe we could—at the very least—cast grave doubt that the man who's strutting his stuff to sit on the Supreme Court of the United States is who he claims to be, that he really isn't as squeaky clean as a new rubber duckie."

The senator turned away from them when they finished their explanations. He gazed out the window and said nothing, merely unconsciously entwined his fingers into "here's the church, here's the steeple, open it up and there's the people" over and over.

Then he turned back to them. He spoke the words softly but with an intensity that shouted so loud Jack's ears rang from the sound.

"I've been grasping at straws…asking, pleading for something. You boys are my answer. You're all I have, but apparently you're all I need. The hearings start Friday. That gives you six days. You go out there and get me evidence—you hear me! And I will bury Chapman Whitworth with it."

Chapter Twenty-Five

1985

It had taken some doing for Becca to talk Jack and Daniel into hiking with her up to Red Rock, but she'd been cooped up in the house for so long she was desperate. Her father was almost never home and neither knew nor cared what she did or where she went—well, he'd never in a million years have let her set foot in Bishop and Theresa's house so she'd told him her weekly Bible study was at Reverend Burke's. Unfortunately, her father happened to be in town on Tuesday when all the bad things happened, and when he got home, he'd barked at her to "stay in the house," in that awful, gravelly voice she still hadn't adjusted to. He used to sound normal, sang along with country music songs on the radio. But the day after his birthday, he'd come home and couldn't talk at all. When his voice finally did come back, it was ragged and hoarse, and it had been that way ever since.

Jack and Daniel had left their bikes at the barn behind her house—the barn where they'd gone that night last winter to find out why everybody said drinking was so much fun and had gotten so hammered they'd had to spend the night there.

Daniel's was a standard ten-speed bike. Jack's was a strange-looking hybrid of the parts from several dead bikes. Both had racks extending out over the back bumper, space to carry the picka-nick basket and sometimes for Daniel to carry Jack when his old bike had a flat tire——which it often did. Neither of them had a bike as fine as Becca's——a real motor scooter with all the bells and whistles her father could lavish on it. He hadn't been home on the Christmas morning he gave it to her, but the housekeeper had shown her where to find it in the garage. Without their bikes, Jack, Daniel and Becca could never have become the Three Musketeers.

Little more than a stone's throw from each of their houses was the railroad. Tracks snaked through town and then crossed the river on a small trestle and cut a trail through the woods to a tunnel under the mountain behind Becca's house. The actual rails had been taken up years ago, but the smooth cindered track remained. Though a lot of geography separated them, they could all meet at any of their three houses in ten or fifteen minutes, depending on how fast they pedaled.

After they turned up an old logging road, overgrown and barely visible, Becca reached down and removed the leash from DD's collar, then watched in delight as he raced after a fluttering butterfly, then stopped to sniff every rock, branch, bush, stick, leaf or dirt pile they came to, his tail wagging so furiously it was only a blur of brown behind him.

"I wish I had a dog's nose," Daniel said.

"You'd look dopey," Jack said, "but we'd love you anyway."

"I mean I wish I could smell like a dog."

"Stinky fur and doggie breath? That 'love you anyway' thing—there are limits."

Becca couldn't hold on to her giggles. They were always like that, teasing and cutting up—but never mean, never hurtful. Just silly.

"I mean I wish I had the olfactory organs of a canine so I could discern a level of smell of which human beings are incapable—that get it?"

Though their manner with each other looked comfortable and easy on the outside, Becca could sense a strand of tension within that surprised and saddened her. There were things they couldn't—wouldn't—talk about, now. There never had been before.

Daniel was hopping from one slick rock to another in a creek, showing off, when he slipped and landed on his butt in the water—a dunking feat he'd been avoiding all day. That's when Becca noticed McDougal was missing.

"Dougal Dog," she called out. "Here, DD." She expected the dog to burst out of the bushes and come running. But he was nowhere around.

"We can see him from up there," Jack said, pointing to the crest of a hill up the trail from them.

Daniel was ahead and he suddenly stopped. Jack was behind him, still blocking her view. When Jack moved out of the way, all the air was sucked out of Becca's lungs as if somebody had punched her hard in the belly.

Standing beside a big rock next to the trail were Jacob and Victor. McDougal had bitten Victor that day in the woods, and now Victor had the dog clutched tight to his chest with his fingers around McDougal's snout to keep his mouth closed so he couldn't bark. Jacob's wasp demon was laughing maniacally. Victor's lizard-faced demon merely eyed her with lidless red eyes, flitting its forked tongue out of its mouth. From where she stood, she could smell the stench of brown goo that trailed from him and feel the icy blast of the cold that surrounded them.

She finally found enough air to cry out, "McDo!" and started toward them.

"I'd stay right where I was if I's you," said Jacob. "Wouldn't want anything bad to happen to your worthless mutt."

"Don't hurt DD."

"Give Becca back her dog," Jack said and started toward them.

"Say please," Victor said.

Jack ground his teeth together. "Please," he said.

"Ok, since you asked so nice—sure, we'll give him back to her."

Then Victor lifted the dog up, holding him in one hand by the neck. McDougal was wiggling frantically, squirming and whimpering, trying hard to break free.

"Here, you go," he shouted. "He's all yours."

Vic reached up and took the dog's head in both hands, then twirled the dog's body around it, the way you wring a chicken's neck.

Around and around the body went—once, twice—then Jacob snapped his wrist like popping a whip, and the dog's body flew out into the air and plopped into the dirt a few feet away. Dougie's legs were running…running, and then they were still. Blood gushed from the bloody hole above his shoulders where his head had been.

Becca let out a horrified wail, and Victor and Jacob turned and ran off into the woods. She knelt in the dirt beside DD's body and lifted him tenderly into her lap. Then she rocked back and forth, sobbing.

"It's my fault." Her anguished words were strangled by tears. "I shouldn't have let him out of my sight. All those other dogs, you know the Bad Kids killed them, too." She closed her eyes, felt the warmth of the animal in her lap and continued to sob.

Daniel knelt in the dirt beside her. "Becca, we need to go now," he said with great tenderness in his voice. "I'll—we'll—carry McDougal for you. Jack and I will dig a grave and we'll bury him."

"I shouldn't have let him off the leash. But he loves to run in the woods, and I never thought…"

She opened her eyes then, looked at her dog's bloody body, and then at the dog's head that Daniel was holding and burst into hysterical sobbing again, hugging the limp ball of fur in her arms and shaking her head.

"Dougie. Precious DD."

She felt Jack's hands on her shoulders. "We have to go," he said.

She knew he was right. Drawing in a shaky breath, she eased McDo's body out of her lap, and Jack helped her stand.

"We'll go to the sheriff now, the three of us. We have proof!" Daniel said.

But Becca knew nobody would believe a twelve-year-old boy could kill a dog that way. Any more than they'd believe a boy could pull a man's arms right off his body. Just snap. She was repulsed by the memory, horrified anew by the brutality. That was when she saw the Bad Kids at the foot of the hill. Jack saw them, too, and elbowed Daniel.

All six of the Bad Kids were there. They weren't looking at Jack and Daniel. They all were staring at her, their demons glaring, hatred distorting their already grotesque features, cold flowing from them in a wave. The combined force of their evil was a hammer blow that staggered her, left her alone and cowering. Mindless horror rose in her, threatening to tear loose every mooring she had to life in a world with sunshine and blue skies, and cast her out into a darkness so profound it had substance. She couldn't breathe or think, and she felt herself begin to slide . . .

Then there was warmth beside her, all around her. The warmth shoved the cold away, pushed it back as if it were a snowball on ice, and then wrapped itself snug around her. Becca felt like she'd been immersed in a sweet-smelling bath. Golden light shone, making the world beyond it look shadowy and unreal. There were gold sparkles floating in the light, and Becca longed to reach out and touch one, put it in her pocket and take it away to be with her always.

Becca felt a warm, soft hand take hers. She looked up then into beauty so pure it almost hurt to see it, into eyes the color of robins' eggs in a porcelain face, with black hair cascading down beneath a silly red-and-white striped hat.

"I said I'd come to hold your hand," the angel said, "so you wouldn't be afraid."

When the Bad Kids started up the hill toward them, Jack leaned close to Becca and spoke softly. "Danno and I are going to take them. When we jump them, you run as fast as you can all the way home. Don't look back until you get there."

"No," she said, then looked past him at the approaching evil that turned the very air black with its approach.

"I see you and I'm not afraid of you," she called out to the demons. "You don't have any power over me."

Jack and Daniel looked at her, uncomprehending. The Bad Kids stopped, motionless. The demons began to scream, cries of rage and hatred so ugly it would have savaged her ears to hear them, but the warm glow sealed her in.

Like Tupperware.

And the barrier it formed around her was impenetrable by six demons or a thousand demons or ten thousand demons.

"Really?" Jacob said. He reached down into a gunnysack he carried, pulled open the drawstrings, then flung the sack at her so that the contents came out in the air. "Not afraid of this?"

The snake landed in the dirt not three feet in front of Becca. The diamondback was huge, probably five feet long, and it curled instantly into position, its head in the middle of the coil, its tail sounding a rattling alarm as it drew back its whole upper body to strike.

Becca didn't flinch.

Tupperware.

"A rattlesnake?" Cole Stuart roared at Jacob, grabbed a handful of his shirt front and yelled in his face. "You stupid—"

The angel lifted her hand, causing the light that was fabric to shimmer, sparkling with a million tiny points of golden light. When she lifted her hand, the snake also lifted off the ground. The six boys started backing up as soon as the snake began to rise. When they turned and ran down the hill toward the woods, the angel made a slight gesture with her raised hand and flung the snake into the air after them. It hit the ground with a plop and slithered quickly into the undergrowth.

2011

Daniel held his cell phone against his ear with his shoulder so he could use both hands to turn the newspaper page to the jump from the front-page story. Jack picked up as Daniel was composing the message he was going to put on Jack's voice mail.

"You do know what time it is," Jack grumbled.

"This morning's Enquirer has a story about Senator LaHayne and Chapman Whitworth."

"Read it to me. I don't get the paper." Jack was fully awake now.

Daniel began to read.

A reliable source inside the office of U.S. Senator Thomas LaHayne revealed yesterday that the senator intends to present evidence—

"Evidence?" Jack was incredulous.

—at next week's confirmation hearings that Supreme Court candidate Chapman Whitworth has committed grave improprieties. The source said that the senator, who has long opposed Whitworth's confirmation, will provide documentation—"

"Documentation?"

"Stop repeating everything I say, Jack. You sound like a parrot."

"We don't have documentation!" Jack was practically shouting.

"Don't shoot the messenger. Shut up and listen to the rest of it."

The rest of the story said that the senator had only just come into possession of the material regarding Whitworth and that the information would kill his chances of being confirmed.

"Why would the senator put out a story like that when he knows we don't have any proof?" Jack said.

"How do you know the senator leaked the story to the press?"

"What, you think Whitworth did it—went rushing to the media because his reputation is whiter than a virgin's wedding dress and he couldn't wait to spill punch all over it?"

"Well, the boring confirmation hearings just went from a ho-hum story to front page above the fold," Daniel said.

Jack sighed. "Apparently, all this is part of the senator's plan."

"It's part of somebody's plan."

Chapter Twenty-Six

2011

When Theresa heard the name "Chapman Whitworth," she whirled around and looked at the screen. Then she went to the set and turned up the volume and sank down in Bishop's favorite chair to watch.

It was a news show, the kind of thing they used to fill up Sunday morning programming when wasn't nobody interested in watching television.

"We have invited Mr. Whitworth to join us here on Meet the Press this morning," said the talking head in a suit, "in light of the allegations against him coming out of Senator Thomas LaHayne's office yesterday."

"I don't know what I can say in my own defense since the senator has never said what it is he thinks I've done," Whitworth said.

The talking head opened his mouth to speak again, but Whitworth kept talking, looking right into the camera, speaking slowly and distinctly. "This has to be some misunderstanding. Senator LaHayne opposes my nomination. I don't know why that is, but it is certainly his right to do so."

Theresa leaned in toward the striking, square-jawed man with a scar on his face who was speaking so sincerely to her.

"But the senator is a good man, an honorable man who has served our common state of Ohio with integrity and a humble spirit for almost three decades. Someone has misled him. He would not, he is not capable of, making something up out of whole cloth."

Obviously, he was telling the truth, and Theresa admired his generous spirit, that he would speak so highly of a political opponent. She felt the confidence he exuded, and it buoyed her up, carried her along in a sense that no matter what happened to be going wrong at that minute, everything was going to be fine in the end. He would see to it that it was.

"My reputation is absolutely clean, my conscience clear, so I have nothing to fear from the senator or anybody else. But I would stake that reputation right now on the senator's honor. He is a deceived man, not a dishonest or malicious one."

Theresa heard a noise behind her, only a little squeak, and turned to see Becca staring in wide-eyed horror at the television screen. As soon as Theresa looked away from it and was no longer paying attention to Whitworth's voice, her impression of him changed, and he didn't seem capable and sincere and honest at all! She was shocked by how completely she'd been taken in. His voice, more than mesmerizing, stronger than hypnotic, was the voice that had spoken to Eve in the Garden.

Becca's face was white, contorted in an expression of such terror and loathing her features were almost unrecognizable. She'd been doing better. In the week she'd been staying in the spare room in Theresa's basement, she had lost some of that hollow-eyed, haunted look. She was clean —still too thin, but Theresa thought she might be putting on a little weight. She still wasn't beautiful like she'd been before, and maybe she never would be again. She had the fragile quality she'd had as a child, though, like she was a porcelain doll that was in danger any moment of shattering into a thousand pieces.

And in the next few moments, that's exactly what she did.

Theresa instantly understood Becca's reaction. She'd responded like Andi had when she'd seen the man on television. But Becca was way more profoundly affected than Andi'd been. Neither had ever met Chapman Whitworth, but Becca had met the monster that controlled him.

THE BEAST FIXED lidless eyes on her and spoke to Becca out of the mouth of the scar-faced man on the television screen.

"I am so glad to see you again. I've been looking everywhere for you. Why haven't you come when I summoned?"

The questions were innocent, spoken in a soft voice that had a bit of an edge to it, a purr, like the sound you can barely hear when you pull velvet slowly through your fingers. But the words tore at her ears like clawed beasts, ripping at the insides of them until blood ran out and down the side of her neck. They resounded in her head like a gong, so loud the vibration shook her skull, and the pain of it, slamming into the insides of her head was excruciating. But she could only whimper as blood began to run out her nose and down her lip.

Her diaphragm banged against the hard edge of the terror in her chest like waves against the rocks on the shore. A black frame appeared around what she could see, and it began to close, leaving a smaller and smaller field of vision. She knew that when the frame closed all the way, when it banged shut with a clang like a jail cell, she would be trapped in total darkness with the monster who was made out of hate. And he would feast on her, gorge his belly full of the pieces of her body.

A face appeared between her and the face of the beast. A black face and it got closer and closer, filling her vision. The lips on the face moved, though she could not make out the words spoken, drowned out as they were by a sound like pounding surf in her ears. She felt hands on her shoulders, and from a great distance she heard a voice calling her name. "Becca! Becca!"

Becca dropped to her knees and curled up in a fetal position, whimpering. Then he came. He reached out of the screen and touched her. It touched her—pure evil, as silky smooth as the belly of a spider.

She began to scream.

THERESA CALLED OUT TO BECCA, but the girl didn't respond, then she collapsed on the floor and began to scream. The look of absolute terror on that child's face like to broke Theresa's heart.

Theresa didn't know if that demon really was reaching out to Becca in some way and tormentin' her soul or if it was Becca herself, reliving what happened or imagining things that wasn't real—awful thoughts coming from a mind that had been beat very nearly all the way to death with evil.

Easing her bulk down onto the floor beside Becca, Theresa patted her back. Wasn't nothing else she could do. And as she sat soothing the horrified girl, Theresa came to understand some things.

Chapman Whitworth had a power she hadn't counted on. Somehow he'd wielded it even on her. His voice had been hypnotizing, paralyzing that day in Miss Minnie and Mr. Gerald's parlor. But she'd heard it for what it was, then — pure evil, wrapped in a pleasant baritone. Now, the evil was hidden, cloaked in sincerity, and all the power was channeled into persuasion, control. When he spoke, it was like you had to believe what he was telling you. Afterward, when he wasn't talkin' no more, you could look back and not even be able to figure out what it was he'd said that you'd so totally bought into. At least Theresa could do that. But could other people? Did some people still believe him even after he quit talkin'? She bet they did, some of 'em. A lot of 'em. And that was a terrible thing, maybe the terrible-est thing of all.

But there still was something Theresa couldn't figure out, a niggling itch that wouldn't leave her alone. Why would a demon as powerful as an efreet settle for taking a position as one of nine justices on the Supreme Court? Powerful as a judge might be, he wasn't in charge of nothin' his own self. That didn't stack up with what she knew about demons.

The next morning when Theresa went down to call Becca to breakfast, the girl was gone. Theresa wasn't really surprised by that. Sad, but not surprised.

"Where'd she go?" Jack wanted to know when she called and told him about it.

"Out there, I suppose. Another little minnow being carried along by the current."

"No telling how long it'll take for us to find her again."

"What for? She'll just run off again if we do."

"But she and Daniel and I...somehow the three of us have to..."

His voice trailed off. Yes, indeed, somebody was going to have to find that efreet, wherever it had secreted itself like a dung beetle in a hole, and send it packing. It wouldn't be Becca, though. Theresa already knew how this was gonna shake out, and she figured the others did, too, if they'd ever let their minds go there. When it came time to go up against that monster evil, Andi would take Becca's place.

~

1985

Jack leaned his bike next to Daniel's against the mailbox post in front of Bishop's house. They hadn't called to tell him they were coming, to ask if they could come. Hadn't even discussed it with each other. It was like that all the time. He'd think something, look over and see Daniel was thinking the same thing. After they'd carried McDougal out of the woods to Becca's house, dug a hole in the ground beside her rose garden and buried the dog, they'd gotten on their bikes and started back to town. When they got to Daniel's house, he didn't stop, just kept riding toward Bishop's. That was it.

If Bishop was dismayed to see them, he hid it well. At least they weren't interrupting a basketball game. Bishop was a Chicago Bulls fan, had bent Jack's ear during the whole season about one of their new players, a guy named

Michael Jordan--but the Bulls had gotten beat in the playoffs.

Bishop greeted them at the door with a solemn but not disapproving face, showed them into the living room and asked if they wanted anything to drink.

"I'll fetch two glasses of lemonade with lots of ice," Theresa said, without waiting for their replies. "See if I can rustle up some blueberry muffins. I made some for breakfast, and if Bishop didn't gobble the lot of them, I'll warm 'em up in the oven for you."

"What's happened?" Bishop asked as she turned to leave. There was the slightest hesitation, like maybe she'd stop, sit down and listen to their story. But then she continued into the kitchen and left the three alone in the living room. "Ain't nobody hurt, is they?"

"Becca's dog's dead. The Bad Kids killed it," Daniel told him.

"And Becca...?"

"Just the dog. Becca's fine."

"No, she's not," Jack said. "She couldn't be fine. She watched them murder her dog and then we helped her bury it. How could she be fine?"

He and Daniel had taken turns carrying the dog's body out of the woods and digging its grave. Once they'd covered the grave with dirt, tamped it firmly down with the shovel, they'd stood together, silent.

Then Becca had turned to Daniel. "Would you...say something?" Her trembling voice had threatened to break down into sobbing.

Daniel had begun to speak. His voice was strong, but gentle and kind, too. Jack couldn't remember now what he'd said, only that he'd thought while Daniel was talking that he'd never again in his life have a friend as good as Daniel Burke.

"Tell me what happened," Bishop said. "All of it. Don't leave out nothin'."

Theresa came and went during the telling, bringing lemonade and near the end of the story, warm blueberry muffins that smelled delicious. But Jack and Daniel didn't touch them, and they sat on a plate on the coffee table, getting cold again as Daniel told Bishop what Becca had said, and Jack described the rattlesnake rising in the air and flying toward the retreating boys.

"That all of it?" Bishop asked.

The boys nodded.

Bishop sat back. He'd been leaned toward the boys as they talked, sitting side by side on the couch facing him. Now, he settled back into the chair.

"You boys need to go wash your hands," he said.

That was when Jack realized his hands were covered with dried dog blood and the dirt of McDougal's grave. "Then come on back in here and eat them muffins and drink that lemonade Theresa fixed for you. You're gone need to listen close to what I'm 'bout to tell you."

When the story came, told in Bishop's deep rumble, Jack was so stunned by the revelations that some essential part of him pushed back from the reality and stood outside, watching the two boys and the big man from a distance. He could only catch pieces of what was said. Those fragments were what Jack took away with him, images and scenes dangling and frayed on the ends.

The six Bad Kids were...possessed by demons. And Becca could see them.

Then Jack was yanked back into his own mind like he'd been pulled by an overextended rubber band. Bishop's words sucked all the oxygen out of the room, and Jack was no longer an observer.

"Isaac had the knowing, too," Bishop said. Jack

stopped breathing. "Boy had it strong, strong as my Grampa Rufus." Bishop's voice thickened and sank almost to whisper. "I need *my son*. The two of us together…but it's just me now. Just me."

And that was Jack's fault. Whatever had happened to Isaac, it was Jack's fault.

Chapter Twenty-Seven

2011

Daniel sat in his office, his morning coffee bitter in his mouth, Andi's words when he'd tucked her in bed last night ringing in his head.

"Daddy, what does rape mean?"

By the casual way she dropped the bombshell, he knew she had no idea what she was asking.

"Why do you want to know?" he said, stalling.

"Bethany said at school today that you did that—the rape thing—and that her mommy said you should be arrested and put in jail. What does it mean?""

"Well, I didn't," Daniel said, reeling, trying not to stammer. "Do the...that. So the word doesn't mean anything at all."

"But what—?"

"Enough talk now. Time for sleep. Don't forget you have a piano lesson after school tomorrow."

That did it. Andi went off on how much she hated piano lessons and forgot all about the word. This time.

So what do I tell her when I am arrested? What happens to Andi if I go to prison?

His phone rang. He saw the unfamiliar number and almost didn't answer it. How could a reporter have gotten his cell phone number? It rang again. He told himself to relax, probably a telemarketer and hey, you never knew when you were going to need a not-a-slicer, not-a-dicer, cutter-upper, chipper-chopper available for the next thirty seconds for a mere nine, ninety-nine, ninety-nine.

The call wasn't a slicer-dicer.

"Please hold for Senator LaHayne," a woman's voice said into his ear, and he spent an uncomfortable minute or two trying to figure out what the senator wanted, given that the hearings began tomorrow, and they had nothing.

Jack and Crock had worked all but nonstop ever since Senator LaHayne issued his "get me proof" directive, and the two police officers had amassed a wealth of information about a certain Edgar Wallace Boskowitz. They knew just about everything there was to know, in fact, except where he was.

Suddenly, the senator's pleasant gravel voice spoke into Daniel's ear.

"Daniel, I want you to come to Washington. Now. Today."

"Excuse me?"

"It's all arranged. My secretary will give you the details. There will be a car waiting for you at Dulles and we'll meet tonight in my office."

"Why do you want me in Washington, sir?"

"Jack doesn't have anything, and we're out of time. I need you to help me implement Plan B."

~

"YOU READY, HONEY?" Mrs. Beavers called up the stairs. "Don't forget your music."

As she tied the shoestrings of her bright-red Converse sneakers, Andi tried to come up with any possible way to get out of going. She could pretend to have a stomachache. But there was pink stuff in a bottle in the medicine cabinet that Mrs. Beavers thought would cure anything. Andi bet if she broke her leg, Mrs. Beavers would try to force some of that Pepto Bizzard down her throat.

She decided she'd rather go to the piano lesson than swallow that nasty pink stuff.

Mrs. Powell's house was only a couple of blocks from Andi's. As she walked down the sidewalk toward it, Andi thought about last night when Daddy said the rape word didn't mean anything but she knew it did, too. Something really bad or why would they put you in jail for doing it? She hadn't told Daddy how Bethany and Sophia had taunted her, calling her "Jailbird! Jailbird!" Today in school, she'd told her teacher she had a headache during recess so she wouldn't have to go out on the playground and hear them chanting.

Was Daddy really going to jail?

Her stomach yanked into a knot, like it'd felt when Daddy told her Becca had left. She heard Daddy tell Miss Theresa on the phone that "Andi took the news pretty well," but the truth was Andi was devastated. Becca gone, too. Just like Mommy. She wasn't dead like Mommy, but if she never came back, she might as well be.

Andi's world was crumbling around her, and she couldn't do anything to hold it together.

Her shoe came untied, and when she knelt to tie it, she noticed a man lounging against a tree next to a white van parked at the curb half a block away. He looked familiar. Where had she seen—?

Dreadlock Man! The man from her dream, her vision. What was he doing here?

Her heart began to pound painfully. The vision hadn't been scary, but she was afraid now all the same. She didn't want to be anywhere near Dreadlock Man or any of the other men she'd seen. What should she do?

Run home! Run!

She dropped her music on the sidewalk and bolted back down the street the way she'd come. She thought she saw Dreadlock Man move away from the tree as she turned, but she couldn't be sure, and she wasn't going to look back now to find out. She ran as fast as she could down the block, made it to the Henderson's house on the corner and cut across their yard and around their hedge. She burst out on the sidewalk on the other side and bumped into a man with a cell phone to his ear headed in the opposite direction. She hit him hard, and he grunted, reached out his hand to steady her so she wouldn't fall down.

"Whoa," he said. "Jew need to be a leetle more careful—"

Speedy Gonzales.

Instead of letting her go, his fingers tightened around her arm, but she wrenched free. He grabbed for her, and she kicked him in the shin as hard as she could—wished she'd had on boots instead of sneakers—then darted out of his reach and ran back toward the Henderson's house.

She hadn't thought to scream, but right now she was so scared and winded, she didn't have enough air to scream. The Hendersons would help her. They'd call the police.

A white van—the one she'd seen parked near Dreadlock Man—whipped into the Henderson's driveway and blocked her path. She dodged around it as the driver's door flew open, and Dreadlock Man leapt out and almost tackled her. She dodged his grasp and bolted up onto the Henderson's porch and banged on the door.

"Let me in," she cried. "Help me."

She sensed rather than heard the two men closing in on her, coming up the sidewalk.

"Help me, please," she cried and banged hard enough to rattle the stained glass in the inset on the door. "Hel—"

A big hand fastened over her mouth and cut off her words. Big fingers dug into the flesh of her upper arm. She found the air to scream then, shrieked, but the sound was too muffled to be heard. The man behind her yanked her backward off balance, then half carried, half dragged her kicking and struggling to the open back doors of the van.

When he took his hand off her mouth, Dreadlock Man hissed, "Keep quiet." But apparently he saw her take in a huge breath to scream again because he hit her.

No one in her life had ever struck Andi. She didn't know whether or not her parents even believed in spanking because she'd always been a good girl, didn't talk back or disobey—the things other kids did to get spanked.

The force of the slap snapped her head violently to the left, and she would have staggered and fallen if the man hadn't picked her up into his arms like she didn't weigh anything at all, tossed her into the van, hopped in behind her and slammed the door shut. Then the van reversed, whipped a turn and sped off down the street, leaving one red high-top Converse sneaker behind in the Henderson's driveway.

~

1985

Today was picture day. A photographer from Turner's Photo had shown up as Bishop was getting out of the car. He said he wanted to take the individual photos first. Each boy was s'posed to have two poses from several different angles. When he was finished with the individual shots, he'd arrange them boys the way he wanted for the team picture.

"I'd like to get the individual shots over there in front of that tree, use it as a background," Matt Turner said, pointing to a majestic maple tree on the far side of the parking lot.

Bishop looked around. Daniel had started to suit up in his catcher's uniform, pads and face mask. His mother had dropped him off on her way to have his little sister's ears pierced. Several other boys was playing catch or switching into they team jersey T-shirts. But Mikey wasn't here. Hard to figure that boy not being here. Even more concernin'—Jack wasn't here neither. And not one of the Bad Kids and they monsters was anywhere to be seen.

Bishop told the boys to go on with Mr. Turner across the parking lot to the tree to get they pictures took. Daniel started to go with them, but Bishop put his hand on the boy's shoulder and asked if he'd seen Jack this morning. He hadn't.

They both heard Mikey calling before they saw him, huffing and puffing down the woods trail toward them, his fat face beet red, his breathing coming in gasps. "Coach…" Gasp. "Washington! You gotta…" Gasp. "Help Jack."

He practically fell on his face at their feet and had to catch his breath enough to speak. When he did, it come out so fast it sounded like a woodpecker tapping on a tree.

"Heard them in the woods, beating up Jack so I hid,

and then Jacob had a knife and wanted to cut Jack's ears off, but Cole wouldn't let him because they had a job to do and that would bring the police—"

"Where's Jack?" Bishop demanded.

"Up in a tree. They stuck a screwdriver in his leg and then threw him up into a tree. I'll show you."

Mikey started running back up the trail, fast for a kid his size, with Bishop and Daniel behind him.

When Bishop seen Jack, sprawled on his belly across a big limb that must have been twenty feet off the ground, he called out to him.

"Jack, you all right, son?"

"I can't get down," he said, his voice raw. "And my leg…"

"What do you mean they stuck a screwdriver in his leg," Daniel asked Mikey.

"A Phillips head. Cole stuck it on his shin and then began grinding it into the bone."

Bishop felt a flash of hot rage wash over him. "You hang on now, boy. We gone get you down."

He boosted Daniel up into the tree to help Jack, and in a few minutes Jack was on the ground, pulling up his pants leg to examine the small hole in his right shin. It was red and swollen, but didn't look like it was paining Jack nearly as much as it must have been.

"Cole said nobody'd know, that it'd look like I banged my shin on something," Jack said, his voice tight.

"Can you stand?" Bishop asked.

Jack got carefully to his feet with Daniel's help, then tested putting weight on his injured leg. It was clear the wound hurt somethin' fierce, but he managed to limp forward.

"Daniel, can you help Jack?" Bishop asked, and Daniel

draped Jack's arm around his shoulder and nodded. "Good, 'cause I got bidness to do!" Bishop turned and thundered off through the woods toward the baseball field.

Chapter Twenty-Eight

2011

When the flight attendant instructed the passengers to discontinue the use of all electronic devices, Daniel started to press the off button as a text pinged into his phone.

Again, he didn't recognize the number, though the area code was Kentucky.

The message said simply, "You give me back mine and I'll give you back yours."

What in the world could that mean? He mulled it over as the big jet lifted off the ground from the Cincinnati International Airport and pointed its nose eastward toward the coast.

You give me back mine, I'll give you back yours.

He'd borrowed a putter from Hugh Beddingfield a three-month lifetime ago, back when playing golf and other mindless activities filled up all the cracks of his mundane life. But Beddingfield didn't have anything of his to trade back, not that Daniel knew of.

What did Daniel have that belonged to somebody else, something they wanted back?

The punch in his gut was so painful he could not imagine that somebody hadn't kicked him in the belly. What did he have that somebody wanted back—Becca! At least Billy Ray thought he had her. And that meant…

It couldn't possibly be. No.

But it made such nauseating sense that he was afraid he was going to have to use the sick sack in the seat back pocket in front of him. He had Billy Ray's daughter, which meant Billy Ray…had his.

With trembling hands, he turned his phone back on. The flight attendant spotted him and leaned over to tell him, "I'm sorry, sir, but the use of cell phones is not permitted at any time during the flight."

He ignored her, punched messages as soon as the phone sprang to life.

Sure enough, the message he'd received a few minutes before read: "You give me back mine and I'll give you back yours."

He touched the number of the message.

"Sir, I have to ask you to turn that off. The use of cell phones can interfere with our navigational equipment."

Daniel had never believed that, by the way. He'd always suspected it was the one thing they'd thought up to say that would scare people into compliance. "Then you better hope the pilot can see the Washington Monument from here."

"Sir, I will have to inform…"

"Inform anybody you like. Do whatever it is you people do when you don't get your way. My little girl is in trouble, and I am making this call."

But he didn't make the call. He had no bars. No coverage.

He looked up pleadingly into the flight attendant's eyes.

"In-flight phones. You have those, don't you? I have to make this call."

"Some flights do but not this one."

As the plane passed over the Blue Ridge Mountains far below, he punched redial again and again and again, dozens, maybe hundreds of times. Just as the aircraft began its descent into Dulles, the call connected. Daniel was so surprised, he wasn't really prepared when Billy Ray answered on the second ring. But it didn't matter. Billy Ray was as chatty as he could be.

"Daniel. Wondered when you'd call. What took you so long?"

"Where is she? What have you done with my daughter?"

"Why, Daniel, I don't have any idea what in the world you might be talking about. All kind of folks could be listenin' in to what we say. Technology's like that these days. All I done was text you about that grubbing hoe you borrowed. You remember. I found a baby chick belongs to you, and I was thinkin' we might make a swap…your chick for my hoe."

"Billy Ray, if you hurt…"

"Now, Reverend, I don't think you are in any position here to be makin' threats. Chicks is fragile things—wouldn't take nothin' to hurt one real bad. But I ain't got no reason at all to hurt yours. Fact is, if I's to harm a single feather on that little bird's head, a world of hurt would come down on me so fast I'd be the one winds up in a cage. It's in my best interests—and if there's anything I'm real good at, it's lookin' out for my own best interests—to make sure that baby chick don't even ruffle up its down."

"I don't know where Becca is! I already told you that." And this time it was true. He really didn't know where she was now.

"Then best you find her—quick! I figure to hand off this chick while she's still all chirpy like—not had time to miss the barn and her own nest. Any more than twenty-four hours and baby birds is susceptible to all kinda problems."

"I'm on an airplane, Billy Ray! On my way to Washington."

"Then you best get on another plane soon's you land and fly right back to Cincinnati. We got bidness to do, you and me, 'fore the sun goes down tomorrow night. I'll be in touch. Oh, and one other thing. You call in the…you know, the game wardens, the ones that look for lost chicks, then it becomes in my best interests to see to it your little birdie don't never chirp again. Like I said, I always look after my own best interests! I'm a man of my word; ask anybody. You might not like me, but you know that's true. I tell you your chick's safe, you can b'lieve it." He paused. When he spoke again, his voice was soft and menacing. "And if I tell you she's gonna get plucked and fried if you don't give me what I want, you can b'lieve that, too."

The line went dead and the wheels squealed as the big plane touched down on the runway of Dulles International Airport.

~

"SLOW DOWN, DANIEL!" Jack said. "You're not making any sense."

The fear in Daniel's voice made a great thundering sound in Jack's head, like it was league night at a bowling alley.

"Billy Ray has Andi. He kidnapped her. He wants to trade her for Becca."

Bam! Somebody on the bowling league got a strike.

"How do you know that?"

"He texted me, then we talked on the phone and… none of that matters, Jack. It's true—Andi's gone. I called Mrs. Beavers, and she was freaked out, said she'd been trying to reach me. She thinks Andi ran away because she didn't want to go to her piano lesson, dropped her music on the sidewalk and left one shoe in the driveway of a neighbor who's out of town."

The last few words came out with a choking sob, and Jack could hear the rising timbre of panic in Daniel's voice.

"Daniel, calm down and tell me what Billy Ray said. Exactly what he said. Word for word."

Daniel repeated the conversation.

"You told him you didn't know where Becca was?"

"He didn't believe me any more than he did the last time I told him that when I did know where she was." He paused. "He said if I called the police, he'd…Jack, what do I do?"

Jack suddenly understood on a visceral level why surgeons refused to operate on their own children. How could you do your job, make the hard, perhaps risky, calls you make every day with other people when the kid going under the knife is your own?

Get a grip.

Daniel suddenly burst out, "Andi knew it, Jack! She saw this. In a vision, just like she did the triangle and the square and the rope. She told me about it, but it didn't make any more sense than the other one did. She was seeing what was going to happen."

"Tell me about the vision. Everything she said. Every detail, no matter how small."

As Daniel spoke, Jack wrote furiously in his officer's notebook, stopping him constantly to ask questions.

"She said the license plate read 'Land of…something' but she couldn't read the next word. Had an Indian design on—"

"Yellow license plate with a Navajo design, Land of Enchantment—that's New Mexico. Did she see the numbers?"

"It was splattered with mud—red mud."

Jack peppered him with questions and learned about the train, three men, the tattoo and the dreadlocks, about groceries from BetterBuy and beer with two x's that was still cold.

"One of the men was Hispanic, sounded like Speedy Gonzales, said they should have eaten his mother's tacos."

Jack questioned Daniel for another five minutes. When he was finally satisfied, Daniel went back to his original question.

"Jack, what do I do? Do I call the police? The FBI?"

Jack was slow to answer. "This is a federal crime," he said. "Not just because it's kidnapping. She heard one of them say 'the south side of the river,' which means they transported her across the state line into Kentucky. If you call the police, they'll hand it off to the FBI. When you tell the FBI about Billy Ray, they'll be all over him."

"They'll arrest him?"

"They might. They might storm his house with a SWAT team. Or maybe bring him in for questioning. At the very least, they'll blanket him with surveillance, trying to track where he goes."

"Even if it's only surveillance, he'll know," Daniel said. "Imagine trying to track Billy Ray Hawkins through the woods and him not catch you at it?"

"The FBI has resources—technology they can use where he'll never know a thing. Heat sensors so they know who's in a house. Other things. And they've got the manpower to check all this—to check the BetterBuy stores south of the river, find out who owns satellite dishes, the location of railroad tracks and times of trains. They even have a database of tattoos on convicted felons. The problem is—"

"How can I tell them what I know about where she is and get them to believe me?"

Jack was silent, then said in a resigned voice. "You can't. Try explaining to a 'suit' that you know a guy in dreadlocks and another dude with a dragon tattoo kidnapped your daughter because she had a dream about it. At the very least, they'll blow you off."

"Or think I'm crazy. Or that I know all this because I'm involved in it somehow. Ok, then I won't tell them the part about the vision."

"If you don't, they'll be useless. We know Billy Ray didn't act alone, but the FBI doesn't. They'll channel all their resources into targeting Billy Ray—because he's all they've got. And we know that where they're holding her isn't anywhere near Billy Ray."

"So what do I do?"

Jack said nothing.

"Jack…?"

"I'll find her."

Jack had been coming around to that conclusion all along. A surgeon operating on his own kid.

"Can you do that?"

"I have a whole lot better shot at it than the FBI. At least, I won't get Billy Ray's back up and I'll be looking in the right place."

"I haven't had time to find the next flight back to Cincinnati. I don't know what time I'll be—"

"Stay where you are, Daniel."

"Stay here? My daughter's been kidnapped, and I'm going to help you find her!"

"Do that! Help me find her—by staying right where you are."

"Jack, I'm not going to—"

"You'll get in my way, Daniel!" He hadn't meant to sound brutal, but maybe that was the only way he could get Daniel to listen to him. He continued in a kinder voice. "You won't mean to, you'll be trying to help, but you'll slow me down. I don't have time to coddle an anxious father."

The silence from Daniel's end of the phone was so profound Jack feared Daniel had hung up on him. When he spoke, his voice was barely a whisper. "Find my baby."

Jack sat very still after he hung up, his rapid heartbeat stitching a gauzy web of fear around him, white and sticky and inescapable. He was a police sergeant in a suburban department, a beat cop with zero experience as a detective. He didn't have the skill to do this. Or the manpower. If that little girl died, it would be his fault—and it wouldn't be the first time someone he loved had died because of him.

Chapter Twenty-Nine

1985

When Bishop came out of the woods, the six Bad Kids were milling around the dugout that was between them and the bleachers and parking lot. Bishop charged at Cole Stuart, grabbed him by both shoulders and slammed him so hard against the post holding up the net behind the catcher that the netting swayed back and forth from the impact. The look of surprise on Cole's face morphed into rage in an instant. He put his hands on Bishop's chest and shoved him. Bishop flew backward and landed on his backside in the dirt halfway to the pitcher's mound.

He got up slowly, a great angry bear. When he spoke, his voice was the sound of cannon fire in the distance. He had let his rage carry him, and it was all he had. The only thing that kept the terror at bay was the red curtain of fury that shrouded his eyes and obscured the features of the demons screeching at him.

"Good! That's what you gone have to do when I come after you."

He strode menacingly toward them until he could lean

in and spit words into Cole's face. Cole and all the others were so surprised they only stared at him.

"You listen up. All six of you—hear this. I am done with your evil, mean torture. What you done to Jack…" For a moment he was overcome with such rage he couldn't form words. Only for a moment though, then he drilled his booming voice into their faces. "It's over. You hear me? Over. You dare touch so much as a hair on the head of any one of them children again, and I will come for you."

Now, he poked his finger into Cole's chest. All the other demons were screaming and growling so loud it was hard to think, like being in a room full of wood-chippers—but Cole Stuart's demon was silent, glaring at him in malignant fury.

"I'm gone find you somewhere public, lots of people around, and tear into you like a chain saw." He poked Cole again. "You listenin' to me? When I do, I ain't gone stop 'til I kill you or you kill me, but one way or the other, it will be the end of whatever it is you got planned!"

Cole's demon responded to that. He ground his razor teeth, and his scorpion tail twitched back and forth.

Bishop leaned over Cole and growled the next words. "Case you ain't noticed, I'm a whole lot bigger'n you are, son! Ain't no way in the world you gone beat me 'thout using superhuman strength—and that big ol' crowd of people gone see it when you do. By the time we're through, everybody will know you ain't human!"

The hot rage in Bishop's chest suddenly cooled, became a steely frozen resolve that rang out with the pure clarity of a hammer striking cold steel. "Explain that to the one who sent you. How one big ol' black man done outsmarted all his hired help and spoiled his grand plan!"

Now the demons were quiet.

"Are. We. Clear?" Bishop dropped each word individually, like tossing pebbles into a pond. "Or we can settle this right here and right now." He gestured toward the bleachers, blocked from view by the dugout, where moms, grandmothers, little sisters and brothers waited to watch the day's practice. He pointed to the parking lot, where two cars had just pulled in and other cars could be seen turning in off the street. "I'd be glad to destroy your 'mission' and end it all in the next thirty seconds. There'll soon be plenty of folks to bear witness." His huge hands balled into fists like sledge hammers. "You in?"

In the silence that followed, Bishop became aware for the first time of the freezing cold that emanated from the demons. And now that his anger wasn't hammering courage into his veins, he felt oily black terror slither in.

Then Cole Stuart spoke.

"We're so sorry, Coach Washington, if our horseplay with Jack got a little out of hand. It won't happen again, promise." He draped a smile on his lips. "Looks like we'll soon be ready for the team picture." He flattened his Mohawk and seated his ball cap firmly on is head. "I'd be glad to help you get everybody lined up."

The rest of the practice was surreal. With every word he spoke, every direction he gave, Bishop felt the silent hatred of six monster creatures. Their combined malice pummeled him like physical blows, battering him, and he struggled every second not to be beaten down by their collective evil. The demons didn't make a sound, only watched him with their nightmare eyes while the bodies they'd hijacked were totally cooperative, couldn't have been more polite, performed excellently—but not in any superhuman fashion, of course.

Jack sat out the practice. Mikey had found some ice somewhere and wrapped it in an unused team T-shirt so

Jack could hold it on the wound on his leg. Jack and Daniel were the last to leave, had waited behind to talk to Bishop.

"What did you mean by that, when you said somebody sent them, that they were just the hired help?" Daniel asked.

Bishop suddenly felt very old and tired. And this battle hadn't even really begun yet. At least he knew now. Last night, going through them ancient texts in his study, he'd realized that the answer he was lookin' for wasn't in them books. He knew now what he was up against. And these children had to know about that, 'cause if he was interpreting everything right, they was gone be part of it.

"I'll lay everything out for you to see at Bible study Thursday night," he said.

SHERIFF BILL CUNNINGHAM took off his glasses and rubbed his eyes, then put them back on and studied the time sheets on his desk. It was done, over. He had used up the whole year's overtime budget in the past week. There had not been a single act of vandalism since what he had come to call Black Tuesday. No dead dogs. No snakes. Nothing.

Of course, it was clear to Sheriff Cunningham that anybody smart enough to do what they'd done and not leave a trace was also smart enough to figure out that no small town could keep up that kind of vigilant surveillance for long. Sooner or later, it would have to end, and life would return to normal.

And deep in his gut, Sheriff Cunningham believed that

as soon as the patrols stopped, the horror would start all over again.

The sheriff got up from his desk and wandered over to the window, pulled back the flowered curtains his wife had insisted on hanging there and stared out at the town square. The late-afternoon sunlight was shades of burnt-orange and pink, and the shop windows smoldered with reflections of that fading fire. It looked totally unremarkable. People going about their lives. Mammas pushing strollers, stores selling shoes and cosmetics and spark plugs, Pete at the Gulf station changing the gas price sign to $1.09 a gallon, two little boys in white Karate uniforms practicing their "wax on/wax off" moves. Normal. But now it seemed like airbrushed reality. Ever since he got the first look at the mutilated corpse of Ella Fletcher's Jelly Belly, it had seemed to the sheriff that he'd been granted a peek behind the curtain, a view of —not the Great Oz pulling cranks and pushing buttons —but of something sinister, dark and ugly. And frightening.

He shivered. Ok, admit it. He was scared. He didn't know what he was afraid of, but he was terrified. He knew, without any idea how he knew it, that what had happened last week in Bradford's Ridge was going to pale in comparison to what was going to happen as soon as he called his officers off the street.

His grandmother had lived through the Battle of Britain, had been in London when Hitler's buzz bombs terrorized the city. She'd told him that the hardest part, the scariest part, was when you heard the buzzing engine of the rocket cut off. The silence that followed meant the bomb was falling. You didn't know when or where it would hit and explode, destroying everything and everybody anywhere near it.

The horror last week was a buzz bomb. It was silent now. The engine had cut off, and an explosion was coming.

~

2011

Becca wished the water were clear, like the pictures you see of coral reefs with colorful fish flitting here and there and the bubbles from your scuba tank, little round sprinters, racing each other to the surface.

She would lie back in the clear water, her hair floating like a halo around her head, and watch the bubbles of her last breath rush up to burst into the bright sunlight that filtered down through the water's depths in rays like sparklers.

But the Ohio River was muddy, not clear. It flowed lazily beneath the L&N Pedestrian Bridge, ugly brown water that would swallow her up with no bubbles or pretty fish or sunlight rays. Just cold, wet and dead.

Becca walked slowly up the Cincinnati approach to the Purple People Bridge, an old train trestle converted into a scenic walkway between Ohio and Kentucky. The bridge, the beams and guiders painted purple, called out to her with an air of silliness. Silly was a good last place to be in life.

She pretended to look down at the water as she studied the girders and posts and wires that fit around the bridge, a spider's silver steel web that held it in place. As soon as there was a break in the foot traffic, she would hoist herself to the top of the railing, holding on to a support post to balance on the narrow metal beam. She'd have to move quickly because if anyone spotted her and figured out what she was doing, they would undoubtedly try to stop her.

No one was going to stop her this time. She'd tried before to escape the black monsters that slithered around on human hosts and crawled around in her head. She'd had her stomach pumped twice when she was in the mental hospital. After that, she'd tried to tough it out. She really had. She had lived with horror inside and outside, took every breath with her whole chest constricted, a guitar string pulled so tight you couldn't tell anymore if the sound it made was music or crying.

Last night, he came to her. He was inside Chapman Whitworth, and he saw her, glided into her through the black spots in her eyeballs. Rumbling a mighty roar of rage inside her head, he had ripped her apart in a frenzy of destruction, shredding all she was, who she was.

Now, she was only the tatters of a person flapping in the wind. Ripped pieces with no substance and only the one thin cord of life holding them together. When that was severed, the pieces would float away free into oblivion. And whatever or whoever it was who had been Becca Hawkins would be no more.

She saw her chance, glanced both ways and then climbed up onto the railing. She felt the sun on her face and a breeze lift her hair off her neck. Down below was brown death, waiting for her, and Becca Jean Hawkins lifted her foot to step off into nothing.

That's when she spotted the hat. Floating in the water below her was a tall, floppy hat with red-and-white stripes. She gasped.

The Cat in the Hat's hat.

Becca looked at it in wonder, realizing as she did that it wasn't moving. Sticks and other pieces of debris floated along with the current under the bridge past the hat, but it remained steadfastly where it was.

That kind of hat wouldn't even float—would it? It

would turn into a shapeless red-and-white striped lump. This hat didn't even look wet. The muddy brown water hadn't stained the pure white of the stripes, either. And it was bobbing up and down...as if somebody wearing it were dancing.

"Hey, lady!"

Becca turned to see a man only fifteen or twenty feet away. He was big, with a huge chest and brawny arms, wearing a gray jumpsuit with his name and a logo—Harrison County Electric and Gas—stitched on the pocket.

The man started toward her.

"What do you think you're doing up there?" he said.

"I...I dropped my hat," Becca heard herself say. She looked back down at the river flowing in an endless brown expanse and saw the hat still bobbing in place where it'd been before.

"Well, it's gone now, and you're going to go with it if you don't get down from there."

"No, it's not gone. See,"—she pointed to the hat in the river—"it's right there."

The man glanced where she pointed. "Like I said, the hat's gone. Now come down off that railing."

The man didn't see the hat. Couldn't see it.

Becca never took her eyes off the hat as she climbed back down. When her feet touched the bridge floor, the hat floated slowly away.

Chapter Thirty

1985

Theresa had made chocolate-chip cookies, and Bishop was glad. The smell was wholesome, and these children was gone need wholesomeness around them tonight. He was about to open up the back door to Hell and give them a peek inside. He glanced at the tattoo on the top of his left hand—1John 4:4. He'd gotten the tattoo after he came home shattered by his experience in Vietnam, so he'd never forget: He who is in me is greater than he who is in the world.

He tried to gather his wits about him, what few he had left. Since the day two weeks ago when them six demons come tearin' out of the woods, he'd hardly been able to sleep a'tall, kept wakening up in a cold sweat. His dreams was stalked by monsters too terrible to think about, demons crawling over each other like maggots on road-kill…and beyond it all, in the background of every night-mare, was an awful red glow and a pillar of black smoke. Hidin' inside that smoke was pure evil.

And now he had to tell these children 'bout it.

Jack and Daniel—he sometimes thought of them as Tweedledum and Tweedledee, but he didn't tell them that —sat side by side on the couch in his living room, and he faced them in his big recliner. Becca sat on the floor cross-legged at his feet, watching the silver ballerina go around and around on Theresa's old music box to the hinky-tinky tune of The Blue Danube Waltz.

Bishop leaned over and put his elbows on his knees and looked earnestly into Jack's and Daniel's faces.

"What you children needs to understand is that all them old stories—they's mostly true. Some of them creatures we laugh about now, they're real."

Becca spoke softly to Jack and Daniel. "Cole's demon has the ugly face of a dragon."

They musta talked about it! After he told Jack and Daniel that Becca could see demons, they must have discussed it, the three of 'em. Good! Meant they was close, didn't have no secrets separating 'em. They was gone need that close bond if they was gone do what they was gone have to do.

"Them demons that's doin' they mischief right now in Bradford's Ridge—six of them don't show up in one place for no reason, workin' together like they was out selling Girl Scout cookies. They ain't powerful enough to have got here by theirselves. They had to a'been sent."

"That's what you meant when you said they were just the hired help," Daniel said. "But if they are the servants, who do they serve?"

They musta talked about that part, too.

Bishop squared his shoulders then and spoke words out into the air that had until this moment only haunted the darkest, blackest caverns of his own mind. He was 'bout to share the horror he carried…with three little kids.

"Ain't a who, it's a what," Bishop kept his voice quiet,

but it seemed loud in the small room. "From what I've seen and heard—only explanation that makes any sense to me is that there's an efreet hereabouts somewhere, here in our world."

When Bishop went lookin' for answers in his demonology texts—he'd stayed up all night after he'd snatched Becca back from them demons—he'd shied away from jumpin' to conclusions. Lookin' back, he could see now that he'd known all along, somewhere deep in his guts, what monster from Hell they was dealin' with. But in the beginning, it'd seemed too obvious.

Bishop had first started studyin' demons after the horror he'd seen in Vietnam. And he'd become fascinated by efreets. He'd been like a mouse starin' into the eyes of a cobra—utterly horrified but powerless to look away. Bishop had dug into Middle Eastern and Iranian literature for years, pullin' out a little bitty piece of information here, a single line of reference there. The Caverna County librarians knew when they seen Bishop comin', he was gone ask for some obscure text they'd have to send off for; the mailman finally give up askin' what he was doin' with all them strange books. In fact, there had been some small part of Bishop way down in his soul that was scared his interest would draw the beast, that it would feel his fascination, feed on it, somehow follow it here. Maybe it had. All Bishop knew for sure was that what they was facing was an efreet. He hadn't figured that out by reading demonology texts, though. He just knew.

"What's an efreet?" Daniel asked.

"It's an enormous winged creature made out of fire."

Bishop got up and went to his study. Years ago, he'd happened across the picture of a painting in one of them old books, had spent six months trackin' it down and had to pay almost a hundred dollars to get a reproduction. But he'd a'paid ten times that if he'd had to. He'd felt a compulsion he couldn't control any better than he could understand it. He had to have that image. And that should have warned him there was some power tuggin' on him. But it hadn't. Now, he lifted the reproduction down off the wall where it'd hung all these years and took it into the living room.

The children stared at the image. Hidden by smoke rising out of a lake of fire was a pillar of darkness, a black hole in the world, a shape with wings.

"Efreet ain't no ordinary demon," Bishop said. "Bible says that "our battle is not against flesh and blood but against the rulers, the powers, the authorities of this dark world.' An efreet is a ruler, an authority. A powerful, powerful evil."

"This efreet…where is it?" Jack asked.

"Here in our world—somewhere close by."

Then Bishop told Jack, Daniel and Becca what Grampa Rufus had told him all those years ago. Their eyes grew wide with wonder—and fear.

"What I can't figure is how anybody could have summoned an efreet 'cause what you have to use for the ceremony—the implements don't exist no more. I've read about ancient scrolls that tell how folks called forth demons from Hell, but them scrolls have been lost for centuries, and even if you could lay hands on one, they was in languages ain't nobody spoke for a thousand years."

Though he couldn't figure out how it could possibly have happened, he had finally come to accept that it was almost inevitable. The darkness was magnetic, and the veil here in Caverna County was too thin to hold it back.

"Only thing's still around is the blood."

The children already knew the significance of blood sacrifices. He'd taught in their Bible studies how the Jews were required once a year to bring a lamb to sacrifice on the altar in Jerusalem.

Becca asked if that meant somebody had sacrificed an animal to summon the efreet, and he shook his head, wishin' he didn't have to say it but knowin' he had to.

"No, sugar. Didn't nobody sacrifice an animal. To bring forth a demon like this one"—he pointed to the monster in the picture——"out of the spiritual realm and into the world, you got to sacrifice a person."

"So if someone in Bradford's Ridge summoned an efreet," Becca said, her voice so soft it was barely audible, "they had to…murder somebody?"

Bishop nodded. But you couldn't murder just anyone, he told them, had to be somebody who'd been singled out, somebody evil had put some kinda mark on. Bishop had first read about that part prob'ly ten years ago and had scoured every text since, tryin' to find out what it meant for evil to "put a mark on" somebody. He never found out. But in the past week, a possible answer had begun to form. That awful day he'd stood on the edge of the woods and first seen six demons in one place—that experience changed him. Couldn't nobody see a demon, experience a demon, and be the same person afterwards. That kind of evil left a scar, a mark. Maybe that's what "the mark of evil" was talkin' about.

He cleared his throat and went on, talked about the pentagram, that whoever called forth the efreet had drawn a pentagram and summoned the efreet into it.

"That day in the woods," Becca said, "the demons were trying to find 'the summoner.'"

"Why wouldn't the efreet know who summoned it?" Daniel asked.

Bishop shrugged. He had no idea. He explained that a pentagram was a hole in the barrier between the human and the spiritual world, a place where demons could crawl out. The pentagram outlined the boundaries of where the efreet, and the other demons that had come along with it, could go in the human world. The only way to escape the pentagram was to possess a person.

"So the efreet brought six other demons with it when it was summoned," Jack said.

"Six that we know of," Bishop said. "Ain't no telling how many they is. That pentagram is a hole—a door. And you know what happens when you leave the door open. You come home, and they's wasps and flies and all kinda creatures you kept out with that door closed. Somebody summoned the efreet—don't know who or how or where or why, but it musta happened. Somehow them six kids stepped inside the pentagram used to summon it, and six of the demons there escaped the pentagram by possessin' the kids. But that don't mean them six was the only demons there."

"Is the efreet in one of the Bad Kids?" Jack asked.

"No, that demon's too big and powerful to possess a child. That'd be like putting rocket fuel into a toy truck. It'd burn up. The person who summoned it—that's who the efreet possessed. It's called perfect possession when somebody invites a demon in, and then the evil don't just control the person, it's a part of 'em—milk in coffee, all stirred up together. They soul is completely gone, nothing left but a black hole where it'd been."

"So the Bad Kids must have found the summoner," Becca said.

"Uh-huh," Bishop said. "And that's who's calling the shots now. He's got them kids out doing awful things for a reason. I can't imagine what that reason would be, but it's not just random demon mischief. Whatever the efreet-possessed summoner's got planned, it's a powerful, terrible thing."

He paused then. Now that he had come to it, he wasn't sure he could do it. But he didn't have no choice. Wasn't like he was the one who'd picked out these children to be involved in this. There was a reason for that, too. It made no sense a'tall to him. All he did know was that they all had to play the part they was called on to play—whatever it was. Adult or child.

"And we"—he made a gesture that indicated himself and the three children—"we got to do two things." He took a breath. "First, we got to find that efreet and—"

"I thought you said the efreet was in the summoner," Jack said.

"I did and it is. But demons come from a spiritual world that don't work the same way the human one does. An efreet ain't bound by our rules of what's possible and what ain't. That monster is in the summoner. But it's still inside that pentagram, too. Both at the same time. We got to find the efreet in the pentagram..." He paused. "And we got to send it back to Hell."

Shock drained all the color from Daniel's face. "Us?" His voice croaked like it'd just started changing, right there, that minute.

"God wouldn't a' brought us here and shown us what we've seen less'n he intended to use us to make things right."

Jack sounded like a parrot. "Us?"

Bishop couldn't help the smile that sprang to his lips at the looks on their faces.

"Not all by our lonesome. We gone have help." He smiled down at the little girl at his feet. She was as beautiful, pure and good as any human being he'd ever known. He was deeply saddened, but not at all surprised, she'd been picked out for this. "Becca, sugar. Why don't you tell us about the angel."

She'd already shared the story with Bishop, and he watched the looks on the boys' faces as she recounted it again. Theresa had come into the room, drying her hands on a dish towel, and she stood leaned against the door frame, listening to the child's words spoken in a voice like tiny bells.

"She's just…there sometimes. It's not like I can call, and she'll show up. I don't know when she's going to come to me…except that she said when the demons appeared, she'd be there to hold my hand so I wouldn't be afraid." She stopped, seemed to realize something. "They're afraid of her!" She turned to Bishop for confirmation, and he nodded. "The demons. She scares them. I can tell by how they act when she's there. She's stronger than they are."

"And I figure she's been sent here to help us do what we got to do," Bishop said.

"Find the efreet…" Jack said, awe in his whispered voice.

"And send it back to Hell," Daniel finished softly.

Chapter Thirty-One

2011

After Dreadlock Man slapped her and threw her into the back of the van, Andi was so scared she couldn't get a breath all the way down into her chest, felt like she was panting, probably sounded like a dog on a hot day.

The van was a cargo van with no seats or windows in the back. She sat on the floor, huddled up into the back corner while Speedy Gonzales sat on an upturned milk crate near the front and talked to Dreadlock Man, who was driving. She wasn't tied up or anything, and she eyed the back door handle, wondered if she pulled on it, could she jump out. But they were going fast, and she didn't know if it was possible to survive hitting the pavement at sixty miles an hour, and if they were on a highway, the car behind them would run over her before it had a chance to stop. Besides, the door was probably locked.

The fear kept her stomach all squeezed up in a knot until they finally stopped. When they dragged her out of the van, she saw that it was parked in the backyard of a house out in the country. They took her inside, shoved her into a room and locked the door behind her.

She'd seen all this before, been in this room with the dangling bare light bulb and the blankets on the floor and the boarded-up window. Of course, she hadn't really been here, just seen it.

She sat down on the floor and leaned her back against the wall, trying hard not to cry. Daddy would come get her and take her home. Or maybe Uncle Jack. Everything would be all right.

But everything hadn't been all right when that man came to the church that time with a gun, and Andi'd hidden in the pageant storage room. Mommy said it would be, but it wasn't. She got shot. Mommy died.

She reached down and tenderly fingered her mother's cross necklace that Uncle Jack had fastened around her neck the day of Mommy's funeral.

Would Andi get shot this time and die and have a funeral? She put her hands up over her face and started to cry.

~

1985

The fog was so thick it was like trying to drive through cotton candy when Theresa Washington set out for Potter's Funeral Home that morning. She hadn't seen fog this thick since…well, she couldn't remember that she ever had, and she thought the unseasonably cool, damp weather was fitting somehow, almost like the world was mourning with Amelia. It was a terrible thing to have to say your final good-byes to a child, but it'd somehow be worse if you had to do it on a bright summer day when the birds was singing and you could hear the sound of healthy children playing. Theresa was glad she wasn't the one sittin' on the front row in a funeral home with her son lying dead in a casket in front of her! Glad Isaac was fine…just gone somewhere, that's all—and he'd be back. He'd be home soon. He was just…

Her eyes welled with tears. She wiped them roughly away, shook her head and concentrated on the road. Hard enough to see through this fog 'thout making it worse with tears when there wasn't nothin' to cry about!

Amelia Grant had been one of Theresa's best friends since they was both in grammar school. She'd gotten married and had five children—four little girls and finally the son her husband had always wanted. Christopher had been barely two years old when they found out he had leukemia, and Theresa'd always known Christopher wouldn't make it. He was so small and frail and…docile—there didn't seem to be any fight in him at all.

Now, Theresa was dressed in her good black dress with the acres of full skirt for the funeral service at nine o'clock. There'd be a brunch in the fellowship hall of the First Baptist Church after the service, and burial would follow this afternoon. Folks was saying Amelia was taking it real hard and wasn't nothing you could do when a friend was grievin' a loss except stand beside her and grieve with her. She'd left Bishop at home, asleep. He'd said he'd go with her, but the poor man hadn't come to bed at all last night after he told them children about the efreet. She'd found him asleep in the recliner this morning, and she'd left him there.

The parking lot was full but not jammed. She made her way toward the building through air so wet it left water on every surface it touched, and for some reason the fog didn't seem so welcoming anymore. It swirled in little clouds around the cars, drained everything of color, made the familiar alien and foreign. She felt an unusual sense of foreboding as she stepped up onto the porch and greeted the funeral director.

"Morning, Mrs. Washington," said Elmer Potter as he held the door open for her. Elmer was the third generation of his family to operate the facility, and they was a time when it was for white folks only. Black people had they own place. Elmer'd been the one who'd changed all that, and she liked him for it. He was a reserved little man who seemed a mite frazzled this morning. She looked around for his sons, who helped with the business, but they was nowhere in sight.

"Mornin' to you, Mr. Potter," she said. "You doin' all right?"

"Can't complain. You?"

"Where's you boys?"

"I'm flying solo this morning."

"It's a lot to do all by yourself, ain't it?"

"Not now. Everything was done yesterday. The graveside service is the thing, and they're going directly there from the airport. They were supposed to be home from their grandmother's yesterday, but their flight got canceled."

Most everybody was in the viewing room already, so Theresa hurriedly signed the guest book, stepped inside and took a seat in the back row of folding chairs that was arranged neatly in double rows across the room with a center aisle cleared between them. Almost all the seats was taken.

After a small group of people in the hallway had seated themselves, Mr. Potter quietly closed the big double doors at the back of the room. Probably didn't nobody like funeral homes, but Theresa suspected she disliked them more than most. Amelia and her family didn't go to church so Theresa understood, but having a funeral service in a place like this seemed almost…despairing. At least in a church, there was a sense of the presence of God all around, and a church had windows. Theresa's church had three huge stained glass windows on each side of the building. This room was a dark, dignified cave, with no windows at all and only the big double doors at the far end. Even open, they didn't admit much natural light, though, particularly on a dreary day like today.

Theresa could see the tops of the family's heads seated on the front row. Four little stair-stepped girls and Amelia with her head on her husband's shoulder. In front of them, resting on a curtained platform with wheels on the bottom, was the casket, with a huge spray of roses and gardenias resting on top. It was a grownup's casket, looked like, not small for a child. Special-made little ones was probably more expensive, and with all Christopher's medical bills, Amelia's family didn't have hardly nothin' left.

Set back on a small dais behind the casket was an old-fashioned wooden pulpit, wide and bulky, must have been five feet high. If the minister hadn't been a tall man, he'd have looked like a munchkin behind it. He said a prayer and then nodded, and Mr. Potter moved quickly and efficiently to the casket. He lifted the spray of flowers and placed it on a shelf behind the curtains of the platform. He stepped to the end of the casket, so as not to block the family's view, reached out and released the catch and lifted the half lid on that end.

Somebody gasped, and Reverend Peterson staggered back.

There was…movement. Something was moving in the casket! That's when the screaming started. It began in the front of the room and washed through the crowd back toward where Theresa was seated, a wave of screeching horror. At first, Theresa couldn't understand what—

Then she saw it—saw them. Two enormous snakes had slithered out of the opening and wriggled up to the top of the casket. Black rat snakes, maybe six feet long, they slid together down the length of the casket to the end as other snakes———smaller ones, bull snakes or garter snakes—swarmed out of the opening in a tangle of writhing motion.

It took Theresa a moment to process the reality of it.

Oh dear Lord, that casket's full of snakes.

~

2011

"What's wrong, Daniel?" Senator LaHayne peered at him over the top of the Ben Franklin glasses parked precariously on the end of his nose. "Daniel."

Focus!

"I'm sorry. What did you say again?"

"I'm not saying anything until you tell me why you're giving me about ten percent of your concentration. Where's the other ninety percent?"

All the way to the senator's office from the airport, Daniel had bounced around the emotional pinball machine, lighting up terror, rage, fear, hope, guilt—each bright red when he bumped into it. And when he could wrench his thoughts for even a moment away from Andi, he considered what he'd say when the senator asked him that question. How could he possibly tie all this up in a way the senator would understand—what had happened to Andi that really had nothing to do with Chapman Whitworth. And yet it had everything to do with him because it was about Becca.

He now sat before the man the country expected to take the mantle of the presidency of the United States only a few months from now and had no more idea what to say than he had in the car.

"Bad things are going on back home," he said. "Worse, even, than we told you about."

The senator didn't speak, waited expectantly for Daniel to continue.

"A long time ago, something happened to Jack and me —and Chapman Whitworth. Something indescribably horrible." He actually shuddered, felt chill bumps pebble his arms. "It's how we know…who…he is. But it wasn't only Jack and me. There were three of us—Jack, me and Becca. And now, Becca's in trouble—and so's my little girl, Andi."

"Would you tell me the whole story if I asked?" the senator said. He leaned across toward Daniel and put his elbows on his knees. The skinny arms, the big head…Jack thought of a praying mantis.

The two of them were seated alone in some kind of sitting room that Daniel assumed was in close proximity to the sena-tor's office. The aide who'd picked him up at the airport meandered up and down the halls of the senate office building for so long that Daniel couldn't have found his way back out if he'd left a trail of bread crumbs. The chairs were comfortable, leather, well worn by the backsides of uncounted men who'd gone out from this room and made a difference in the world.

"I thought we settled that."

"If I asked?"

"Yes sir," Daniel said. "But don't ask. Please."

The man studied him.

"One day I will. You know that, don't you?"

"Yes, sir, I do."

"Right now, we keep the main thing the main thing," the senator said. "Are you able to do that? Can you give me your full and undivided attention? What I'm about to talk to you about will require every bit of your strength and focus."

No. Absolutely no way! But he had to. Daniel resolutely shoved Andi out of his mind and slammed the door hard behind her.

"I will do my best, sir. But…I don't understand what you need me to do here, what either of us can do. We haven't found Bosko. Jack told you that."

"I've checked in twice a day, every day. I know the status of the investigation."

"Then you know we don't have any proof."

"I do know that. But Chapman Whitworth does not."

Daniel merely looked at him.

"Clearly, you are not a poker player. When you've been dealt lousy cards, you have two choices. You can toss your cards onto the top of the chips and give up. Or you can bluff. We're going to bluff."

"Sir?"

"Whitworth knows you've come to me. That's all he knows."

Daniel wanted to ask why the senator had leaked information about their meeting to the press, but didn't.

"Seeing you here with me will rattle him." The senator leaned back, in that relaxed pose that was anything but. He was stretched as tight as a bow string. "I intend to get him to fold, to withdraw his name from consideration for the seat on the court by getting him to believe we can prove way more than we really can."

"But why would he do that? Withdraw? Why would he give up without a fight?"

"Because I'm going to make him an offer he can't refuse. I'm going to give him a Get Out of Jail Free card."

Daniel had absolutely no idea what Senator LaHayne was talking about.

∼

JACK LEANED over the gigantic map of the greater metropolitan Cincinnati area—which included all the suburbs and small towns on both sides of the Ohio River.

He'd spread it out on the break room table, not concerned someone would stop by and ask what he was doing. Since he'd become persona non grata at the station, he could have been disarming a nuclear warhead and the other officers would have walked right past him and out the door without comment. For a moment, Jack felt the pain of their disapproval and hostility. He wasn't one of the Good Guys anymore. But then maybe he never had been.

He shook it off and wondered yet again if he should have asked for Crocker's help to find Andi. But he couldn't bring himself to divert Crock from chasing Bosko. It was likely futile, but they had to keep trying.

Now, he sat alone, staring down at the map in front of him, and felt utterly defeated. He'd used Google maps to locate all the BetterBuy stores in the Cincinnati area—twenty-eight of them—and another nine in Boone and Kenton Counties in northern Kentucky.

Then he thought about the ice cream and narrowed the search to the southern half of Cincinnati—which lopped off seventeen of the stores. Bright red stickpins now marked the locations of the remaining twenty BetterBuys.

The blue stickpins were Tony Barroni Pizza carryout shops. He'd drawn a semicircle bulging out south from the river that encompassed the BetterBuys and the fourteen pizza parlors. And that wasn't counting liquor stores. When Jack did a Google Earth search for them, there were so many little red dots on the screen, it looked like the map had measles.

Train tracks crisscrossed the area, and tomorrow morning when somebody was in the office, he could start narrowing down which trains had run through this piece of real estate and on what schedule. Given enough time, he could canvas the stores and pizza parlors one at a time, ask about New Mexico plates and dragon tattoos, and eventually he'd scare up a rabbit.

Trouble was, he didn't have time.

Had he been wrong to advise Daniel not to call in the FBI? But even if they'd believed him, their manpower and resources weren't unlimited. They couldn't check out thirty-four different businesses and more liquor stores than he could count in less than a day. It would take an army of investigators to do that.

Jack froze for one beat. Then two. On the third beat, he grabbed his cell phone and punched in Daniel's number.

Daniel answered on the first ring. "What have you found?"

"Nothing yet."

"Do you know anything?"

"I know I need your help to find her."

"What can I do from here?"

"Everything."

Chapter Thirty-Two

1985

Even from the back of the room, Theresa could identify the big brown snake that next rose out of the opening of Christopher Grant's casket.

It was a rattlesnake. A diamondback.

Panic went off in that room with the force of a stick of dynamite.

Shrieking in terror, people lurched to their feet and bolted for the door in the back of the room. They didn't make their way down the rows of chairs to the aisles in the middle and on both sides. They turned and crashed through the chairs behind them, knockin' the chairs and the people that'd been sittin' in them out of the way, pushin' and shovin', their eyes wide and wild.

A blond man, probably near as big as Bishop, got to the doors first, pushed down the flapper handles and shoved the doors outward. Or tried to. The doors wouldn't open. They weren't locked. The handles released and the fasteners unlatched, but something on the outside was preventing the doors from moving apart.

Theresa was one of a handful of mourners who'd gotten to the doors before most everyone else. Seated on the back row, she hadn't had as far to go as the rest of the fleeing throng. Even aware as she always was that for a woman of her size and girth, running didn't usually end well, she'd nonetheless dropped her purse and raced mindless to the room's only exit, as panicked as everybody else. But soon's she seen that them doors wasn't gone open, that there wasn't nowhere for everybody to go, she wiggled back out of the tangle of bodies and turned around—just as another wave of hysterical people broke on the doors, plowing headlong into her and the blond man and the half dozen or so other people already there, mindlessly crushing them up against the doors. And people kept coming, jamming themselves into the crowd, screaming and clawing at those ahead of them, shoving and elbowing others aside, using whatever brute force they could muster to break through the dam of people, get to the doors and escape.

Held in place by the crowd with her back to the doors, Theresa watched in revulsion as the casket continued to vomit horror. Two more copperheads slipped out, over the side and onto the floor, followed by king snakes, green snakes and rat snakes. Behind them was a cottonmouth and two monstrous timber rattlesnakes, must have been five feet long, the sound of their furious rattles drowned out by the screaming crowd.

Theresa might have been the only person who noticed when the nature of the screaming changed, or maybe just the only person who knew why, who watched shrieks of terror become cries of pain as the snakes began to claim their prey.

Old Man Gregory was probably the first snakebite victim, certainly the first fatality. He used a walker, and when the crowd stampeded toward the back of the room, it was kicked aside, and he was knocked to the floor. The first snake got to him before he made it to the walker. A water moccasin struck him in the neck as he crawled. He screamed and went rigid, then fell face-first and lay there, his legs twitching like a chicken's legs after you'd wrung its neck.

Clarice Singletary, Dr. Clements's office nurse, lay on the floor on her side in a pile of collapsed folding chairs, holding her right leg. Blood drained down from twin holes in her calf where fangs had ripped through her pantyhose. She was trying to get to her feet, to get up and away from the snakes on the floor when another one—a timber rattler, looked like—struck her in the shoulder. It stuck to her shoulder, hanging there, until she reached up and knocked it away. She didn't cry out, only looked confused for a moment, then sank back down to sit on the floor, unaware of the snakes slithering by her and over her.

Tyrone Adams fought back. The eighteen-year-old high school basketball star dumped the flowers out of one of them tall vases and was using it as a club, hammering any snake that got near him. Theresa watched in horrified fascination as a timber rattler and a copperhead, slithering toward the crowd at the door down what had been the center aisle between the chairs suddenly turned aside and joined the snakes encircling Tyrone where he stood with his back against the wall near the casket. He'd taken off his Michael Jackson jacket and wrapped it around his left arm, holding it out in front of him like a shield. It was probably made of red and black vinyl instead of leather but it still offered some protection. That boy was in a rage, hollerin' obscenities as he kicked some snake butts, if snakes'd had butts. A handful of crushed snakes lay at his feet.

"Want some of this?" he yelled at a diamondback on his left. "Huh? Well, come and get—"

A water moccasin got him on the ankle. He shook it off, continued to hammer at the other snakes, but his movements were slower now. He looked unsteady on his feet. They moved in for the kill then. A diamondback coiled—Theresa knew a coiled snake could strike farther—and lunged, sinking its fangs into his groin through the thin fabric of his gray parachute pants. Tyrone didn't cry out. He was breathing funny, though, and seemed to be having trouble holding onto the vase. A copperhead got him on the calf, and he staggered, went down on one knee. Another water moccasin lunged at his chest and planted fangs deep into his flesh, and the front of his white shirt showed a growing red circle, like the bull's eye on a target. His arms went limp, and he dropped the vase, fell to his other knee and remained like that, on his knees as snake after snake struck him, like he was a punching bag. When he finally fell forward on his face, Theresa knew that boy wasn't gone be using that basketball scholarship to Western Kentucky University this fall.

Theresa couldn't make no sense of what she was seein'. It was like the snakes was singlin' out prey and stalking 'em, which went against everything Theresa Washington knew about snakes. She wasn't no expert by any means, but she'd always had a garden, had dealt with her share of rat snakes, king snakes, corn snakes—even a few rattlers. Ever' last one of them'd slither off in the grass the instant she came anywhere near, hightailed it one way fast as she was runnin' the other. Her mama'd told her snakes was more scared of her than she was of them, and she'd always found that to be true. But this…she'd never in her life seen snakes…attack like this. Yes, that's what it was. They was attackin'. Not just the poisonous ones, neither. They was all striking. A big black snake had sunk its fangs into Simon Gosset's calf. Didn't have no venom, but poor old Simon was horrified, batting at it, shrieking, then he got a funny look on his face, grabbed his chest and collapsed.

Two of Amelia's daughters had clambered up onto the pulpit at the front of the room, the one Reverend Peterson had stood behind to say the prayer. They stood there, huddled together on the flat shelf in the middle where preachers put their sermon notes. Every one of them snakes could climb, though, and the girls watched rat snakes glide up into them big sprays of flowers and black racer snakes slither up into the limbs of them fake trees, danglin' down like they was in a jungle.

They seen the big rattler soon as it started up the pulpit toward 'em. The oldest, Shamika, kicked at it, trying to knock it off with her black patent leather shoe. She succeeded once, but it come right back at her, smarter this time. When she kicked, it dodged and struck her in the leg right above the white socks, folded over neat so the lace on the top edge would show. It hung there, didn't let go when she tried to shake it loose. She fell to one knee, unsteady. Her little sister tried to hold onto her but the child wasn't big enough, and when Shamika went limp, she toppled off the pulpit to the floor, her body lost in a writhing tangle of serpents. The other little girl, her face a mask of terror, remained on top of the pulpit, watching the snakes swarm around the bottom of it, wonderin' when one of 'em was gone come climbing up after her, too.

They was so many snakes spread out now that they come at the crowd like waves of infantrymen. The folks at the back shrieked as snakes sank fangs into their calves. They tried to crawl up the backs of the people in front of them to get away but fell back or was flung off by the folks in front. The snakes slithered into the crowd, striking at ankles and bare feet where folks had lost they shoes.

Theresa felt a snake glide over her shoe and brush up against the skin of her ankle. Her heart was thumping in her chest so fast it was the whirr of a hummingbird's wings. She tasted terror, like her mouth was full of pennies, and cringed away from the pain she'd feel when the viper sank its fangs into her leg. Then the woman next to her screamed, and Theresa knew the snake had passed her by and struck that woman instead. Shrieks like that were coming from all over the crowd now, sending everybody else into hysterics.

Someone stepped on Theresa's heel, stood on the back of her shoe, and she lost her footing. She slipped downward slightly—just enough for her full skirt to touch the floor. When it did, the people around her stepped on it, nailing it down so Theresa couldn't straighten up. Half crouched, unable to stand upright, the crowd suddenly lurched to the right when a snake struck somebody on the left, and Theresa felt a searing pain in her lower back that sent agony up her whole body like a blast from a flame thrower. Snakebite couldn't have hurt worse. Bein' struck by lightning couldn't have hurt worse. The pain was so bad, the world began to gray out.

That's when Theresa heard it above the cries of the mob around her, a scream that sounded like ripping cloth. Amelia was shrieking in revolted horror, a wail of disbelief and grief so despairing and desolate it surely must have ripped open the very throne room of heaven.

It was the cry of a woman gone completely mad.

Theresa saw her up front beside the casket. She was reaching into it and grabbing handfuls of snakes, shrieking inarticulate hatred and fury at them as she threw them on the floor and stomped them. Handful after handful. She'd been bitten twice, and the snakes still clung to her. A green snake hung by its fangs from her right forearm. A small blacksnake had struck her in the face and dangled from her cheek. Neither was poisonous, but Theresa thought Amelia would have gone on screaming and grabbing snakes out of the casket even if they had been.

Her husband tried to pull her away and was struck several times before he staggered back and collapsed on the dais. Amelia remained focused, intent on ridding the casket of every serpent, desperately trying to uncover her son from the monsters writhing on top of him. It wasn't long before the floor around the casket was slick with snake blood and guts and their trampled bodies.

Amelia's youngest little girl, Stella was her name, about four years old, was on the floor at the foot of the casket. Theresa'd watched, horrified, as a big diamondback struck the little girl in the face, and now that side of the child's head had a softball-sized lump on it. Suddenly, her little body went rigid, and she began to shake, convulsing again and again, lying among the bleeding snake bodies on the floor at Amelia's feet. Her mother didn't notice.

The casket had been jammed full of snakes when Elmer Potter had opened the lid. But when Amelia finally reached the bottom of it, cleaned out every last one, her son's body wasn't there.

"Christopher!" she cried in a bone-chilling wail. "Where's my son? Where's my baby?"

~

SHERIFF CUNNINGHAM HAD BEEN SERVING a summons at the south end of Caverna County when he heard the call go out over the radio. At first, he thought the dispatcher had made a mistake. Code 10-34 was a riot. How could there be a riot at a funeral home? The dispatcher filled him in as he drove. Lights and siren were useless driving through fog as thick as Elmer's Glue, so he was not the first emergency responder to arrive at Potter's Funeral Home. But even half an hour in, with every deputy, every Bradford's Ridge Police officer, emergency medical technician and paramedic in the county working to establish order, the carnage was hard to fathom.

The double doors on the first viewing room on the left off the main hallway were mangled. One had been ripped off its hinges, torn from the frame. It lay on its side, still fastened to the other door by a padlocked chain that affixed the doors' handles together.

Injured, bleeding people were everywhere. So were snakes. The sheriff had almost stepped on a small garter snake when he walked into the building. At the sudden sound of a shotgun blast, Cunningham jumped and reached for his service revolver before the EMT standing beside him put his hand on the sheriff's arm.

"They're killing snakes," the man said, a kind of skin-crawling horror in his voice you couldn't miss. "When we got here, they were all over the place—every kind of poisonous snake I've ever seen. Rattlesnakes, water moccasins—"

A boom sounded again.

"Seven confirmed fatalities from snake bites, but there could be more—will be more," he said. "I've seen several I know aren't going to make it."

The EMT wore the uniform of Ballaster County Emergency Medical Services. Caverna County EMS had apparently called for assistance from neighboring counties.

Victims, some conscious, most not, were wheeled past the sheriff on gurneys to waiting ambulances. He spotted

Victor Hernandez, the barber who wouldn't likely be cutting the sheriff's hair anytime soon because he appeared to have a broken arm. Theresa Washington lay strapped to a spine board on a gurney with an oxygen mask over her face. She was dragging in great heaving gulps of air. And he watched the paramedics hurry down the hallway to a waiting ambulance pushing a gurney with a small woman who looked like Tweetie Bird's grandmother. Ella Fletcher didn't appear to be breathing. And who knows what the body count would have been if the weight of the crowd hadn't torn the door off its hinges.

The sheriff heard another blast and then became aware of a high keening, a sound that almost wasn't human, coming from inside the viewing room. He stepped to the opening where he could see paramedics struggling with an obviously hysterical woman. She had snakes dangling from her face and arm, but she held fast to the edge of the casket screaming, "Where's Christopher? Where's my baby?" Then she slumped into the arms of one of the paramedics, finally sedated by the injection he'd given her.

A deputy stepped up to the sheriff.

"The little dead boy's body—we found it. And that's not all we found."

The sheriff felt a sick dread in the deepest pit of his stomach as he drove through the swirling mist out to the Caverna County Cemetery on the edge of town. At the end of a winding lane, the cemetery occupied a wooded hilltop where the view was spectacular on a clear day. More than a century old, the graves were like the rings of a tree—the oldest at the top of the hill and subsequent generations down the sides so the newest plots rested near a small creek at the bottom of the hill beside the road.

The mist granted everything an otherworldly look, cast

ghost shadows, swirled and contorted around the head-stones so as to make everything foreign and other. That's why the sheriff couldn't figure out what he was seeing when he passed the first one. It vanished from view before he could decide what he'd seen, and by then, he had come upon another. He stopped the car, killed the engine, got out and strode nearer, horror and revulsion rising in his chest and threatening to choke him.

It was a grave. A disemboweled grave. The headstone had been knocked aside, the grave dug up, and the casket hauled out. The contents of the casket lay in a pile beside it. This was a fairly recent grave. The stink of moldering decay reached his nostrils, and he swallowed hard not to vomit. He got back into his car and drove on in mounting horror. Though it was impossible to tell in the thick fog, it appeared that graves had been desecrated all over the cemetery. They all bore the same signature. Headstones shattered, graves unearthed, caskets removed, and bones and bodies strewn all around.

He saw bright colored lights through the fog that resolved themselves into the bubblegum machine on the roof of Kentucky State Police Trooper Craig Wilson's cruiser. He'd been dispatched after a hysterical 911 call from Elmer Potter's two sons. The boys were there, in the back seat of the trooper's cruiser, obviously in shock. Their father, Elmer, had tried to slam the coffin lid shut to contain the snakes in the viewing room, but had been swarmed by snakes, bitten repeatedly before he had a chance. That's what the EMT had told the sheriff, said the funeral director was one of the seven confirmed fatalities.

"I think this must be the little boy from the funeral home," Trooper Wilson said, his voice tight with restrained emotion. He walked through the mist to a freshly dug grave that was awaiting Christopher's burial that afternoon. The funeral home tarp with its crank that lowered the casket gently into the grave remained, as did the rows of folding chairs for the mourners. The headstone was in pieces.

The little boy's body sat on the ground with his legs dangling into the grave. A folding chair placed behind him held him upright. Rigor mortis had made the body as stiff as a plank. His back and both legs had been snapped to get his body to sit at the proper angle. Lying in the little boy's lap and draped around his neck were snakes, dead ones, missing their heads.

The sheriff turned aside and was sick, splattering his breakfast on his shoes.

Chapter Thirty-Three

2011

At 8:30 Thursday evening, the following was posted on Daniel Burke's Facebook page and on the page for Voice of Hope Community Church: "A good friend has often teased me that our congregation is bigger than the army of some small countries. I always tell him that we're not an army, we're a family. Families love each other, help and support each other—and I need my family to do that for me right now. I need your help to save the life of a little girl. I have to find someone—quickly! Unless the man can be located in time, a little girl will die."

Daniel didn't lie. But he carefully crafted the wording of the post so it didn't set off any alarm bells, either, so it sounded like the child needed the man for medical reasons, as a blood donor, maybe.

"I don't know the man's name or very much about him. But I do know that he was in a BetterBuy in Cincinnati or northern Kentucky today, bought chocolate ice cream, and he ate dinner at a Tony Barroni Pizza Parlor—maybe with some friends, a Hispanic man and a black man with dreadlocks. The child's loved ones can't go to every BetterBuy and Tony Barroni in Cincinnati and northern Kentucky looking for him. But their 'family' can."

Daniel explained that the man he was seeking had a red, black and green dragon or sea serpent tattoo on his arm that reached from his shoulder to his fingers. He was driving a blue car with New Mexico plates.

"Would you help these desperate members of our church family? Please, go to the BetterBuy store and the Tony Barronis in your neighborhood and ask about the man. Ask the checkers and the managers if they saw him today, the stock boys and bag boys. The man has no idea anyone's looking for him, doesn't know how frantic this family is to find him—because unless he can be found, a precious little girl with pale blue eyes just like her mother's will not live to see another sunrise."

Then Daniel listed a phone number to call if anyone had any information. The phone number was Theresa's.

Jack read the post through twice, then called Daniel.

"You don't suppose Billy Ray's on Facebook?" Daniel asked, suddenly horrified.

Jack had considered that—when they'd visited him in prison, Bill Ray had Googled them before they got there—but decided it was an acceptable level of risk.

"Billy Ray Hawkins strike you as the kind of man who frequents social media? Who even has internet service back in that hollow where he lives?"

Daniel was silent.

"Do you think these people will do it, that they'll help?" Jack asked.

"Oh, they'll help. Trust me, they'll help." Then he was silent. "I only hope it's enough."

WHEN ANDI WOKE up on the pile of blankets on the floor, she could still taste pizza from last night. She needed to brush her teeth, but didn't dare ask any of the men for a toothbrush. She doubted that kidnappers gave the little kids they kidnapped toothbrushes.

Her eyes felt puffy and like they had sand in them. That was from crying. When she'd cried all the time after her mother died, they'd felt like that. And she'd cried herself to sleep last night. For some reason, seeing the room in the daylight calmed her, made her feel better. God knew this room was in her future, and he'd shown it to her, and maybe that was so she wouldn't be scared. So she tried not to be.

Now, she was going to have to get somebody to let her out to go to the bathroom. She hoped Dreadlock Man or Speedy Gonzales answered her knock. She was afraid of all of them, but Tattoo Man scared her most of all. She'd never seen him, had only heard his voice, gruff and scratchy and mean-sounding.

She finally couldn't wait any longer, went to the door and knocked. But before anybody had a chance to answer her knock, the door vanished, went away like it had been turned to glass, and she could see through it to what was on the other side. And what was on the other side was a jumble of images, each one more horrific than the last. There was a mighty rumble, like somebody had gathered up the thunder from a thousand storms and set it loose all at once. There was red-orange fire everywhere. Unrecognizable things—and people!—were flying through thick smoke. And not just whole people. Arms and legs and— a bloody piece of a person, but she couldn't tell what piece, hit something with a horrible splat sound and slid, leaving a bloody snail trail in its wake. Everything was burning, flames were eating up the world. Melted, mangled pieces of —she didn't know what it was—were tangled up with bloody people in black smoke that smelled awful, like——

Andi heard a voice calling and felt someone shake her shoulder.

"Hey, little girl. Something wrong with you?"

She heard the voice call out to somebody else.

"She got epilepsy or something? She's just standing here, staring like she's blind."

"Her name ees Meeranda," said Speedy Gonzales. "Meeranda, wake up. What's the matter wi' choo?"

The world of solid things you could touch and feel returned so suddenly it was jarring. Andi was staring at carnage, and then she was here in the doorway of the room where she'd slept on the floor last night. She focused her eyes. Speedy Gonzales was staring at her; Dreadlock Man was shaking her by the arm.

"I…I need to go to the bathroom," she said.

"See, ees nothing wrong with her," Speedy Gonzales said and turned away while Dreadlock Man shoved her down the hallway to the bathroom. It was gross, like bathrooms in gas stations where her mother told her not to touch anything. Dreadlock Man was waiting outside the door. He held a paper plate with two stale doughnuts on it and a can of Coke and gave them to her, then pointed to the open door of her "prison room" at the other end of the hall.

She'd only gone a step or two toward it when the front door of the house opened and in stepped Tattoo Man. He took one look at her and went postal.

"What's she doing out of that room?" he roared.

"She had to pee," said Dreadlock Man.

Andi could tell that Tattoo Man scared him, too.

Tattoo Man let fly a string of expletives—words she had never heard in her whole life, then yelled. "Get her back in there and don't let her out again, you hear me."

Dreadlock Man shoved her into the room and locked the door behind her.

She looked down and saw that the plate with the doughnuts was shaking because her hands were trembling. She whimpered, the images from the vision still as fresh as wet brush strokes on a painting. She stumbled to the corner of the room, set the Coke and doughnuts down on the floor beside her and sat with her back to both walls. She drew her knees up in front of her, wrapped her arms around them, closed her eyes and tried to summon Princess Buttercup. After all, she'd had a vision and the lady had always come when she had a vision. But she'd tried before to summon the woman made out of light, and it never worked. She wasn't a genie in a bottle. She came when she wanted to talk to Andi, not when Andi wanted to talk to her.

Andi rested her forehead on her knees and started to cry again.

~

1985

Friday morning dawned as crisp and clear as the day before had been gloomy. Thin pewter clouds scuttled by high overhead, sharp as sabers slicing open the sky. No one could remember a fog like the one Thursday that had shrouded the county in mist until almost sundown. The fog had granted yesterday's events an otherworldly, horror-movie quality, but it had also kept the worst of the rubber-neckers and lookie-lous away from the cemetery. It wasn't until the fog cleared right before dusk that anybody spotted the message spray-painted in red that dripped like blood down the front of the Halverson family crypt—the largest in the cemetery: The rest of the dead will rise tomorrow.

The day's bright sunshine brought out the immediate world to gape at the carnage. Though the state police set up roadblocks on the road leading to the cemetery, it did no good. They couldn't have kept away distraught families with a twenty-foot electric fence and razor wire. People parked their cars beside the road and walked past the road-blocks. No, ran. They surged into the cemetery and joined a growing crowd of people deranged with horror. You could hear them everywhere, shrieks as thin as paper cuts. When family members discovered the remains of their loved ones, their bones or decaying bodies scattered, they screamed—wailed—wept, fell to the ground or simply stood gaping, too dumbfounded and shocked to do anything at all.

The sunshine brought the press, too. Two huge satellite news trucks drove past Daniel, Becca and Jack as they rode through town early Saturday morning—their lunch stowed in the picka-nick basket strapped to the back of Jack's bike and Daniel riding behind Becca because this time it was Daniel's bike that had a flat tire. One of the trucks was from the CBS affiliate in Louisville and another from the ABC station in Bowling Green. These trucks were the big dogs, could broadcast events live, as they happened. The three stopped at the courthouse to get a closer look at the big, white WCOH Action News First truck with the gigantic satellite dish on top, in Bradford's Ridge to cover the "strange happenings" that had so far claimed eleven lives and left fifteen people hospitalized. And, of course, to cover—live— the spectacle of the dead of Bradford's Ridge rising out of their graves. Michael Rutherford was at the courthouse and joined them. Jack was actually glad to see him this time. His non-stop babble was, if nothing else, distracting.

Even Jack's father had been shaken. He'd come home early from the bar last night almost sober with the tale of rattlesnakes and disemboweled graves he'd heard there. Becca was so upset she appeared close to tears, and Jack heard her mumble something under her breath about pulling the wings off a fly. Daniel noticed, too, of course, and suggested they go explore the labyrinth of antiques in the second floor of the furniture store to take her mind off what had happened. Maybe this afternoon they'd go skating. The old Arista Theater building had been transformed into a skating rink, with a revolving light ball in the center of the ceiling that sprinkled colored sparkles on the walls, and a sound system that blasted music. Madonna, mostly-- "Like a Virgin" and "Material Girl." All the boys looked forward to "Crazy for You" because on a slow song you got to hold hands with your girlfriend. He, Daniel and Becca always sat that one out and went for a Coke--that tasted disgusting ever since they changed the flavor a couple of months ago.

Old Mr. Walker was glad to let the kids poke around. He pulled down a rickety ladder that extended through a trapdoor like the entrance to most attics. Then he shut and latched the door behind them so they wouldn't accidentally fall through it and told them to holler for him when they were ready to leave.

The attic ran the whole length of the building, a dusty museum of strange-looking lamps, hat racks, vases, clocks and pictures of ugly, unsmiling people in big gilt frames. There were floor-to-ceiling windows on the front of the building overlooking Commerce Street and on the back overlooking the back side of the Eastern Orthodox Church about half a block away. But the windows didn't open, so there was not a hint of a breeze, and their movement disturbed ancient dust that hung in the air like yesterday's fog.

Daniel was examining an elephant-foot stool, and Mikey was looking through a silver kaleidoscope when Becca suddenly cried out. She was standing at one of the back windows and when all the boys rushed to her, she pointed to the church across the alley. Five-year-old Joey Roberts was making his way along the narrow ledge that ran around the edge of the round roof of the church toward a soccer ball that lay in the gutter. In the side yard of the church thirty feet below him were the six Bad Kids.

Jack raced to the trapdoor and banged on it, hollering for Mr. Walker to come and let them out. But the old man never came, either he didn't hear or was busy. The four of them were trapped in the attic, forced to watch helplessly while the Bad Kids threw rocks at the little boy on the church roof.

"They're trying to knock him off there," Jack whispered.

"That's why they got him to go up there in the first place," Becca said.

"I don't think so," said Mikey. "If they wanted to hit him, they could. I think they're trying to scare him so he'll cry."

"Why would they want—?" Daniel began. The Bad Kids suddenly dropped their rocks and ran around to the other side of the building out of sight. Beatrice Cunningham, the pharmacist's wife, was coming down Baxter Street along the side of the furniture store toward the church.

She heard Joey, looked up, and her scream rattled the

windows. After that, it didn't take long for a huge crowd to gather.

As the wail of a distant siren grew louder, they heard the catch on the trapdoor open, and they thundered past a bewildered Mr. Walker and out the side door of the store. The six Bad Kids were sauntering toward them. Jack put out his hand, motioning the others to stop there, out of sight in an alcove between the furniture store and the dry cleaners next door. They could hear the Bad Kids' voices as they approached, but the boys never even glanced in their direction—their eyes were glued to the developing emergency on the other side of the alley.

"...should keep them busy for a while," Cole said. "Get your bikes and meet me at Allsup's Station in five minutes."

Then they heard an odd sound, like laughter—but with a harsh, vulgar ring, an ugly parody of amusement.

"We're gonna make 'em squeal." That was a voice none of them recognized. Not a human voice. The Bad Kids walked on down the alley, rounded the corner and disappeared.

Becca spoke softly after the awful sound died away.

"The demons are so excited they're hopping up and down, jumping around like the monkeys in that cage at the zoo."

Michel stared at her, uncomprehending.

"This is some kind of distraction to get everybody's attention, focus it here so they can get away with something else that's even worse. We have to do something," she said.

"We don't have time to go find Bishop," Jack said. "Whatever they're planning, it's now. We can follow them and—" He stopped as a new thought struck him. "They might even be going…you know—there, where it is, to its…lair."

"Lair?" Daniel was incredulous. "Jack, this isn't an episode of Wild Kingdom. There's a monster demon out there!"

Jack saw Mikey look from one to the other of them in growing fright.

"They're up to something awful." Urgency made Jack's already-a-man's voice gruff. "But nobody will believe that! If we don't stop them, who will?"

There it was then, the end of all things, the edge of ancient maps where it said "beyond this point be dragons." If they stood by, didn't at least try to stop them, the Bad Kids would do something horrible…and people would die. They hadn't even been able to talk about that part yet. The unthinkable had finally happened. The snakes the Bad Kids had put in that little boy's casket yesterday had killed people.

"Don't act like you're going alone," Daniel said.

"The bike'd be too slow with both of us on it. We'd lose them. You and Becca and Mikey go get Bishop."

Then Jack leapt on his bike and tore out down the street in the direction the Bad Kids had gone.

2011

Jeff Kendrick's secretary tapped timidly on his door. It was still "personal time," the fifteen minutes before the switchboard went on and the law firm of Taylor, Murray and Kendrick was open for business. Personal time had been Jeff's idea, and it'd been a good one. Productivity was up, morale was high, and he'd come to be seen as "the guy on their side" by the staff—the secretaries, the paralegals, the file clerks, the receptionist and housekeeping. That was worth its weight in billable hours. In a crunch, sometime when Jeff really needed it, they'd march down the barrel of a cannon for him.

Not a bad return on investment for the half hour it took him to convince the senior partners that the staff was doing it anyway—no way to police a thing like that. He argued for granting fifteen minutes in the morning and an extra fifteen minutes at lunch during which they could Tweet or Pin, watch a YouTube video or check their Facebook page———in exchange for their pledge not to use social media any other time.

Appeared to be working better than buying expensive software to limit their access to the Internet.

Which was why Jeff was surprised that his secretary wanted to talk to him.

She had brought her iPad with her.

"I thought you might want to see this, sir. Isn't he one of your clients? This seems a little bit…odd."

Jeff read Daniel's Facebook post from the night before.

"Odd" was a gross understatement. Jeff thanked her for her diligence—and was calling Daniel's cell before the door closed behind her.

The call went directly to voice mail.

The phone number listed in the bizarre Facebook post was Theresa Washington's. She was in on it—whatever "it" was. He called but got her voice mail. Her phone wasn't turned off; the line was busy. So he waited to call again, trying to figure out as he did what in the world Daniel Burke was thinking.

The perception of Daniel mattered in his case. He needed to look, act—even smell like "a minister." He needed to appear trustworthy and dignified. Posting something as bizarre as this on Facebook would not contribute to that image in the minds of prospective jurors.

Why would he unleash a twenty-five-thousand-member congregation on a grocery store chain and a pizza parlor?

He tried Daniel's office and discovered that he wasn't even in town. He was in Washington.

Chapman Whitworth.

Jeff had ping-ponged back and forth on what he believed about the Supreme Court candidate—and, in consequence, what he believed about the honesty/sanity of his own clients. He'd arranged for Daniel and his police officer friend to see Senator LaHayne because he was absolutely certain nobody could con the senator! And if there was any possibility that the Supreme Court candidate really was involved in murder and extortion…

Did this strange Facebook post have something to do with Whitworth?

Jeff tried Theresa Washington again. Still busy. He instructed his secretary to try the number every ten minutes. If he couldn't get through to her by lunchtime, he'd go to Theresa Washington's house and ask her in person what in the Sam Hill was going on.

Chapter Thirty-Four

2011

"No, ma'am, the man with dreadlocks don't have red hair," Theresa said.

The phone had rung nonstop. Oh, there hadn't been any sightings of the kidnappers, but it was human nature, she supposed, for folks to want you to know they'd tried to help.

She punched the off button on her iPhone and watched it die. A woman had to deal with calls of nature, phone or no phone. Besides, her poor old back had been aching fiercely ever since she set her feet on the floor this morning, and she was gonna have to put on that brace else she couldn't sit here and answer the phone. When she come back down the stairs, she noticed the smell of cinnamon and vanilla. There was a time when they would have been the smells of real cinnamon and vanilla from her baking, not the artificial scents from air fresheners with little bottles that stuck into outlets and had an underlying aroma of some petroleum product. The minute she turned the phone back on, it rang in her hand.

"Jack, honey," she said, "I can't believe you got through. Phone's been ringing off the hook all morning." As she said it, she realized that was another one of them phrases that didn't mean nothing anymore. Wasn't no hook to hang a phone on these days. In fact, even "hang up" didn't make no sense. "I told you I'd call you soon's I heard anything that was even a tiny bit helpful, but the folks I'm talkin' to want to give me a description of everybody they talked to and what they said. I'm getting calls from far away as Louisville and Lexington."

Daniel had told people "Cincinnati and northern Kentucky" but she supposed "northern Kentucky" could be interpreted in pretty broad terms. And besides his twenty-five-thousand-member congregation, untold thousands of people all over everywhere watched Daniel's sermons on television every Sunday morning—and read the church's Facebook page.

"Thanks for doing this," he said, and she hated the disappointment she heard in his voice.

"It's gone happen, sugar," she told him. "You"ll see. The Lord's gone lead us to wherever it is Billy Ray's got that little girl hid out." She sighed. "Wherever Becca is, I'm glad she don't know her monster father snatched Andi to get her back."

Theresa thought she heard a sound behind her, but with the brace on, it was hard to turn around. It was only the old house creaking.

She punched the off button, wiggled in the chair trying to get comfortable, and the phone rang again immediately.

~

1985

Maybe I'll die today.

Oliver Marshal had started every morning for the past twenty years with that thought and so far it had proved an empty promise.

The old man sat in his wheelchair inside the front doors of the Twin Oaks Nursing Home, had been parked there by that juiced-up crackhead of an orderly. Oliver had that guy's number alright, could tell he was a druggie by the way his eyes were always dilated and how he was as antsy sometimes as a little kid who needed to go to the bathroom. But do you think anybody would pay attention to Ollie if he ratted the guy out? He made a humph sound in his throat. Not likely! They'd all sworn allegiance to the Great Sovereign Gospel of Nursinghomedom: anybody over the age of sixty-five is either senile or an idiot, and either way you're free to ignore them.

"Thank you for telling us, Mr. Marshal," they'd say soothingly, giving each other the look right there in front of him like he was blind instead of only a little hard of hearing. "We'll check into it right away."

"Check into it" meaning pretend the old coot hadn't said a word and "right away" meaning never.

It wasn't Oliver's fault he'd lived so long! He hadn't wanted to, hadn't asked to. Who wants to be eighty-nine years old and can't get around anymore? Shoot, he hadn't stood up on his own like a man since they kicked Nixon out of the White House. Millions of people, young people, dying every day, and his heart kept ticking like a Timex watch.

Since everybody believed he was senile, Ollie played along and let them think so, sat with his chin on his chest and his eyes blank. It took too much energy to get the attention of people who looked right through you as if you weren't there. He'd stay here where they'd parked him with a blanket over his lap—why'd they always truss him up like a Christmas turkey? He'd never said he was cold. It was summertime, for crying out loud!—and watch what little life there was in this place go on around him. Eventually, they'd come and get him and park him somewhere else.

He saw a group of boys on bicycles cruise by the nursing home on the road out front as he heard Mrs. Booth's high heels click, click, clicking on the shiny ceramic tile floor behind him—her on-a-mission gait.

"Robert," she called out to the crackhead orderly who was probably on his way to snort some coke, "is the phone in the TV lounge working?""

"Don't know, ma'am, haven't tried to use it today.""

"Well, try," Mrs. Booth said. "I think all the phones on the first floor are dead. I'm on my way to see about the ones on two and three."

She went clicking off to the sweeping stairway on Ollie's right, one of two that swooped down in an elegant curve from the second to the first floor of the old building, with an elevator tucked unobtrusively between them. On the second floor, the elevator and staircases opened onto an internal balcony with a wrought iron railing that ran the width of the west wing where second and third floor residents could sit in rockers or wheelchairs and stare off into the elegance of the atrium—those who could see that far, that is.

The beauty and grace of the original Twin Oaks mansion had been preserved when the structure was converted into a hotel in the 1930s, and miraculously most of it survived the renovation into a nursing home in 1978, retaining sufficient style and architectural niceties to keep the building on the National Registry of Historic Places.

The structure was U-shaped, nestled in the woods on the north and south, with the west wing of the building backed up against the Big Puddle River. There were no resident rooms on the first floor, leaving all the original grandeur intact, the whole sweep of it an open atrium with ceramic tile flooring in an intricate mosaic design, marble pillars, columns and glass-top tables that held huge vases filled with a jungle of tropical silk flowers. Ollie couldn't decide which he thought was the more ostentatious—the historic chandelier or the fountain. The antique wooden chandelier hung above the front doors, suspended by four chains from the third floor ceiling, a fifteen-foot-wide, detailed scale model of Twin Oaks with lights shining out its windows and from a later-added lattice attached to the bottom. The fountain sat in the middle of the atrium, pristine white marble with a six-foot-tall porpoise standing on its tail in the center with water squirting out its mouth.

The kitchen was located in the south corner of the ground floor, the administration offices the north corner. Facing a parking lot in the center of the U, a wide plank porch stretched the length of the building, enclosed not by white balusters but by a black wrought iron railing. The wrought iron was mirrored in the decorative window grates on the second- and third-floor rooms. Frosted glass in the double entrance doors featured the entwined oak trees logo.

So prestigious was the facility, its waiting list ensured that within forty-eight hours after a resident "passed," another showed up to take his place. Right now, the sixty-four rooms housed one hundred and fifteen residents—which meant they'd be bringing somebody in to take the place of Ollie's former roommate any day now. He'd already outlived half a dozen or so; he'd lost count.

The six boys on bicycles cruised by on the road out front again, going the opposite direction, not cutting up like boys out for a ride but serious as soldiers on a mission, playing some game, probably. One of them had a Mohawk haircut. Looked like a punk. One day he'd wish he could grow back some of that hair he'd shaved off. Three cars pulled out of the parking lot, and the boys on bikes stopped on the side of the road directly across from where Ollie sat and watched as the cars drove away, leaving only a handful of vehicles—staff and maybe a visitor—in the lot. Once the cars were out of sight, one of the boys got off his bike and ran off into the woods across the road from the nursing home. He returned a moment later hauling some kind of sign, a big one mounted on what looked like a sawhorse but couldn't have been because he carried it in one hand. He placed the sign across the driveway that led from the road to the parking lot and started back to his bike. One of the other boys called out something to him, and he turned back to the sign and used his shirttail to wipe the sign where he'd been holding it. Then he got on his bike again, and all the boys raced away west down the road and disappeared from view beyond the sunroom.

The sign was blocking the entrance! Whatever was written on it was facing the other direction, and Ollie couldn't read it. Probably said, "Screw you!" The boys' prank wasn't going to seem at all humorous to the first person who tried to pull into the parking lot and had to get out of the car and move the sign to get past.

A couple of cars drove by, but none tried to turn in. A few minutes later, Ollie saw a lone boy—a black kid carrying something—walking down the roadside in front of the building, coming from town, opposite the direction the other boys had ridden away. He crossed the road, walked past the sign set only a few minutes before in the driveway, then crossed the parking lot and loped up the steps to the porch and in the front doors of Twin Oaks. He was wearing a Bradford's Ridge Rangers All-Star team baseball shirt and looked hot, tired and winded. Had he walked all the way from town?

"Excuse me, sir, is there a pay phone in the building?" he asked Ollie.

Ollie said nothing, pretended he didn't hear.

The boy figured out Ollie wasn't going to answer and looked around, apparently saw the sign pointing to the administrative wing and headed off in that direction. When the boy turned his back, Ollie read the name printed on his jersey in big block letters: Carpenter.

The boy hadn't been gone out of the atrium for ten minutes when Ollie saw the six boys who'd twice cruised by on the road out front come around the edge of the sunroom on foot. As they jogged toward the parking lot, he saw the big gym bags they carried, bags that they had not had on their bicycles. When they got to the parking lot, they divided up. The north and south wings had double doors that opened onto the porch and steps that extended to sidewalks leading to the parking lot. Three boys headed up the sidewalk to the north wing and three headed up the sidewalk to the south wing. None of the boys entered the building through the double doors in front of Ollie.

He saw one of the boys, his hair all fluffed out like a sissy girl, cross to where Gladys Overstreet was sitting on the porch in a rocker. He grabbed the back of the rocker and dragged it backward, with Gladys aboard, across the porch and into the building and closed the double doors behind him.

Ollie felt a chill. He hadn't felt cold like that since the day he'd watched the Krauts toss mustard gas canisters into a school and then shoot the kids when they came running out, him sitting helpless in the trees, unable to do a thing to stop it.

The six boys came straight down the hallways into the

atrium. A blond kid with a rat-tail that must have been a foot long hanging down his back set his duffle bag on the floor and took a length of chain out of it. He went to the double doors on the front of the building, closed them and then wrapped the chain around the handles, fastening them together. He took a padlock out of the sack, hooked it through the chain links, snapped it closed and dropped the key into his shirt pocket.

Ollie's heart began to hammer in his chest, but he sat with his chin down, slack-jawed, and the boys blew by him like he wasn't there. Harold Castleback wasn't pretending senility, though. When he saw the boy begin to chain the door shut, the seventy-five-year-old former high school principal stood up from where he'd been reading a newspaper in one of the chairs by the window and hurried in his shuffling gait across the atrium.

"Hey, there," Harold said. He had reached the boy who had dropped the padlock key into his pocket. "What do you think you're doing?"

The boy turned to Harold. He had a plump bottom lip that made him look like he was pouting, but he didn't behave like a petulant child.

"Keeping the world out and you in," he said. Then he grabbed Harold by the neck with one hand. Ollie couldn't see what he did exactly without turning his head, and he didn't intend to move! Whatever it was, all Ollie heard was a kind of strangling sound, a grunt, and when the boy released his hold on Harold, the old man collapsed on the floor like a marionette with broken strings.

"The floor plan shows six entrances," said a redheaded kid who appeared to be the leader. "These three on the front of the building, a big service entrance next to the kitchen"—he pointed toward it —"and two back doors on the river." He indicated the hallway leading to the back of the building. "And you saw the two fire escapes on the way in. Seal everything, chain the doors and nail the windows shut. Nobody gets in or out. Kill anyone who tries to stop you."

One of the boys had been carrying one of those big stereo things, a boombox, and he set it on the floor and punched a button and sound blasted out of it in the most awful racket Ollie'd ever heard. Wouldn't call it *music*. The pulsating rhythm attacked his whole body, the screeching and shrieking sounded like somebody was feeding cats into a meat grinder.

The redheaded boy turned to the remaining boys and indicated the "administration" sign with his chin.

"Come on," he said, and the parody of a smile curled his lips. "This is going to be payback for all the times we were 'careful not to hurt anybody.'"

Chapter Thirty-Five

2011

Senator LaHayne's office sent a car to pick Daniel up at his hotel. He stepped out into sunshine so bright it made the world look overexposed. He patted the cellphone in his pocket, willing his fingers to leave it alone. And he slammed shut for the one millionth time the door leading down into the dark dungeon of monsters in his mind. Where the Wild Things Are. He'd read that book to Andi when she was little. Only the wild things behind the door in his mind were real, they walked around in the world, and his daughter could see them. One of them had kidnapped her and was threatening to kill her.

No, that wasn't right. Theresa'd said Billy Ray wasn't possessed by a demon. He was just an evil man all on his own. She said there were a whole lot more bad people like him out there than people possessed.

Daniel literally shook his head to fling thoughts of Andi out of his mind, then got into the back of the sleek limousine. The sights along Pennsylvania Avenue blew by the window in a blur. Daniel wouldn't let himself think about the time he and Emily had brought Andi to Washington. She'd wanted to climb up into Abraham Lincoln's lap.

When the car bearing Daniel to his meeting with Senator LaHayne and the demon-possessed Chapman Whitworth turned left off Constitution Avenue onto First Street, Daniel glanced right. Half a block down the street on the left stood the grand edifice of the United States Supreme Court building.

The senator's office was on the fifth floor of the seven-story Dirksen Senate Office Building, across the street from the Russell Senate Office Building and diagonally across the grounds from the senate wing of the Capitol.

The clicking of his heels echoed ominously as he walked down the long, brightly lit hallway, past the doors of other senators—each with flagpoles on both sides. On the left was the American flag, on the right the flag of the state the senator represented. He spotted the Ohio state flag with its distinctive triangle of stars and swallowtail design beside a door about halfway down on the right.

He was ushered immediately into the senator's inner office. Surrounding a sitting area and a huge cherry desk, the walls were painted a dignified forest green and inset shelves were jammed with a somehow uncluttered array of family photos and books. Daniel wondered if he'd actually read all of the books and decided he probably had.

The senator looked up from his work, rose from his chair behind the desk and indicated for Daniel to take a seat in one of a pair of stately wingback chairs across a glass coffee table from a sofa covered in incongruously bright-yellow fabric. Arranged on the table was a tea service set for three—white china with a simple gold rim and the seal of the senate on each cup, and a small plate of cookies. The senator was famous for his proud devotion to tea over coffee. LaHayne seated himself in the other wing-back and indicated a manila folder on the table beside the teapot.

Daniel picked it up but didn't look inside. He knew what the folder contained.

"My grandmother would have said you look like death on a cracker," the senator told him. "Did you even go to bed last night?"

He hadn't.

"Of course I did. I just didn't rest well," Daniel said. "Guess it shows, huh."

"The steamer trunks under your eyes are big enough to pack up a fashionista for a month-long tour of Europe. Things aren't any better back home, are they?"

"No, they're not."

"I'm looking forward to hearing the whole story of what's going on with you and your police officer friend."

"Don't. It's not a story you want to hear."

The senator reached out and patted Daniel's knee. "We're writing the most important chapter in it today, son. You ready for this?"

The senator had an uncanny way of making a question sound casual, when it was anything but. The calm and peace around the man was no facade. It went all the way to his core. He was not tense about what was to come—not because he foresaw the outcome but because he was totally prepared to deal with what happened, however it turned out.

Daniel tried to let the senator's presence calm him.

The senator laid out the plan again for Daniel, such as it was. He'd described it yesterday, and it hadn't altered since then. Daniel represented the chips the senator intended to stack up in the middle of the table, his whole bankroll bet on one hand. On a cell phone the senator had provided that was now in Daniel's coat pocket, he had a copy of the surveillance video linking Whitworth to a man named Edgar Wallace Boskowitz and the murdered "rape victim." It was his job to display that "evidence," along with the contents of the manila folder, to make it appear the senator was holding four aces—instead of a couple of twos, a three, a seven and the joker.

~

2011

Becca moved as silently as a cat in house shoes. It was a skill she'd learned during years on the run. Don't wake up the other derelicts—they could be like junkyard dogs, vicious if roused. Don't disturb the cattle when you sneak into the barn to sleep in the hay. Don't let the security guard hear you slide in behind the boxes to keep warm or the produce trucker hear you fill your duffle with carrots.

Theresa kept her car keys in her purse. She kept her purse upstairs on the dresser beside her bed. As Becca eased up the stairs, she listened to the rise and fall of the old woman's voice on the phone. The second step from the top squeaked so she stepped over it.

With the keys snug in her jeans pocket, Becca went back down the stairs as quietly as she had gone up them. Theresa was still talking as she had been when Becca came in earlier—when Becca heard her say that "Billy Ray's got Andi hid out."

That monster had stolen sweet Andi to trade for her.

She eased the kitchen door open again. This time, she moved the screen so slowly the spring didn't squeak as it had earlier. The car was parked in the driveway. Becca hoped it had gas. She had no money to buy any. She hoped it had an automatic transmission, too. She hadn't driven a car in twenty years and didn't know if she could manage a clutch. She scored on both counts, backed slowly out of the driveway and drove away.

~

1985

Jack had tried, but it'd been hopeless almost from the very beginning. The Bad Kids had ridden a normal speed through the town streets, and even on his colossal wreck of a bike with the picka-nick basket strapped to the back, Jack was able to keep up with them, far enough behind that they wouldn't notice. But as soon as the boys got out of the clusters of houses along the river, they pulled out the stops, and Jack watched them blow away out of sight so far in front of him there was no hope of ever catching up.

He'd lost them.

Think. Where could they have gone?

Jack knew that whatever they were planning, it was on this side of town since they'd gone to considerable trouble to create a diversion on the other side. But what or where it could be, he couldn't imagine. There wasn't much of anything here—subdivisions had snuggled up next to the Big Puddle as the town expanded south. There was a small marina and dock where the river widened out, a nursing home on the riverbank a couple of miles away, and beyond that a strip mall with a grocery store, a beauty parlor, and a branch of Kentucky State Bank. Could that be it—were they planning to rob the bank? What for?

Even though he'd lost sight of the Bad Kids, Jack kept going. What else could he do?

The nursing home finally appeared ahead on his right.

It sat on a small hill. Jack was starting up the incline toward the building when the chain came off his bike, the back tire locked up and he went flying over the handlebars and landed in the road, peeling much of the skin off the palm of his right hand. The wreck also tore the right knee of his pants and bent the handlebar on the bike. He could fix the chain—it wouldn't take very long—but he had already decided it was pointless to continue. He'd walk up to the nursing home and borrow a phone to call Bishop for a ride. Maybe they could drive around in Bishop's truck until they spotted something—which he didn't believe for a minute would do any good.

He dragged the bike—it wouldn't roll with the back tire locked up—off the road into the edge of the woods and leaned it against a tree, didn't bother to hide it. Who in their right mind would steal a battered-up old bike with a bent handlebar and a broken chain? It occurred to him for the first time that he was hungry, so he unstrapped the picka-nick basket and took it with him as he trudged up the hill toward the huge white building on the summit. Jack had never been inside the place. Daniel had been there dozens of times. On Saturdays, his father took communion to the nursing home residents, and Daniel often went along.

"There's a fountain on the ground floor that I'm dying to put dishwashing soap in," Daniel had said. "The bubbles would be epic!"

The banisters on the two curved staircases would probably provide a decent enough ride, he'd said, but there were always too many people around for him to try. And he'd found a "not exciting" crawl space under the floor one day when he spilled grape juice. No creepy cool basement, though, only a dirt hole with a coal chute for a furnace that wasn't there anymore.

Jack got to the driveway leading to the nursing home from the road and found it blocked by a sawhorse and a sign that read "Danger!" in bright-red letters on the top. "Restricted Area, Natural Gas Leak," was printed below next to the Bradford's Ridge Gas and Electric Company logo. Jack looked around but saw no truck or G&E Company workers. He skirted the sign, crossed the parking lot and went up the steps to the main entrance—double doors flung wide today to admit the summer morning air. Each door had an oval-shaped pane of frosted glass in the middle with a single tree etched in the glass. When the doors were closed, the two trees side by side with entwined limbs formed the Twin Oaks logo.

An old man sat in a wheelchair beside the door, but when Jack asked him where he might locate a pay phone, the man sat with his head bent, looking at nothing. Then Jack saw a sign: "Administration." There'd be a phone he could borrow in the office.

The office complex opened with a frosted glass door that matched the ones on the front. There was a broad reception counter, with an area behind it where women were working in individual cubicles. He approached the receptionist, who was absorbed in paperwork at a desk behind the counter, and set the picka-nick basket down on the floor beside him.

"Excuse me. My bike broke down on the road. May I please borrow a phone to call somebody to come pick me up?"

She didn't get up, but did drag her gaze away from her work long enough to give him a distracted glance. "I'd be glad for you to borrow a phone, son, but we have a line down somewhere, knocked out all the phones in the building."

She noted Jack's disappointed look. "I'm sure it'll be

fixed soon, and you're welcome to wait." She indicated the empty chairs in the reception area. Then she seemed to think of something. "My grandson is about your age and when he comes to visit me, he likes to take a comic book"—she pointed to a pile of tattered ones on the coffee table with equally worn copies of Reader's Digest and National Geographic—"and read it back there."

The receptionist gestured to a space between the wall of the room and the wall of the first cubicle. "This old building is full of interesting nooks and crannies, and Bobby has explored them all. Apparently, you can crawl in there and go around a corner, and there's this nice open space where a window trains a beam of sunlight like a reading lamp—or so he says." She bent her head back to her work.

Obviously, her grandson was not actually Jack's age but several years younger. Crawling in tunnels was a little-kid thing to do, way too childish for a twelve-year-old. Still… he wanted to see the open space with the beam of sunlight—then he'd know something about the nursing home Daniel didn't—and it'd be a cool place to eat a sandwich. So he knelt down and crawled into the cubby hole, which it turned out did, indeed, have a veritable sunroom about five feet by five feet. Jack leaned back against the wall in the sunshine, took a peanut-butter-and-jelly sandwich out of the picka-nick basket and began to eat.

<h1 style="text-align:center">Chapter Thirty-Six</h1>

2011

After a couple of dozen calls, Theresa had a response down that shut up all but the most talkative callers.

"The reverend sure does appreciate your effort. Why don't you send him an email and tell him all about it 'cause I got to keep this line clear for somebody who did find out somethin'."

Soon's they heard that, the person on the other end of the line hung up.

"On the other end of the line." That didn't make no sense anymore, either.

The phone in her hand rang.

"Is this the number you're supposed to call if you found out something about the man the reverend Daniel is looking for?" a woman asked.

Theresa was instantly alert. Nobody'd asked that.

"Yes, it is. Did you find someone who's seen him?"

"It just shows what kind of man our pastor is that he's trying to help this poor family whose little girl is sick. I don't believe a word about what they said he did. The reverend would never—"

Theresa heard a voice in the background.

"They don't care what you believe about the reverend, Roberta. Tell them about the car."

"Well, I think the reverend needs to know we support—"

There was a rustling sound and a man's voice spoke. "Name's Herbert Black, and we didn't find anybody'd seen the man, but we did find somebody'd seen the car—a blue car with New Mexico plates, right?"

Theresa's heart began to pound. "Yes, that's right."

"We had about given up, asked everybody we could find in the store. And, by the way, they're getting tired of being asked, said they'd already had almost a dozen people this morning come in to question them. Anyway, we were walking out to the car when we saw this boy in the parking lot pushing carts back into the store. Long blond hair—in a ponytail." Theresa could hear the disapproval in his voice. "He said nobody'd asked him anything, and he definitely remembered the New Mexico plates. Said he plays a game with himself to see how many states he can find, and this is the first time he'd seen a car from New Mexico."

"Where are you? Which BetterBuy?"

"The one on Barstow Avenue in Florence. One other thing—the store manager told us that one of the checkers who was working yesterday afternoon doesn't come in until after lunch. So maybe she knows something."

When Theresa touched Jack's name on her favorites list, her hands were shaking.

"The BetterBuy on Barstow in Florence," she said when he answered seconds after the first ring. "I been there. Take the Lakewood exit south right after you cross the river. Make a left on Fourth Street. Parking lot boy—

long blond hair in a ponytail—seen the car. He's sure of it."

"Thanks!" Then the line went dead. Without no dial tone, did lines even "go dead" anymore?

The phone rang again, and she wondered if she needed to answer it now that they'd found what they was looking for. Probably should. But first things first. Time for another potty break. When she passed the front window on her way to the bathroom, she stopped and stared out, forgot all about how bad she needed to pee. Her car was no longer sitting in her driveway.

Who'd steal an old car sitting in a driveway in a quiet neighborhood? Musta needed a car real bad to do a thing like that in broad daylight.

Then her heart took up the rhythm in her chest her heart doctor said didn't do her blood pressure no good at all. You don't s'pose…

She hurried up the stairs as fast as an old fat woman could climb them. Her purse where she kept her keys was lying open on her bed.

That noise behind her. Becca had been here. She'd heard about Billy Ray and Andi.

~

1985

Jack heard the sound of Van Halen and his head snapped up. Who in a *nursing home* would play…? "Runnin' With the Devil." His heart slammed into a rhythm faster and harder than the beat of the music.

"What can I do for you boys?"

At the sound of the receptionist's voice, Jack stopped breathing.

Boys?

"Is this everybody, the whole staff?"

Cole Stuart!

"I beg your pardon," the receptionist was still only confused, not frightened.

"How many people work here? Total?"

"Son, I don't think that's any of your business. Why do——?"

Jack heard the swish of the half-doors in the counter that separated it from the waiting area. Then there was a clunking sound as something was knocked to the floor—a lamp or the lady's purse—and a squeaking sound, an awful squeaking sound like somebody had stepped on the tail of a mouse.

"How many?"

"Twenty-five," came a strangled response from the squeaking voice. The receptionist was scared now.

"They all here today?"

Apparently, she shook her head because Jack heard no reply.

"Where?"

"…in here, in the office—eight, no ten, I think. Yes, ten. Please, don't hurt anybody. We'll give you whatever you want, just let us——"

"Where else?"

"The kitchen, the laundry—Sylvia and Grace are doing sheets—physical therapy and the game room. And the caregivers, nurses and aides and orderlies on the floors with the residents."

"How many?"

"I don't——"

Cole hit her, you could hear the slap sound of his palm connecting with her face. She started crying then, trying to talk through her tears.

"There are…six or seven on each floor—I don't know how many exactly." He must have threatened to hit her again because she continued in a rush. "Thirteen! Yes, there are thirteen timecards—that's all I know."

"Nobody working outside?"

"No, today is the groundskeeper's—it's Tomás's day off."

"Lucky Tommy," said another voice. Victor Alexander.

An ugly chuckle followed. Roger Willingham.

"That everybody?"

"Yes, that's every—"

Her voice cut off with a choked noise. Jack heard a thump and the sound of things falling to the floor and knew Cole must have tossed her back into her chair or onto her desk.

The rest of the room erupted in screaming, the office workers at first responding to what had happened to the receptionist but quickly erupting in terror for what might be in store for them, too. Jack lay down and put his face to the floor and could see a small slice of the room from under the back panel of the cubicle.

From what little Jack could see under the wall, the Bad Kids tore into the crowd of women like a pack of attacking wolves. It sounded like a slaughter house. Women screamed, things were knocked over and crashed to the floor, hysterical voices cried out, begged for their lives.

"No, don't! Please—"

"Why, what are you do—?"

"I have little children. They need—"

It did them no good to plead for mercy. What inhabited the bodies of those twelve-year-old boys was incapable of mercy.

The Bad Kids slammed bodies into walls, the workers' cries cut off abruptly in midscream. He thought of what they'd heard the boys—the demons——say as they passed by the alcove beside the furniture store. "We're gonna make them squeal." Was this what they meant?

A woman's voice nearby wailed.

"Don't. I'll pay you—please—"

There was a strangling sound, and she slammed into the partition Jack crouched behind. He could hear her feet kicking, thrumping the wall uselessly, like maybe she was held up in the air. Then her body dropped down to the floor, blocking his view. The woman had blonde hair, and her face was only inches from his. Her clear blue eyes were looking right at him or would have been if the eyes had not been sightless. Her throat had been ripped out—with what? Bare hands? Fingernails? Teeth? Jack could see her spine through the gory hole in the front of her neck.

He felt his stomach begin to heave at the sight, but he clamped his jaw shut and forced himself to swallow. If they found him right now, while they were in this feeding frenzy of killing, they would literally rip him apart with their bare hands.

It didn't take long for three twelve-year-old boys to murder ten women. Not long at all.

The room was finally quiet and Jack could hear the music again. Motley Crue blasting out "Shout at the Devil," singing about putting "the thrill back in death." He could hear the boys panting on the other side of the partition, barely three feet from him. The smell of blood was everywhere. Were the other Bad Kids inflicting similar carnage in other parts of the building?

Bishop had said the efreet intended to commit some heinous act. But who could have imagined anything like this? That woman had said there were twenty-five employees here. Had the Bad Kids killed all of them?

Twenty-five murders. And there were probably more

than a hundred old people still in the building. Why would they kill the staff and—?

Jack exhaled shakily and then drew air back in slowly. No, he hadn't been mistaken. He smelled gasoline.

~

2011

Daniel looked at his watch. Whitworth was late. Maybe he didn't intend to show up at all. Daniel was instantly ashamed of the thrill of joy that thought shot through his body. Oh, how he did not want to do this.

Though Daniel understood in general terms the process of a Supreme Court nomination and confirmation, the senator outlined it briefly as they waited for Whitworth to arrive, speaking in the even tones of a college professor lecturing a class. Daniel could see no sign of tension at all in the man, no hint of apprehension. But he was sure he displayed enough apprehension for the both of them. He was equally sure the senator was giving him the mini civics lesson to distract him, to keep him from winding tighter and tighter as the minutes ticked away.

"You do know that Whitworth's nomination won't be decided by this committee, don't you," LaHayne said, but didn't wait for Daniel to answer before he continued. "All the committee will do is vote on whether or not to send the nomination to the full senate for confirmation. Only takes a simple majority vote of the committee." The senator paused, then continued matter-of-factly. "I've counted my chicks, and on this committee, I don't have enough votes to quash the nomination."

"So, unless he's willing to withdraw…?"

"The full senate has only rejected about a dozen candidates—the most recent was a long time ago, Robert Bork in 1987. But if you and I can't get Whitworth to fold his hand here, I can filibuster his nomination once it hits the senate floor. I do have the guns to pull that off. I can delay the vote indefinitely if I have to." He smiled a small smile. "Until Hell freezes over, if that's how long it takes."

"But that only puts it off, doesn't change—"

"A lot of things can happen during a filibuster, son."

LaHayne's phone rang in decorously subdued tones and Daniel's heart sank. Apparently, Whitworth had arrived and was waiting in the outer office.

LaHayne reached out a hand and placed it gently on Daniel's shoulder. "Just remember…we've read the end of the book. We know how it all comes out."

That's what Clayton Abernathy had said.

The senator picked up the receiver, listened and said, "Send him in."

As soon as Daniel looked into Whitworth's cold, shark eyes, he knew theirs was a fool's errand, that nobody could stop this man from getting whatever he wanted.

~

1985

Oliver Marshal could barely get it into his head that what he'd seen was real, that he wasn't hallucinating or having some crazy reaction to the pills they were always shoving down his throat. Six boys—just boys—had come into the building less than twenty minutes ago, and Ollie would bet his Social Security check there wasn't a nursing home employee still alive anywhere in the building.

He'd heard pandemonium break out on the upper floors after the boys disappeared up the stairs. Yelling, screams and shrieking, furniture crashing, shouts and running feet. Along with whoops of excitement mingled with laughter, maniacal laughter, an ugly, vicious animal sound that put Ollie in mind of mad dogs. All of it on a background of the tortured sounds coming from the box on the floor, the throbbing rhythm jarring his bones and making his teeth ache.

He'd watched, without moving his head, of course, as one boy chased Mrs. Booth out to the balcony, then picked her up and tossed her over the railing, like she was no heavier than a doll. She lay on the tile floor now, about twenty feet from Ollie, with her head facing the wrong way on her neck. One of those clickety-clacking high heels had come off when she fell and landed right in front of his chair. Hard not to look at it, but he'd been practicing his blank stare for going on fifteen years now, and he had the thing down.

He'd seen the big orderly, Joe, put up a fight on the second-floor balcony where the kid had tossed Mrs. Booth to her death. He'd swung a roundhouse punch at one of the other boys that would have dropped a mule if it had connected. But it hadn't. The kid was as fast as a rattlesnake—faster than it was humanly possible to be. He dodged the blow and grabbed Joe's arm and...broke it, snapped like it was a potato chip. The kid slammed a punch into Joe's belly, bending him double, and then the boy grabbed Joe's collar and rammed him head-first into the slab of white marble wall beside the elevator. From where he sat, Ollie could see the gory trail of blood and brains Joe had left as he slid down the wall to the floor.

One boy dragged Agatha Willingham out to the railing of the third floor balcony. Ollie could see her talking to him like she knew him, crying and pleading, calling him "Roggie." Then he grabbed her by the throat and tossed her over the rail and as she fell, he called out, "So long, Grandma."

Her body crashed down on the boombox and the music died in mid-shriek. Ollie let out a sigh of relief, figured Aggie gave her life for a good cause.

Now he could hear voices--weak, terrified voices from the upper floors, pleading for help and mercy. The monsters had likely killed anybody strong enough to put up a fight. Those left were bedridden, in wheelchairs, knocked off walkers. Easy prey.

So far, the boys had expended no attention or energy on either him or Maude Franklin, who sat on the other side of the atrium beside the window. Her dowager's hump had so bent her back that she couldn't lift her head up at all, could only look at her own lap. And she was almost completely blind, so she didn't see much there.

The two of them were just furniture. Even a gang of ruthless murderers looked right through both of them as if they didn't exist.

The boys gathered in the atrium, their clothes torn, and blood smeared on their hands and arms and faces, so keyed up they couldn't stand still. The one who'd brought in the boombox shoved Agatha's broken body off it and punched ineffectually at the buttons. When nothing happened, he stood and gave Agatha a vicious kick. One sucked blood off his fingers like it was the last of the cake batter out of the mixing bowl, another unconsciously crimped his hands into claws. That one accidentally bumped into another one, and they were at each other so fast you couldn't even follow the action. Snarling and growling—growling!—ripping at each other's eyes and faces. For a moment it looked like they were all going to join in the fray, until the redheaded kid pulled them apart.

"Kill each other when we're finished," he barked at them.

They glared at him with unmasked hatred, a glint of madness—or something worse—in their eyes that left no doubt they'd turn on anybody, or each other, at the slightest provocation and literally rip them to pieces.

Then Ollie smelled gasoline. It was all he could do to keep his head down, to look like a blithering idiot who didn't see or hear anything, certainly wasn't sitting there watching as the redheaded kid distributed cans of gasoline and sent the remaining boys off in different directions in the building.

They're going to burn the place down.

Yes, sir, they intended to burn it to the ground with everybody in it! Ollie gasped, couldn't help it, but nobody noticed.

Why?

What would possess six preadolescents to do a thing like that? Were they drugged? Hypnotized? And how could they possibly expect to get away with it? Somebody would see them leave the building. And speaking of leaving the building, how did they intend to pull that off after they'd locked, chained and nailed shut every exit? All the windows had that fancy wrought iron grillwork that essentially served as prison bars to keep the inmates in the asylum. The two fire escapes were on the ends of the north and south wings—right out by the road. There was a balcony on the third floor on the back, overlooking the river, but it wasn't like they could all do swan dives off it into the water. The riverbank was a good sixty feet from the building. It'd be another fifteen feet to the deep part in the middle. What were they going to do—fly? Maybe they didn't intend to get away with it, maybe this was some monstrous murder-suicide pact. But what kid commits suicide by setting himself on fire?

Still, it was what it was. Maybe those boys had a way out, but Oliver Marshal did not. It had finally come to it. He really was going to die today. That was fine with him, of course, but he'd be danged if he'd let a pack of slobbering jackals send him on his last ride without putting up a fight! He'd been in the Great War, had marched off to battle at eighteen—not much older than these boys—and had fought all the way across Europe. These monsters in human being suits thought they had this all planned out perfect—that nothing could possibly go wrong. Well, he—Oliver Marshal—intended to find some way to plunk a turd into their punchbowl. Just as a parting shot going out.

Chapter Thirty-Seven

2011

The only indication that Chapman Whitworth was surprised to see Daniel in Senator LaHayne's office was a slight widening of his eyes and a tightening around his mouth. He didn't offer to shake Daniel's hand, for which Daniel was profoundly grateful, merely acknowledged his presence with a slight nod of his head and addressed the senator.

"You didn't tell me we'd have company for our little tea party," he said.

The senator smiled pleasantly and offered a seat on the yellow sofa to Whitworth.

"He's small," the senator said. "He doesn't eat much."

Whitworth sat. Daniel sank back into the wingback chair, and the senator busied himself pouring tea into three cups.

"Sugar?" he asked Whitworth. "Or do you take it with milk like the Brits?"

"Just black."

"Daniel?"

Daniel shook his head. "I don't care for any, thank you." In truth, he couldn't possibly take a cup. The way his hands were shaking, the cup would rattle on the saucer like a bucket next to a jackhammer.

The senator settled himself into the wingback next to Daniel's, took a long sip and sighed audibly. "God created tea on the fourth day, you know," he said. "Right after the sun, the moon and the stars and before the birds and fish. Says so right there in the book of Reservations."

If the senator was trying to make Whitworth uncomfortable, it didn't appear to be working. The man only smiled affably.

"Last time I looked, blasphemy was still a sin, senator," he said. "I'd be watching the ceiling for any sign of a crack if I were you."

Daniel was aware of the voice then. Like the hum of a transformer under Whitworth's words. Energy restrained. But there, definitely there.

"I shall take your warning in the spirit in which it was intended," the senator said. The smile never left his face. There was nothing special about his voice at all, but Daniel was acutely aware of his "presence." The man had a power of his own.

He took another sip from his cup and then set it back in its saucer on the table.

"I see no reason to beat around the bush here," he said. "I invited you to see me today before the hearings this afternoon to avoid certain...unpleasantness. No need to share dirty laundry with the world when the right purpose can be served without doing so."

"I'm not sure whose laundry you might be talking about, senator," Whitworth said. The hum turned up a notch. "The press has been digging around in my clothes basket for months and hasn't found so much as a single stinky sock."

"That's because they only looked in the basket set out for them to see," the senator said. "But you and I both know you have other baskets." The senator's demeanor never changed. His voice remained level, his manner almost offhanded. Yet somehow he managed to convey a clear threat with his words.

"Oh?" Whitworth took a sip of his tea and said nothing more.

The senator turned toward Daniel.

Showtime.

Daniel found his mind remarkably still, a glassy pond in the mountains. Without a word, he withdrew the cellphone from his pocket, punched a couple of buttons, and when the video began to play, he handed the phone to Whitworth.

"It won't win an Academy Award for cinematography, but it's clear enough. Scenes of the 'hired help' doing what you paid them to do."

Whitworth stared at the screen for a moment, then snapped. "I don't know these people." The voice was a growl. A leopard before it pounced.

"Really? Then I guess you must have been hitchhiking the night Minnie and Gerald Cohen were murdered, and Mr. Edgar Wallace Boskowitz just happened to stop and give you a lift."

Whitworth shot Daniel a glance, then turned his eyes back to the tape.

"Right before he went to the Centurion Hotel and punched out Lily Saunders, the woman I supposedly raped."

Daniel reached into the manilla folder and took out a still-frame shot of Whitworth in the backseat of Bosko's car, his face unmistakable. He placed it on the coffee table beside the teapot, then slid it toward Whitworth.

"I'm not sure you're to that part yet, but at the end, your face is caught in very good light."

Whitworth looked from the video on the phone to the still-frame shot of his face and back to the video.

"Or maybe you weren't hitchhiking that night at all. Maybe you paid for a ride." Daniel slid a second photograph out of the folder, a picture of the envelope stuffed with money, and placed it on the table. "You could go a long way on a twenty-thousand-dollar fare."

Daniel pointed to the black smudges on the envelope forensics had left when they lifted fingerprints off it. "Your prints," he said. "Next to Bosko's."

Whitworth stared at both photographs, but didn't touch them. Obviously, the tape had played to the end, but he made no effort to hand the phone back to Daniel. Merely clutched it tight in his hands. Were they…shaking?

"I don't have any idea what you're talking—"

"Save it, Chapman," The senator's voice was forceful, but not loud. "Mr. Boskowitz is cooling his heels in a jail cell, started singing like a songbird in a cage as soon as we offered immunity in exchange for his testimony."

The senator had taken the handoff and would handle it from here on out. That's how they'd planned it. LaHayne was the poker player, not Daniel. He was the man who could run a bluff if anybody could. Daniel was merely 'a useful idiot.' He could state the facts, tell the truth, but he was an absolutely terrible liar.

"Who'd believe—?"

"Show that tape and the envelope to a jury and then try to convince them you were only paying your friend Bosko for some Girl Scout cookies. Good luck with that."

Whitworth said nothing.

"And then there's the gun in Bosko's murder case that must have fallen down behind a filing cabinet somewhere."

Whitworth's head snapped up. Another gut punch he hadn't counted on. He looked at the phone in his hand, and in a sudden fit of rage, hurled it across the room, where it hit the wall and bounced down next to a bookshelf. He grabbed hold of his emotions immediately, slid back into the sincere-public-servant persona he wore like a thousand-dollar Armani suit, and smiled a tight smile. He hadn't meant to let the temper show. He understood that this was a game for people with ice in their veins, and he'd lost points there.

"Why are you doing this? Showing this to me?"

"Because I want to make a trade. I give you that," the senator gestured toward the bookcase the phone was beside, "and all the rest of the evidence slips down behind a couch cushion and is never seen again. You know how that works, don't you."

Whitworth flinched.

"It'll be like nothing ever happened."

"What do you want from me?"

"You withdraw your name, respectfully decline the president's nomination. You tell the committee this afternoon that you've decided to step down for "personal reasons.""

Whitworth was incredulous. "What? You think I'd walk away from this based on the testimony of a known druggie? Are you serious? The rest of it's circumstantial evidence, all smoke and mirrors. I can beat this with one eye tied behind my back. Why on earth would I give up without a fight?"

"Because a fight will get ugly," the senator said, with a razor edge to his voice. "You lose and you go to prison for a long, long time—worst case scenario, they slide a needle into your arm. You win and…even then, with the accusations, all the bad publicity, the president will run from you like a rabbit from a pack of hounds."

"No, he won't," Whitworth snapped. "The president and I have…an agreement. He will support me no matter what."

If Daniel hadn't been looking directly at the senator, he wouldn't have seen the rapid blink that showed he had not expected that card. Had not expected it at all.

"You'll have no such support from the next president."

"And let's say that is you. Even the president can't touch a hair on the head of a Supreme Court justice."

"No, but if you don't manage to grab this Supreme Court brass ring to protect you, you're done." The senator leaned forward and focused the full force of his persona on Whitworth. "As President of the United States, I will bury you."

Whitworth was shocked by the force in the senator's words.

"And if I back down, withdraw—what then? When you're president, what then?"

"Then…I will leave you alone. I will neither help you nor hinder you. You'll be free to carve out your destiny on your own."

"How do I know you'll keep your word?"

"Because I am an honorable man, Mr. Whitworth. Honor is something your kind can't begin to understand, but it matters to those of us who don't walk in darkness."

Whitworth just stared at him. Then, without a word, he rose and strode out of the room.

Daniel said nothing. The senator slumped back in the chair, and Daniel realized for the first time how much strength and energy it had required to defy Whitworth as he had done.

"Do you think he'll do it? Withdraw?" Daniel asked.

LaHayne looked at him with tired eyes. "Son, I have absolutely no idea."

∼

OUT OF UNIFORM, dressed in a T-shirt and jeans, Jack stepped into the air-conditioned interior of the BetterBuy "super store" in Florence and looked down the rows of grocery carts parked inside. Two boys were jockeying the carts into position. One had a blond ponytail.

"Excuse me, son," Jack said, "Are you the young man who told some friends of mine you saw a car with New Mexico plates in the parking lot yesterday?"

The boy noticed Jack's service revolver holstered at his side with his badge clipped to his belt. That got his attention. Jack had put the badge there for effect, where you could see it but probably couldn't make out the words on it ——that it was an Ohio badge, which granted it the same level of authority in Kentucky as a badge out of a Crackerjack box.

"I never should have said anything," the boy said.

"Why not?" Jack asked.

"I don't want to get fired."

"Why would talking about what you saw get you fired?"

"Because the manager's pulling his hair out."

The boy nodded to the checkout lane nearest the door where a woman with no groceries in sight stood talking to the checker—while a line of customers waited.

"It's been like this all morning, a constant stream of people asking questions." He looked at the other boy. "A couple dozen, maybe?"

"More than that," the other boy said.

And Jack had been worried nobody would respond to Daniel's request.

"I'll talk to the manager, son, and apologize for any inconvenience the questions have caused. I'm the one who started all this, and I'm sorry. But if I don't find this man, a little girl will die."

"That part's true then, that there's a little girl with a rare blood type who needs a transfusion, and this guy you're looking for is like one of only three people in the whole country who has the same blood type?"

"It's…something like that, too complicated to explain. But please believe me, this really is a life-and-death situation."

"There's not a whole lot I can tell you," the young man said. "Like I told those other people, I always notice license plates. It's a game I play"—he grinned sheepishly at the other boy—"to have something to do. And I saw a car in the lot yesterday with New Mexico plates."

"What color was the car?"

"Blue or maybe gray. It was old, rusted out around the wheel wells. There was mud over the words on the license plate. 'Land of Enchan--' was all I could see, but I knew it was Land of Enchangment, New Mexico."

"Red mud?"

"Yeah, how'd you know that?"

"You grow up around here?"

"No, I'm from Louisville." He gestured to the other boy. "But he did."

Jack turned to the other boy.

"Know anywhere around here where there's red mud?"

The boy shrugged.

"Mollie might have seen the man," the blond boy said. "She's the only checker nobody's talked to yet. She was on the register when the car was in the lot, but her shift doesn't start until one o'clock."

That was half an hour's wait.

After he apologized to the store manager, Jack spent that time talking to the other checkers, who'd been answering questions all morning. None had anything substantial to add. One thought he'd seen a man with a big tattoo on his arm, but...maybe not.

He asked everyone if they were native to the area and did they know where there was red mud, and the butcher said Turner's Bluff on the riverbank had red mud. He grew up around there, and his mother used to get mad if he tracked it into the house.

Mollie came in late, harried, but the manager gave her a nod, and she cooperated. Yes, she had seen a man with a dragon tattoo on his arm. He came through the line with a Hispanic man who was cheery, cutting up a little, had tossed a package of Mentos into the order as she was ringing it up, and the other guy gave him a dirty look.

"How did he pay?" Jack was praying for "credit card."

"Cash."

Sitting in his car a few minutes later, Jack tallied up what he'd learned. He'd narrowed the search area down to somewhere within a twenty-mile radius of this parking lot, probably in the northern part of the county along the river because the mud was red there. He looked at his watch ——roughly six hours until sundown.

He couldn't help thinking about Crocker's angels. Where was Andi's angel when Andi needed her? Coffee break, maybe? He banged his fist on the steering wheel in frustration so hard that three Hispanic children running past his car into the store looked his way.

A phrase from their conversation drifted into his head and hung on a nail there.

"Mi madre's..."

My mother's. Andi had heard the Hispanic man say they should have eaten his mother's tacos.

But what if what he really said was ...

He punched the button and spoke to Siri in his iPhone.

"Find a restaurant called Mi Madre," he told her.

"There is no restaurant called Mi Madre near you," she said, and his heart sank. "I was only able to find Mi Madre's Tacos."

"I love you, Siri!"

"I bet you say that to all your Apple products."

Chapter Thirty-Eight

2011

Most of the time, Becca didn't know how much of what was real to her was something other people could see or hear or smell or feel, too.

Oh, sure, it was probably a safe bet the average person couldn't see the slithering maggot with its face buried in an ugly woman's neck. Or the darkness that sometimes slid down the sky like paint running down a wall until the clouds stood out against an utter blackness, snowballs on tar. Other things, though—the cry of lost children on the wind or the ever-present underlying stench, like a rat had died under the porch—was that reality for other people?

Every once in a while, though, Becca experienced the world the same way everyone else did. She came up out of the darkness of her own soul like a swimmer breaking the surface into the sunlight, gasping for breath, sucking in great lungfuls of clean air.

That had happened to her the moment she stepped down off the railing of the Purple People Bridge. One last glimpse of the Cat in the Hat hat in the river before it vanished, and suddenly it'd felt like a bucket of cold water had been dumped on her head. Then the whole world was bright and beautiful and clear.

That kind of clarity never lasted more than a few minutes, but this time, for the first time in—she had no idea how long—the clarity had remained for hours. All afternoon yesterday. And last night, she'd hardly slept a wink in that little alcove she'd found in the corner of an alley. She didn't want to close her eyes and miss a single second of the calm clarity of her mind. No lurking black shapes, no sickening dread, no terror only barely held at bay. She'd been able to *think*—not just for a few minutes, but for hours. She sorted out a lot things during those lucid hours, untangled so many knots. She'd decided to go back to Theresa's—and it was a good thing she'd shown up there when she did.

"Is that it—is that why the clarity came now?" she heard her own voice ask out loud, speaking words into the interior of Theresa's car that smelled of the oil the old woman used on her hair mixed with the pine scent of the little green tree dangling from the rearview mirror.

There was no answer, of course. There was just the fact of it, and right now that was enough. Becca rolled down the window and rested her elbow in the opening, felt warm wind tousle her hair. For this time, for right now, she was real, normal. Sure, she was driving into the mouth of a crocodile who would clamp his teeth shut and never let her go. But she refused to allow her mind to go there. If Becca had learned anything in all these years on the run, it was to enjoy the good when it came along, drink fully from that cup, because it could—it would—at any minute get snatched out of your hands.

Trees lined the narrow, winding roads leading back into Caverna County, casting shadows of black lace across the pavement. She smelled pine and cedar, wildflowers and rich, black dirt, and looked with wonder at a beauty she'd taken for granted as a child—green forests and mountains painted in oils on the bright blue sky, still shiny and wet. How had she not noticed this as a little girl; why had she not longed for it with a bone-deep ache all these years since?

The house where she had lived as a little girl with her father and mother appeared around a bend, with oak and maple trees in the front yard and a rose trellis beside the front porch. It was the house where her mother died. And after that, they'd moved into the big house, the mansion where Becca had been locked in the broom closet for punishment. Or for sport. Where she never saw the hand coming that slapped her and knocked her off her feet. The house where her father always left the bedside lamp on so he could see.

She pulled up in the gravel driveway and sat for a moment, gathering herself, conjured Andi's face before her to give her the courage to get out of the car. When she was halfway up the sidewalk, her father stepped out the front door, holding a .22-caliber rifle in the crook of his arm with the offhanded ease of a man who'd shot his first squirrel at five. His lips twisted in the half smirk that said you'd lost and he'd won.

"Well, would you look at this, my own baby girl, come home to her Papa where she belongs."

She'd forgotten how hoarse and gravelly her father's voice was, like wind-driven sand scouring stone or the whispery, brittle click of cockroaches when you turned on a light.

"What happened to you?" He looked her up and down. "You used to be a pretty little thing. You're so ugly now you'd make a train take a dirt road."

"Where's Andi?" Becca said, her own voice remarkably level and strong. "What have you done with her?"

"Why I don't believe I know anybody by the name of Andi."

"Let her go. That was the deal. Trade her for me. Well, I'm here. Are you going to keep your end of the bargain?"

She had him there, and she knew it.

"You gotten real pushy since you been gone," he said. "That ain't an attractive trait in a woman, you know. But we'll see to that now you're here to stay."

The menace in his words was unmistakable, and it occurred to Becca for the first time to wonder if he was going to kill her outright. Oh, eventually he would—he'd accidentally hit her too hard in a rage or maybe beat her to death on purpose. But perhaps he intended to do it right now. Shove that .22 up against her temple and pull the trigger.

As she watched her father slide a cell phone out of his pocket and heard him speak into it, Becca felt the real world begin to warp, change, leaving her standing on a tiny island in the middle of black water swirling toward a drain. The bright sunlight shifted down like someone was using a dimmer switch. Smells vanished, the sense of calm and clarity slid slowly away. She was naked and vulnerable now, trapped on the island while she heard the footsteps of the monster trudging toward her.

She whimpered, hunched her shoulders from the blow she could feel was coming. Then she dropped to her knees to make herself small, curled up in a ball in the dirt. Closer and closer he came, and she began to scream, to shriek and wail in unadulterated terror.

A small part of her registered the genuine shock on her father's face as he stuck the phone back into the pocket of his overalls, and that part celebrated for the briefest of moments. Then Becca Hawkins was gone.

~

1985

Motley Crue was replaced by Twisted Sister, growling "We're Not Gonna Take It," after the Bad Kids left the office area. Jack cowered in the "sunroom" behind the cubicle with the wet-penny smell of blood filling his nostrils. The music stopped abruptly but his own heart continued to pound like a drum, each beat rumbling in his ears so loud he couldn't think. And he had to think! He had to figure out a way to get out of the building. Since he had no idea where the exits were, he decided his only chance to escape was to make it across the atrium to the stairs leading to the second floor and climb down one of the fire escapes he'd seen on the ends of the building when he'd crossed the road.

He sneaked out of the office and hid behind a marble pedestal holding a statue of somebody he didn't recognize. As soon as the Bad Kids left the atrium, he bolted across it, running harder than he'd ever run from third base heading for home. He almost made it. Another step or two and he'd have been there. But he suddenly felt himself yanked backward off his feet, and he landed painfully on the tile floor. Jack sat up slowly, his eyes fixed on Cole's Stuart's blue shark eyes.

"What in the world are you doing here, nigger?" Cole asked, surprised and clearly delighted.

"Visiting my grandma," he lied.

Jacob Dumas had returned with an empty gasoline can by this time, as had Ronnie Martin and Roger Willingham.

They all stood staring down at Jack, a pack of hungry wolves encircling a rabbit. Then Jacob took a step toward him. "Like I said before, nigger, I'm gonna get me some dark meat."

He reached out to grab Jack, but Cole stayed his hand.

"Think this through," he said. "Rip him to pieces…or toast him like a marshmallow? Tie him to something and let him burn with the rest of the little piggies."

That idea appealed to Jacob.

Cole reached into the sack at his side and took out a length of chain, then looked around for somewhere to tie Jack. He spotted the dolphin in the fountain and laughed out loud.

"We'll tie you up in the fountain, Jack," he said. "That way maybe your eyeballs won't melt before you get to see the rescue that's going to be broadcast live all over the world."

The three shoved Jack up next to the dolphin in the fountain, where Walter and Jacob started at his throat and wrapped chain around and around his body so thick he looked like a parody of the damsel in distress chained to the railroad track. Walter fastened two links of the chain together at the bottom with a padlock, snapped it shut and threw away the key.

"You gonna fry, nigger—sizzling dark meat," Jacob said.

With water pouring over his face, Jack watched Cole instruct Ronnie Martin to "go get the old guy." In a matter of minutes, he'd wheeled an old man in a bed out of the elevator and parked him on the far wall between two of the glass tables holding flower vases. The skinny old man in wet pajamas kept ineffectually trying to get out of the bed until Cole shoved him back hard.

"Want me to tie you down?" Cole snarled.

The man settled back on the bed. Cole turned to the other boys with the evil distortion of a smile on his face and a gleam of pure hatred in his eyes.

"Let's do this."

Roger and Ronnie ran down to the ends of the north and south wings on the ground floor and set fires to the trail of gasoline they'd poured on the floor. Jack could see the red glow behind them. The carpet had soaked up the gas like a wick, and now fire spread quickly and evenly down it. If the floor'd been wood instead, the gasoline would have pooled on it, and the fire might have beat the boys back to the atrium. The other boys climbed the stairs and apparently did the same drill—set fire to a trail of gasoline at the far end of the hallways to burn toward the center.

"Unlock the front doors, Jake," Cole said, and Jacob Dumas retrieved a key from his shirt pocket, removed the padlock and tossed it and the chain aside.

When all six were back together in the atrium, Cole spoke to Jack. "You, nigger, are about the see the making of a hero—if you live that long."

Then the Bad Kids wordlessly climbed the stairs to the third floor and disappeared down a hallway leading toward the back of the building.

Jack could hear old people begin to cry out when they smelled the smoke and felt the heat. But he neither heard nor saw any further sign of the Bad Kids. Where had they gone? They'd set fires between themselves and the fire escapes. They must have some other plan to get out of the building. But Jack had no plan. He wasn't going to get out at all. Jack Carpenter was going to die here today.

Chapter Thirty-Nine

2011

Jeff Kendrick pulled his shiny gray Mercedes into the empty driveway in front of Theresa Washington's house and firmly slammed the door on the self-analysis that'd been playing ring-around-the-rosy in his head all the way from his office in downtown Cincinnati. The truth was simple; why try to dodge it? He knew precisely why he was expending so much extra effort on this case.

It wasn't because of Theresa Washington or Daniel—though he was convinced neither had committed the crimes they'd been accused of. He'd come here today for one reason—Emily.

Emily Burke had sailed into his life on a breeze that smelled of honeysuckle and jasmine, had brought laughter and joy and…love—was it love?—into it for the first time. When she wouldn't see him after Andi was shot, the emptiness was so oppressive it had threatened to drive him mad.

Then he got that text, the last one she ever sent, only minutes before she died. He'd texted her right back, but by then she had been murdered. If there was even a miniscule chance that Chapman Whitworth was somehow responsible for her death, then yeah, Jeff would give up his lunch hour to nail him—and all the other hours in the day, too.

Jeff stepped up on the porch to ring the bell, but the door flew open before he had a chance. Theresa Washington looked at him, smiled broadly and lifted her eyes skyward.

"Thank you!" she cried to the clouds. Then she smiled at Jeff. "You probably don't know it, but you's the answer to my prayer. God sent you here for a reason. Let's git."

She brushed past him, hurried out to his car, got in on the passenger side and closed the door behind her. When he didn't move, she called out something, then fumbled around for a moment before opening the door and calling out through the crack between it and the car.

"How you roll down the windows in this thing?" she asked, but didn't wait for a response. "Don't just stand there, we got to get going. Way I figure it, she probably ain't got even an hour's head start. We can catch her if we hurry."

Then she closed the door again and looked expectantly at Jeff.

He couldn't help it—he had to strangle a sudden impulse to burst out laughing. Instead, he went to the driver's side of the car and got in. But he didn't put the key in the ignition.

"Who only has an hour's head start?"

"Becca." She gestured at his car keys. "Go on now, start this thing up. You can talk and drive at the same time, can't you?"

∼

MI MADRE'S Tacos was a battered white building that had no indoor sit-down service. The establishment served tacos and other Mexican food out a window to walk-up customers.

Si, the cheery Hispanic woman told him, she remembered the man with the tattoo. She grinned at the younger girl beside her, who was making a burrito.

"Rosa always flirts with his friend, Jorge."

"Do you know where Jorge lives, where I can find him?" Jack said, keeping his voice level, the urgency at bay.

"She doesn't speak much English," the older woman said, and translated the question. The younger girl shook her head, then ducked it, embarrassed.

She knew more.

"Please, Rosa, this is very important," Jack said, then picked up the story folks had made up and ran with it. "There's a little girl who…needs a blood transfusion and… I have to find the man with the tattoo, or she'll die."

Though Rosa still looked reluctant after the older woman translated the question, she said something else in Spanish.

"She doesn't know for sure, but she thinks it might be somewhere near Meadeville because he keeps trying to get her to meet him there for a beer. They sell Dos Equis at the Food Mart."

Jack sent gravel flying out behind the back tires of his car as he sped away.

～

CROCK COULD FEEL that niggling itch, a mouse taking a delicate nibble off a piece of cheese in his gut. He had missed something with Bosko. He was sure of it, some tiny detail. He concentrated. Nothing. In frustration, he picked up the Harrelton News-Enterprise on his desk and turned to the crossword puzzle. Sometimes, he came up with his best ideas when he was thinking about something else.

The puzzle was in the back section beyond the obituaries, across from the movie listings. Crock never got to the puzzle. As soon as he opened to the page, his eye fell on the advertisement for the movie playing at the Dynamo Complex. Harry Potter and the Dealthly Hallows—Part 2. The premiere showing in Harrelton was a performance scheduled for this afternoon.

The biggest movie poster on Bosko's wall, the one he woke up to every morning, had had no ticket stub attached…because the movie hadn't opened yet.

You don't suppose …? Surely, a parole-jumper who'd committed three homicides and tried to kill a police officer in the past week wouldn't be that stupid. But in the words of that great philosopher and theologian Forrest Gump, "Stupid is as stupid does."

Now, Crock sat in an unmarked car across the street from the ticket booth of the Dynamo Movie Theatre complex in south Harrelton, gnawing on a cinnamon toothpick, scanning the slow-moving line as it inched its way to the ticket booth. He heard a shrill, high-pitched shriek, which either meant somebody nearby was using a "silent" dog whistle or Cher needed to go into the shop for an oil change and a lube job, and Crock was reaching up to pop out the hearing aid when he spotted him. A man wearing a Cincinnati Reds windbreaker, sandwiched between a group of teenagers and a woman holding a sleeping toddler, lifted his head so Crock could see his face. Edgar Wallace Boskowitz. Bosko to his friends.

Bosko paid his money, the ticket agent slid a ticket

under the glass partition, and he disappeared instantly into the crowd flowing in a solid wave through the door.

Crock sat back and took out another toothpick. Bosko would be here for the next two hours and four minutes—well, a few minutes more counting the previews. He'd be right there, in theater 11—with two hundred civilians and another five or six hundred outside waiting for the next showing. Two hours and ten minutes was how long Crock had to figure out a way to pluck Bosko out of that crowd like a daisy—without damaging so much as a petal on any of the other flowers.

ANDI WENT to the door when the shouting began, put her ear to it and listened—not that she needed to do that to hear what they were saying. They were yelling, all three of them, having an awful argument—about her.

"It's your fault," Tattoo Man roared. "You're the one let her out to go to the bathroom."

"We got paid to do a job, and the job's done," said Dreadlocks Man. "I didn't sign on for anything else."

"Think you'd like prison, do you?" asked Tattoo Man. "Think you'd enjoy the food, maybe? Or is it the friendly atmosphere where 'everybody knows your…number?' I ain't going back there."

"Nobody's gonna catch us," said Dreadlock Man. "We dump the kid and bail. We got enough money to stay hid for a long time."

"We touch a hair on that leetle one's head, and they never stop looking for us. Choo know who her daddy is?" Speedy Gonzales said.

"You idiots just don't get it, do you?" said Tattoo Man.

"They'll look, sure. They might even find us, but what if they do? They can't prove nothing, not without a witness. That kid's seen us. She can identify us. She can identify me."

Andi began to get the drift of the conversation and felt cold and sick. Goose bumps pebbled her arms and neck.

"A reggae bass player and a chicken farmer—the only place there's a picture of you two is on your drivers' licenses and in your high school yearbooks. The law's never gonna find you. You'll blend back into the scenery and disappear. But I have a record. All that kid's got to do is describe my arm, and they'll pull my mug shot out of a database faster'n you can say 'life sentence.' And that, my friend, is your fault. If you hadn't let her get a look at me, I wouldn't have to do this."

"Billy Ray said a bar of gold to babysit a kid for twenty-four hours," Dreadlocks Man said. "I ain't gonna hurt a kid."

"I don't leave witnesses behind who can identify me, pick me out of a police lineup and say, 'That's him. He's the man kidnapped me.' That's not happening."

"Jew can count me out. You're loco, man."

"Fine," Tattoo Man roared. "Get out, both of you. If you ain't got the cajones to do what has to be done, leave. I'll clean up after us all."

Andi heard Speedy Gonzales spew out a flood of words in Spanish so fast, she couldn't follow, heard doors slam and then thought she heard the blue car start up in the driveway. She was about to turn to go to the window to look when the door where she was listening suddenly flew open. She was standing so close, it smashed into her, hit her in the face and knocked her backward onto the floor.

The room swam for a moment, and then Tattoo Man was standing over her.

"I'm sorry, kid," he said, but he didn't sound sorry at all.

Then he pulled a knife from a scabbard at his waist. It was huge, bigger than the one Daddy used to carve the turkey at Thanksgiving. The blade was shiny, sparkled in the light through the crack in the window. "This is the way it's got to be."

He reached out, grabbed a handful of her hair and yanked her head back. The feel of the blade against her throat was cold. Only for a moment, though. After that, Miranda Burke made only one final sound, a wail of terror, "Daddy!"

DANIEL'S HEAD snapped up like he'd been slapped. Some sound, some…cry…echoed in his mind just outside the range of his hearing. It sounded like Andi.

"You sure you're ok, Daniel?" Senator La Hayne asked.

An image appeared in his mind. Andi on a hospital bed. He could hear the beep, beep, beep of a heart monitor grow slower and slower. Then the beeps stopped. Until Jack called her name—Andi.

"You don't have to stay for this, you know," the senator said.

But, of course, he did have to stay for this. That was, after all, the only thing left he could do. He had to be here, had to sit unafraid, in utter defiance, right here in the front row of spectators.

The Senate Judiciary Committee that would decide the fate of Chapman Whitworth's journey to the full senate for confirmation convened in the Dirksen Building in room

226, three floors down from Senator LaHayne's fifth-floor office.

Daniel and the senator had just entered the room through the wide doorway in the center of the back wall, where doors with designs of concentric squares opened by the ornate doorknobs in the center. Facing them on the far wall of the wood-paneled room was a raised platform with a huge semicircular desk that looked a little like the bench where a judge sits in a courtroom. Committee members were already beginning to make their way to seats behind the desk on the platform, arranging papers on the wide desktop.

A long table was located directly in front of the semicircle where those testifying could face all the committee members to make statements and answer questions. Behind the table were the rows of chairs that constituted the gallery. Though seating there was limited, the proceedings would be broadcast live on the United States Senate Committee Channel.

A week ago, the gallery for this routine committee hearing would have been virtually empty. Today it was jammed, spectators and the press jockeying for position to watch proceedings nobody'd cared about until the leak Monday about the senator's "evidence."

As chairman of the committee, Senator LaHayne secured Daniel a seat on the front row and then moved to take his place in the center of the semicircle desk behind his nameplate.

Daniel actually felt rather than saw Whitworth enter the room. Almost against his will, Daniel turned to face him. Whitworth was smiling and glad-handing reporters and committee members as he made his way through the crowd and could not possibly have missed Daniel, seated in the front row of the gallery. But he never acknowledged Daniel's presence, merely pulled out the chair behind the table, laid a single manila folder on the otherwise clear tabletop, leaned back and opened one of the two water bottles aides had set out on the table and beside the nameplates of each senator. Water beaded on the sides of the bottle. It was still cold.

As soon as all the seats behind the big desk were filled, LaHayne rapped a gavel, and the room instantly hushed. The press seated behind Daniel leaned forward expectantly.

LaHayne spoke in a sonorous voice.

"This is the first meeting of the Senate Judiciary Committee to consider the president's nomination of Chapman Wainwright Whitworth as federal judge for the U.S. District Court for the Southern District of Ohio to fill the vacancy on the U. S. Supreme Court caused by the death of Justice Alexander Grant."

LaHayne looked squarely at Whitworth and asked affably, "Would the nominee like to make any opening remarks before we proceed with our questions?"

Daniel saw an almost imperceptible squaring of Whitworth's shoulders. Those not seated close to him saw only a calm, confident exterior, but Daniel could see a big vein in his left temple begin to pulse rapidly.

His hands were clasped casually in front of him as if he were about to address citizens at a school board meeting or perhaps a group of high school civics students on a tour of the federal building in Cincinnati.

"Thank you, Senator LaHayne," he said.

The voice. Whitworth had the dimmer switch on the strange power it possessed dialed full bright now, each individual light casting a fierce glow. The force of it felt to

Daniel like the blunt trauma of running full speed into a brick wall.

"I do have a brief statement I would like to make," he said.

Showtime.

Chapter Forty

1985

Fire enveloped the Twin Oaks Nursing Home with a mighty whump sound that was stunning in its ferocity. Jack never dreamed fire could move that fast. One minute he could see a red glow at the end of the hallway, and the next minute yellow flames licked up from the floor at the edge of the atrium with a sound like a pigeon beating its wings. Jack watched in fascinated horror as the blaze ate the hallway walls and ceiling and then burst through to set the whole plank veranda outside aflame.

With water gushing over his head and down his face, it was hard to see. But Jack heard the wailing of a thousand sirens and could make out through the narrow windows that framed the front door that a collection of firefighters and firefighting equipment had sprung up, like mushrooms after a rain, in the parking lot.

The firefighters probably hadn't yet discovered that all the windows and doors had been chained or nailed shut. Maybe they never would. Maybe no one would even attempt a rescue, and the structure would burn all the way down, and they'd find the chains in the ashes. Or maybe the fire would burn so hot the chains would melt, and nobody would ever know they'd been there.

The Bad Kids had not poured gasoline in the atrium—why not?— and its walls were marble rather than the dry old wood that had ignited like cardboard in the rest of the structure. Only the atrium's ornate ceiling three floors above was on fire. Smoke began to puddle here, though, like pouring coffee into a cup, and Jack was glad of that. Surely, he'd pass out when he breathed enough of that smoke—he'd already started to cough. Maybe it'd even kill him. Either one was fine—just so he didn't have to…burn to death.

Please, kill me now. Don't let me burn. Please!

The blazing ceiling would eventually collapse, raining fiery death down into the atrium, and Jack wanted to be long gone before that happened.

Then the front doors were suddenly blown open by the force of water firefighters had trained on them. A trio of firemen in full masks and gear—the one in the middle carrying a squirting hose—burst into the atrium. The swirling smoke obscured the fountain and Jack, but when they got farther into the atrium they'd spot him, and there was still time to—

Hope had no chance to bloom in his heart. Seconds after they made it inside, two of the four chains holding the Twin-Oaks-replica chandelier came loose from the burning ceiling and the whole right side of the model broke off and crashed down on top of them, almost like it'd been aimed at them. It hammered two of the firemen and slammed them to the floor, knocking the fire hose out of the middle one's hands so it snaked around, shooting water randomly. The remaining fireman scrambled to lift the debris of the mangled chandelier off the others. He was only able to free one man, and he grabbed the man's collar and dragged him out the door and into the spray of water trained on that part of the burning porch from fire hoses out front just as the rest of the chandelier fell. It crushed the fireman still pinned down and blocked the doorway with a pile of rubble that quickly caught fire into a wall of flames.

No one else would be coming through that door.

❧

2011

Billy Ray was totally unprepared for what Becca did while he was calling his flunkies, telling them to cut the kid loose. One minute, she was standing defiantly in front of him and the next she was rolling around on the ground. Course he figured out quick it was an act. She was puttin' on. Wasn't nothing really wrong with her. Was there?

He came down the porch steps and approached the girl curled up in a ball in the dirt, inspected her like she was a bug on a pin.

"Shut up that squalling," he told her.

She acted like she didn't hear him. He drew back his foot and kicked her as hard as he could with the blunt toe of his work boot. The boot caught her in the hip. Becca had no meat on her bones, and he was surprised the blow didn't break something. She kept on screaming.

"You shut your mouth, girl, or you're gonna be swallowin' every tooth in it."

Still no response. In fact, she had been screaming so fiercely, she was beginning to lose her voice. But she kept on.

Billy Ray felt suddenly uneasy. What if she really was

crazy? He'd spent years planning in minute detail exactly which one of her bones he intended to break for every year he'd been locked up. Wouldn't nobody hear her scream where he was gonna take her. Just like didn't nobody hear Isaac Washington when Billy Ray took to him with a chain saw.

But wouldn't do no good to hurt her if she didn't even know you's doing it. What if this wasn't no act? Well, he'd by golly find out. He grabbed a handful of her blond hair, cut as short as a boy's instead of long and pretty like it used to be. He dragged her across the yard to the car she'd parked in the driveway and dropped her beside the passenger side door. She was all curled up in a ball. He leaned the .22 against the car, pulled her left hand loose and uncurled her fist so her index finger was extended.

"You listen here to me," he said. "You stop that hollering. Stop it now." He reached over, opened the car door and placed her finger on the frame of the door opening. "You're gonna wish you'd shut up."

Then Billy Ray slammed the car door on her finger.

No response. She continued screaming as she had been, making no sound at all now, screaming in silence.

Crying out in the dark, but there's no sound. His voice is gone—not from screaming on and on but from one explosive scream so powerful it shreds his vocal cords. The ugly red glow is everywhere…

Billy Ray trembled. Why'd he keep remembering that dream? Why couldn't he forget it?

He shook his head violently. Then he opened the car door and released Becca's finger. She slumped forward and curled up in the dirt again, her hand with the smashed finger balled into a fist as it had been before. He picked up the rifle and stood looking down on her, trying to figure out—

A silver car, a Mercedes, suddenly shot up his driveway and ground to a stop, throwing rocks and gravel in every direction.

Out the passenger door come none other than Theresa Washington! The fat old crone come waddling fast as she could to where Becca lay, knelt on the ground beside her and started patting her on the back and saying soothing things, like you'd say to a scared kid. Never even acknowledged Billy Ray was standing there.

The man in the suit did, though. He got out of the car more slowly, came around it into the yard. He barely even looked at Becca. The man never took his eyes off the rifle in Billy Ray's hands.

~

1985

Sheriff William Cunningham got out of his cruiser in the parking lot of the Twin Oaks Nursing Home. The heat from the blaze felt like standing next to the forge in the Hazelwood Works, the Pittsburgh steel mill where he was a crane follower as a teenager. He got it now. He understood that the massacre of the animals on Black Tuesday, the snakes in Christopher Grant's casket and the desecration of the cemetery—all that had been the silence his grandmother'd talked about after a buzz bomb's engine cut off, the silence as some great evil hanging over the community fell out of the sky.

The Twin Oaks fire was the explosion.

Someone had set this fire on purpose—used gasoline or some other accelerant. Even old wood didn't catch fire this quickly on its own. Fires that ignited naturally started somewhere and spread; this fire was everywhere at once. And the sheriff had known the moment he pulled off the highway that nothing short of dumping a lake of water on the building would extinguish a blaze like this.

Then he heard the cries for help.

Looking up, he could see them. All the windows were shut, with faces pressed against the glass. In a room on the end on the second floor, someone had broken out the window glass—why not just open it?—and he could see arms waving through the wrought iron grating, hear voices crying out in terror. Glass had been broken in three windows on the third floor, too, the people there trying desperately to squeeze their bodies through the grates so that arms and legs hung out. But even the smallest resident would have been unable to fit between iron bars set six inches apart.

The cries from the old people trapped on the upper floors sparked feverish effort among the firefighters, so frenzied it was almost insectile. The fire chief only paused for a moment beside the sheriff's cruiser to tell him that the sunroom doors were chained shut, then he and two other firemen made an unsuccessful attempt to get inside the building through the open front doors. One fireman was killed, and the front doorway was blocked with flaming debris.

The crowd that police was trying to keep at bay stretched along the road and deep into the woods on the other side. The onlookers weren't merely rubberneckers. They were the friends and family members of the people inside the burning building, hysterical with horror as they watched loved ones die in flames before their eyes.

And before the eyes of the whole world. The news crews already in town with their satellite trucks to cover the rising of Bradford's Ridge's dead descended on the scene like crows on road kill. Within minutes, they were set up and broadcasting the nightmare blow by blow around the world.

Suddenly, a young man in a blue shirt broke free from the crowd. Crying, "My father's in there!" he dodged the police line and raced up the sidewalk toward the front steps and porch. Sheriff Cunningham took off after him, but the man was so fast, he was up onto the burning porch and into the building before the sheriff could stop him. The sheriff stayed on his heels, though. Hoping to tackle him and drag him quickly back out, Cunningham leapt over the blazing pile of chandelier debris right inside the door, the pain of the burns on his legs a distant agony his mind put aside to process later.

The young man was right in front of him, but the smoke was so thick…and then the smoke moved away, like a fan had blown it back from the man in the blue shirt. The flames moved away, too—this was crazy!—leaving the young man in a smokeless, flameless bubble, and he seemed almost not to touch the ground at all. The sheriff dived, grabbed him in a perfect tackle around the ankles and brought him down with a thump on the mosaic tile floor.

And there was no smoke, no flames around him, around either one of them. It was like the two of them were sealed in a fishbowl and nothing could get in. The young man flipped over on his back as fast as a coiling rattlesnake. Then he offered the sheriff a resigned smile.

"There's only going to be one hero here today—and it's not you." the young man said, and now that the sheriff could see him close-up, he recognized him as that Whitworth kid—Chase or Chapman. His father had been an archeologist or something like that before he'd had a stroke a couple of years ago.

Scrambling to his feet, the sheriff extended a hand to

the still recumbent Whitworth. "Come on! I'm sorry, son, but your father's gone. We've still got a shot at getting out of here."

"Oh, I have more than a shot at it," Whitworth said. "But you, unfortunately, do not."

Then the sheriff saw an outline form around the young man—a glow that was a deeper red than the flames. The glow seemed to morph into a shape.

The sheriff gasped, and the scream in his throat froze there behind his lips. A hideous, deformed face with cat-slit eyes and lumps of horns materialized around the young man on the floor at his feet. It opened its mouth—rows of dagger-sharp teeth—and roared at him. The sheriff did scream then, staggered backward and fell. The face grew. As Whitworth got to his feet, the face surrounding him loomed in the air above the sheriff. He looked into its eyes and saw there pure evil, all the hatred and devastation that had ever been and ever would be were in the bottomless pit of those eyes, deaths unnumbered, war and famine and pain, and a future of absolute desolation.

Then Whitworth reached out—only it was the monster shape reaching out a clawed hand—and grabbed the sheriff's thick beard. In one yank, he ripped most of the sheriff's face off his skull. As the sheriff shrieked in inarticulate horror and pain, his body rose up into the air, into the boiling smoke above the bubble. Then a force flung him across the atrium and into the flames in the north hallway.

Bill Cunningham breathed fire when he tried to scream, his whole body burning. The last sight he ever saw was the shape shrinking back down into Chapman Whitworth, glowing red around him as he headed toward the stairs on the back wall.

Chapter Forty-One

2011

The proprietor of the Hooperton Food Mart easily recognized Jack's description of the men in the blue car with New Mexico plates. They'd purchased beer from him several times—Dos Equis—not his best-selling brew. Before Jack even had a chance to ask, he added, "On my way home from work yesterday, I seen that car. It was parked next to a cabin about three miles from town, on the bluff above the river."

Jack closed his eyes and allowed a little of the wound-tight strain to ease. He'd found her! He realized then he'd been clenching his jaw so tight his teeth hurt. This wasn't over yet, but he didn't have to go it alone anymore. Now, he could call in the troops, return to solid police procedure. He'd call the Kentucky State Police and the Boone County Sheriff's Department. He flinched at the thought of needing a trained hostage negotiating team from the FBI, but it could come to that.

He pulled his cell phone out of his pocket, considering as he did how much trouble he was in—an off-duty, suspended, Ohio police sergeant chasing bad guys in the woods of Kentucky. But the other law enforcement agencies would bag all those issues for later as soon as he said the magic words, "kidnapped child."

The food mart manager was talking and Jack tuned back in at "…almost ran me down."

"I'm sorry, I missed that. Who almost ran you down?"

"Those guys you're looking for, well two of them anyway. They came roaring through here like they's being chased by a mad dog. Had to jump back up on the curb, or they'd have—"

"How long ago?"

"Half an hour, maybe. The ugly guy with the tattoo wasn't with them."

One kidnapper had stayed behind with Andi.

Jack felt like he'd reached the end of a bungee cord and had been breathlessly yanked back up. It would take at least half an hour for help to arrive and get set up. The nearest Kentucky State Police post was in Dry Ridge, thirty miles away on Interstate 75 South. The Boone County Sheriff's Department was located near the airport—at least fifteen minutes away and more likely twenty. And right this minute, Andi was alone with only one kidnapper.

Jack had to seize the opportunity.

He shoved his phone back into his pocket and leapt into his car.

Jack cruised by the cabin once, saw it was more shack than cabin, not quaint but rundown and dilapidated. A screen door dangled from a single hinge on the front of the structure, and a shiny new satellite dish grew incongruously from the north wall right below the eaves. The windows had been boarded—recently. The unpainted wood hadn't weathered. A white van was parked in front.

He parked his car half a mile away, snatched his M4

patrol rifle and his tactical vest with twenty-eight rounds of ammo off the backseat floorboard and cut through the woods. As he knelt behind a pile of brush and examined the building, his heart was hammering in his chest so hard his vision pulsed with each beat.

A surgeon operating on his own child.

He drew all his will into a single point of light and focused it on calming his heartbeat, slowing his breathing, dispelling the black cloud of panic that was impairing his judgment. Then he circled the house, out far enough in the woods that if somebody spotted him and fired a shot with the weapon of choice in this neck of the woods—a deer rifle—the bullet would likely be deflected by tree limbs or brush.

He studied the building from the trees, concentrated, tried to remember every detail of Andi's vision that Daniel had described to him. She'd said there was a "crack between the boards that covered one of the windows," and she'd looked out it at the driveway. A room with two windows was likely a corner room, with windows facing two directions. The corner room by the driveway, then.

Andi was probably alone in that room. She'd said there was nothing in it but blankets on the floor and a dangling light bulb, so the kidnapper probably wasn't sitting in there with her on the floor, but rather had locked her alone in the room while he made himself more comfortable in another part of the cabin.

Approaching the cabin through the trees, Jack stayed on a diagonal from the driveway-side corner. When he reached the last of his cover, he bent low to the ground, scurried to the house in a Groucho crouch and flattened himself against the wall beneath the window overlooking the driveway. Then he froze, remained utterly still. Using a military term, he made himself an LPOP: Listening

Post/Observation Post. He concentrated on trying to hear any sound coming from the house. Voices. Music. A television. A toilet flushing. Even the hum of a refrigerator or the whir of a fan. He listened with his whole body, a tautness in him like a bowstring with the arrow ready to fly.

Nothing.

Then he raised up by inches until he could take a quick peek through the crack Andi'd looked out. The lone bulb shone brightly in the room. Through the small strip of his visibility, he could see no one. But the bulb did reveal one corner of the pile of blankets Andi'd described.

The blankets were bloody, and Jack could see blood on the floor, too.

~

1985

There it was!

Oliver Marshal gave the right wheel of his chair a shove while he held the left one still, and the chair pivoted around, leaving Ollie sitting in front of the key on the floor that loudmouth punk threw away after he used it to padlock the chains holding the kid to the dolphin in the fountain. Ollie rolled closer, leaned over and picked up the key.

Now he just had to make it back. Smoke was everywhere. He only took little sips of breath, like he'd done when they were afraid the Krauts had laid out mustard gas. It was hot, flames licked out at him from debris that had fallen from the ceiling, but the ceramic tiles wouldn't burn, and he could make it if he concentrated, tried.

Ollie gave both wheels of the chair a mighty shove—

well, as mighty a shove as he could manage, and propelled himself toward the fountain, dodging the bodies--Harold Castleback's, Mrs. Booth's and Agatha Willingham's-- where they lay crumpled on the floor. Another shove. Then one more and his footrest connected with the marble base.

Water gushed down over the boy chained to the dolphin. His eyes were closed.

"You, boy!" Ollie called out. "Don't you give up on me!"

A survivor to tell the world what they'd done! Yep, Ollie bet that wasn't in the playbook of the punk monsters who'd staged this massacre. If this boy lived, he could take a royal dump in their punchbowl—a fitting memorial to Oliver Marshal.

The boy opened his eyes when he heard Ollie's voice.

"I've got the key, gonna unlock those chains."

Which might prove easier said than done. Ollie would have to get up out of the chair, step over the lip of the fountain, kneel down beside the boy and unlock the padlock. Ollie literally could not remember the last time he'd stood upright.

How hard can it be? Just stand up, that's all. Gotta be like riding a bicycle. It'll come back to me.

He reached down, picked up his right leg, lifted his right foot out of the footrest and carefully set it on the tile floor. He did the same with the other foot. Then he locked the wheelchair wheels. Now, all he had to do was grab the chair handles and lift himself out of the seat.

2011

Like the other Harry Potter freaks seated in row after row above him, Bosko was reluctant to move when the movie was over. After the last riveting scene, it was jarring to come back to reality, to sitting in a darkened theater in a world not peopled by wizards with magic wands.

It wasn't as good as *Harry Potter and the Half-Blood Prince,* Bosko decided. Oh, it was good, but not as good as that. And *nothing* was as good as *Harry Potter and the Prisoner of Azkaban.* Though the house lights had not yet come up, other movie patrons had begun to rise from their seats, gather purses and sweaters and sleeping children from the seats around them. Bosko had just let go of the fantasy, exchanged Hogwarts for the reality of an October day in Ohio, when an announcement was broadcast into the theater.

"The Dynamo Movie Theatre complex has a special prize for one lucky movie-goer today," the voice said. "Warner Brothers Pictures has provided movie posters signed by Daniel Radcliffe, Rupert Grint and Emma Watson as prizes to give away to the premiere audience."

There was a murmur all around him. Bosko froze. He tried not to think about his movie posters, the most precious possessions he owned—gone. Whenever he thought about them, he envisioned a cartoon character banging his own forehead with a sledge hammer. Why'd he run? Why'd he shoot? The police couldn't possibly know he'd killed Lily. It had been a monumentally stupid knee-jerk response. He'd been so on edge, he'd panicked. Bosko had hardly slept since he strangled her, and when he did, he had nightmares about her terrified face. He'd never killed anybody before, but Chapman Whitworth had told him to do it, and he couldn't refuse. Not merely because the judge who'd "lost" the evidence against him in that bank robbery case could just as easily find it again. It was more than that. Bosko was—go on, admit it—he was terrified of the scar-faced man with the dead-fish eyes.

But he wouldn't allow himself to think about what Whitworth had done that day to those old people. How he had done it. It could not possibly have happened like Bosko thought it did. Whitworth couldn't have—no, he would not go there! Now, he was on the run, everything that mattered to him gone.

"We randomly selected a single seat in the theater before we opened the doors," the announcement continued, "and the lucky person who chose that seat will walk out of Dynamo with more than just a ticket stub. He'll have a signed Harry Potter movie poster to go with it."

Bosko could feel perspiration break out in little beads on his forehead.

"So look down at the numbers on your seats, folks. This poster goes to the person sitting in seat number twelve in row B."

Bosko stared in stunned disbelief at the twelve in silver letters on the back of his seat, as the people around him searched their seats and then groaned in disappointment. The little boy sitting next to him, who'd wiggled, squirmed, whispered and spilled popcorn like confetti through the whole movie, looked at him in defiance. "I was there first!" he said.

Bosko scowled at him.

"I sat down there before you did. Seat number twelve was mine…until my *mother*"—he cast a murderous glance at the haggard woman to his right—"made me move so I wouldn't be sitting next to Brittany. That poster's mine!"

"Would the person in number B12 please remain seated until an usher comes for you. He'll accompany you to the projection office where your poster will be waiting for you."

The team of Clydesdales that pulled the Budweiser Beer Wagon couldn't have dragged Bosko out of that chair.

And it was about that difficult for the mother of the belligerent little boy to drag him out of the theater. The kid went into a full-bore temper tantrum meltdown, kicking his mother when she took his hand, yelling and crying.

Then Bosko spotted a red-coated usher swimming upstream against the last of the tide of people emptying the theater, and the howling youngster became the sound of a gnat by your ear on a summer day.

"Guess this is your lucky day," the usher said.

"Sure is," Bosko said, then got up out of seat number twelve and followed the usher as obediently as a lamb to the slaughter.

Chapter Forty-Two

2011

Jack's heart tried to jackhammer a hole in his chest at the sight of the blood on the blankets and floor of the room where Andi'd been held in the cabin. He grabbed hold of the emotion welling up into his throat and clamped down with all his willpower on the urge to leap up and go running into the house. If she were…dead…she'd be just as dead in five minutes as she was now, but if she were only injured and he blasted in like Sherman plowing through Atlanta, he could get them both killed.

He had to get inside the house without being seen, and he couldn't do that through the window. Even if he could pry the boards loose without waking the dead, the window was probably locked—or more likely in a place this old painted shut. Odds were the back door lead to the kitchen or if he got real lucky, a laundry room—like a bathroom, not as statistically likely to be occupied as a living room or kitchen.

Crossing beneath the windows to the back door, he tried the handle. It was unlocked. He pushed it slowly inward and stepped into a small kitchen, his head on a swivel, not merely scanning three hundred and sixty degrees but seven hundred and twenty. Up at the ceiling to rafters or the entrance to an attic, down at the floor where…there were drips of blood on the floor in a line across the kitchen and out onto the porch.

He knelt and touched them. They were sticky, still wet. They were small, too, not the kind of blood you'd see from a catastrophic wound. Jack still had to clear the house before he checked them out. Room to room, swiftly now, in a crouch, rifle extended, sweeping each room as he entered. The house was deserted. In the back bedroom, he examined the bloody blankets. If the kidnapper had stabbed her, the room would have been awash in gore. It wasn't. So he'd hurt her, injured her in some way, and then either carried or dragged her out the back door.

Jack returned to the blood drops. Blood was hard to follow. Where it dripped on dirt, it soaked in, leaving black marks that were almost impossible to spot. But he found a drip on a leaf and another on a rock, then spotted a trail that cut through the trees up the hill to the north. Though Jack didn't know the exact lay of the land here, he understood the general geography well enough to know that there was nothing in that direction but the wide, muddy Ohio River, where tall bluffs overlooked the water on the Kentucky side.

Why would the kidnapper be taking Andi to the river?

1985

An old man in a wheelchair emerged from the swirling smoke like some kind of apparition. He was the man Jack had asked about the telephone when he came into the building. He'd been slumped comatose in a wheelchair by the door, his chin on his chest. Now, he was upright and alert. His eyes were clear, his voice strong.

The man said something to Jack about not giving up. Jack couldn't hear him clearly. But he heard all four words of the second thing the man said. "I got the key." He brandished it like a Samurai sword. "I'm gonna unlock those chains."

The old man lifted his feet up out of the footrests, pushed upward with his hands on the arms of the chair to lift himself upright. Nothing happened. He pushed again, but he only got a couple of inches off the chair seat before tumbling back in.

"Please…" Jack bleated, trying not to cough. He hated how childlike and scared his words sounded, but he couldn't help it. He didn't want to die! "Help me, mister… who are you?"

"Ollie Marshal," the old man barked and tried a third time to heave himself up out of the chair. But he had no more success than he'd had twice before.

Jack was seized by a chain of coughing that went on and on until his throat was raw, and he was afraid he was going to throw up. The old man was struggling to rise out of the chair again. Weak as he was, he was trying, doing everything he could to help somebody he'd never met.

As soon as Jack could catch his breath, he cried out, his voice ragged from coughing and thick with unshed tears, "Thank you, Mr. Marshal."

The old man's head snapped up, and he stared at Jack, who looked into his eyes and didn't blink. They froze like that for a beat, then tears welled up in the old man's eyes—must have been the smoke—and he looked away.

"Can't unlock the dad-gum padlock from here," he

said, seemed to consider a couple of options, then shrugged.

Marshal took hold of the arms of the chair, using hands so arthritic they resembled turtle flippers, and shoved, leaping/falling forward out of it. He tumbled over the low fountain rim and splashed down face-first into the foot-deep water. He struggled, fought to get his head up, turned over on his back and rested on his elbows. Then he shoved and scooted himself to the base of the dolphin. Jacob Dumas had ended the chain wrap-around at the bottom so the lock was there by Jack's feet. Jack watched in fascinated terror as the old man fumbled with the wet key in his crippled hands.

The man grasped the padlock to hold it steady and shoved the key at it. He missed the hole. When he started to try again, the key slipped out of his wet hands and plopped into the water. Marshal felt around on the bottom of the fountain, groping for the key. It seemed to take a hundred years for him to find it and another thousand for him to grab the padlock and point the key at the hole again. He shoved and missed, jabbed at the hole a couple more times. His hands began to tremble. Now both the lock and the key were moving targets. He tried again. And again.

Jack burped out a sound that was half cough, half sob. Then he found he was crying in earnest, tears of fear and frustration. Marshal fumbled the key again and it plunked back into the water. Jack was sobbing and coughing, unable to control either. When the old man fished the key out of the water a second time, he mumbled words as he stabbed it at the lock.

"…old fool…stick a key in a lock for crying out loud… can't even—"

Then the key slid into the padlock, the old man gave it

a twist and the lock opened. He pulled it free from the chain links and dropped it into the water. The straight-jacket of chains instantly loosened, but Jack still couldn't get it off without help.

"I'll unwind far as I can," the old man said, spacing his words out between hacking.

The unwinding took interminably long. Jack wiggled and sobbed and coughed and squirmed and as soon as Marshal unwrapped his arms sufficiently, he shoved at the chain binding his chest, loosening it, forbidding himself the great intake of air his lungs were begging for. He clawed the rest of the chain off his neck, dropped the chain into the water, and staggered a couple of steps away from the dolphin. Then he reached down and grabbed the old man's collar and began dragging him toward the edge of the fountain.

"Hey, what do you think you're doing?" Marshal struggled to shake free of Jack's hold on his shirt.

"I can't carry you!" Jack barked out another chain of coughing, then spoke in gasps. "Dragging is the only"—gasp!—"way I can get you out of here."

"Who said I want out of here?" The old man jerked backward out of Jack's grasp and splashed down into the water. "Other folks are always deciding what I want and what I don't." He was coughing hard as the smoke settled around him. "Leave me alone!" He waved his hand dismissively. "Had an appointment on this day for going on twenty years." Cough. "And I'm finally going to keep it."

Flames were all around Jack as soon as he stepped out of the fountain. The heat was harsh without water running over him. Pieces of the ceiling had fallen to the floor and formed mini bonfires everywhere. The stink of burning flesh from the bodies on the floor made Jack gag. The over-stuffed furniture was on fire, and the silk flowers in vases had been turned into torches. Jack could hear the horrified screams of the old people trapped in their rooms on the second and third floors as fire came for them.

There was a sudden agonized shriek in the swirling smoke that now obscured the spot where the fireman had died. Jack tried to see who had cried out, but the smoke was too thick. Then a figure appeared in the flames. He seemed familiar, someone Jack had seen before. And it looked like…the flames backed up from him, moved out of his way as if shoved by an invisible hand. Jack recognized him—it was Chapman Whitworth, the son of the man Jack's father called a "sticky-fingered anthropologist." Was he possessed, too? How could he move through the smoke and flames like that?

Jack watched in horrified fascination as Whitworth crossed to the hospital bed that contained the feeble old man in wet pajamas that Cole had threatened to tie down with straps. The old man was trying to push Whitworth away, shaking his head no. Whitworth turned around and faced where Jack stood, dripping water into a puddle. Then he reached out to the table beside the old man's bed —his eyes never leaving Jack's face—and picked up a vase that flaming silk flowers had turned into a torch.

Holding the flaming flowers in his right hand, he did an odd thing. He touched the fingertips of his left hand to his forehead and snapped them upward in a strange salute to Jack. Then he dropped the torch of flowers on the old man. The man was an instant fireball from head to foot. His wet pajamas—that was gasoline! Whitworth watched him burn and scream, writhe, and twist—did nothing, merely stood with an odd little half smile on his face. Then he picked up the blanket on the end of the bed and smothered the flames on the lower part of the old man's body. He left his shirt burning though, and when he lifted the old man into his arms, those flames snaked up the side of Whitworth's face. He didn't seem to notice or care, merely gave Jack a crooked smile, and turned for the door, an invisible bubble shielding him from the flames he passed through. When he reached the barrier beams, the bubble vanished. Whitworth's shirt and hair were on fire now—and he leapt over the timbers and out the door.

"You just going to stand there and burn up?" barked the old man in the fountain.

Suddenly, Jack knew where to go.

"Which way's the kitchen?"

The old man pointed.

~

2011

There was very little in police work Crock enjoyed more than seeing the look on a perp's face when he figured out he was the one who got conned. As soon as Bosko stepped into the projection room, the two uniformed officers stationed by the door grabbed him, and one of them cuffed him quicker than a rodeo cowboy in a calf-roping contest.

"Good afternoon, Mr. Boskowitz," Crock said.

"Where's my poster?" Bosko asked.

Crock burst out laughing. "You want a poster, maybe we can see you get one to hang on the wall in your cell on death row," Crock told him. "They'll probably make a whole new movie by the time all your appeals are denied, but that's part of the fun, don't you think? The anticipation. Looking forward to the movie…and waiting for the feel of that needle sliding into your arm."

"I want a lawyer," Bosko said.

Crock went on as if he hadn't heard him. "Of course, you could get to see it the next time J. K. Rowling starts hallucinating--seeing boys in nightgowns flying around on sticks. I could make the whole death row scene go bye-bye. All you have to do is answer a few questions."

"I'm not saying nothing."

"Ah, but in this case, silence is not golden. It is deadly. You tell us who hired you, and the death sentence for three —count them, boys and girls, three—premeditated murders is off the table."

Crock had absolutely no authority to make any such offer. Prosecutors made plea bargain arrangements, not police officers. But Bosko didn't know that. There was no law against a police officer lying, and most had perfected it to an art form.

"I don't have to talk. I said I want a lawyer, and you got to get me one."

He'd apparently learned something from watching cop shows on television. Crock did, indeed, have to provide him a lawyer. But in the grand scheme of what really mattered in life, violating this scumbag's civil rights was more than a few rungs down the ladder from stopping a monster demon from sitting on the U.S. Supreme Court.

Did I just think that?

It still hit Crock like a blow to the solar plexus to tack words onto what he now understood to be the reality of the true functioning of the universe.

"Get him out of here," he told the uniforms, and they escorted the handcuffed Bosko out the door and down the hallway to the stairs leading out of the building. They'd leave by the side door to avoid the crowd out front.

Crock paused in the hallway to shake hands with the theater manager and thank him again for his cooperation. That's why he lagged a few steps behind the other officers, why he didn't see exactly what happened once they stepped out into the parking lot.

He heard part of it, though. A little kid's voice yelled something like, "That's him, Daddy. He stole my poster," followed by the sounds of a scuffle. When Crock opened the door that had closed behind the other officers, one of them was cuffing a large man sprawled facedown on the asphalt beside a little kid in the full throes of a temper tantrum. And he could see the bright red of Bosko's University of Louisville jacket, zigging and zagging between parked cars in the lot with the other officer only a few steps behind him.

Chapter Forty-Three

1985

Jack started in the direction the old man pointed, making his way past burning debris from the rapidly disintegrating ceiling. The smoke was so thick now, he couldn't see, couldn't breathe. Coughing until there were spots in front of his eyes, the world began to gray out. Dizzy. Couldn't stand. He staggered and fell to his knees. No air, only smoke. Then he was on the floor, the tile cool on his cheek. He'd tried, done the very best he could. The world began to gray, and he was aware enough to be grateful he wouldn't feel it when the fire got him. The pigeon-wing sound of flames faded gradually away.

A great cracking roar high above roused Jack, and he covered his head with his arms and squeezed his eyes shut, waiting for death as the ceiling fell down three floors to land on top of him. But only a few small pieces of debris clattered on the tile around him. He opened his eyes and squinted. The smoke wasn't as thick as before. In fact, it was clearing away, not puddling on top of him but flowing upward, away from him. He looked up. The roar had been the fire in the ceiling breaking through the roof. Like a chimney, the hole was now sucking the smoke and heat up and out. The air around Jack cleared. Still woozy and disoriented, with the room swimming in and out of focus, Jack began to commando crawl forward, sucking in little sips of the much cleaner air off the floor. Above the crackling of the flames and the crashes of collapsing walls, Jack could hear…nothing.

The old people had stopped screaming.

Jack continued forward, grasping frantically at the vague memory he had of one of the times he and Daniel had talked about the nursing home.

"I was filling the tray of communion cups in that little room off the kitchen on Saturday, and I spilled half a bottle of grape juice," Daniel says.

They are fishing, sitting on the bank of Buzzard Roost Creek, leaned up against a tree as the corks atop their baited hooks lounge languid in the slow water. Becca is playing with McDougal, tossing him a Frisbee. Her bell-clear laughter wafts to them on air scented by the honey-suckle vine climbing the tree behind them.

"How much trouble did you get in for making such a mess?"

"None. No mess. I grabbed a rag to wipe the floor where I'd spilled it, but there was hardly any juice at all. Most of it had leaked down through cracks between the floor planks…like maybe there was a hole there or something. So I tried to pry up one of the planks. It was a trapdoor."

"Cool!"

"Most of the trapdoor was covered up by a big rug. So I waited until Dad was busy on the second floor, moved the rug, pulled the door up and crawled down through it."

"And you found a huge room like the one under the opera house in Phantom of the Opera?"

"Nope. I didn't find anything at all. There was nothing there but a crawl space and a big dirt hole. Must have been where the furnace used to be because there was a coal chute."

If Jack could crawl down into that hole under the floor, he could get out through the coal chute.

He finally made it to the edge of the tile flooring where the atrium opened into the big hallway that housed the kitchen in the back corner. The carpet on the hallway floor was burning, and the plank flooring in the kitchen beyond was on fire, too. And Jack had no idea where the little room was where Daniel's father filled up communion cups.

~

2011

Jack had only gone a few dozen yards up the trail in the woods when he saw a tuft of white fabric stuck to a bramble. Then he spotted a twig on a bush, broken and dangling. Odd. A few yards farther on there was another. It was out of place, which was, of course the point. Andi had done it—to leave a trail so somebody could follow.

Andi believed her Uncle Jack was coming for her.

I don't ever have to be afraid, Uncle Jack, because you'll always keep me safe.

That's what she'd said in the hospital the day after he'd shot her—had called him "Uncle Jack," when she'd never met him.

He ruthlessly shoved those images out of his mind before they could muddy his focus and cloud his judgment. He still didn't know exactly what he was up against so he shifted off the trail into the woods and moved parallel to it, proceeding as fast as possible without sounding like a water buffalo stampeding through the trees.

If the man were packing a .30-.06 deer rifle, it would have a scope. It'd be easy with a scope for the man to sight in on Jack if Jack were coming straight at him. But trying to focus a scope on an object moving laterally through woods with limbs and trees and other things that'd take the focus would be far more difficult. It could give Jack the edge, a couple of seconds. That's all he needed to drop the guy.

Jack slowed as he reached the slope that stretched to the top of the ridge. The trail led up it and then out across the summit to the edge of the rocky bluffs. He moved from tree to tree, peering through the undergrowth at the trail. When he reached the top of the bluff, he spotted the man. A big guy in a white shirt.

Jack took in details instantly.

He was armed, but not with a rifle. He held a big hunting knife in one hand.

The man was standing with his back to Jack about twenty-five yards away. Just standing there, staring off the bluff at the river below.

He was alone.

IN A SLOW, almost lazy motion, Billy Ray Hawkins lifted the .22 rifle and pointed it at the chest of the suit-clad man in his front yard.

"You wanna tell me what you're doin' here?" he asked. Not that he wanted to know. It was of no consequence whatsoever why the man had come. All that mattered was that he wasn't never going to leave. It was his own fault, showing up unexpected like he done. He'd seen Billy Ray with the gun, and that was a parole violation that'd land Billy Ray back in prison. And Billy Ray was not going back to prison.

"I brought Mrs. Washington here to get her friend, Becca," he said. He was scared, you could see that. But he was handling it pretty well.

"You figure to take Becca away with you, do you?" Billy Ray was stalling, needed time to figure out the best way to kill him.

"If she wants to leave, then yes, we'll take her with us."

"Well, now see, there's the rub of it. My Becca girl belongs here with her daddy."

The fat nigger woman kneeling in the dirt had been magic. She'd soothed Becca with her words and her patting, and the girl had stopped screaming altogether. Was lying there, curled up in a ball, whimpering and moaning.

"Look, we don't want any trouble. All we want is—"

"You ain't smart as you look, Mr. Suit-and-Tie Man, if you think it matters diddly-squat what you want. Only thing that matters is that you's trespassing on my land. And around here, we shoot trespassers."

Billy Ray loved the look on the Suit's face when he said that, how all the color drained out of it 'til he was chalky pale. He thought to wonder how pale the man'd get if he knew Billy Ray absolutely did intend to shoot him, put a bullet square in the middle of the red tie on his chest— which is where he'd have to put it to drop the man with a single shot from a .22. Not a whole lot more powerful than a glorified pellet gun, the rifle was for small game—a squirrel, a rabbit, maybe a fox. But a .22 could still kill a man if you knew where to shoot him. Billy Ray knew, and he'd prefer the back of his head if he could manage it.

But instead of shooting him, Billy Ray really ought to

slap the guy on the back and thank him for delivering Theresa Washington into his hands. Never in his wildest dreams did Billy Ray envision having both Theresa Washington and Becca under his thumb, so he could extract a full measure of payment from Becca for what she'd done and kill Theresa just 'cause she was a nigger. If he'd learned anything from his useless father it was that a man ought never pass up a chance to kill a nigger. But before he killed her, he'd tell her how her boy squealed when that chain saw blade cut into him.

Have to do it in the barn, though. Couldn't never get that fat pig through the crack in the rock down into the boxcar. He'd run Theresa's car off Scott's Ridge, but he'd sell that fancy Mercedes. A friend of his ran a chop shop on his farm on the other side of the county. That car'd go in whole, and inside twenty-four hours it'd be in more pieces than Isaac Washington.

The Suit had started talking while Billy Ray was planning it all in his head.

"…intend to trespass and will be glad to turn around and drive right back out of here."

The man glanced at Theresa and Becca on the ground.

"As soon as we collect our friend," he finished resolutely.

Had some backbone, that Suit did. Becca was quiet now, only whimpering. Theresa was rubbing her back and murmuring to her.

Theresa spoke to him for the first time, and the very sound of her voice raised the hackles on his neck like the hair on a mad dog. "You planning on doin' murder here this day, ain't you Billy Ray?" She was looking up at him, squinting a little at the sun. There was no fear in those eyes so black you couldn't make out the dot in the middle.

His lip curled into a snarl, but he dialed back his anger.

Needed to fool the Suit long enough to get him out of the front yard before Billy Ray shot him.

"Why Theresa Washington, why would I do a thing like that, you being an old family friend of my daughter and all?"

She made a humph sound in her throat and went back to tending to Becca.

"I tell you what, Mr. Suit-and-Tie-Man, you pick up my daughter and carry her around to the backyard where we can lay her in the shade of the sycamore tree out of the sun until she…comes back to herself."

He gestured at her with the barrel of the rifle.

"I didn't do nothing to her to make her like that. She come here of her own free will and was right as rain until she dropped down into the dirt and had some kind of a fit."

Becca was quiet now, breathing the herky-jerky way a little kid breathed after a crying jag.

"She comes around, and we'll ask her does she want to stay. If she says no…well, then I guess that's that. All of you can get in your cars and drive back out of here the same way you drove in. That sound fair to you?"

"Billy Ray, you'd lie when the truth'd sound better," Theresa said without even bothering to look up.

"I ain't talking to you," he snapped. Then he turned back to the Suit. "Come on now, pick her up. She's so skinny, she don't weight nothing a'tall. We need to get her out of the sun and give her some lemonade—"

"Lemonade?" Theresa barked out a laugh. "Right, Billy Ray. Like you got lemonade."

"And then she can tell us her own self what she wants." He dropped the conciliatory tone and gestured with his gun barrel. "I said, pick her up. That ain't a request."

The Suit knelt down on one knee—got dirt all over his

clean silver trousers—and rolled Becca over onto her back. Her eyes were open, but she was as limp as a rag doll. He got his arms under her neck and knees and with surprising ease lifted her and stood up. Stronger than he looked.

"Get going," Billy Ray said and nodded toward the back of the house. He looked pointedly at Theresa, who was still down on one knee on the ground. "Both of you."

She struggled to get her fat old body upright and started for the backyard, her walk stiff and pained. The Suit carrying Becca fell in behind her. Billy Ray followed, the rifle pointed square between the man's shoulders. Soon's they cleared the house…he'd make it a headshot. Less blood and a sure thing. With his arms full of Becca, the guy was totally helpless.

Theresa passed around the corner of the house. The Suit was right behind her. Billy Ray raised his rifle and pointed it square at the base of the man's skull.

Goodbye, Mr. Suit-and-Tie Man.

He raked in a bullet and squeezed the trigger.

THE OFFICER outside the theater door held the struggling, cursing man on the ground with his arm twisted behind his back while he spoke crisply into the microphone clipped on his uniform at the shoulder, broadcasting Bosko's position and direction of travel.

Bosko was booking! But they'd catch him. It was hard to run with your hands cuffed behind you, and there were half a dozen police cars less than a minute away.

Bosko reached the end of the parking lot and never broke stride as he leapt out into the street. The big red garbage truck hit him square, right in the center of the front grill, knocked him into the air and over the hood of the truck.

Crock had no memory of crossing the whole length of the parking lot to the spot where Bosko's crushed body lay in the street. He was just there, with his heart hammering a painful hole in his chest and his breath heaving into his lungs in gasps.

Ignoring the popping of his knees, he knelt down beside the man as the officer who'd been chasing Bosko held back a growing crowd of people gathered around them, talking in hushed tones as they looked at the man sprawled on his back on the asphalt. The whole right side of his face was smashed, unrecognizable. His right arm, wrist still handcuffed to his left, was clearly broken in several places, both legs were skewed at unnatural angles, and the gurgling in his chest with every breath bespoke a man who was drowning in his own blood. He'd be dead before the ambulance got there.

"Bosko," Crock gasped, his breath almost as ragged as the man lying beside him, whose every exhalation produced bubbles of blood that ran out the corners of his mouth and down the sides of his face.

Bosko turned his eyes toward Crock but didn't move his head, maybe couldn't.

"You're not gonna see another sunrise, Bosko," Crock said. "You're dying." No time to beat around the bush. "You need to come clean before you stand before your maker. You know the man who hired you is...from the other side."

Bosko's eyes widened, then something like recognition settled on his features.

He struggled to speak. "We made it look like that black woman killed that old couple, the Cohens...but she didn't." He coughed and splattered blood on Crock's pants and shoes. "He did it with an ax. I watched him hack…" The voice came out through a gurgling red puddle rapidly forming in his mouth. "Me and Lily made it…look like that preacher raped her." He began to cough again, spraying blood on Crock's shirt and face. "Practiced so the cameras would…Then he told me to kill her…I didn't want to but—"

He began to cough, deep ragged coughs that wracked his body like seizures.

"*Who* hired you?"

Bosko continued to cough, the sound growing weaker and weaker.

"Who was it?" Crock prodded.

Bosko locked his gaze on Crock, willing himself to stop coughing, to draw a single clean breath. But recognition slowly drained out of his eyes until they were staring sightlessly in Crock's direction. Another breath, the chest rose for another cough, but then sank back down again and was still.

Crock sat back on his heels.

"You heard that?" he asked the officer at his side.

"I heard." He held up his phone. "Recorded it."

Theresa and Daniel were clear, then, but the only witness against Chapman Whitworth lay dead on the street at Crock's feet.

Chapter Forty-Four

2011

Chapman Whitworth looked from one senator to next, starting with Senator LaHayne and moving to the right. Then back down the row and moving to the left. He made eye contact with each man. Locked into his gaze.

When he had grabbed the absolute attention of every one of them, Whitworth began to speak, his voice honey poured over jagged shards of glass.

"We live in momentous times. Our land is graced with unimaginable opportunity, and our future is fraught with insidious peril—from enemies both without and within—growing menace that gnaws at the very fabric of our society, threatens our national character as a people and our honor as individual human beings."

He had them.

"These fifty United States of America are poised on the brink, balanced on the knife blade of history. Something more than chance has brought this particular group of men together in this room, gentlemen, and nothing less than destiny will be fulfilled by what we do here this day."

They were spellbound, hanging on his every word. During his week in the national spotlight, Whitworth had captured the imagination of a nation, of ordinary Americans from Bangor to Bakersfield, Portland to Pensacola. Now, he focused all the force of his persuasive powers on the men seated around a semicircular table within rock-throwing distance of the nation's capitol.

The crowd was so mesmerized, if Whitworth had laced in a pledge of "our lives, our fortunes and our sacred honor," Daniel doubted anyone would recognize the reference. He didn't know why he could sit outside and watch the proceedings as an observer, why he was not being hypnotized like all the others by the force of Chapman Whitworth's personality and the power of his words.

Could it be that he was behind Whitworth, that the man cast power outward somehow at those before him? That those not looking into his face didn't fall under his spell?

Daniel looked around at the people sitting in the gallery around him. Since he was in the front row, he couldn't get a good look at more than a handful of people, and what he saw was a mixed bag. All seemed captivated and fascinated. A few seemed in a trance. None appeared to be impervious to his power—except Daniel.

Perhaps it was because Daniel had gone behind the facade, had pulled back the black curtain and found the "wizard." But the Wizard of Oz had had no real power. Chapman Whitworth had one of the greatest powers in the universe—the power of evil.

He listened as Whitworth described what everyone in the room already knew in terms that somehow seemed new and fresh. He talked about the cases facing the court, the momentous nature of the decisions that had to be made that would "shape the future of this great country for generations." He talked about the absolute need for haste, for a swift resolution to the judgeship appointment.

Whitworth paused, looked pointedly at each senator individually, let the growing silence build until it assaulted Daniel's ears like the pounding of surf on rocks. When he spoke again, his voice was a whisper that rang out louder than a shout.

"You must fill this position without delay. You must find not just any man, but the one uniquely qualified by expertise, skill and integrity to fulfill the weighty responsibility and wield the might of the power that will be his."

Another pause. Another wave of silence crashed into the rocks. Another whisper.

"I am certain, gentlemen, without a shadow of a doubt that I am that man."

Well, there it was. Game over. Whitworth had called their bluff. And when Senator LaHayne was forced to spread his cards out on the table, Whitworth would gloat over the senator's consummate defeat and his own unqualified victory.

CONSIDERING THE CIRCUMSTANCES, the voice in Jeff Kendrick's head spoke with remarkable calm.

He's planning to kill all three of us.

Something in the hillbilly's eyes said so.

Even though Jeff had never in his life seen a look like that, it was somehow unmistakable, universal and primeval, and he recognized it, understood it on a gut level. Any second now, the man would pull the trigger on that rifle and send a bullet tearing into Jeff's chest.

His own arrogance had landed him here. The sense of

being bulletproof that provided just the right swagger in a courtroom to convince a jury—subliminally—that his was the just cause, that his expensive brown leather briefcase was the repository of all truth. He believed he was indestructible—a belief that sent him free climbing when his fellow rock-climbers were safely roped in, a belief that relished risks of all kinds—from sky-diving to hang-gliding, playing fast and loose with life and relationships, certain he would walk out of whatever circumstance he found himself unscathed.

Emily had changed all that, of course, the relational part of it anyway, had left him broken and bleeding. But he was still an arrogant fool for all that, and that character flaw was about to get him killed.

Theresa had told him the story of the kidnapping as they flew south down Interstate 71, and he'd grown cold all over. Emily's daughter was missing. He'd never met the little girl, but understood without Emily ever saying it that her love for the child knew no bounds. His relationship with Emily had run off the rails the day of the school shooting that had put the little girl in the hospital—a shooting that had occurred while he and Emily had been together. The last time they were together.

Now that little girl, that part of Emily, was in danger. Emily's Miranda. Andi. She'd been kidnapped, a hostage to trade for someone named Becca—and nobody had called the police! That was insanity. Trying to find a missing child based on some daydream she'd had was absolutely unconscionable. But in that calm way that Theresa Washington was so certain about all manner of other things, she'd been adamant that her police officer friend Jack would find Andi and keep her from harm.

Theresa'd told him that Billy Joe, or Billy Dan, or whatever his stereotypical Southern double name was—

was dangerous and "mean as a wasp shook up in a Mason jar." She'd wanted Jeff to drop her off at the end of the driveway. Of course, he'd refused. But he could see now how foolhardy it had been to come driving in here and expect to pick this Becca up like she'd been waiting at a bus stop.

How could he have been so stupid? He dealt with criminals every day, knew the brutality they were capable of. But he was here, facing a wild man with a gun, feeling responsible in some way for the old woman who knelt in the dirt beside the hysterical girl. Clearly, nobody was going to come along and get them out of this mess.

Billy Dan instructed him to pick up Becca and carry her to the backyard, and Jeff understood the ruse for what it was. When Jeff heard the racking sound of the rifle—all this time he hadn't even had a round in the chamber!—he reacted on pure instinct. He dropped Becca, and even as she was rolling out of his arms, he was shifting all his weight to his left leg. He leaned his whole upper body forward, had no time to look, merely kicked backward and up, about chest high, with his right foot, putting all the force he could muster into the blow.

At the moment Jeff's foot connected with the rifle, it fired. The bullet whizzed past Jeff's head so close he could almost feel the air rearranging itself. He heard a grunt. Then Theresa Washington dropped to her knees and pitched face-first into the dirt in front of him.

~

1985

Mikey, Daniel and Becca rode as fast as they could to Bishop's house from the furniture store, which wasn't very fast with Daniel perched like a parrot on the back of Becca's scooter and Mikey struggling to keep up.

Bishop's truck was parked in the driveway, but his car wasn't. There was a note to someone named Bill taped to the front door.

"Had to take Theresa to the hospital in Louisville. Her back's hurt real bad. We'll have to move that piano some other time."

They stepped off Bishop's porch, and Mikey pointed to the western sky.

"Look at that smoke!" he said.

When Daniel and Becca turned to look, Becca gasped and her face turned chalk white.

"What do you see?" Daniel asked her.

Mikey looked from Becca to the boiling tower of smoke in the sky and back, confused. Duh, she saw smoke.

"There's a…shape in the smoke." Her voice trembled, and she backed away from it as she spoke. "Red. A red thing. Its face…" She stared, transfixed with horror. "Horns and rows of teeth…" She began to shake her head. Her eyes filled with tears. "And hate. It's so angry, so—"

Daniel took her shoulders and turned her to face him, away from the smoke. She was frozen for a moment, like she didn't see him. Then she relaxed, put her hands over her face and started to cry. He put his arms around her, and she leaned into him, sobbing.

Mikey had no idea what was going on, but something was, something the others understood and he didn't. And he wanted to know what it was more than he'd ever wanted anything in his life. No, he wanted more than that to have his arms around Becca as she cried.

He looked back at the smoke. "It's the nursing home,"

he said. "Twin Oaks. It's the only thing out that way big enough to make that much smoke."

"The Bad Kids did it," Becca said, her voice strangled, her face still buried in Daniel's chest. "The demons set it on fire."

Demons? No, she didn't mean…Then a thought struck Mikey. "So if the…Bad Kids set the nursing home on fire and Jack was following them…where's Jack?"

"Jack!" Becca pulled back out of Daniel's arms, wiping the tears off her face. "We have to find him." She climbed on her bike, and Mikey saw that she was careful not to look directly at the smoke as she set out toward it.

By the time the three of them got near the nursing home, Mikey was exhausted. The building sat on the crest of a small hill, and he did not want to ride up that incline with Daniel and Becca. They didn't have to pedal to continue traveling forward. He did.

The road leading out of town had been as jammed with traffic as the exit ramp from a rock concert. They'd weaved their bikes in and out among cars with horrified and frantic drivers, honking uselessly at the cars that had stopped in front of them. Helicopters from television stations in Louisville, Cincinnati, and even Bowling Green buzzed overhead like flies around road kill. The closer they got to the nursing home, the more it seemed to Mikey that the smoke darkening the sky cast a shadow, a finger pointing directly at the three of them. But that was crazy, couldn't possibly be.

When they finally got within sight of the building, Mikey was done, "Wait up, guys!" he cried, and to his utter delight they didn't ignore him, but pulled to the side of the road and stopped, and he pumped as hard as he could to make it up the beginning of the incline to where they waited.

Then he and Daniel stood gaping at an inferno. Becca covered her eyes and refused to look. Even from here, they could see the tops of flames licking the bottom of a column of smoke that smeared tar on the sky above. Becca did look at the mob that stretched down from the top of the hill, and Mikey figured she and Daniel were wondering the same thing he was. Was Jack in that mob? Or in the burning building?

The look of despair on Becca's face told Mikey where she believed Jack was. Her sorrow broke Mikey's heart.

"Hey," he said, as soothing as he could manage with a Mickey Mouse voice that hadn't yet started to change, "we don't even know that Jack followed them this far."

"Oh, yes we do!" Daniel cried and jumped off the scooter. Leaving Becca to hold it upright, he took off down the side of the road and into the woods—where Jack's bike stood leaned against a tree.

"The chain's off," Daniel said. "He must have left the bike here when he couldn't go any farther."

"And walked to the nursing home to get help," Mikey said, hating every word as it left his mouth.

"Which means," Becca said, her voice so soft she was hard to hear, "that he's…in there, now. Jack's in the fire."

Mikey could think of nothing to say. Daniel didn't speak, either, merely set about fixing the chain on Jack's bike so he could ride it instead of riding double on Becca's scooter.

Daniel had recovered some by the time he got the chain in place.

"We don't know Jack's in that building," he said with what Mikey thought was remarkable conviction, given that he didn't believe his own words. "He could be in the crowd out front—but the police are never going to let us get close enough to find out."

He stood and wiped grease off his fingers onto his pants. "Here's what I think we should do—ride back to the intersection and turn down Pullman Lane so we can come at the nursing home from the south. If the crowd's not as thick on that side, we can get past the police barricade."

"Do you think Jack's…ok?" Becca's voice sounded so frightened it broke Mikey's heart all over again. "Sure he is," Daniel said.

Mikey was silent, just gave Daniel a look that said he wasn't buying what Daniel was selling. Then the three got on their bikes, turned around and headed back toward Pullman Lane.

Chapter Forty-Five

1985

Jack bumped into a wheelchair as he crawled. He'd been trying to figure out how he was going to get across the burning kitchen floor to the other side, where there were three closet-sized doors. One of them must lead to the room where Daniel's father had filled communion cups.

Maybe the chair could be his ride. He looked around and found a small rug that hadn't yet caught fire, folded it over three times and placed it on the wheelchair seat. Then he stood, grabbed the hand rests on the front of the wheelchair and began pushing it backward as hard as he could toward the burning kitchen.

When the chair passed over the last of the tiles, he leapt into the seat on his knees and rode the momentum across the burning carpet and plank floor into the kitchen. He'd never have made it if his clothes hadn't been soaking wet. The soggy denim of his jeans wouldn't ignite, but the heat and flames from the burning floor blistered the skin on the front of his legs from his ankle to his knee.

The wheelchair rolled to a stop in front of the middle

of the three small doorways, and he leapt into the room. If this wasn't the right room, Jack would die. He'd never make it to either of the other rooms to look there. The door frame was on fire, and the flames had spread to a rug on the floor, so he tossed it back out into the kitchen. The moment he'd stood up into the thicker smoke in the hallway, he had begun to cough violently. Now, he was coughing so hard his watering eyes left him almost blind. He dropped to his knees and felt around on the plank flooring, looking for a crack, a handle, something to indicate there was a trapdoor somewhere beneath where the rug had been. He could feel nothing…the smoke was so thick.

There! There it was. Deeply inset in a space between wood planks was something cool, something metal. Jack fumbled with the piece of metal, drawing it up out of the crack to form a handle.

There was a crash and whooshing sound behind him. The kitchen ceiling was giving way. Another thirty seconds…

He pulled up as hard as he could on the handle and a whole section of planking around it rose away from the floor. He could see darkness beneath. Daniel hadn't said how far the drop was from the floor to the dirt below, but Jack didn't care. He dove into the hole blindly and hit hard, tucked his head and rolled with the momentum, doing a somersault before coming to a stop under the floor about ten feet from the trapdoor opening. The subflooring above his head had not ignited yet, but it was hot and smoking, eager to admit the fire to the crawl space. There was a rumble, flaming debris and sparks crashed down through the trapdoor opening.

Backing away from the opening, Jack looked around for the hole Daniel had described. He spotted it about thirty feet away. It was just what Daniel had said, nothing but a hole dug into the ground under the building. Scrabbling across the old, gray dirt of the crawl space, with the heat from the flooring above his head burning his back and neck, he got to the hole and tumbled into it. It was deep enough that when he stood up, the smoking subflooring was five or six feet above his head, so it was considerably cooler and the air was better.

When he wiped the dirt off his hands on his pants, he noted that the palm he had injured when he fell off his bike—how long ago?—was now burned as well. But that didn't matter because the rest of what Daniel had described was right there in front of him. Outlined in light on a sloping wall were double doors that opened out, like a storm cellar.

Jack scrambled up the dirt incline, reached up and shoved on the doors. They were stuck. He shoved again. And again. As his eyes adjusted to the darkness, the terror he'd managed to keep at bay clamped iron manacles around his chest.

No. Oh, please, no.

The doors weren't stuck. He could see through the crack between them the rusty lump of padlock on the outside that held the doors pinned together. He shoved a couple more times in frustration, then slumped down on the dirt slope littered with chunks of coal.

This was it. There was no way to get out of this basement, and the flooring above him would soon ignite, turning the crawl space into an oven were Jack would…cook.

~

2011

Andi swiped at the blood running down her upper lip and off her chin. When the door where she was listening to the men argue had suddenly flown open, it hit her in the face and smashed her nose, and now it was bleeding. Tattoo Man had grabbed her hair, held the big knife up against the skin of her neck and she'd cried out for Daddy. Then the man had told her not to make so much as another peep or he'd cut her throat. She'd been so terrified she'd thought she might wet herself.

She was still that scared now as he dragged her by the arm across the backyard and into the woods to a trail that ran up the hill. Maybe even more afraid because she couldn't think of any reason why he'd drag her out of the house into the woods except…She stumbled, caught her shirt on a bramble and ripped off a small piece of fabric.

Somebody would see that!

Whoever came up the trail behind them would notice it. And she knew who that person would be. Uncle Jack. She knew he was looking for her and she sensed—or imagined she sensed—that he was nearby.

Andi wished she had a brooch, a bright-green leaf thing like Pippin had had! She'd have dropped it on the ground like he did so Strider, Legolas and Gimli would find it. But she didn't have a brooch.

The next time she brushed past a limb, she reached out and broke off a tiny piece and left it dangling. She'd seen that once in a movie. That would have to do since she didn't have a brooch.

She broke off another twig and then another.

The trail got more steep, then flattened out, and she realized she was on the top of a hill and you could see the Ohio River.

The trail ended here.

Why would Tattoo Man bring her up to the top of a hill where the trail ended?

She knew why.

In a burst of panic, she yanked her arm out of his grasp and turned to run back down the trail. He grabbed at her, got hold of her shirt and swung her back around, but she wiggled free. She was in front of him now. Nowhere to run. She looked around, frantic. He had her trapped. And he knew it.

She moved away from him, her back to the river. The wind ruffled her curls and tossed them into her eyes. Only a glance over her shoulder told her she was much higher than she'd imagined. Higher than the top of a Ferris wheel. There was nothing but a drop-off, a cliff behind her.

She began to whimper. Tattoo Man was advancing slowly on her, his arms out so she couldn't run past him, his knife shiny in the bright sun. She took another step back. Now she was only one step away from the rim. She had nowhere else to go.

That's when she heard the voice in her head. She'd heard it before. That day when Mommy got shot. Mommy'd told her to "Go hide, Andi. Hide where nobody can ever find you." And she'd climbed up into the Easter pageant storage room, crawled back deep into it and down into a big basket that sat beside the stack of firewood from the woman-at-the-well scene.

But then the voice had told her to come out. The voice in her head, gentle and kind. It was the voice of the lady made out of light, Princess Buttercup, and the voice had told her to climb out of the basket, run to the vestibule of the church and ring the bell. Andi hadn't wanted to, was scared to come out of hiding, but the voice said she must, and she couldn't not do what the lady wanted even though it was scary.

What the voice told her to do now was way scarier than climbing out of a basket and ringing the church bell.

Play Catch Me, Andi, the voice said, like you do with Daddy.

Fall backward? Here?

When she played Catch Me with Daddy, he was right there behind her. There was nothing behind her now but the river. Andi couldn't swim. In three miserable months of swimming lessons, she hadn't even learned how to tread water.

The kidnapper was advancing on her with the knife. Another step or two, and he'd be close enough to grab her.

Play the game, the voice insisted.

No! Andi cried in her head. Who'll catch me?

I will, the voice said.

Tattoo Man was within grabbing range now. He reached out his beefy hand—

Andi stretched out her arms, leaned her head back, closed her eyes and fell backward off the rocky cliff above the river.

JEFF KENDRICK DIDN'T ALLOW his focus to shift to Theresa's still body in the dirt. He continued the spin. In a fluid arc, he brought down the foot he'd kicked backward with, transferred his weight to it, and hammered out with the other foot in a forward punch. He could see his target this time and slammed his seven-hundred-dollar Burberry leather wingtip brogue into Billy Boy's surprised face. He actually heard the crunch sound when the man's nose broke. Blood squirted from it and his split lip as his head snapped back. Catapulted backward, his body collided with the side wall of the house, and he crumpled to the ground unconscious, limp as a sack of doorknobs.

Jeff stood over the body, panting not from exertion but from the adrenaline rush that throbbed now in his temples. He reached down and snatched the rifle off the ground, a rage coursing through him like he'd never felt before. He snapped the handle and cocked it, aimed it at the bloody hillbilly's head.

"Don't shoot him!" Theresa said.

Jeff turned slowly and stared at her in disbelief.

"We can't kill the mangy dog," she said. "But it'd be fine with me if you wanted to kick him in the face another time or two."

She was on all fours, in the final stage of trying to stand. Jeff ran to her and offered his hand. He couldn't seem to get his mouth to form words, knew when he spoke he sounded mentally challenged.

"He shot you," he said. "Why aren't you—"

"Dead?"

"At least…injured."

"You sound disappointed," she said and grinned up at him. "I ain't hurt 'cause my Bishop protected me."

Bishop. Her dead husband.

"A ghost? Well, shoot, why not? I mean, we got demons and murderous hillbillies—what's one spook more or less?"

He could hear in his voice the ragged edge of what had to be incipient hysteria, and he gritted his teeth to keep from bursting into a hail of giggles, or shrieks like—

He looked for the first time toward the rag doll woman he'd dumped in the dirt. She was sitting now, too, not making any effort to rise, though. But there seemed to be nothing wrong with her. She was there, present, not curled up in a fetal position howling at the moon. She was cradling her left hand, maybe injured it when he dropped her.

"Not no ghost," Theresa answered reasonably. "Ain't no such thing as ghosts."

"Well, that's a relief."

"I told you when we started all this you wasn't gonna b'lieve everything we said, but I wasn't talking 'bout fairy tales. Spooks and such. My Bishop ain't no spirit floating around in a white nightshirt. He's in Heaven with Jesus. He 'saved' me 'fore he left."

She turned slightly. Jeff could see the motion pained her, reached around and knocked on her lower back with her fist. It made a clunking sound.

"Made me this here cookie-sheet corset to help stabilize my back so it wouldn't pain me so bad."

Jeff reached out and touched her back. It was like she was wearing a suit of armor.

"Course God was the one done it. He knowed I's gonna need this thing, and that's why he put it in Bishop's head to build it."

Jeff said nothing. His mind had returned like paper clips to a magnet to the little kidnapped girl, Emily's daughter. He strode over to the hillbilly and kicked him.

"You! Wake up."

The hillbilly groaned. His eyelids fluttered open and then closed. Jeff kicked him again.

"Wake up. You're going to tell us where to find Andi Burke."

"He doesn't have her anymore," said the woman called Becca. Her voice was ragged and husky, hoarse from screaming—and breathy, too, the way you talk when something hurts. But she seemed rational enough.

The hillbilly opened his eyes, but didn't focus. He wasn't fully conscious yet, but he was on the way.

"How do you know that?" Jeff asked her.

"I heard him. When I got here, he called whoever had her. Told them to let her go, to take her to a McDonald's somewhere, give her five dollars for a Happy Meal, then drive away and leave her there."

A sweet flood of relief flowed over Jeff so profound, he only then realized how frightened he'd been.

The hillbilly rolled over on his side and sat up slowly. Then he fingered his broken nose gingerly and grunted in pain. He looked up at Jeff with such naked hatred it was chilling. He was back now.

Jeff kept the .22 leveled at him, then nodded to Theresa.

"My cell phone's in my jacket pocket," he said. "Get it out and call the police."

Before Theresa could reach for it, Becca cried, "No, don't do that." She had risen to her feet and crossed to stand in front of the hillbilly on the ground.

"Don't call the police?" Jeff was incredulous. "We're not playing that game anymore. They should have been called the instant that child went missing yesterday!"

"I didn't have nothing to do with no kidnapping," the man said, his words muffled like he had a bad cold.

"Then we'll start with attempted murder and work our way back to kidnapping."

"No," Becca said. "Please."

"He tried to kill—"

"We're even now," she said, not to Jeff but to the man sitting in the dirt holding a bleeding nose. She took a step toward him, holding her left hand to her belly with her right, and glared down at him. "I was a teenager, just a kid, and the police told me if I'd testify, you'd be locked up long enough for me to vanish, and I had to get away from here, from…the evil. But the police lied. They said it'd only be for a couple of years—didn't say anything about a mandatory twenty-year sentence or tacking on time when you refused to cooperate. Whether you believe it or not, I never intended that."

She pressed her lips together in a tight line. "Well, this balances the books. I sent you away to prison once. And now I'm keeping you from going back to prison. We're even."

The man said nothing, only looked at her.

"Are we done—yes or no?" she said.

The man scowled at her, loathing so distorting his face he looked like a Halloween mask.

"We're square," he mumbled.

"So you're not going to—?"

"I said we was square, didn't I?" he snapped. "I'll leave you be. Billy Ray don't never go back on his word!"

Chapter Forty-Six

1985

What's it feel like to die?

Jack addressed the question silently to the hot dusty darkness around him that was rapidly filling with smoke.

Does it hurt? Up to dying, getting burned will hurt, but the dying itself—is it painful?

Though he didn't know exactly what he meant by the word, he wanted to die with as much dignity as possible. He didn't want to fall apart and cry, scared and desperate, begging God to save him.

What was it Theresa always said?

"God's gone do whatever God's gone do, and if he's set on it ain't much sense trying to talk him out of it. What you need to talk to God about is how the two of you is getting on. 'Cause if your relationship with God's what it ought to be, it won't matter much one way or the other what he does."

Jack closed his eyes and bowed his head. Then he remembered that Bishop had said there was nowhere in the Bible that said you had to bow your head when you prayed. So he lifted his chin and opened his eyes.

"Guess I'm going to find out now if all the things Theresa and Bishop have been saying are true."

His voice sounded small and hollow against the background of the fire's roar and the distant rumble of the front part of the building beginning to collapse.

He turned his face to the smoky ceiling and cried out, "Are you there, God?"

Then he looked around as if he expected to see some sign—an angel, maybe, like Becca saw. But there was nothing but the dust and smoke in the air and the cavorting red-yellow flames where the subfloor had caught on fire near the trapdoor. Behind him, streaks of sunlight from slits in the coal chute door stuck in the dirt at his feet like flaming arrows.

"I need help! To…die like a man. So Bishop would be proud of me." He paused as another rumble reverberated in the ground around him.

"And…I'm scared, ok! I'm really scared." Now that he'd let that out, set those words free, the rest that he'd wanted so badly not to say came tumbling after it. "I don't want to die! I want to grow up and be a soldier…or a cop…or…a minister." He only threw that last part in because he thought he should, and then realized if God was who he was supposed to be, he knew that. And if he wasn't…the rest of it didn't matter. "Ok, not a minister. But a good man. Please…don't let me die. Do something!" That sounded whiney and like a little kid, but he couldn't help it. "Please show me a way out of here."

There was no voice, no apparition, no sound but the roar of the blaze.

Then Jack saw fire move out from the burning floor around the trapdoor, and he watched with the fascination of a mouse watching a cobra as a single strand of red-yellow flame, almost like a candle, moved toward him. It lit up the crawlspace as it came his way, casting shadows. When it got to the area over the dugout hole where the furnace had been, it grew brighter, almost like someone had turned up the wick on a lantern. In its glow, Jack saw what he'd been unable to see before. A pipe.

Set in the dirt across from the incline leading to the coal chute doors was a black opening maybe eighteen inches across. Jack ran to it and tried to see what was inside, but the flame's glow only extended in a couple of inches. What was the pipe for? Drainage? Sewage? He stuck his head into it and sniffed, trying to detect if there was clean air in the pipe, but there was so much smoke and dust around there was no way tell. Did the pipe travel through the ground and on to an opening somewhere? The riverbank, maybe. Or was it only a piece of metal junk left in the ground, open here but long since plugged up at the other end?

"You want me to…to get out through this?" he cried out, and the response was the crackling of burning wood. "I can't crawl in there—what if it doesn't go anywhere? I'll be trapped."

The pipe was so small he would barely be able to get his whole body into it, no room to turn around. If he crawled into it, he would have to follow it wherever it went. There'd be no coming back and nowhere to come back to when the building collapsed. And if the pipe was blocked off or went nowhere at all, Jack would die in there.

Die in the dark, squashed up in a pipe!

Die how? Suffocate? Stuck until he died of thirst.

And if he died in there, nobody…nobody would ever know what happened to him. Jack Carpenter would vanish, like he'd never really been here at all.

"I can't, God!" he cried. "I…"

He put his head and shoulders into the pipe and pulled himself forward on his elbows. Only a little way. Most of him still dangled out at the end. He could still change his mind.

It was dark and tight, cold and scary. Nothing but inky blackness ahead.

"I can't!" he cried and scooted frantically backward. He popped out of the pipe like a cork and fell on his butt in the dirt. The heat above was cranking higher and higher. It was like lying on the rack in an oven set for broil.

Cook? Or suffocate?

Choose.

"Nooo!" he wailed. Then stood, stepped to the pipe and started down it again. "Nooo!" he cried out in the darkness, then shoved himself forward as far as he could, again and again until he was so far in there was no going back.

2011

Andi didn't know what she'd landed on until she opened her eyes. It was soft, and kind of sticker-y and the smell of it was familiar. When Daddy took her to the zoo in the summer and the workers were hosing down the enclosures, you could stand close and lean over the railing and smell the animal poop. And another smell, too. This one. The smell of the wet hay.

She opened her eyes and saw the hay all around her, almost covering her, stuck to the almost-dry blood on her upper lip. But she could see sky through the hay and the top of the cliff. And Tattoo Man staring down at her in disbelief. Then he shoved the knife into the scabbard at his waist and began to climb like a monkey down the side of the rocky cliff face.

Andi tried to get up out of the hay so she could run. Where? But she'd fallen into it hard and was buried down deep in it. She tried to stand, but she couldn't get her feet under her and she had nothing to grab to pull herself up. It was like trying to get out of Jell-O.

Tattoo Man was coming fast down the side of the cliff.

Maybe she shouldn't try to get out of the hay at all. There was a lot of it. It must be one of this huge hay rolls she saw when they passed by farms on the highway. When there was snow on top of them, she thought they looked like Frosted MiniWheats. Maybe she should try to burrow down deep in it, roll up in a tiny ball where he couldn't find her. She didn't really have to decide to do that. She couldn't stand, so she rolled over on her belly and began to dig her way through the hay. She'd dig all the way to the bottom. He'd have to tear the whole pile apart to find her.

She knew he'd reached the ground and was wading into the hay because he was cursing, saying awful things. Which was good because as long as he was making noise, she'd know where he was and he didn't know where she was.

He must have figured that out because he shut up. Then it was quiet, except for the sounds of digging and swishing hay. Andi hunkered down as far as she could, rolled in a tight ball, bit her lip hard to keep from whimpering.

In her head, Andi cried out to the voice that had spoken to her, the lady made out of light.

Help me. Please. I'm scared. Where are you?

But the voice said nothing.

Then she heard a grunt, close by. How did he find—?

Big fingers closed around her ankle. He'd spotted the

red striped socks she'd put on with her red Converse sneakers. He yanked on her leg, and she kicked at him with her other foot, but it didn't do any good. He pulled her up to the top of the hay. He wasn't even trying to stand up. He was down on his knees. When her head came up out of the hay, she could see him crouched there. He grabbed her by the hair again, pulled her toward him as he drew the knife out of the scabbard.

Andi shrieked, "Mommy!"

He raised the blade in the air—

"Drop the knife!"

The words came down to them from the top of the ridge, spoken with Uncle Jack's voice.

The man froze in surprise, jerked his head around so he could see who was yelling. Tattoo Man was between Andi and Uncle Jack so she couldn't see him. But he must have looked as mad and mean and scary as he sounded because Tattoo Man remained frozen.

"You got seconds to live, pal." Uncle Jack said. "Open the fingers of both hands. Slowly. You so much as twitch, and I will put a bullet square in your right eye socket."

"I'll cut her throat!" Tattoo Man threatened, but he didn't sound near as mean as Uncle Jack did, and he didn't move when he said it.

"No, you won't. Try and you'll be dead in a puddle of your own brains." Uncle Jack paused, then ground out the next words in the meanest voice Andi'd ever heard. "I want to kill you so bad I can taste it. That's my little girl. You will not draw in another breath after this one unless you drop the knife now!"

Tattoo Man dropped the knife into the hay and let go of Andi's hair.

Andi knew better now than to try to stand up and walk in the hay. She merely scurried away from Tattoo Man on all fours over the top of the hay roll and crawled/slid off it to the ground.

"Run away, Andi," Uncle Jack called out. "Run!"

She bolted down the small strip of muddy shoreline where the river lapped up against the rock wall of the bluff.

Chapter Forty-Seven

1985

Jack started to cry, to sob. Terror welled up in his chest, like pulling the cord and inflating one of those navy dinghies he'd seen on TV, and he couldn't breathe. But there was only forward, so he continued to crawl. Crushed on all sides by the cold metal, dragging the skin off his elbows and burned knees and legs, his hands out in front of him, feeling…air. Fear that any second he'd touch something solid in the darkness ahead was worse than the fear of the fire when he'd been in the building.

He crawled and crawled. He had been in the pipe for—what? Ten minutes? Two hours? Each moment was the longest moment of his life—until the next. It felt like his time in the pipe was as long as the whole rest of his childhood, and with every scooting motion forward, he left a piece of his childhood behind him. How far had he gone—thirty feet? Fifty yards? Half a mile? There was no gauge to use to measure anything, time or distance. He realized he was still sobbing when he heard the sound and wondered for a moment what it was. When he stopped crying, the pipe was still, silent.

A tomb.

Buried alive.

Panic rushed in, a hairy black monster gorging its belly full of the meat of his soul. The walls slowly tightened, began to crush him, squeezing the air slowly out of his lungs.

"Let me out! I want out!" he cried, his voice ragged. "I'd rather die, burn—anything."

He fought the walls around him, tried to push them away, bawling in terror, kicking his feet and banging with his fists. He lifted himself up on his elbows and screamed, "God, get me out of here!"

Some part of him registered the act of rising and he froze, his cries echoing in the silence.

Had the pipe gotten bigger? He hadn't been able to rise on his elbows before, had been ducking his head to keep from dragging it across the roof of the pipe. Now, it seemed that the space above him was larger. He was breathing hard, panting as he crawled on another few feet.

Then his hand in front connected with something solid. He felt around on it desperately, scratching, clawing, feeling for some kind of opening.

But there was none. He'd reached the end of the pipe. He was going to die in here.

A deep, guttural wail of horror rose out of his chest, a sound he'd never heard any other human being utter—a desolate cry of bone-deep terror that reverberated around him as if he were inside a huge bell. He shrieked, threw his head back and—

His head didn't hit the top of the pipe.

He lifted his hand and felt above his head, reached up as

high as he could, but he couldn't feel the pipe overhead anymore. Slowly, he twisted his body until he was lying on his back. Then he reached both hands up…into empty air. He felt around, waved them around, but he couldn't reach the top.

How big was the opening above? Had the pipe not ended, but merely turned—upward?

Jack rolled back over onto his belly and began to scoot forward. When he got to the solid wall in front, he moved up it, pulling himself forward and pushing with his feet. He wiggled and squirmed and scooted until he was on his knees. Then he carefully stood. The vertical pipe he was in now was not as tight a fit as the horizontal one had been. He had room, air around him. But there was only blackness everywhere, like being blind. And nowhere to go but up. How could he…climb up? The pipe was smooth, no handholds. He stood thinking, trying to puzzle it out, trying to stop the wild hammering of his heart that thundered in his ears far louder than the fire had. He leaned his back against the cold pipe wall, and the toes of his shoes bumped into the wall across from him.

Before he had a chance to form the intent to do it, he flattened his back against one side of the pipe and began walking his feet up the other. Then he scooted his body upward. He did it again. And again, developed a bit of a caterpillar rhythm. Pushing his body upward, scooting and pulling.

Light!

No.

Yes. It was light.

Only a tiny glimmer of it trickling down through some pinhole above. He dragged himself upward toward the light, which didn't get any bigger or brighter as he approached. Then other lighted shapes emerged out of the gloom. A semicircle of light around the first light. A familiar shape. It was light coming in around some kind of round lid!

He shoved himself frantically upward, now, the light growing brighter, until his hands struck something metal overhead. It was a cap of some kind blocking the pipe. Jack pushed. It didn't move. He shoved again, but only succeeded in shoving himself back down the pipe. He had no leverage. He scrambled his toes around, trying to find—there! Something was sticking out of the pipe maybe an inch, right above his right foot. He didn't know what it was, but it didn't matter. He rested the toe of his shoe on it, put all his weight on that foot and shoved upward.

The lid moved. Only a little. But it moved. Which meant it wasn't locked down.

Frantic with hope now, desperate with pent-up claustrophobia, he shoved with his arms, shoulders and legs. The lid moved again. It had been set down in some sort of groove, and Jack managed to move it out of the seating. Now light and air flooded in—smoky air—and heat. Wherever this pipe came out, it was still very close to the fire.

Jack shoved his fingers into the crack between the lid and the edge of the pipe and pushed sideways. The lid scooted five or six inches to the right. He did it again. Another six inches. And again. Crying now, sobbing, bordering on hysteria, Jack shoved the lid one final time, then pulled himself upward by grasping the rim.

The top of his head peeked out of the pipe. He was on the south side of the building, in the lawn at the edge of the woods. There was nobody here. Firefighters and equipment were out front where there was water. Jack would have to move the lid off the pipe, then leap out of the hole and run for the woods to get away from the heat of the blaze. He took a deep breath of pipe air, shoved the pipe lid all the way off the pipe into the grass, grabbed with both hands, pushed off with his foot on whatever he'd been standing on and got the top half of his body out of the hole on his belly. He dragged himself forward, flipped over onto his back, yanked his legs out of the hole and staggered to his feet, trembling all over. Then he headed toward the woods at what was as close as he could get to a dead run.

He hit the boundary of trees, stopped for a moment and looked back, then kept going, deeper into the woods, away, away from the smoke and the heat and the flames. He came to a small clearing and dropped to his knees, panting. Then he started to sob again, great, gulping sobs for what he had endured and for the murdered people in the building and for—

"How did you get out of there, nigger?"

Jack's head snapped up.

Cole Stuart stood in front of him with the other Bad Kids arrayed behind him. They were all cleaned up, no blood or gore. They wore clean, ironed shirts, their pants were unwrinkled. Victor Alexander's mop of brown hair was combed, Cole's Mohawk stood up straight and stiff. It appeared they'd all taken a shower.

"You look like you crawled out of a rat hole," he said.

Compared to the Bad Kids, Jack was a filthy, tattered, bloody, burned mess.

"Now, I'm gonna kill him," Victor Alexander snarled. "Ever since his girlfriend's dog bit me, I've been wanting to do one of 'em." He advanced a step toward Jack.

"Uh-uh, he's mine," said Jacob Dumas. He glared at Jack. "You didn't roast after all, nigger, but I like my dark meat raw."

"What about the other two?" Cole said and put out his

hand between them. "Where are they? And the light? Do they know what we—?"

It was almost too fast to follow. Victor jumped at Jacob, who almost dodged the lunge. But Victor managed to get a handful of his shirt and pulled Jacob to the ground with him. Then they were a tangle of arms and legs, angry, snarling animals.

Ronnie tried to pull them apart. Roger knocked him away, and Ronnie came up swinging. In seconds, they were all at each other—clean clothes forgotten in their untamable rage.

Jack staggered to his feet and ran away through the trees. If he could make it to the road, there'd be cars and people and—a hand grabbed him from behind, yanked him backward off his feet and threw him down. He was again on the ground, looking up at Cole, whose split lip was dripping blood on a shirt smeared with dirt and missing two buttons. Cole glowered at the other boys, who now stood disheveled but no longer violent in a circle around Jack. Cole held the others in check with a murderous gaze.

"We're not going to kill him until he answers some questions," he said, looking from one of the Bad Kids to the next. There was an uneasy rustle among them.

Jack's mind flitted to Becca's words: Cole's demon looks like a dragon, don't you think?

"We'll take the nigger back. Let…him do the asking."

"How are we going to get him back there without somebody seeing?" Walter Stephenson sneered. "Look at him. It's pretty clear where he's been."

"Then we'll clean him up," Cole said. He looked pointedly at the boys' soiled clothing. "We'll all clean up."

The others didn't argue this time. Ronnie Martin grabbed Jack's arm and hefted him off the ground, and they set out through the woods toward the river, dragging Jack along.

When they got to the riverbank, Jacob and Roger took off their shoes and socks, rolled up the legs of their pants and shoved Jack into the shallow water. Then they started scrubbing him, cleaning the filth off his clothes with their hands and with sand from the river bottom. Jack cried out in pain when they scrubbed his raw arms and burned legs, but they paid him no mind.

Cole and the others used the water to clean the dirt off their own clothing and the blood off their faces and hands.

"How did you get out?" Jack asked, then cried out in pain when Jacob Dumas rubbed sand across his injured, burned palm.

"Jumped off the back balcony into the river," Cole said, obviously proud of the accomplishment. "Not another soul in the world could have leapt that far."

When the other boys dragged a dripping Jack out of the water, Cole grabbed him by the hair and snarled into his face. "We're going to take you to meet a friend of ours. The sight of him could scare you to death. Literally *scare you to death.*"

~

2011

Jack held the rifle steady, didn't relax a muscle or move his aim from the man's right eye until Andi was well out of grabbing range. A few seconds. If he'd been a few seconds later…

He'd thought he had been too late. When he'd seen the man standing alone on the bluff, he'd been certain Andi was dead, and a white light had burned the world away.

He'd lifted his rifle and aimed at the back of the man's head. Nothing existed except the feel of the M4 in his hands with his finger on the trigger. He flashed on the image of Andi, limp in his arms, her warm blood soaking into his shirt that day in her classroom, and he began to squeeze.

Then the man suddenly dropped out of his line of fire and began climbing down the side of the cliff. Jack raced to the cliff's edge, saw the pile of hay and knew Andi must be buried somewhere in it.

So, would he have killed the man, shot him down right there in cold blood? Jack shoved the question out of his mind. The answer might mean acknowledging a darkness in his heart that he wasn't prepared to examine right now.

"Put your hands on your head and slide down off that hay roll."

A hay roll. Two or three of them, he thought, though it was hard to tell because they'd mostly come apart, spreading hay all along the sliver of riverbank below the cliff. Andi must have jumped off into them.

How'd she know they were there? How'd they get there? Washed out of a field in a flood? Hay rolls did float, looked like brown marshmallows bobbing in the water. And that explanation would work, except there hadn't been a flood.

Down below Jack, the man's feet hit the ground. And the instant they did, he bolted. Not after Andi. Out into the river.

"Stop! Stop right there!" Jack knew as the words left his mouth that there was absolutely no way for him to make the man stop short of shooting him in the back. And outside the white-hot glare of rage, Jack wasn't prepared to do that.

The man kicked off his shoes as he ran and began

gliding through the water with firm, steady strokes. He obviously intended to swim across the river to the Ohio side more than half a mile away! Jack would see to it there was a reception committee waiting for him when he waded into shore there.

Or would he? Now that it was over, that Andi was safe, were they going to go "official" with the fact that she'd been kidnapped? That he had come roaring after her—not just out of his jurisdiction but into another state?

He stood and watched the man swim farther out into the river, no longer slicing through the water. His pace had slowed. He was tiring now, paying for the burst of energy and speed he'd used to get away from the shore and Jack. Maybe he'd bitten off more than he could chew trying to swim the river. The river was sluggish, almost no current here, but still, half a mile was a long way to swim in street clothes.

Jack called out to Andi—she'd stopped running after fifty yards. There was nowhere else to run because the cliff bank came right down into the water. He slung the M4 across his back and started to climb down the side of the rock wall to where the little girl with brown curls was walking back toward the hay rolls, her striped socks coated with sticky, black river mud. That's when he saw it. Apparently, the man swimming in the river hadn't seen it yet because he kept slogging slowly ahead—oblivious to the behemoth bearing down on him.

For all their size and girth, Ohio River coal barges traveled almost silently. The engine rumble of the tug pushing them trailed a thousand feet behind the lead barge. Hidden by a bend in the river, the barge snaked out past the point like lead screwed out of a pencil. A single barge was thirty-five feet wide and a hundred and ninety-five feet long. This was a standard tow, fifteen such barges, three wide and five long, winched together with cables. Loaded as it was with Pennsylvania coal destined for the Mississippi River, it sunk at least ten feet down below the water line.

It was useless to yell out a warning. The man was too far out to hear. Swimming at a snail's pace now, he continued inexorably out into the shipping channel in the center of the river—oblivious to the oncoming barge.

The man couldn't possibly be stupid enough to think the barge would stop to keep from hitting him! The tugboat captain could not see what lay in the path of the lead barge—which was thirty-three football fields out front of him—and even if he could, it would take the leviathan two or three miles to stop.

Jack stood where he was on the bluff and watched the silent drama. When the man finally caught sight of the barge, or maybe felt the vibration of the tug's engines in the water, he began to swim frantically toward the Ohio shoreline. But even as desperate as he was, he was too exhausted to propel his body through the water fast enough to get out of the barge's path. At some point, he must have figured out he wasn't going to make it because he stopped swimming and faced the oncoming giant, treading water as it closed in. He began to yell something. Jack couldn't make out the words, but the tone was unmistakably defiant.

The man was likely screaming obscenities when the front hull slammed into him, shoved him down into the cold, muddy water and moved inexorably over the spot where he had been.

Jack scanned the river after the barge glided past, rounded the next bend and slowly disappeared. He saw no sign of the man, but he didn't expect to. His body would float to the surface somewhere downstream in a day or two. Or it wouldn't. The Ohio had claimed many victims who had slipped down into its muddy depths, and no trace was ever found of them.

"Uncle Jack!" Andi had climbed up the side of the cliff face during the drama. She flung herself into his arms and burst into tears. Holding her close, he pulled his phone out of his pocket and hit Daniel's number. Daniel had his phone turned off. Jack left him a cryptic message. "I've got her, Danno. Andi's with me. She's safe."

Andi continued to hold him tight and cry. Jack slipped his phone back into his pocket and eased down onto a rock and drew the sobbing child into his lap. He pulled out a handkerchief and wiped at the blood on her upper lip. A bloody nose. *She'd had a bloody nose.* Then he held her, rocking unconsciously back and forth, totally in the moment, relishing the feel of her and the smell of hay in her hair. Relief untied the knot that had cinched his belly so tight his muscles ached.

"It's ok, sweetheart. It's over. The bad man is…gone." She hadn't seen what happened to him. Why add that image to her ever-growing repertoire of horrible memories. "You're safe now."

She hiccupped words out between sobs. "No, I'm not. I'm going to burn up. We all are."

"What are you talking about?"

"I saw it, a vision. Everybody's going to die."

Then she told him about it.

She stopped crying in the telling of it. But by the time she was finished, it was Jack who felt like crying.

So far, Andi was two for two with visions. What she envisioned had happened. Exactly like she saw it. Twice. Was the horror she'd seen in this vision also…destined to be? Unstoppable?

Chapter Forty-Eight

2011

Whitworth's voice echoed in an oil drum in Daniel's head.

I am certain, gentlemen, without a shadow of a doubt that I am that man.

He let his words hang out there in the air of the room. None of the senators spoke. Perhaps they couldn't speak. Daniel had the sense that until Whitworth released his hold on the men, they would remain motionless and mute.

"I am that man," he repeated. "The one you've been looking for. I am uniquely qualified for the position. I possess the skills necessary to perform the task."

This time there was only the barest heartbeat of a pause, no crashing wave of silence. He continued speaking, almost interrupted.

"But I am not the only man so qualified and skilled. There are others who could bring to this position a stellar record and a sterling character. I have no doubt that the president will find such a man to bring before you for confirmation, because I am withdrawing my name from consideration. I informed the president before I came here today to make the announcement."

The silence that followed his words was not an animate, almost sentient thing like before, crashing against the shores of the mind. This silence had no life in it. Without the energy Whitworth imparted, it hung dead and empty in the room.

That's when Daniel realized that everyone had been released, set free from whatever "spell" Whitworth had cast over them. They came back to life, reinhabited their minds and bodies without any real awareness that for the past few minutes they had been imprisoned, held totally captive by Chapman Whitworth's power.

With their release came the restless shuffling movements so glaringly absent before. People moved and shifted in chairs, coughed, sneezed, lived, and the surprise that flowed across the room was like The Wave flowing across a stadium.

Senator Morrison, seated to the committee chairman's right, was the first to find his tongue. "But why?" he asked the question almost plaintively, making it clear that he, at least, was still bound by Whitworth's spell. Maybe every last one of them, except Senator LaHayne, had been eager to give him the rousing confirmation and endorsement he so richly deserved.

"Because the future of this nation is far more important than the vicissitudes of one man's fortunes," Whitworth replied. "This seat must be filled now, without delay. I cannot in good conscience be a further hindrance to the swift resolution of this matter. My nomination and confirmation would undoubtedly cause great delay, and that is simply unacceptable to me."

He looked then at Senator LaHayne, who had spent the entirety of Whitworth's remarks sitting peacefully in the chairman's seat. To the observer, he had seemed neither positively nor negatively affected by the words. Daniel wondered if Whitworth's spell had had any impact on him at all.

"The chairman of this committee, the senior senator from Ohio, Thomas LaHayne, opposes my nomination. He has made no secret of his opposition, though he has not, to my knowledge, ever given any explanation for it. Apparently, he intended to present information about that opposition at this hearing. As I have said repeatedly in the past week, I have nothing to fear from any revelation he might make because I don't have any skeletons in my closet." He glanced down, momentarily, when he said that, and Daniel thought about what Billy Ray had said about people's behavior when they lied.

"Presenting that information, will, however consume some amount of time. Refuting it will take time as well. I am absolutely confident about what the outcome of all that debate will be." He looked around at the rest of the committee. "The senator does not have the votes on this committee to prevent my nomination from going to the full senate."

The senator had said as much to Daniel, and now, as Daniel looked from one senator to the next, he suspected that if the vote were taken right now, Senator LaHayne's would be the only one dissenting.

"But there is something else we all know about the senator." Again, he focused his gaze on LaHayne, who showed no hint of being intimidated by it. Whitworth smiled ingratiatingly. "We know that he is a man of character and determination. Though we are on opposing sides on this issue, I admire and respect the fact that the senator will not be dissuaded from a course of action when he believes he is right."

Whitworth shifted his gaze back in a sweeping glance that took in the whole committee and sighed almost melodramatically. "Which means, gentlemen, that he will filibuster my nomination once it reaches the senate floor." His eyes snapped back to LaHayne. "Won't you, senator?"

LaHayne smiled an enigmatic smile but did not reply.

Whitworth sat back in his chair and looked both sad and tired. "And that is unfortunate. A filibuster can drag on indefinitely. This country does not have time to wait 'indefinitely' for the appointment of a new justice to join the court in the resolution of the issues before us. When I spoke to the president this morning, he said he would present the name of another candidate to this committee by Monday. Barring"—he paused and focused the punch of his jibe at LaHayne—"unforeseen and unexplained opposition, the matter should come before the whole senate by the end of the week."

He let out a dismissive sigh. "That is all I have to say, gentlemen. Thank you for your time and consideration, but if you have no further questions, I'd like to be excused."

A couple of senators started to speak, but LaHayne cut them off. He rapped his gavel down once.

"We thank you for appearing before us today," he said, cordially. "We have nothing further to discuss. You may go."

And that was it. It was over.

We won. We did it. We stopped him!

Then Daniel grabbed his phone and switched it on. He scanned the list of messages until he came to Jack's. He played it through three times, then lowered his chin to his chest to keep himself from bursting into tears of joy.

∼

1985

Becca, Daniel and Mikey were about half a mile down Pullman Lane, the spur that would take them back to the nursing home from the north side, when they heard them. The Bad Kids were yelling and snarling at each other, making a racket you could hear long before they came into view. The three hurried into the woods and hid, then peeked out through the bushes.

When they saw that Jack was precariously balanced on the fender rack of Roger Willingham's bike, Becca had to stifle a cry of relief. He was alive! Until that moment she hadn't realized that she really believed she'd never see Jack again.

"They must have caught Jack following them," Mikey whispered. "Why didn't they just …?"

"Kill him like they did all those people in the nursing home?" Daniel finished for him.

"They must want him for something," Becca said.

Terror washed over her as the six demon-possessed boys drew nearer, the primitive fear that they'd somehow sense her presence in the woods and come after her. The combined horror of the monstrosities that rode by in the summer breeze was enough to stop her heart. She began to tremble, couldn't stop shaking. But she had to. She and Daniel and Mikey had to see where they were taking Jack.

They followed the Bad Kids through Bradford's Ridge, as deserted as a ghost town, its inhabitants gathered around a burning hulk of a building where an unthinkable mass murder had just been committed. The whole world had seen it all, watched it live.

The Bad Kids rode out of town on the other side and took Bethel Park Road, which followed the riverbank and then connected to U.S. 31.

Daniel, Mikey and Becca had stayed so far behind they

feared at every curve that the road in front of them would be empty—the Bad Kids taken off some direction they hadn't seen. If Mikey hadn't spotted the six bicycles in the bushes beside Milkstone, they'd have passed right by them.

Named for an outcrop of pure white limestone that extended out into the river, Milkstone was a popular hangout for teenagers in the summertime because the rocks blocked the channel, and water rushing around them had formed a small, deep pool to swim in. The mouth of an enormous cave gaped in the hillside on the shore, a hundred feet tall and probably twice as wide, blocked in the back by a rockfall. The dirt area in front of the cave opening was littered with trash, beer and soft drink cans. Inside the cave mouth were black spots in the dirt, the remains of campfires, and the roof had been blackened by smoke from generations of teenage parties. It was anything but secluded and isolated. The three of them had driven by this spot with their parents all their lives. Becca's house was on the opposite side of the mountain from Milkstone, probably not two miles away--if you moved the mountain.

They pulled off the road into the grass and sat looking at the six bicycles.

"At Bishop's barbecue—this is where they wanted us to go drinking with them," Daniel said.

"Who did?" Becca asked.

"Cole and the others. We almost got into a fight when we said no."

"Where'd they go?" Mikey asked, looking up and down the riverbank.

"They're in the cave," said a voice from behind them, where no one had been standing only a few seconds ago. Becca turned to the sound of the voice, but Daniel and Mikey only turned because she did, and then they began to squint.

As horrible as everything was, Becca still managed to smile. She wondered what the boys were thinking about the lady made of light who had appeared out of nowhere wearing a silly red-and-white striped hat.

She turned from the woman to ask them, but swallowed the question. It was clear they couldn't see the angel, only the glow of her that almost blinded them.

"You can't see it from below, but there's a crack in the rock up there at the top," she said, pointing to a pile of boulders that appeared to reach all the way to the roof of the cave in the back right corner.

Becca lost her breath for a moment, the wind knocked out of her. She'd never in her life been so frightened—or so calm, both at the same time. Terror almost ate a hole in her, but she knew with the certainty of absolute truth what she was supposed to do, wondered if perhaps she had been created by God for this very moment.

"We have to go get Jack," Becca said. Daniel stood looking at her, his face unreadable.

"No! Don't!" Mikey suddenly cried. Though it was easy to forget all about him, the little fat kid was making his presence known now. "Don't go in there." He almost grabbed Becca's arm but stopped a moment before he touched her. "Please, don't go in there. The Bad Kids will kill you for following them. And…there's something horrible in there, and if you go in you'll never come back out."

Becca said nothing, only smiled at him. Then she turned and followed the angel toward the base of the rockfall and began to climb. When Becca got to the top and looked back down, Mikey was nowhere to be seen. Daniel was right behind her.

She wordlessly took the angel's hand and the three of

them passed through the crack in the rock into the dark cavern beyond.

~

2011

When Daniel felt a hand on his shoulder, he looked up into the kind eyes of the next president of the United States. Senator Thomas LaHayne smiled down at him. To most other people, the man's demeanor hadn't changed throughout the whole proceeding. But Daniel had seen it, little signs of tension and pressure around his mouth.

His face bore its usual calm, marked now with what Daniel knew was a profound sense of relief.

The senator gestured to the phone that Daniel still clutched in his hand.

"It would appear you have had good news from the home front," he said.

"Is it that obvious?"

"Son, the smile on your face would melt frost off a windowpane at thirty paces."

Daniel actually laughed. He stood and fell in beside the senator as the other man started for the door of the meeting room.

"My secretary will set up an appointment—at your convenience, of course—with you and your police officer friend." LaHayne fished for the name for a moment, then found it before Daniel could provide it. "Jack Carpenter."

"I am ready now to hear what Paul Harvey always called, 'The Rest of the Story.'" He looked concerned for a moment. "You do know who Paul Harvey is, don't you, because if you don't I must be a whole lot older—"

A journalist from CNN with a familiar, yet unplaceable

face touched Senator LaHayne's arm. "If you have a minute, sir, I only have a couple of questions—"

"I'll have a statement for you." Daniel either saw or thought he saw the senator cut him a knowing look. "I'm just as surprised as you are about all this and I'll need some time to—"

That's when it happened. Though what exactly "it" was would be a matter of debate and conjecture, would probably provide fodder for conspiracy theorists for the next fifty years.

Senator LaHayne tripped. Except there was nothing there for him to trip over. Footage from stationary cameras in the room later revealed only that he appeared to stumble over his own feet. But that didn't explain how forcefully he fell forward and that he never put his hands out to break his own fall. He'd been walking slowly beside Daniel, and then he was hurling toward the floor. There was a chair in his path, and his forehead collided with the wooden railing between the back legs of it. His momentum carried his body forward; his head was shoved backward.

Daniel believed forever afterward that he actually heard the senator's neck snap. He was dead before he settled in a limp heap on the floor.

Ruthlessly shoved to the side, out of the way, Daniel found himself standing alone, an island in the middle of a sea of scurrying, frantic people. Only one other person was standing back from the crowd, observing.

When Chapman Whitworth saw that Daniel had noticed him, he turned to face him. Whitworth's expression was decorously solemn as would befit such a sad and tragic event, but there was malicious glee sparkling in his eyes. He touched two fingers of his left hand to his forehead and gave Daniel his snappy little salute. Then he walked out of the room.

Chapter Forty-Nine

1985

Mikey Rutherford had wet his pants. Twelve years old and he'd wet his pants! He couldn't help it, though. When Becca and Daniel and that bright light left to go into the cave, he was suddenly so terrified, for them and for himself, that he ran mindless down the riverbank and his bladder let go. He couldn't control it.

When he was able to get his breath again, he took his shoes and socks off and waded out into water up to his waist. That drenched him, of course, but it looked better than having a giant wet spot on the front of his pants.

Then he waited.

He wished he could go get Bishop. Maybe he was home by now.

He waited some more. He searched for flat rocks and skipped them over the surface of the water, actually got three or four that skipped instead of sinking like...well, like rocks.

Had it been hours? It seemed like it. Mikey had no

watch, but he didn't think he had ever waited so long for anything in his whole life.

Then he heard noise at the top of the rockfall. He looked up and froze in terror. Climbing down over the rocks were the Bad Kids—all six of them.

Hide!

Where?

There was nowhere to go. Only flat riverbank. No sense trying to run, they'd be on him in a second. And they were coming fast. They weren't merely climbing down the rockfall, they were scrambling down it. Hopping from one rock to another, slipping and sliding and falling. Victor Alexander lost his footing and went down hard on his backside. Ronnie Martin, who was right behind him, helped him to his feet and—

Helped him?

Cole Stuart was the first one down, and he ran right at Mikey.

Mikey squeezed his eyes shut. One of the dozens of Woody Allen lines he'd memorized popped into his head. "I'm not afraid of dying. I just don't want to be there when it happens."

Cole bumped into him when he ran past.

"Sorry," Cole mumbled.

Mikey's eyes snapped open!

Cole had reached his bike. He yanked it out of the bushes, leapt on it and pedaled frantically away, going no faster than Mikey could have gone—well, than Jack or Daniel could have.

Others had made it down the rockfall now and were running all-out to their bikes. One of them, Jacob Dumas, was crying. Tears streamed down his cheeks and snot ran down his lip, but he was in such a hurry, he didn't even wipe it away.

None of them paid the slightest attention to Mikey.

In no time at all, they were gone. He watched them pedaling madly until they were out of sight around the curve. Then Mikey turned slowly back to the rockfall beneath the crack in the rock, shaken and confused—and there at the top was Becca! She began climbing down, with Daniel behind her. And there was Jack! They'd found Jack!

The bright light was nowhere to be seen.

But something was wrong. They weren't clambering frantically down the rocks like the Bad Kids. They were slow and deliberate. They weren't smiling or talking. They looked like robots.

Mikey ran to the base of the rockfall, but when Becca climbed off the last rock, she walked right by him without speaking. He stood dumbfounded as Daniel did the same.

"Jack!" Mikey cried as Jack completed his descent. "Are you all right?"

He certainly didn't look alright. He was beat up. His elbows, palms and knees were skinned and bleeding, maybe burned, too. It was hard to tell. His clothes were wet and dirty. The right knee on his jeans was torn out, and the bottom of both pant legs were blackened —scorched.

Jack walked right past as if he hadn't heard a word Mikey said.

Mikey watched, so surprised and confused that for once in his life, he couldn't find a thing to say.

The three of them wordlessly went to their bikes. Daniel slid onto the rack on the back of Jack's bike, but there was no conversation. He did it in silence.

Mikey was finally able to blurt out, "What's wrong? What's going on?"

Nobody answered him, but Daniel appeared at least to

have heard the question. He looked confused, then mumbled distractedly, "I don't know."

Then the three rode away, leaving Mikey on the riverbank to watch until they were out of sight.

~

2011

Theresa hated to call it a celebration, hated to think about getting together all happy like when there was still a powerful demon on the prowl, roaming out there free in the world, and three little kids in Bradford's Ridge enduring the horror of being taken over by creatures from Hell.

And there was Jack. The Harrelton Police Department had made official what Crock'd done so's Jack could look for Bosko—they'd suspended Jack pending the outcome of the ATF investigation. Wasn't no way to change that until he or one of the others remembered what'd happened at Twin Oaks that day.

Besides, she still hadn't been able to shake the sense that somethin' wasn't right about all this. Daniel said Chapman Whitworth had killed Senator LaHayne. So why did Whitworth wait to do it until after he had withdrawn his name? The senator was all that stood between him and the nomination. There was somethin' out there they wasn't seein'.

So she hadn't used the word "celebrate" when she'd invited them all to come over for her famed chili. Chili'd been one of Bishop's favorites. He'd slide up behind her on cold winter nights when she was fixing it, slip his arms around her and lean over her shoulder to smell the fragrant steam rising up off the pot on the stove.

"I do love me some of that chili, woman," he'd say. "'Cause it reminds me of you."

"How you figure that?"

"Well, it smells good, it's brown and it's spicy and—"

"Now, don't you be sayin' somethin' that's gone embarrass me."

"And it warms a man's heart and makes him feel loved," he concluded. But there'd been a chuckle in his deep voice that brought a flush to her cheeks anyway.

She smiled at the memory, looked over at Bishop's picture on the mantle, and the ache to feel his arms around her throbbed with every heartbeat. But it was a tender pain now, didn't take her breath away no more.

And when she thought about it, she decided it was, too, a good thing to call this a celebration. They was lots of good to celebrate. Andi was safe. They hadn't indicted Daniel, and they'd dropped the murder charges against her —Thank you, Lord! Which put her in mind of Jeff. She'd invited him, but he'd said he couldn't come. Made up some excuse, but she knew it was 'cause Daniel'd be there, and there was something between the two of them they wasn't talking 'bout.

Then Daniel and Andi showed up, and it was like the whole family coming in for Christmas, Andi squealing with delight when she spotted Biscuit, the dog running around and around in circles, barking at everything and nothing. And after that, the evening was filled with talk and laughter soft as confetti and silly good humor. It was easy to forget the awful that was still looming out there. Andi's vision— which stopped Theresa's heart in her chest every time she thought about it. And they was gone have to come up with some kind of plan to rid the world of a monster—permanently. They'd talk about that later, of course, all of them together. But not right now.

The doorbell rang after everybody'd been served. When she opened the door, Jeff Kendrick was standing outside.

"Why, you decided to come after all," she said.

"Don't you ever answer your telephone? I've left half a dozen messages, and you never call me back."

"Get on in this house, son, and don't be pesterin' an old woman 'bout somethin' unimportant as a telephone."

Truth was, Theresa had no idea where her phone was. Coulda fell off behind the dresser or maybe under the seat in the car. She hoped it wasn't in one of her pockets 'cause she'd done a full load of laundry this morning. The phone store had replaced the one she broke, and the last thing she needed was to have to buy another one of them things and try to figure out how to use it.

Jeff stepped inside, and she saw his eyes lock briefly with Daniel's. Then he turned to her.

"I didn't come here to crash your party. I'd have told you what I had to say on the phone if I'd been able to reach you."

"I ain't near as attached to my phone as some folks is," she said, and cast an eye on Jack.

"What she's trying to say is that the only serious female relationship Jack has in his life is with Siri," Crock said. "He needs therapy."

"You need to hear this," Jeff said. And it was only then that it registered with her and the others that Jeff wasn't smiling, and there was no good humor or banter in his tone. Whatever news he'd come to deliver, it wasn't good.

He spotted the television in the corner and said, "Better yet, you need to see it."

He picked up a remote off the coffee table and turned it on. Theresa had the most horrible sense of foreboding when he did. The sense of déjà vu was so strong you could almost see it, thick as fog or smoke floating in the air. She looked from Daniel to Jack and saw they'd felt it, too. So had Andi. She climbed up into her daddy's lap and snuggled tight in his arms.

Jeff found a news broadcast and turned the volume up, dumping too-loud words into the room in midsentence.

"…announcement has taken even the shrewdest politicos by surprise. Until the controversy surrounding Whitworth's Supreme Court nomination, the American public didn't even know his name, and now Chapman Whitworth appears to be the man of the hour."

Theresa sat down hard on the arm of the overstuffed chair where Daniel and Andi sat.

"He definitely has momentum, as any dark horse must to have a prayer of succeeding," said some national news anchor she probably ought to recognize but couldn't place. All those talking heads looked the same to her. "Senator LaHayne had the nomination all but sewn up. Now, with no apparent frontrunner to take his place, the party's scrambling, searching for somebody who can catch the imagination of the electorate."

"Whitworth might just be that candidate," said the other talking head. "Apparently, President Barker thinks so and his ringing endorsement of Whitworth goes a long way."

Theresa wanted to look around to see how the others were reacting, but she couldn't take her eyes off the screen, the dread rising up in her throat like warm bile.

"At this point, anything's possible," said the first news anchor. "He might carry the day. Let's show that clip again of his announcement."

Chapman Whitworth's face filled the screen. Somebody in the room groaned like they'd been punched in the gut, but Theresa didn't—couldn't—take her eyes off the screen to see who. Andi whimpered and started to cry softly.

"A man must rise to the occasion, accept the call placed on his life by a higher destiny than he had imagined." His sonorous tones flowed like butter off hot pancakes. "Though Senator LaHayne and I were political opponents, we were close personal friends. That is why he never once in all the time we stood on opposite sides of the Supreme Court nomination issue, criticized me, never once had a hard or disparaging word to say about me. We disagreed on issues, but we loved each other like brothers and no one in Washington feels the pain of his loss more than I."

His voice appeared to choke on the last words. And he had to pause before he continued.

Jeff murmured beside her. "Close personal friends? That's not what I heard."

"I am honored and humbled to take up his mantle, to lift the banner from his hand where he has fallen and to carry his vision and ideals forward in his stead. It is in his great light that I stand here today to announce that I will seek my party's nomination for the presidency of the United States of America."

Becca backed out of the room, her eyes huge, and ran to the bathroom where Theresa could hear her vomiting.

The scene shifted to the two talking heads again.

"The man has magnetic charisma—he's already being compared to the Kennedys. JFK's style, Clinton's charm and—" said the first anchor.

"Ronald Reagan's gift for saying the right pithy thing at the right time," said the second.

"There is, of course, the thorny issue of campaign financing," said the first anchor. "Whitworth hasn't raised a dime, no war chest. He's going to have to pull this off on a shoestring, and there's something glamorous and gallant about an underdog effort. But what really can't be stressed enough is what I said earlier. Whitworth would have passed into political obscurity if it hadn't been for Senator LaHayne's opposition to his Supreme Court nomination. Now, he's got as good a shot as anybody to become the next president of the United States."

"Turn that thing off," Theresa said. Her voice was shaking. Jeff punched a button on the remote still in his hand, and the screen went dark.

"We been tricked!" she said. Her heart was hammering in her chest so hard she could see her dress move with each beat. "That sly fox done outsmarted us."

"What are you talking about?" Jack asked.

"I know what she's talking about," Daniel said. He held his little girl tenderly on his lap and spoke softly. "He used us. He needed notoriety. He needed an excuse to take his dog-and-pony show on the road, a chance to mesmerize the public with his evil voice. And we gave it to him."

Jack shook his head slowly, back and forth, awed. "You're saying you think that was his plan all along?"

"I didn't see it in time," Theresa said. "Demons is smart, crafty creatures. We underestimated this 'un, played right into his hands." She paused, and when she continued, wonder and revulsion colored her voice. "Now, he could become the most powerful man in the world."

The horror of that thought struck them all silent.

"Did you ever pull the wings off a fly?"

Becca spoke from the back of the room. Her voice was eerily flat and emotionless. It was such a non sequitur that no one knew how to respond.

"Becca, honey…" Theresa began.

"That's what he said that day, and then he pulled the fisherman's arms off."

Theresa exchanged looks with Jack and Daniel, who

appeared as bewildered as she was. Only Andi was unfazed.

"One of the demons did that, didn't he," Andi said, "and you watched him do it, and it was awful. In the visions, I watch what demons do." A tremor went through her whole small body. "It's awful, too."

Becca seemed to come back from some faraway place then, and her eyes fastened on Jack. Her voice was still soft, but it was tremulous now, and it was clear it took an emotional effort to get the words out. "It was in the woods. You and Daniel found me with the Bad Kids. I can't see all of it. There's fog swirling around. I can hear DD barking but I can't see him. Do you remember?"

Jack shook his head. "No, Becca. I'm sorry."

"I do," said Daniel, and Becca turned to him. "They were going to take you with them—to the efreet, I guess. I don't remember anything except how scared you looked."

"I remember it crisp and clear--no fog--like the images are sealed in a crystal bubble. I hid in a crepe myrtle bush with Dougal Dog and watched the Bad Kids murder a fisherman. No reason. Jacob Dumas just tore his arms off. Then they tied his body down in the river and piled rocks on it."

Though Becca was making sense now, Theresa still couldn't figure how that connected to what they'd just found out about Chapman Whitworth.

"All these years, that man's family never knew what happened to him." She didn't even realize she'd put her hands into her armpits, hunched her shoulders and was hugging her own self. "I never told a soul because it hurt too bad to talk about it. It was so painful I couldn't bring it up. And I've been refusing for years to face other things I know are true because they terrify me." She paused. "Me, me, me. It's always about me."

Both Jack and Daniel started to protest, but she waved them off.

"I understood it for the first time after I saw the hat floating in the river." No one had any idea what she was talking about. But what she said next confirmed what Theresa and Bishop had long believed. "I'm the one who failed when we were twelve. I don't know how or why, but I've been running away and hiding from that failure ever since. It's my fault he's come back. I have to stop him."

"Sugar, we all gone have to—"

"You don't know how!"

Becca looked from one to the other of them, all the way around the room. "Do you know what to do—any of you?" No one spoke. "I know that creature better than any other human being. I've been in his presence, heard his thoughts, smelled his…"

She took a deep, shaky breath and crossed the room to the hallway. From where she sat, Theresa could see her walk slower and slower as she neared the door of Bishop's study, like she had to push her way through some invisible force trying to keep her away. Might be that force was her own self. Might be it wasn't. She stopped in front of the door. Stood there. Then she reached out and turned the knob.

When she spoke, she wasn't talking to nobody Theresa could see. But maybe Becca could.

"I'm going to find out how to destroy you," she said.

Then Becca Hawkins stepped into Bishop's study and closed the door behind her.

Epilogue

2011

A voice came out of the shadows, and Billy Ray jumped in spite of himself.

"You clean up good for a country boy."

Billy Ray pulled at the tie in the stiff collar around his neck.

"I'd a'stuck out like a dog in a duck parade if I'd shown up here looking normal. And you said you wanted discreet."

"Indeed, I do." Chapman Whitworth stepped out into the light and smiled, a shark smile that never reached his strange, light-green eyes. "Silent partners need to blend in so well they disappear altogether."

"It's good you should mention that 'partner' thing 'cause that's what I'm here to talk about," Billy Ray began. "I want to nail down exactly what it is I'm payin' for before I hand over—"

Billy Ray began to rise in the air. His face went white

and he looked down in horror as his feet lifted farther and farther off the floor.

"What the—?"

Then his body flew across the room and slammed into the wall so hard a picture nearby fell off and shattered.

Billy Ray's eyes were so huge he looked like a baby owl. Then he began to rise off the floor again, and he looked around in terror, trying to see how it was done, find some way it was an illusion, some kind of trick.

"How do you…put me down," he whined, his gravelly voice whimpering like a frightened child. "Put me down… please." Billy Ray suddenly dropped in a heap on the floor.

"A deal's a deal, Billy Ray, and you can't back out now." Whitworth laughed, a dark parody of the real thing. It had an ugly, sinister edge to it. "Didn't your mama ever warn you not to make a pact with the devil?"

He stood over where Billy Ray lay cowering on the floor.

"I'll walk you through this—use little bitty words so I don't have to draw you a picture with your crayons. You get clemency, a pardon. You don't have to spend the next decade walking a tightrope, sucking up to a parole officer. And in exchange, I get certain 'contributions' to the Whitworth for President campaign."

"You gonna use my money to buy the White House."

It was a statement, not a question, but Whitworth answered it anyway. "No, I'm going to use it to buy an army."

"What do you need an army for?"

Whitworth leaned toward him and spoke softly. "To start a war."

The End

A Note from the Author

Thank you for reading *The Deceiving*.

If you enjoyed this book, would you please consider writing a review of it on your favorite bookseller site so other readers might enjoy it too? Just a couple of sentences. That would mean a lot to me.

Thank you!

Ninie Hammon

About the Author

Ninie Hammon (rhymes with shiny, not skinny) grew up in Muleshoe, Texas, got a BA in English and theatre from Texas Tech University and snagged a job as a newspaper reporter. She didn't know a thing about journalism, but her editor said if she could write he could teach her the rest of it and if she couldn't write the rest of it didn't matter. She hung in there for a 25-year career as a journalist. As soon as she figured out that making up the facts was a whole lot more fun than reporting them, she turned to fiction and never looked back.

Ninie now writes suspense--every flavor except pistachio: psychological suspense, inspirational suspense, suspense thrillers, paranormal suspense, suspense mysteries.

In every book she keeps this promise to her Loyal Reader: "I will tell you a story in a distinctive voice you'll always recognize, about people as ordinary as you are--people who have been slammed by something they didn't sign on for, and now they must fight for their lives. Then smack in the middle of their everyday worlds, those people encounter the unexplainable--and it's always the game-changer."

Also By Ninie Hammon

Cornbread Mafia

Fire In The Hole

Blown' Up A Storm

Ridin' For A Fall

Nowhere, USA

The Jabberwock

Mad Dog

Trapped

The Hanging Judge

The Witch of Gideon

Blown Away

Nowhere People

Through The Canvas Series

Black Water

Red Web

Gold Promise

Blue Tears

The Taken Saga

The Taken

The Changed

The Hidden

The Saved

The Unexplainable Collection

Five Days in May

Black Sunshine

The Based on True Stories Collection

Home Grown

Sudan

When Butterflies Cry

The Knowing Series

The Knowing

The Deceiving

The Reckoning

The Fault

Stand-alone Psychological Thrillers

The Memory Closet

The Last Safe Place

www.ingramcontent.com/pod-product-compliance
Lightning Source LLC
Chambersburg PA
CBHW010518100726
47903CB00011B/2804